HOUSE OF GRACE

A Family Saga

Patricia M Osborne

White Wings Books

Published 2017 in Great Britain,
by White Wings Books

British Cataloguing Publication data:
A catalogue record of this book is available from
the British Library

This book is also available as an ebook.

In Memory of

my dearest mum,

Lila (1932-2014)

and

Sister,

Heather (1956-2009)

Two courageous and inspiring women

A light went out in my heart when you both left this world

PART I

(1950)

Chapter 1

I closed my sketchpad and crossed the room to the window. Seagulls flocked on the rocks, waves splashed high. I'd miss Greenemere but I was now a talented dress designer and full of dreams. One day, Grace Granville would change Britain's vision of fashion.

The door creaked. Katy, my roommate, strolled back in. 'Well?'

I turned around, mulling over her earlier words.

'Well don't just gawp.'

'I don't know.'

'Come on Gracie, it'll be fun. You can see how the other half lives.'

'Wigan though.' I twiddled my hair around my finger. 'Father isn't going to like it.'

'It's nineteen fifty, not the nineteen-hundreds, you know?' She huffed. 'Does he need to know about Wigan? It's only for the dance. Just tell him you're going to Bolton and that my Dad owns a cotton mill there.'

'Maybe.'

'Surely that should be respectable enough, even for your parents.'

It did sound thrilling. Would Father let me go? Katy was right, I didn't need to tell him about Wigan or the dance.

'Your parents are such snobs Gracie, best not mention Dad started off in a two room terrace. Or that Mum was in service before she got married.'

After I finally agreed to phone my parents, Katy jumped off the bed, grabbed a small purse and waltzed into the bathroom.

'What are you doing in there?' I called.

'Lippie.'

By that I assumed she meant lipstick. I'd never worn any. Would I need to? Should I be buying some? Maybe Katy would help me choose? I'd no idea what colour to get. I picked up a magazine with Bette Davis on the front cover. She was wearing bright red. Katy and I had seen her earlier in the year in *All about Eve*.

If we were going to a dance I needed to buy material to make a dress. I could see it now, a full skirt, fitted waist and belt, showing off my slim figure.

The door slammed shut as a new Katy rushed back in. What a metamorphosis. I wondered if I could change like that.

'Dad said he'll send his driver with the Rolls to collect us. Forgot to say, my cousin Jack can't wait to meet you.'

Golly, she'd never mentioned him before. Better not mention Jack to Father. I wondered what Jack was like. Probably a spotty faced, lanky lad. He'd be no threat to my chastity.

'Katy, shall we take a trip to the market before we leave here and get some fabric so I can make us new frocks as I've got nothing to wear to a dance?'

'Sounds a marvellous idea, anything particular in mind?' she asked.

I passed my notebook from the desk. 'Well I was thinking this? Red for me?'

'Yes I can see you in that. The colour will show off your dark hair.'

'I could make yours the same design but a different colour. Soft blue to accentuate your blonde curls?'

'Yes please.'

We were going to have an adventure. A pang of guilt hit me as I remembered my sister, Elizabeth. In her last letter she mentioned counting the days until I was back home. It must be hard with only Nanny and dreary Daphne, the dullest governess ever, for company. Mother and Father were far too busy working and socialising to spend time with their children. I consoled myself that I'd be home in time for her thirteenth birthday and buy her something special or maybe make an unusual gift.

Greenemere taught every girl how to dance as part of the curriculum. In fact there wasn't much they didn't cover to ensure we graduated as fine young ladies. Father had his own idea of education, to groom me into a good wife for someone of his choosing. Katy's parents sent her for refinement because she was a tomboy but she was still down to earth Katy, always up to mischief. We were a bit like salt and pepper.

I couldn't believe it had been three years since we first shared the sparsely but tastefully furnished room. She liked telling stories about her cousins, how they lived on the breadline, unlike her mum and dad who lived in a big house with servants. Her grandfather had been a coal miner, uncles and cousins followed in his footsteps. It must have been awful working down there in the dark. I couldn't think of anything worse. I was even scared of shadows at night. Katy's father managed to avoid the pits because he made enough money through gambling to buy a cotton mill which became prosperous. I'd never been to Bolton but I'd seen pictures in books of mills with tall chimneys. In fact I'd never been further north than our home in Gerrard's Cross.

'Come on Gracie,' Katy said, 'are you going to make that call?'

I couldn't put it off any longer. 'Will you come with me?'

'Of course.' She linked her arm in mine and we made our way to the large winding staircase. She gave me a little shove, her eyes glinting.

'Come on Gracie.'

I wasn't sure, but at the same time something inside me made me.

'Live a little. What can they do? It's almost our last day.'

'Go on then.' I threw my legs over the wooden banister and she climbed on behind, tugging gently at my waist.

'Ready?' She nudged me.

We slid down the thick shiny rail, helter-skelter style. Footsteps, oh dear. We were rumbled. Oh no, it had to be...

'Katherine Gilmore and Grace Granville, my office now.'

Miss Allison turned her face but not before I spied the fleeting grin. Maybe we'd caught her on a good day? Subdued, like naughty children, we stepped towards the heavy mahogany door with *Headmistress* engraved on a brass typeface.

'Come in, girls. Sit down. Haven't we taught you anything these past years? Young ladies graduating from Greenemere don't behave like kindergarten.'

'Sorry Miss Allison,' we said in unison, trying not to laugh.

'And what's that on your face, Katherine?'

Katy touched her face. 'It's for drama,' she lied.

'Very well. Make sure you wash it off before leaving the building.'

'Yes Miss Allison.'

'Please may I use the telephone?' I asked. 'I need to call Father to get permission to stay with Katy for a couple of weeks.'

'What an excellent idea, Grace. If you need me to speak to him to vouch for Katy's family, then I'm happy to do that.'

'Thank you, Miss Allison. Sorry about the banister.'

'Don't worry.' She smiled showing white teeth. 'It's tradition that graduates have one last ride on Bernie.'

'Bernie?' Katy rolled her eyes.

'You don't think you're the only adventurous ones, do you? Sliding down Bernie the Banister was popular in my day.'

Katy and I giggled.

Shaking, I dialled the number to *Granville Hall* and asked for Father. I hung up and turned to Miss Allison.

'It was the maid, she said Father isn't in. She'll get him to call later.'

'You girls go and get ready for dinner. I'll speak to Lord Granville when he phones.'

I'd miss this place and wasn't sure how I'd cope if Father didn't allow me to go on to college. The thought of being stuck at home in isolation with Nanny and dreary Daphne worried me. In fact, the idea horrified me.

Chapter 2

A Silver Rolls pulled up outside the school building. The chauffeur got out of the car. He reminded me of Father's drivers, the same grey uniform and matching flat peak hat. Katy ran over and addressed him by his first name leaving me shocked.

'James, this is Gracie, my best friend.'

He offered his hand but I ignored it and nodded. It was unheard of to speak to the staff. I worried what Father would say. First name basis too. I supposed that was the difference between Katy and me.

'I'll get the trunks.' James moved towards the stone steps.

Katy called up to him, 'Just a suitcase for Gracie, her trunk's already gone home.'

James loaded up the boot while Katy and I climbed onto the back seat. She pulled down a flap, took out two glasses and a bottle of dark coloured pop.

'Drink?' she offered. 'It's Sarsaparilla.'

Katy chattered as we sped along. I'm not sure how long we'd been travelling when my tummy started to feel queasy.

'Gracie, are you all right?' Katy asked. 'You've gone awfully green. James, pull over, I think she's going to be sick.'

James dutifully obeyed. I managed to open the car door just in time, leant over and let the contents of my stomach spill to the ground. I was so embarrassed. It was hardly ladylike. Mother and Father would be ashamed to see me in this manner.

Katy patted my hand. 'Why didn't you tell me you suffer from travel sickness?'

'Probably because I didn't know. I've never been further than Brighton from home before.'

'Don't worry.' Katy poured water into a beaker and passed it to me. 'Drink little sips. Maybe you shouldn't have had the Sarsaparilla?'

I gave a little laugh. I'd never tried Sarsaparilla before that day. It wasn't the type of drink Father would have approved of.

'James, do you know somewhere close, where we could stop?'

'There's a park about a five-minute drive away, if your friend can manage?'

Katy turned to me, I signalled yes and we both clambered into the back of the car. James closed the door behind us.

'I'll open the windows, it should help,' he said, before driving off.

Katy stroked my face and reassured me all would be fine. Before I knew it the driver eased the car through tall arched iron gates and switched off the motor.

'There's a little café up the footpath if you want to get something, or I could go?' he offered.

'I think the walk will do Gracie good,' Katy said.

We got out of the car and strolled up the enclosed track adorned with Black Night Buddleias on either side.

'We'll buy some travel sickness tablets before you go home. Look.' Katy pointed at the ice cream sign. 'The café. Maybe we should sit inside, away from the sun.'

It was almost empty, just a woman with a small child buying an ice cream and a young couple sitting cosy in the corner, drinking cups of tea.

'Cake, that's what you need,' Katy insisted. 'My Dad vows by cake for sickness, he says it lines the stomach. We haven't got far to go, about another forty miles or so.'

My tummy was raw and empty. I was willing to try anything. Katy ordered our snack and we sat by the window. Before long, a slim waitress brought a tray with cups of coffee and slices of Victoria sponge. I nibbled on the cake and sipped the warm fluid. Surprisingly it made me feel a little better.

'Are you ready to cope with the rest of the journey?'

I acknowledged with a nod but I wasn't ready for any of this. I should have gone home. If Father found out about first name terms with a driver and being sick in a car, he'd lock me in my room forever. Katy took my hand as we walked back towards the Rolls. James was standing outside smoking a cigarette.

'Give us a puff.' Katy held out her hand.

James obliged, I couldn't believe it. She took the cigarette, held it between two fingers and drew it to her mouth, inhaled, pursed her lips and released the smoke. She was clearly skilled at smoking. It certainly wasn't her first time to partake.

'Would you like to try, Gracie?' she asked.

I stepped back, shook my head.

'No, you're probably right, not the best thing when your stomach is out of sorts, no rush.'

I couldn't believe what I heard. Surely she didn't expect me to take part in that unladylike behaviour.

'Do your parents know you smoke?' I asked.

'Yes, of course but they don't mind. I mean how can they? Dad's been smoking since he was fourteen and Mum since she was a little older.'

It seemed we lived quite different lives. I was uncomfortable and nervous not knowing what was coming next. I wished I'd gone home.

Katy dropped the cigarette stub to the ground, extinguished it with the heel of her shoe then climbed into the car and patted the seat to instruct me to follow. James slowly drew the car away. A cool breeze from the open window stopped me feeling sick.

'Not long now, girls,' James said, 'we'll be home in about half an hour.'

My eyelids closed and I drifted into deep thought, pondering on the big mistake I'd made by agreeing to this crazy venture. The driver slowed down. I sat up as he steered through black wrought iron gates and followed the road up to a mansion not dissimilar to my own home.

'We're here,' Katy said. 'Mum and Dad are desperate to meet you.'

A short lady with dark curly hair stood waving by the steps. She rushed towards us. 'Welcome home, darling. We've missed you. Dad's caught up with a phone call but will be here in a minute.' She turned to me. 'And you must be Grace? Welcome to *Willow Banks*, we're so happy to have you.'

I offered my hand. 'How do you do Mrs Gilmore, thank you for having me.'

'Call me Eliza, we don't stand on ceremony here. Eric will take your bag.'

A middle-aged man in a dark suit came over.

'Hi Eric.' It seemed my friend was informal with all staff members. 'Daddy,' she shouted, and ran towards a tall man with blonde curly hair.

The man hugged her in his arms and swung her around. 'How's my girl?'

'Better now I'm home. This is Gracie, she's been sick, I think she'd like to lie down for a while.' She turned to me. 'Wouldn't you?'

It sounded like a good idea. 'Please.'

Eliza came to my side and wrapped an arm around me. 'You poor love, Katy will show you to your room. You can freshen up and take a little nap. Max.' She turned to Katy's father. 'Give Grace's parents a ring and let them know she's arrived safely.'

Katy nudged her mum. 'Have you heard from Jack?'

'Yes, there's been a change of plan. He and Eddie are coming to Bolton instead. They'll meet you Saturday evening in the Palais and then come back here for a few days.'

'Yippee, I can't wait.' Katy clapped her hands.

I was confused, Eddie, who was Eddie, he hadn't been mentioned before? Was he another cousin?

'Come on, you've got the blue room.' Katy grabbed my hand. 'I'll show you where it is.'

We walked along the hallway, up a winding staircase and down the corridor. Katy stopped outside a door, turned the knob and led me inside.

'The blue room. Home for the next two weeks. I'm glad you're here.'

I peered in. It looked pleasant enough and someone had certainly gone to a lot of trouble to make it welcoming. A crystal vase sat on the dressing table housing burnt orange cactus dahlias and yellow chrysanthemums. Blue curtains draped the window and a flowery bedspread flowed across the double bed.

'I'll just be next door.' She pointed to the other side of the room. 'Eric's brought up your case so you can get unpacked. Through here is your bathroom.'

Once Katy left the room, I lay down on the bed and cried myself to sleep.

Chapter 3

I awoke to a shaft of sunlight on my face from the gap in the curtains and a chaffinch in full song. If I peeped out of the window, I was sure I'd find him perched on a fence showing off his patterned plumage. There was a tap on the bedroom door. Katy wandered in, wearing a rose-coloured housecoat.

'Good morning Gracie, did you sleep well?' she said, smiling broadly. Her blue-grey eyes shone.

'Actually, I slept very well and I'm looking forward to our day ahead.'

Katy looked relieved. I think she expected me to be drab company for the next couple of weeks. It was strange. Yesterday, I'd been dreading today and wanted to go home but this morning I was excited. I didn't know why. The knots in my stomach had loosened and a daring inner me was craving to get out. Two weeks to find a new Grace before returning to the strict upbringing at home. Yes, I was quite looking forward to it.

'I'll go and get us some tea.' Katy waltzed out of the bedroom.

I popped out of bed and peeped through the window to the garden. The grass was rich green. Burnt orange cactus dahlias, matching those in the vase, shared a flowerbed with purple chrysanthemums and white alyssum. There he was, the chaffinch, sitting as predicted, on a bird table pecking at food in-between tunes. I was happy and contented, ready for my big adventure wherever it may take me.

Katy walked back into the room with a clink of china. She was carrying a tray with a Royal Albert tea set.

'Shall I be Mum?' She tipped the pot, warm liquid trickled into the cups. 'Here you are.'

'Thank you.'

'After breakfast, Mum said she'll do our hair and make-up for the dance. Would you like that?'

'Yes, thank you.' No one had ever set my hair before. Hair and make-up, it was definitely going to be a good day.

'How's your tummy this morning, Gracie?'

'I'm hungry so that's a good sign.'

'We'll finish our tea and then go down for breakfast. Just stick a pair of slacks on after your bath.'

'Slacks?'

'Trousers, you know, like men wear, only designed for women? Can't believe you haven't thought of designing a pair.'

'Oh. Trousers? I don't have any.' I couldn't believe Katy was going to wear trousers and even worse, she wanted me to. It really wasn't acceptable for ladies. At least she hadn't worn them at school, Miss Allison would have had heart failure.

Katy interrupted my thoughts. 'Don't worry, you can borrow a pair of mine. You need to be comfy.'

Katy picked up the tray with the empty cups, left the room and then returned with a pair of brown trousers in her hand.

'Right I'm off for a bath,' she said, and was gone again.

I slid off the bed, strolled into the bathroom and ran the water, adding a box of soap flakes to provide suds. After peeling off my nightdress, I stepped into the bath and let the bubbles cover my nakedness. I closed my eyes and wondered about the upcoming day. When I found myself nodding off I decided to get out. The water had gone cold, anyway. I wrapped myself in a large fluffy towel then sprinkled lavender talcum powder over my body before pulling on Katy's brown slacks and a pink jumper. Keen to join the others I ran a comb through my wet hair and went downstairs.

'Ah Grace, how did you sleep?' Katy's mother asked.

'Very well thank you Mrs Gilmore. The bed was extremely comfortable.'

'Come dear, sit yourself down.' She held her hand out towards the long table. Katy breezed in and sat in a chair opposite me.

'I'll get Maggie to bring in breakfast.' Mrs Gilmore rang a bell.

The maid walked in. 'Yes Miss?'

'Maggie, the girls are ready for breakfast. I'll have mine too.'

'Yes, Mrs Gilmore.' Maggie left the room and returned pushing a hostess trolley. She passed plates of bacon and eggs to us all and set a full toast rack on the table.

'We'll see to the rest,' Mrs Gilmore said, picking up a jug of freshly squeezed orange juice.

Everyone chatted while we ate and I wondered what it would be like if Mother sat this way with Elizabeth and I. Of course it would never happen, everything had to be formal in our house.

Afterwards we cleared the dishes as Katy's mother said it wasn't fair to expect Maggie to do it, she had other chores. I didn't mind. It was fun. We didn't have to wash up, just take them into the kitchen.

'Right girls, what are we going to do with your hair?'

I shrugged. No one had ever asked me this before.

'How about clips to make it curly, Mum?'

'Grace?' Katy's mother turned to me.

'Yes, thank you. That would be nice.'

'Let's go into the recreation room and get started. Grace first. Katy, go and get the Kirby grips out of my bedroom.'

Once I was settled Mrs Gilmore took a few strands of hair at a time, wrapped them around her finger and secured with clips. Next was my friend's turn. Mrs Gilmore did the same to Katy before placing hairnets on our heads turning us into little old ladies.

'Now, what about make-up?' Mrs Gilmore asked.

'I've never worn any, what do you suggest?'

'Well Grace, I think with those lovely big brown eyes, a nice soft green would be the right shade.'

Mrs Gilmore applied a cream foundation to my face and added a flesh coloured powder on top. My skin tingled. She followed with a powdered laurel green eye shadow and then took out a little rectangle box with a black slab and tiny brush to use on my eyelashes.

'Can I see?' I asked.

'No, not yet, I don't want you to look until you're finished.'

'Very well,' I agreed, 'Katy's turn.'

She sat in the chair and her mother repeated the process. Once Mrs Gilmore had finished, we went to sit outside in the garden. I grabbed my notebook, there was nothing like a bit of sun and a bird orchestra to give me inspiration.

The weather was very warm but a welcoming breeze stopped us from feeling stifled. We placed a blanket on the ground to sit on. Katy read a book while I sketched drawings, fashion designs of course.

'Do you think you'll be famous one day?' Katy asked me.

'Definitely,' I said, 'one day I'll have lots of shops and people queuing to purchase my gowns.'

I'm not sure how long we were out there when Katy's mother brought out a hamper basket. 'Lunch.'

'Thank you Mrs Gilmore,' I said.

'Call me Eliza, Mrs Gilmore sounds so formal.'

'I'll try,' I promised.

'Thanks Mum.' Katy ploughed into the picnic.

We munched salmon and cucumber sandwiches on brown bread and drank Sarsaparilla. This time I really enjoyed it and knew it wouldn't come back up.

'Tell me about Eddie. Is he another cousin?' I asked.

Katy laughed. 'No, he's Jack's mate.' Katy's face went tomato red. 'He's my boyfriend.'

I put my hand over my mouth. 'What? You've never mentioned him.'

Katy giggled. The red in her face deepened. 'Can you keep a secret?'

'Of course I can, we've shared a room for the last three years. What?'

She whispered in my ear.

'Golly. You're teasing me?'

She shook her head.

15

'What? All the way? Why haven't you told me before?' I hadn't even kissed a boy.

'I couldn't, not when we were at school. You might have hated me and not spoken to me anymore.'

'Did it hurt?'

'A little, but Eddie was gentle. We love each other. We'll get married now I've finished school so you'd better start designing my wedding dress.'

I was speechless. I half wished she hadn't confided in me. 'Are you having a baby?'

'No, Gracie. He's careful.'

I wasn't sure what that meant. I knew about 'the birds and bees' because they taught us at Greenemere, but not how to be careful. Nice girls didn't do it before getting married. That was the message. Still I wasn't going to judge my friend. She was more like a sister and

I loved her.

'You'll like Jack.'

Sick inside, I smiled.

'Gracie? Are you all right? You've gone very pale.'

I didn't know what to say so I pushed Katy's revelation out of my mind.

Katy looked at her watch. 'It's five o'clock, we should get ready.'

Our lazy afternoon was over, where had the time gone? We went back inside to the recreation room.

I sat in the chair waiting for Mrs Gilmore to complete my transformation. My hair felt soft and bouncy. Without even seeing it, I knew it looked good.

'Wow, you look stunning,' Katy said.

I smiled, knowing that she was telling the truth.

Katy's mother offered a handheld vanity mirror so I could see my face and hair. It didn't look like me, instead a gorgeous young woman stared back. I truly had become a butterfly.

'Is that really me?'

The process was repeated on Katy, she looked beautiful too, but of course I'd seen her made up before, though not this good. Her mother was a brilliant artist.

'Right girls,' she said, 'do you want tea before you go?'

We shook our heads. We were far too excited to eat.

'Go and get dressed then. I can't wait to see the full works.'

We ran upstairs. Yes, I ran too. No hesitation, full of excitement.

I stepped into my red designer dress before going back downstairs to Mrs Gilmore.

'Your frock is beautiful, Grace, which shop did your parents buy it from?'

Before I got the chance to answer, Katy walked in. 'Gracie made it, Mum, and not only made it but designed it. She did mine too. One day she's going to have her own House label.'

'That's very impressive Grace, I'll have to give you my order,' Mrs Gilmore said.

'Of course.' I felt my face flush.

'Well girls you're ready. Just shoes and bags.'

'Grace has red shoes and handbag to match her dress. I have blue.' Katy dabbed me with Yardley English Lavender scent. I wasn't allowed to wear any at home. Father didn't approve.

We rushed upstairs to collect our accessories. I stood in front of the full length mirror. Gosh I looked stunning, like an actress. It was lucky Mother and Father couldn't see me. Strangely, I didn't care. I was going to have fun. For two weeks of my life I was going to be Gracie and not boring Grace.

Chapter 4

'Come on Gracie,' Katy shouted.

I snapped back to reality, gathered my things together and made my way downstairs.

'The car's been waiting, what took you so long?'

My face burned. 'Sorry, I couldn't take my eyes off the new me.'

Katy laughed. 'You do look lovely. Make-up really suits you, and that dress. Red is definitely your colour. The Palais is in for a treat when we arrive.'

Mr Gilmore emerged from the drawing room. 'What a bevy of beauties lies before me.'

Katy rushed up to her father and hugged him.

'Now girls, you need money.' He took a ten shilling note out of his wallet and handed it to Katy. 'This should cover it. Make sure you get coffee and a pastry. For the boys too.'

We thanked him. He walked us to the front door where his wife was waiting.

'You both look exquisite,' she said, 'have a great time.'

The car tooted.

'They're coming, James,' Mr Gilmore called.

The driver got out, opened the car door and we climbed onto the back seat. I looked out of the window as he drove away from Victoria Road. Large houses on Chorley New Road were secluded by tall bushy trees on either side. We left Heaton behind and took a direct route to Bolton's town centre. The sun was starting to set. Before long we stopped outside a large round building on the corner of Higher Bridge Street.

I looked up at the sign. 'Astoria Palais De-Danse.'

'Yes,' Katy answered, 'only we Boltonians call it the Palais. Come on, let's go in.'

We waved goodbye to James. He promised to come and pick us up when the dance finished. The foyer was just inside the door and Katy handed over the banknote to the uniformed cashier who returned six shillings. Katy took my arm and led me towards a door on the left. As we entered, I took in the plush powder room. Big white-framed mirrors hung either side of the wall above swish red and gold chairs. We checked our hair and make-up then descended more stairs to a large cloakroom where we left our coats.

Katy said we needed to meet Jack and Eddie at eight o'clock under the clock in the ballroom. It was nearly time, so we headed that way. Lots of young couples waltzed around the dance floor, the men dressed in plain suits with shirts and ties. Red, blue and spotted dresses twirled in direct contrast to tight black pencil skirts. We headed towards the clock situated by the left of the balcony. There was quite a crowd waiting. Two young men swaggered through the door in long brown draped jackets and narrow legged trousers. As they drew closer I noticed frayed hems and shiny patches on their coats.

'Close your mouth,' Katy said, 'you look like you're catching flies.'

I put my hand over it to stop me sniggering and signalled towards what was making me laugh.

Katy was horrified. 'You're such a snob, Grace Granville.' She waved to the new arrivals.

I realised it must be Jack and Eddie. Shame consumed me.

The young men smiled as they approached.

'Jack. Eddie.' Katy pointed.' Grace,' then she reached out to Jack to give him a brotherly hug and kissed Eddie on the lips.

Jack took my hand, lifted it to his face and kissed it gently. 'Pleased to meet you, Grace.'

Eddie finally took his eyes off Katy to say hello to me. When no one was looking she scowled in my direction. I mouthed I was sorry and sensed her softness returning.

Jack was tall and slim. Although his draped suit was ragged, I could tell the Venetian silk mohair was good quality fabric.

Once he started chatting and I glanced up into his grey blue eyes, the clothes didn't matter. Blonde curls flicked across his forehead.

'Come on, let's dance,' he said. 'It's *The Fat Man*, by Fats Domino.'

He led me to the centre of the floor. Before long he was swinging me under his arms and making me twirl. I hadn't expected him to have such immaculate timing. After a while we went up to the balcony for coffee and a pastry. There was no sign of Eddie and Katy but she'd given me three shillings from the change earlier.

'I'll get them,' I told Jack, but he wouldn't hear of it. He marched up to the counter and ordered cake and two coffees at sixpence each.

We sat down. Jack lifted the cup to his mouth. 'Mmm,' he said, 'sugar, unusual these days.' He smiled. 'I don't know, the war's been over for five years, you'd think sugar rationing would be lifted by now.'

We laughed together. I was having a wonderful time. My heart beat fast, my tummy had more butterflies than a buddleia in bloom. We were so engrossed with each other's company that we didn't notice Katy and Eddie arrive at the table sipping coffees. It was only when I recognised her laugh, I looked up.

'Ah, Gracie,' she said, 'having a good time?'

I smiled, pleased she'd forgiven me.

'Shall we go back downstairs and do a bit more dancing?' Jack asked.

Excited, we all headed back down. I was Cinderella at the ball. I'd only ever danced with girls at school. Yet here I was, gliding around the ballroom with Jack.

We must have danced every Waltz, Foxtrot, Quick Step, Rumba and of course the famous Jive. My feet had never moved so much. The clock struck twelve and the band went silent. Everyone rushed to the cloakroom to collect coats and outdoor shoes. When we walked out of the building, James was ready with the car. We all squashed up on the back seat, leaving me very close to Jack. My heart pounded, I was sure he could hear it and tried hard to silence it, to no avail.

'So what shall we do tomorrow?' Katy asked, 'Queen's Park or the Moors?'

'Maybe the park?' Eddie said. 'We can walk there. Then do the moors in a couple of days?'

'Well we must go to Hall'ith Wood,' she said, 'Gracie needs to visit Samuel Crompton's house and Smithill's Hall.'

I really didn't mind, as long as Jack came too. I'd never felt like this before and I was sure his feelings mirrored mine.

After a couple of miles we turned into Chorley new Road, well lit by numerous lamp posts. Soon we were pulling up the drive to *Willow Banks*.

I was in paradise and never wanted to go back home. Why couldn't I stay here forever? I'd write a letter to Father tomorrow to see if I could extend my visit for the whole summer. We were noisy with chatter when we got out of the car and headed to the open front door where Katy's mother waited.

'Hiya, Aunty Eliza,' Jack said, as he hugged her.

'Hello Jack, good to have you here. Did you manage to get the week off work?'

'Yes, no problems.' He smiled.

Mr Gilmore suddenly appeared. 'Right you young people, it's time you all went to bed.'

Obediently we headed for the stairs to our rooms. I wondered why no one showed Eddie and Jack where to go but decided they must stay quite often. It was such a friendly home, not like my house. When we reached the blue room, Jack kissed me on the cheek. I shut the door behind me and savoured the kiss. Such a shame that I had to wash the make-up off my face as I didn't want to wipe away his kiss. My first kiss. I'd remember it for the whole of my life.

I pulled back the blankets on the bed, climbed in and closed my eyes. Tonight I would have wonderful dreams. I couldn't wait for tomorrow.

21

Chapter 5

The sun beamed through the windows. I stretched my arms above my head and smiled. All I could think of was Jack. I climbed out of bed and sat at the small mahogany desk. Taking a sheet of paper, I wrote...

4ᵗʰ August, 1950,
  Dear Mother and Father...

There was a loud knock on the door and Katy burst in. 'Are you awake?'

I lifted my head from the letter. 'Morning.'

'What are you doing?'

'I'm writing to my parents to see if I can stay the rest of the summer. That's all right isn't it? We did discuss it last night.'

'Of course it is. Do you think they'll let you?'

'I can't see why not.'

'I'm so pleased that I'll have you for company. Hurry up and finish your letter. Do you need a stamp?'

'No.' I dipped into my bag and pulled out a sheet of brown tuppenny stamps bearing the King's head.

'Princess Elizabeth's due her second baby any day. I wonder if she'll have a girl this time,' Katy said.

'I hope so.' I slid my letter into the buff envelope and stuck on a stamp. 'Ready to post. Is there a postbox nearby?'

'Yes, there's one around the corner. We'll post it after breakfast. Let's go and eat, I'm starving.'

I dressed quickly, picked up the letter and followed Katy downstairs. Mrs Gilmore was sitting at the table, reading a newspaper.

'Good morning, girls.' She looked up. 'I'm sure the boys will be down soon.'

'Good morning.' I pulled out a chair.

Maggie pushed a hostess trolley into the room with plates of breakfast. The young girl smiled. Auburn hair tied up in a neat bun showed off her small oval face.

Suddenly there was a loud thud. Jack and Eddie stormed in.

'Morning, Aunty Eliza.' Jack moved over to his aunt and kissed her on the cheek.

'Morning,' Eddie said incoherently, opening his mouth to yawn.

'Come, sit down. Breakfast will go cold.' Mrs Gilmore guided the boys with her hand to their seats.

Everyone chatted over breakfast. The sound of knives and forks, teacups and saucers were only heard during the occasional lull. Jack's eyes twinkled towards me from across the table. I think mine must have sparkled back.

'So what's the plan today?' Eddie said with his mouth full.

'Well, I thought as it's such a lovely day we should take a walk to Queen's Park. Gracie has a letter to post so we can do that on the way.' Katy touched Eddie's hand, their eyes met.

'Sounds good to me.' Jack's chair scraped as he pulled it back. 'How long before you girls are ready?'

'Five minutes,' Katy said.

'Maggie's made up a picnic and put in bread for the ducks,' Mrs Gilmore said. 'Boys, clear up the plates and pick up the hamper while you're in the kitchen.'

'Righto, Aunty.'

Jack and Eddie stacked the plates before striding out of the room.

'Queen's Park, that sounds fun.' I said.

'It's the best park around here,' Katy's mother answered.

We all met at the front door then waved to Mrs Gilmore as we set off.

Eddie and Katy walked on in front, hand in hand. Jack fell in line with me and before we got to the end of the road he clasped his hand into mine. Was Jack my boyfriend? He swung our arms in jovial spirit as we walked leisurely up the road for about two hundred yards. We turned into Chorley New Road where we spotted a red postbox. I took the letter from my pocket, brought it up to my lips and kissed it before popping it into the rectangular mouth.

'Got one for me?' Jack moved towards me.

My face burned so I turned away. We carried on for a short way until we arrived at Queen's Park. The entrance had two Gothic gateposts, like sentries on guard.

I backed away. 'I don't want to go in there.'

'What are you saying?' Katy asked.

'I don't want to go in there... it looks horrible.'

'What are you talking about Gracie?' Katy asked.

'There's danger. I feel it.'

Katy sighed. 'For goodness sake, Grace Granville. We come here all the time. It's a lovely park. The only danger you're likely to encounter is from me if you don't come on. Hold my hand. I'll protect you.'

Eddie and Jack sniggered. Probably thought I was a mad woman. But something wasn't right.

'I thought our Katy was the highly strung one,' Jack whispered to Eddie but loud enough for me to hear.

Katy held out her hand. I took it as we walked slowly through the guarded entrance. Various shades of green greeted us along the path. Tall, bushy trees enveloped us in dark shadows.

'Let's go to the duck pond first,' Katy said. 'You'll see then how wrong you are about this place.'

We wandered along the pathway.

'Look, the children are feeding the ducks. Jack, check the hamper for our bread?' Katy ordered.

Jack pulled out a loaf and broke it into four.

'I was never allowed to feed them when I was a child,' I said.

'No?' Jack stroked my arm.

'Nanny wouldn't let us. Too dangerous by the water, she'd say.'

'Did your mam never take you?' Jack asked.

'No. Mother and Father were far too busy.'

'What a shame.' Jack passed me a quarter of the loaf. 'Never mind, it's fun when grown up too. Break it up small.'

I broke off a piece and threw it into the water. I started to laugh and threw in another as the sun shone on burnished red and golden reeds. Pink and yellow lilies danced. I tried to relax but the dark sensation stayed within me.

Eddie whispered in Katy's ear, she giggled.

'We'll see you two shortly,' he said.

'No, please...'

'Don't be daft, Gracie. What do you think Jack is going to do to you?' Katy asked.

'It's not him.'

She looked at me and sighed. 'Come on Eddie.' They walked away swiftly and soon vanished.

'And then there was two,' Jack said, 'shall we go for a walk?'

I took his hand.

We walked through the park, past the paddling pool where mothers and children gathered. There were shrieks of laughter, and tears.

Jack continued to guide me along. 'Why don't we find somewhere a little more private?'

I wasn't sure what to say, so I just smiled.

We arrived at a patch of grass almost secluded by bushes and trees.

'Shall we sit down?' he asked, softly.

It was a good job I was going to sit because I didn't think my quivering knees would have held me up much longer. I sat down on the prickly grass. The heat from the sun was warm on my hair and shoulders.

'Grace, it's okay. Don't be so tense.'

I giggled like a ten-year-old.

Jack put his arms around me. I jerked away.

'Lie down. Enjoy the sun. I'm not going to hurt you.'

'I know. It's not you.'

He stroked my face lightly, like a feather brushing across my skin. His lips moved towards mine. I closed my eyes but all I could see were the two sentinels at the entrance.

'No,' I said, 'I want to go back.'

He became abrupt. 'Well we can't go back until the others return. For God's sake, Grace. What the hell do you think I'm going to do to you?' He jumped up. 'Come on, we'll go and wait by the bandstand.'

'Don't forget the hamper,' I said lightly not wanting to spoil our day.

He picked it up and we walked along the path. He no longer held my hand but marched on ahead.

'Wait for me,' I called.

Jack stopped. He turned to me, his face like thunder.

I held out my hand, he took it and grasped it within his.

'Sorry,' I said, 'it really isn't you. It's this place.'

He brought his lips to mine. This time when they brushed, I let them stay. Just at that moment Eddie and Katy appeared. She looked dishevelled and was smoothing down her dress. Her face was flushed.

'Did Jack look after you, Gracie?'

'Yes, he did. What have you two been up to?'

'Gracie, you don't ask questions like that.' Eddie winked.

I couldn't believe they could be so brazen.

'Let's eat.' Katy pointed. 'Over there on the grass.'

She began to undo the hamper. 'Spam sandwiches.' She passed them around, then pulled out a bottle of Sarsaparilla and four glasses.

Eddie handed round a bag of sweets. 'Jack and I saved our rations up.'

'Pear drops. Ooh, my favourite,' Katy licked her lips.

'I know, darling.' Eddie kissed her cheek.

We munched on the picnic and listened to birdsong, high up in the trees above us. I wanted to feel tranquil but menacing thoughts haunted me. A wet drop fell on my hand. 'Rain.'

'I didn't feel anything,' Jack said.

'She's right. It's starting to rain,' Katy shouted, 'quick, run for shelter.'

Everything was gathered up and we ran to the bandstand just as torrential rain began to fall.

'Let's pretend we're the band,' Katy said, imitating a trumpet player.

Eddie had a French horn, Jack a drum and I followed suit with Katy. It was fun but I still couldn't relax. The rain stopped after a few minutes leaving behind a rainbow in the sky. Thankfully, it was decided we should make our way back home before it started again. As we walked out of the park, I looked up at the pillars and shivered.

'Grace, what's the matter,' Jack asked. He took out a clean handkerchief from his pocket and wiped my tears.

'I'm just happy,' I lied.

Chapter 6

I was on my way downstairs when Jack caught up with me.

'Morning, Grace, did you sleep well?'

I turned around and smiled. 'Yes, thank you, Jack.'

Chatter came from the dining room. Katy and Eddie were down first today.

'Hey, lazy bones,' Katy teased, 'I hope you didn't spend the night together?'

Thank goodness Mr and Mrs Gilmore weren't in the room. I didn't know where to look.

'Give over, our Katy,' Jack said, 'you're embarrassing the poor girl. You know damn well we didn't.'

Katy laughed. 'Sorry Gracie, I couldn't resist when you both came in at the same time.'

'Well, it's not funny, Katy. Not everyone's like you,' Jack said.

'You asked for that, Katy.' Eddie laughed.

She fidgeted. 'Well, we'd better eat so we can get out. Gracie, the boys go home tomorrow.'

'I know,' I said quietly, wishing that it didn't have to end. The week had gone by far too quickly. Jack had swept me off my feet. We'd been out every day to so many places since our first outing at Queen's Park.

Mr Gilmore popped in. 'I've a letter for young Grace. You're a popular young lady, one yesterday and another today.'

I took it and stared at the writing.

'They haven't changed their minds about letting you stay, have they?' Katy asked.

I shook my head. 'It's not Mother's writing, it's Elizabeth's. I hope she's all right.'

'Open it. You won't find out by glaring at it,' Eddie ordered.

I tore the envelope, pulled out the sheet of paper and started to read, *Dear Grace...*

The others watched in anticipation.

'Nanny's taking Elizabeth to stay with a distant cousin of Mother's. They're going down to Bournemouth. Mother must have decided this after Father agreed I could stay here.'

'Smashing,' Katy said, 'now we can enjoy the rest of the vacation without you feeling guilty. Where shall we go today? It's going to be another scorcher.'

'Why don't we go up the moors?' Jack suggested.

'Sounds like a plan,' Eddie said with his mouth full. He mopped up his egg with a slice of toast.

I wondered what my parents would make of the boys' table manners. Katy's were fine, she'd been taught at school.

'Right, the moors it is then,' Katy said. 'I'll go and ask Maggie to make up the picnic basket while we get ready.'

Katy disappeared from the room. Eddie and Jack talked about down the mines and football.

'How do you feel about going back to work?' I asked them.

'I'd rather stay here with you.' Jack winked at me, making my stomach flutter and my face felt like it was flushing again.

'It brings the bread in, Grace,' Eddie said, 'and it's what we know.'

I wished I hadn't asked such a silly question.

'Come on, you lot. Let's go.' Katy thrust the wicker hamper at Eddie. 'You can carry this. Tar-ra, Mum.'

We trundled off. I was getting to know my way around. It was a long walk to the moors but worth it for the view.

'I'm really thirsty,' I confessed after a couple of miles.

Jack pulled out a flask and poured some water. 'Here, Grace. There's plenty.'

I sipped it and immediately felt better. Jack took my hand and we carried on climbing the hills until we reached the top.

Eddie sprawled out a blanket on the open ground, free from trees and shrubs. We sat down and ate our picnic.

Katy pulled Eddie to his feet. 'Let's find somewhere private. We'll meet you two at...' She looked at her watch. 'Err shall we say four o'clock? Over there, by that tree.'

Jack and I agreed. We watched them run off before gathering up the leftover food.

'Come and lie down next to me,' Jack patted the ground.

I lay down and closed my eyes in anticipation. I wasn't disappointed, until... 'What was that?' I said.

Jack laughed. 'You have to bring your tongue to meet mine. Then it won't feel like you're swallowing it. It's a French kiss.'

'You're so experienced. Have you had lots of girlfriends?'

'Well yeah, but I'm older. I've never had one as lovely as you.'

'Do you mind that I'm so naive? How old are you, anyway?'

'Mind? Of course not. I'm twenty-one. And you? Sixteen?'

'I'll be seventeen in March.'

He came down towards me but this time I was ready.

'Gentle, Grace. Don't push. Softly. Yeah, that's better.'

My heart leapt. I was ecstatic. Something brushed against my breast. It was light and quick making me wonder whether it was my imagination. Then his hand moved up my blouse.

'No, don't Jack.'

'Shh, I only want to tickle your tummy. You don't mind?'

I didn't think there was any harm in that. 'No, of course not.'

Jack's hand crept up my back until he reached my bra strap.

'No, Jack. I'm not ready.'

'Sorry Grace. I'll behave.'

We carried on kissing. He wrapped my hair around his fingers and stroked my face. I started to relax until his hand wandered up my skirt.

'Jack. No.'

'Sorry sweetheart. We should go for a walk.'

'You don't mind? Me not letting you?'

'Of course not, darling.'

I scrambled off the ground with mixed feelings. Part of me wished I'd let him carry on, wondering what it would have been like. But the inner voice of Good Grace assured me that I'd done the right thing. We strolled along, hand in hand.

'Tell me about your parents, Grace.'

'Well according to your cousin, they're snobs. I don't really know them. Most of my time at home has been spent with Nanny and Elizabeth. I'm closer to Katy than anyone else. I've never had cuddles or bedtime stories.'

'That must have been hard?'

'Well, I didn't know any different. That is until I met Katy. How about you? Tell me about your parents.'

Jack's eyes moistened. 'Mam died when I was eleven. That just left Da and me.'

I pressed his hand. 'I'm sorry. What happened?'

'She stuck her head in the oven and gassed herself. Da says she was highly strung one minute and down the next. I don't recollect much. Manic depressive, they told Da. Have you heard of that?'

'No, I haven't.'

'I worry about our Katy, she's the same. High one minute and down the next. Have you noticed?'

'Some days she is high spirited.'

Jack nodded. 'That's what I mean, I think we need to watch her.'

I thought he was overreacting. 'What about your father?'

'Da does his best. Coughs a lot, think it's the last thirty years down the mine coming back to haunt him.'

Just then a family passed by flying a kite.

'Ooh look at that.' I pointed.

'Have you ever flown one?'

'No.'

'Hang on.' Jack ran after the family He came back with the red triangular object in his hand. 'Come on, take this. I'll hold it with you.'

The kite sailed to the skies. Jack released the string to free it higher and then brought it back down to the ground. 'That's what Mam was like.' He chased after the family. 'Thank you,' he said, and handed the kite back.

I checked my watch.

'What's the time?' Jack asked.

'It's almost four o'clock; we should make our way back to that tree.'

'Yeah. Come on, I'll race you.'

Gasping for breath I arrived at the winning post.

He took out the flask and poured water into the cup. 'Of course I let you win.'

'Any of that left for us?' Katy shouted as she and Eddie approached.

'Plenty,' answered Jack.

We sat down and ate the rest of the picnic, drank sarsaparilla, then packed up ready for the long trek home.

I was subdued on our return journey, the week had gone by too quickly.

'What's up, sweetheart?' Jack asked.

'You go back home tomorrow. Will I see you again?'

'Of course, try keeping me away. We'll travel up at weekends or you girls can come to Wigan. You're special Grace Granville and I'm not letting you go.'

I gazed into his grey blue eyes. His soft lips kissed mine.

'Hey, that wasn't supposed to make you cry.' Jack wiped my wet cheeks.

*

After dinner, the boys went to pack before bed.

Katy came into my room and sat next to me. 'Well?' she said. 'How was today?'

'We did French kissing.'

'What?'

'It's where you use tongues.'

'Yes, I know what it is. I just didn't expect it from my cousin. Eddie's never kissed me that way. I've heard other girls talk about it. So? Did you do it?' She nudged me.

I was puzzled.

'You know?' She lay back slowly on my bed. 'It? Like Eddie and me?'

I shook my head.

'Did he try?'

'Well he had hands like an octopus, if that's what you mean?'

'He took no, for an answer?'

'Yes, of course.'

Katy frowned. 'Eddie never did. He said if I loved him then I'd do it.'

'Jack said it didn't matter. I suppose he respects me.'

Katy sat up. 'So you're saying Eddie doesn't respect me?'

'No, that's not what I meant.'

She slapped my face. 'Shut-up, Grace. Little Miss Prim, Virgin Grace.'

My cheek stung. Speechless, I stared at her. No one had ever struck me before. She stormed off the bed, stopped to glare at me and then slammed the bedroom door.

I didn't know whether to laugh or cry. I was in love and elated but my best friend had just hit me. I wasn't equipped to tackle this sort of thing. No one had told me how. Tomorrow Jack would leave and Katy may not be my friend. Maybe I should pack my bags too.

I took my nightdress from under my pillow, undressed, climbed into bed and cried myself to sleep.

Chapter 7

Last night's events played on my mind and I wasn't sure if I should get my case from under the bed.

Katy burst into my room. 'Good morning, Gracie. Did you sleep well?'

Confused, I smiled. I hadn't slept well at all but wasn't going to say.

'The boys are waiting downstairs. James is going to run them to the station to catch the nine o'clock train, so if you want to say goodbye you'd better hurry.'

I slipped on my pink dressing gown and followed her.

Jack and Eddie were at the bottom of the stairs chatting to Katy's parents, duffel bags hauled across their shoulders.

Mr Gilmore passed Jack a pound note. 'Train fare, lad.'

'Thanks, Uncle Max.'

'Thanks, Mr Gilmore,' Eddie echoed.

Outside, James drew up in the Rolls.

Jack turned to me. 'I thought you weren't coming. That maybe you'd had enough of me.'

'Sorry, I overslept.'

'Come here.' He held me in his arms. We kissed goodbye.

The boys climbed into the car. Katy and I watched it drive away. Her eyes sparkled with tears.

'Are we friends?' I asked.

She didn't respond.

'Last night?'

'Oh, that? Sorry.'

'But you slapped me?'

'I overreacted. Forget about it.'

'But Katy, you can't go round striking me just because you didn't like what I said.'

'You're right of course. But now we need to look after each other. You can be Miss Bossy tomorrow.'

'Don't mock me, Katy. You're supposed to be my friend. Am I still welcome as your guest, or should I be leaving too?'

'Don't, Gracie. Of course you're welcome. I'm sorry. I don't know what came over me.'

'Fair enough. I'm going to get dressed for breakfast.'

'Me too, race you.'

She was like two different people. Jack's words echoed in my ear about his mother being manic depressive. Could Katy be like his mother? I saw Katy in a new light.

*

We spent the next few days in the garden enjoying the sun, doing girl stuff. This morning I was working on dress designs while Katy drew birds, flowers and trees. Our closeness returned and I tried to erase last Saturday night's tantrum from my brain.

Mr Gilmore came out, 'Are you girls off to Wigan tomorrow?'

'Yes, Daddy, I thought it would be good for Gracie to see how the other half lives.'

'Hmm, well as long as her parents know,' he said.

'Yes, they don't mind at all,' Katy lied.

We hadn't mentioned Wigan to Mother or Father. In fact I hadn't written to them for over a week. I didn't see the need, they probably wouldn't bother reading it if I did.

'We're going on the train,' Katy continued. 'I thought it would be exciting for Gracie.'

'Good idea,' he answered, 'I'll get Eric to bring you train times. James can bring you back home, I'm not having you on public transport in the dark.'

'Brilliant,' Katy said, in a high pitched voice. She turned to me. 'You'll have to borrow a pair of my slacks.'

I didn't feel comfortable wearing her slacks, but I assumed they were needed for the train.

Maggie kept us replenished with refreshments throughout the day. She brought water, sarsaparilla, milk, sandwiches and fruit. The atmosphere between Katy and I was like old times at Greenemere.

*

I stepped into Katy's checked trews and paired them up with a red turtle necked blouse. My hair was in a high ponytail. Grace Granville, you'll do, I thought.

'Katy, hurry up.' I'd been standing outside her bedroom for ages. My pulse raced at the thought of seeing Jack.

'I'm coming, where's the fire?' She rushed to the top of the landing and mounted the banister. Climb on behind.'

She didn't have to tell me twice.

'We're going down,' she said, 'hold on tight.'

I clung on to her waist. It was Bernie all over again. Oh dear. I sensed my face burn when Katy's father appeared at the bottom of the stairs. He was standing with a newspaper under his arm, his mouth wide open.

'Sorry, Mr Gilmore,' I said.

He roared with laughter. 'This is what I miss when Katy's at school. Good to see.' He tapped me on the shoulder before disappearing into the lounge, laughing. Katy looked at me, we giggled.

I knew the routine now so helped myself to orange juice without being offered and sat down to eat. Katy sat opposite. Mrs Gilmore joined us.

'Has Eric given you the train times, Mum?'

'Yes he has. Catch the ten o'clock if you can, James will pick you up at Wigan Pier at eight in the evening.' She passed a sheet of paper.

James drove us to Moor Lane Station where we bought single tickets from the cashier. The train slid in about ten minutes later.

There was a big gap between the step and platform. It made my head spin when I looked down.

'Be careful stepping up,' Katy warned as she turned the handle of the train door.

We made ourselves comfortable in a first class compartment. A man sitting opposite was reading a newspaper.

Katy nudged me and whispered, 'He's pretending to read the paper but peeping over. Look.'

We looked at each other and burst out laughing.

The smart looking woman next to him wrinkled her forehead, she focused on our slacks and turned up her nose. This made us giggle more.

The train went clickety clack, clickety clack.

'It's telling us to go to sleep, go to sleep.' I tapped my leg to the rhythm.

'It is, isn't it? I hadn't thought of that before.'

The woman tutted. She disembarked three stops later at Hindley Green with the man. This left Katy and I alone in the cabin. The whistle blew.

'Bloody snob,' Katy said, 'who did she think she was? Queen of Sheba? And him? Dirty bugger. Couldn't keep his eyes off us.'

'Katy.'

'Well, he was.'

We pulled in at Hindley. An elderly lady struggled to get on. I got up to assist.

'Next stop is ours,' Katy told me, 'we need to be ready. Have you enjoyed the journey?'

'Yes, it's fun. The train doesn't make me sick. It's strange watching the trees, they seem to move as we whizz by on the track.'

Katy laughed. 'Yes they do. Don't worry, I have travel sick tablets in my bag in case you need them for going home.'

The train slowed into Wigan. Our boyfriends waved from the platform. Jack held out his hand to help me down off the train. His face drew close and his lips touched mine. My knees trembled. Jack was my destiny, I knew that now.

'Hey, are you all right?' He balanced me.

'Just a bit dizzy.'

Lean on me. Maybe we should get some food inside you, there's a little café down the road.'

The others agreed. After walking a few hundred yards we entered a small gloomy café. We satisfied our hunger then took a stroll around the shops.

Katy stopped at a window full of shoes. 'Clogs,' she shouted, 'I've always wanted clogs. I want to try on a pair.'

'The owner's a craftsman,' Jack informed us, 'Wigan Clogs are known throughout.'

We all crowded in. Katy and I both left carrying bags of black wooden clogs.

'Morris dancing,' Katy ordered.

'Morris Dancing?' I queried. I'd never heard of it.

'Yeah, Eddie echoed, 'you and Katy can give us a show. Let's go to Haigh Park, plenty of room for you girls to dance. Might even join in.'

A short stroll out of town brought us to an arched entrance.

'What danger lies behind this stone doorway, Grace?' Eddie teased.

Jack turned to Eddie and put up his fists. 'Leave her alone.'

'What's up Mate?' Eddie laughed.

'He was just clowning,' Katy said, 'don't be so serious, Jack.'

Jack raised his voice. 'Look at her face. It looks as if Dracula has been at her.'

All eyes fixed on me. 'Stop it. You're supposed to be grown men, yet you act like infants in nappies.'

Jack put his arms around me. 'I'm sorry. Eddie shouldn't have upset you. No one upsets my girl and gets away with it.'

'For goodness sake, Jack. I'm not made of bone china. And you, Eddie?' I shook my head.

'I'm sorry Grace,' Eddie said, 'I never meant... It was a joke.' He turned to Jack. 'Come on buddy, we're best buds.'

Jack growled. 'Well watch it mate.'

'It's fine.' I refused to cry.

Katy pushed the boys together and joined their little fingers. 'Shake,' she ordered.

They obliged, then everyone laughed.

'Let's go to the bandstand.' Katy grabbed Eddie's hand.

Jack and I followed. He wrapped his arm around my shoulder making me feel safe and secure but I was upset at how quickly his temper had flared.

'There it is,' Katy shouted, 'come on.' She raced ahead to the bandstand to demonstrate Morris dancing. She danced on the spot. Knees nearly to her chin, arms waving in the air. I climbed on to the platform and copied. Luckily I was a quick learner. Tap tap went the clogs. I loved the sound. The boys joined in and before long a crowd of children stopped to watch.

'What's the time?' Eddie asked.

I looked at my watch. 'It's six o'clock. We need to be back at the station for eight.' 'Well, I'd like a bit of time on me own with me girlfriend, if you and Jack don't mind?'

'No, go.' Jack ushered them off.

Eddie took Katy by the arm and led her away. Jack held my hand as we roamed through the park. Birdsong enveloped us.

'Would you like to sit under that big oak tree?' Jack asked, more like his old self.

We snuggled and kissed, but his hands didn't wander. We stayed like that until Eddie and Katy jumped up behind us.

'Boo,' they shouted.

'Hello.' I turned around to see them.

'It's time to go.' Katy dragged me up off the ground. 'James is meeting us at eight, remember?'

I wished I could have stayed all night.

Jack heaved himself up and took my hand. We walked briskly out of the park to our location.

Katy waved to James as we approached the station. He was standing by the Rolls with a cigarette in his hand and passed it to her automatically. She drew it to her lips and blew out smoke.

Jack held me close. 'Until next weekend, sweetheart.'

Katy and I stepped into the back of the car and waved to the boys. I wound my window down.

Jack came running beside me. 'I love you Grace Granville.'

'I love you too, Jack Gilmore.'

On the way home, I savoured his words.

Chapter 8

We approached the end of August and the evenings had started to draw in. The boys had been up the past couple of weekends but today was our last meeting before I'd return home to Gerrard's Cross. Father was sending a driver tomorrow. I didn't want to go. And even worse was the possibility that I may not be allowed to come back for college. Katy and I had gone along to Bolton Grange for open day. Father's argument was that I needed to learn how to run a household and they wouldn't teach me that at college. Although, he hadn't refused outright, his letter was clear. He saw my designs as a waste of time.

I folded my belongings neatly into the suitcase.

'What are you doing up there?' Katy called.

'Packing, I want it done before Jack arrives. Are they here yet?'

'No, but they will be shortly. You should come and eat, you need to keep your energy levels up.'

'I'm coming.' I flipped the lid closed and made my way downstairs.

Katy grabbed me. 'I'm going to miss you. Say you'll definitely be back for college.'

'I'll try.'

'Have you got the pamphlets?'

'Yes.' I didn't mention Father suggested I couldn't go.

'That's if you don't elope with Jack. I've never seen him so smitten.'

'Really? You really think that?'

'Gosh, Gracie, usually he only sees a girl twice at the most. You're the one. He told Eddie.'

'He's the one for me, too. He did say he loved me.'

'Nothing or no one can stand between true love. Not even your high and mighty parents.'

A car door slammed. 'Was that the Rolls?' I asked.

'Sounds like it, come on. Let's go and meet them.'

We hurried to the door just in time to see the boys climbing out of the car. I ran down the steps and into Jack's arms.

He dropped his duffel bag to the ground. 'I've missed you too, sweetheart.'

'Let the man get in,' Eddie said. Katy got a casual peck on the cheek.

'I couldn't wait either,' Jack said.

We hugged each other tightly. Katy glanced at me. It was a strange look, like she hated me. What had I done? It wasn't my fault Eddie was cold. I didn't trust him. Most days she'd wait for the letter that never came and watch with envy when mine arrived from Jack.

'Hurry, Maggie's got the kettle on,' Katy ordered.

'I'd rather have a beer,' Eddie said, 'you girls don't mind if Jack and I whip down the pub for an hour do you? This heat's given me a thirst.'

Katy opened her mouth to speak but then changed her mind.

'Well I'm not going anywhere,' Jack said, 'I want to spend the short time left with my girl. It's up to you if you want to go to the pub but I'm sure Uncle Max has got beer in the house.'

'He has,' Katy interrupted.

'Fair enough, we'll sit in the garden,' Eddie said.

'Now what have you been up to?' Jack took my hand and led me into the house.

'Missing you.' I kissed him softly.

'I've been waiting all week for that. Grace, do you have to go home?'

'Yes, Father's sending the car tomorrow afternoon. We need to make the most of our time. But hopefully, I'll be back in a couple of weeks to go to college with Katy.'

Jack eyes saddened. 'Grace, I want you to come and see where I live.'

'What, in Wigan? Yes we can do that sometime,' I answered.

'I mean today.'

'Why?'

'I need to know if you can accept me... Accept me for who I am. It's better we find out now.'

Somehow this sounded like a test and I wasn't sure I could cope with failing.

Mrs Gilmore came to the dining room doorway. 'Come on lovebirds, time for refreshment. Where have Eddie and Katy gone?'

'To find beer, Aunty,' Jack answered.

'That lad drinks far too much.' She tutted.

Eddie had been distant to Katy over the last couple of weeks. I wondered if Jack knew something. I'd ask him later when we were alone. Mrs Gilmore rang the bell.

The maid appeared. 'Yes Madam?'

'Can you bring tea, please, Maggie? Send Katy and Eddie in too.'

'Yes, Madam.'

Mrs Gilmore chatted. Jack and I gazed at each other, longing to be alone.

'Ah there you are,' Mrs Gilmore said as Katy and Eddie strolled in.

His smile showed yellowed teeth. Froth covered his upper lip. He wiped it clean with his tongue.

Jack turned to me and saw disgust on my face. He just laughed. 'Aunty.'

'Yes, Jack?'

'Is James free? I'd like him to drive Grace and me over to Da's.'

'Do you think that's a good idea?' Mrs Gilmore asked.

'I want Grace to see where I come from. And Da to meet my girl.'

'Well, if you think that's the right thing. I'm sure it can be arranged. You do know Katy can't come too? Uncle Max will never allow it.'

Jack nodded. 'It'll just be the two of us.'

'Be back in time for dinner.'

'Yeah, sure.' He turned to me. 'Grace?'

He looked so vulnerable, standing there, the question clear in his eyes. I was powerless to refuse.

Katy nudged Eddie. 'That means you and I can go for a stroll?'

Eddie's eyes glinted. 'Yes, Mam.'

'Don't keep Gracie too long, Jack,' Katy said. 'Remember, she's my best friend and goes home tomorrow.'

Jack smiled. 'Don't worry cuz. I'll have her back by six.'

We were silent on the journey. Jack looked thoughtful. I enjoyed being close to him, I could feel his heart beat.

It took under forty-five minutes to reach Wigan. As James drove through the town, I recognised some shops and the café where we ate on our last visit. The roads changed, they became cobbled and narrow. Tiny little houses appeared, like boxes. Almost maze like.

'It's the next street, isn't it?' James asked Jack.

'Yeah, it is. Once you've dropped us if you want to go off for an hour?'

James stopped alongside one of the tiny dwellings. He looked at his watch. 'I'll be back by four?'

'That's ample time. We'll be ready,' Jack said.

James drove off and left us standing on the kerb. Coal dust was everywhere. I wished I hadn't worn white. If only I'd known.

'Sorry, Grace. I expect your skirt will get dirty.'

What could I say? I wanted to say it was one of my favourites. Instead I smiled and hoped it would come up clean in the laundry. 'No problem, Jack. Why wouldn't Mr Gilmore let Katy come?'

'Nothing to worry about. Da thinks Uncle Max abandoned his family for wealth. They had a big row so don't speak.'

'But surely, wouldn't Max help your family?'

'Yeah, he would. But that's not how it works with our lot. Our lives are down the pit.' He took my hand and guided me around the back of the house into a filthy courtyard. The stench was unbearable and I couldn't stop the reflex of bringing my hand to my mouth.

'It's the lav,' Jack informed me, 'over there. See them queuing? It's one between five families. Not what you're used to. Eh?'

I bent my head. I didn't want him to see revulsion on my face. He lifted my head up, held me close and kissed me hard. Nothing else seemed to matter.

'Da's in here.' He pushed open a battered wooden door and steered me in. 'Only me, Da,' he shouted, 'I've brought someone to meet you.'

There was no hallway. We entered a small dismal room. A man with greying hair sat on a couch by the fireplace, but the grate was empty. He was reading a newspaper. I noticed a bottle of whisky on a dresser and a narrow bed by the window. A small gas cooker stood on the other side of the room next to a large sink.

'Da, this is Grace. Remember, I told you about her?'

'How do you do, Mr Gilmore.' I offered my hand.

He looked me up and down. His stare made me uncomfortable.

'I can see why the lad's smitten,' he said. 'Pass the bottle, Jack.'

'It's a bit early isn't it?' Jack asked.

His father spluttered and brought a blackened handkerchief to his mouth, to catch phlegm. Once again I covered my mouth, praying I wouldn't be sick.

'Put the kettle on, girl.' Mr Gilmore turned to the stove.

I wondered who he was talking to. Then realised he meant me.

'I'll do it, Da.'

'What, she too good to make a pot of cha?'

Tears pricked my eyes but I was determined not to cry.

'Come and sit next to me,' his father said, patting the couch.

I sat on the not too clean cover and wondered what disease I may contract. I itched all over.

'It's all right, Grace. We don't have to stay long,' Jack whispered in my ear.

It was quite clear his father didn't like me and the feeling was mutual but we did have one thing in common. Jack. While he was making tea, his father thought it permissible to place a hand on my leg.

I jumped up.

'Problem?' Jack asked.

'Na, Na,' Mr Gilmore said, 'it was a spider. It's gone now. Isn't that right?' He glared at me.

'Yes, a spider.' I shivered.

'We do tend to get some big ones this time of the year.' Jack pressed his lips to my cheek. 'Here's your tea.'

I drank from the stained mug. Willing the time to pass quickly, I tried to be pleasant and sociable, joining in conversation. For Jack's sake. After what seemed an eternity, a car tooted outside.

'That'll be James,' Jack said. 'Will you be all right, Da? I'll be back tomorro' night.'

'Yeah lad, you go.'

'Well you could always come too,' Jack pleaded, 'bury the feud, once and for all?'

'Don't push it, lad. It's bad enough you go up there. Don't be getting fancy ideas. The pit's your life.' He flew an accusing look across to me.

I tilted my head in shame. This was Jack's home, Jack's family and all I could do was feel contempt. If I loved Jack as much as I thought, I should be able to overlook things. Surely.

'Come on, sweetheart, say bye to Da and we'll be on our way.'

I stepped slowly towards him.

He put his hand up to his left cheek. 'Kiss.'

I held back.

'Give me da a kiss, Grace.'

I moved towards his father. For the briefest moment my lips brushed his face. It was horrid.

Jack held my hand as we walked through the smelly courtyard.

'Wait.' I brushed my skirt and looked down at my bare black smothered legs. Tears escaped. 'I'm sure Uncle Max could help?'

'Don't, Grace. You heard Da. My place is down the pit.' He folded his arms. 'This isn't going to work.'

'Yes it will, Jack. I promise.'

He shook his head. 'I love you, but...'

'I love you too.'

'Coal mining is my lot. That's who I am. I don't think you can live with that.' He lifted my face. 'He's not always like that you know? We caught him on a bad day. After Mam gassed herself, it was hard for him but he kept going. He brought me up and didn't do a bad job, did he?'

I gave a small laugh. I was embarrassed for being judgemental.

'Then a few weeks ago the bosses laid him off with Black Lung. Said he wasn't fit for work. So he's given up and started to drink. Especially when I'm not around.'

'I'm sorry,' I said. 'What's Black Lung?'

'It's a respiratory disease that miners get. It's due to coal dust.'

'Will you get it?'

'I'm not sure. Possibly.'

'Why don't you get out? I'm sure Uncle Max would give you a job in his mill.'

'I told you, Grace. Coal mining is me. You haven't listened to a thing. Have you? It's my heritage and if you marry me, it'll be our sons' too.'

My face gave me away.

'Exactly. You can't accept it.'

'I'll try.'

Jack pushed me at arm's length. 'I'm not coming back to Bolton. I need to think. We both need time.' He led me to the car, opened the door and pushed me gently inside. 'Bye, Grace. James, look after her please.'

The driver nodded and started the car. Jack walked away. I called him but he didn't look back. The scene in the dirty little house stayed with me. What I couldn't comprehend was how Jack had been seeded from such a vile creature. Would he come back to me? And if he did would I cope with our future or was he right? The thought of a child of mine going down a pit tore my insides but what was I to do? I didn't want to lose Jack. I closed my eyes for the rest of the journey and prayed that if we had a son, I'd change his mind by then.

Eddie and Katy were sitting on the steps cuddling when the car stopped. They'd obviously sorted out their differences.

'Good God,' Katy said, 'look at the state of you.'

'I'm going for a bath.'

'Where's Jack?' she asked.

'He stayed in Wigan.'

She touched my hand. 'I'm sorry, Grace.'

This Grace needed to toughen up. I'd show them all.

Chapter 9

It was quieter than usual when I made my way down to breakfast. Katy hadn't come to my room and the dining room was empty. Although I'd no appetite I sat down, poured myself a glass of orange juice and nibbled on a slice of toast. Father's car would be here later. This wasn't how I'd planned my last day. Would Jack come back before I left? Maybe I should have allowed his hands to wander. If I really loved him, then I'd have let him, surely? But then if he loved me, he'd wait. I was in deep thought when Mrs Gilmore walked in.

'Good morning, Grace.'

Momentarily confused, I asked, 'Have I done something wrong? Where is everyone?'

'No, of course not.' She sat down next to me. 'We thought you must have overslept, the others have eaten.'

'I was sorting out my clothes.'

'While we're on our own, I wanted a quiet word with you. What do your parents think about you and Jack? Do they know?'

'Please don't tell them.'

'I want you to think hard, your whole life is ahead of you. A holiday romance is fine but it doesn't have to become serious.'

'I don't think Jack wants me anymore. He didn't come back with me yesterday, did he?'

'If it's over, then it's for the best.' She put her arm around my shoulder and smiled.

What did she know? What did she know of my feelings? It wasn't a holiday romance, it was real. 'We love each other, Mrs Gilmore. There's no age limit on love.'

'Well... if you need to talk?' She patted my leg and left the room.

I checked my watch and was about to leave too when Mr Gilmore walked in.

He reached for the teapot and poured himself a cup of tea. 'Are you all right Grace? I heard about Jack?'

I took out my handkerchief to wipe my tears.

'Now, now, dear. I'm sure it'll be fine.' He picked up his copy of *The Times* and disappeared from the room.

A door slammed and lighter footsteps headed my way. Katy strolled in. 'Do you feel like coming to the park?'

'I think I'd rather stay here in case Jack turns up.'

'I don't want to leave you on your own. We can sit in the garden?'

I shrugged my shoulders. I didn't want to witness them fidget, desperate to be on their own. 'You and Eddie go, I'll be fine. I promise.'

'Are you sure?' She brightened. 'We'll be back in a couple of hours.'

From the window, I observed them slope down the steps, hand in hand before I ventured out into the garden to try and work on some designs.

There was a bright blue sky and the sun was still warm. I daydreamed about Jack caressing my body, his fingertips running across my tummy, up my blouse. Our bodies melded. I didn't push him away. A shadow hovered, bringing me to a jolt. I looked up to see Maggie standing next to me.

'I've brought you lemonade, Miss. It's hot out here. Madam said to keep you hydrated.'

'Thank you.'

She looked at me with pity. I didn't want that, so I turned away until she'd gone. Even the servants knew. I tried to concentrate on my drawings but now and then I couldn't help breaking down in tears, soaking my handkerchief. I'd just finished blowing my nose again when I glanced up. Katy was watching me.

'Gracie, I knew I shouldn't have left you.'

'I'm fine, really I am.' With that I let the tears spill again.

'Will you still come back?'

Jack or no Jack I wanted to go to college with Katy. There was no way I wanted to stay at the mansion in that clinical

50

environment. Jack must come back. How could he not? If he loved me, like he said.

'Are you packed?' Eddie came from nowhere. 'Katy's mum and dad are waiting for you. Your driver will be here soon. Come and have tea, before you go.'

How rudely I was behaving. These people had shown me nothing but hospitality for the last six weeks and I'd repaid them by hiding in the garden on my own.

Mr and Mrs Gilmore were sitting in the drawing room. He was reading the newspaper. She was pouring tea. 'Grace, sit down.' She passed me a cup. 'Help yourself to cake.'

I couldn't eat a thing, but thanked her and sipped the warm liquid. I selected a small slice from the slab of fruitcake and teased the crumbs with my fork.

Eric appeared. 'Miss Grace's car is here and her bag's loaded in the boot.'

'Thank you.' I smiled.

Katy and I clung to each other. She was like a sister and I didn't want to leave. 'I wish you could come back with me?'

'Me too, but you heard what Mum and Dad said. You need to spend time with your family. We'll write every day?'

'Yes, of course,' I promised.

As we wandered towards the door, I said my goodbyes to Eddie and Mr Gilmore. Then finally Katy's mother. She embraced me like I was her own.

'I'm such a softie.' She wiped her cheek. 'You're like a daughter. I can't wait for you to return.'

'And you're like a mum.' I hugged her again. 'Thank you. Thank you for everything.'

We walked out to the car in convoy, Katy and I in front, followed by my surrogate parents, with Eddie at the tail. I prayed I'd be back soon.

'You need to take a Kwell.' Katy passed me a small tablet and the thin box. 'Take these with you.'

A familiar grey limousine sat outside the house. The chauffeur stood by the open rear door. 'Miss.'

I hadn't been back to *Granville Hall* since Easter, the thought made me shiver. I bade the Gilmores goodbye. Just one more hug for all. They stood on the steps as I climbed into the Rolls.

The journey home was long and tiresome, no friendly chatter from the driver. I didn't even know his name. Already I missed James's familiarity. I tried to sleep but that made me queasy. The chauffeur eventually drove through the mansion gates at Gerrard's Cross. I got out of the vehicle and knocked on the front door. Martha opened it.

'Good evening, Miss Grace. Your father will meet you in the drawing room at eight.'

'Thank you.' I looked around the familiar hall with new eyes. Although it was furnished similar to the Gilmores' it was cold and uninviting. Large floral vases stood on the sideboard, filled with chrysanthemums that bowed their golden heads but the house held no warmth. This house was soulless. Welcome Home, I thought sarcastically as I went upstairs to my room. Why wasn't Mother here waiting, eager to see me? Why wasn't she more like a mum? And why did Father want to see me at eight? I wished with all my heart that Katy's parents were mine too.

*

The drawing room door was open, my parents were sitting talking to each other. I tapped and entered, my legs threatening to give way.

'Grace,' Father said. 'Come in. I trust you enjoyed your vacation?'

'Yes, thank you.'

'Do sit down.' He ushered me towards the couch. 'I expect you're wondering why you've been summoned?'

Mother looked across at me. Was that a thin smile? Maybe she was pleased to see me?

'As I mentioned in the letter, we've been talking about college,' Father continued.

'But...' I interrupted.

'It's time you put this stupid nonsense about fashion out of your head and learn how to run a household, like your mother.'

'Have you looked at the brochure for Bolton? It has excellent reviews,' I pleaded.

'The sooner you get rid of these fancy ideas the better. I've got a few suitors lined up. They'll be visiting the house over the next couple of weeks.'

'Maybe we're being a bit too hasty, Charles?' Mother interrupted.

If I hadn't been sitting down, I think I'd have fallen, as I became momentarily unbalanced. Did Mother just defend me?

She took the pamphlet from me and flipped through the pages. 'It does look like Grace may benefit from this place.' She passed the booklet to Father. 'Grace is only sixteen after all. I think a couple of years could mature her, ready for marriage?' She faced Father for approval.

'But what about the suitors?' he said.

'Suitors?' I asked.

'Eligible young men, contacts of mine. Their union will build our empire.'

'But, Father, I'm not interested in an empire. I want to be a fashion designer.'

'You'll do as I say, Grace. You'll marry and have a son to become my heir.'

Tears pricked my eyes. I wanted to marry Jack, not some toff like Father. 'No,' I said, 'No, I won't.'

'How dare you? It's your duty.'

'It's nineteen fifty, not the dark ages. I want a life.'

'Did we defy our parents?' he continued.

Mother said, 'Yes, Charles, you're quite right. Grace should do her duty. But give her a couple more years? She's still young?'

Father stroked his chin. 'It's that Boltonian girl that's given you these elaborate ideas.'

'No, it's not Katherine, I promise.'

53

He continued to stroke his chin. 'If I let you go to college for two years, do you agree to cooperate with the arrangement?'

'Yes. Yes, Father. I will.' I had no intention of doing any such thing but it would give me time to sort out what could be done. Katy would help. Mother smiled, her face hinted softness.

'Our first guests arrive tomorrow evening,' he said, 'the Anson twins. They're twenty-eight years old and both interested. I'll advise them you'll be ready to marry when you're eighteen.'

I looked at my feet. Even if Jack wasn't in the equation, these men were far too old.

'Grace?'

'Yes, Father.'

'Make sure you wear an appropriate gown. Dinner's at seven.'

'Will Elizabeth be joining us?' I asked.

'No, of course not. Why should she?' He looked confused. 'You may go now.'

'Thank you, Father. Mother.'

'Grace,' Mother said in acknowledgement.

I left the room. Why couldn't they be warm and loving? Why couldn't Mr and Mrs Gilmore be my parents? Although, Mother surprised me when she'd stood up from the chaise longue and pleaded my case. She'd done her duty as a girl, accepted an arranged marriage but unfortunately she hadn't given Father a son. Perhaps she had regrets and somewhere in that hard heart wanted something better for her daughters? My appetite vanished, I decided to skip dinner.

I knocked on my sister's bedroom door, opening it slightly. 'Elizabeth, it's me. Are you awake?'

She lifted her head off the pillow, sat up, glanced at me and lay back down.

'It's me.'

'I know it's you. You missed my birthday. You promised,' she said accusingly.

Oh goodness, I'd forgotten all about that. I meant to buy something special. My head had been filled with Jack and I hadn't given her a thought. 'I'm sorry. I'll make it up to you. How about I design you a dress? Or slacks. Trews?'

'What?'

'Trousers. Women wear them now too. They're awfully comfortable. I'm going to do a pair for myself so I could make you some too?'

'Father won't like that.' Her voice softened.

'In the morning then?'

'Night Grace. I'm glad you're home.'

'Night, Elizabeth.

In my room I sat at the desk and started to write. There was no way I was going to marry any suitor. I'd play Father's game while biding my time. I wrote to Katy then followed with a letter to Jack. I wasn't sure what to say, except I missed and loved him. I sealed the envelopes ready for posting then pulled a sketchpad from my drawer and began drawing a pair of slacks. Tomorrow I'd take Elizabeth with me to choose fabric.

Chapter 10

Maids shuffled around the house flicking feather dusters. The door of the drawing room was open, I peeped in. Martha was kneeling by the marble fireplace.

The butler walked by. 'May I help you Miss?'

'I'm looking for my parents?'

'They're out I'm afraid. Is there anything I can do?'

'I was hoping for a car.'

'There are two drivers free.'

'Thank you.' At least that made it easier for Elizabeth and I to visit town without questions.

Martha appeared. 'Would you like breakfast, Miss Grace?'

'Is my sister in there?' I pointed to the dining room.

'No, Miss. She wanted to eat in her room.'

'Don't worry, I'll get my own.'

'I'm sorry, Miss, but that's my job.'

'Sorry, I wasn't thinking. Tea and toast will be fine.'

'Yes, Miss.' She walked away briskly, carrying her cleaning box.

The knot in my stomach was still there from last night. Jack was on my mind but so were Father's words about suitors, the Anson twins. It was all such a mess. I decided to try to forget. I made my way to the dining room, sat down and began to draw a design in my sketchpad.

Martha came back with a tray and placed the contents down on the table in front of me.

'Thank you.' I watched her leave before continuing with my drawing. It took a while, but eventually I was happy. My toast and tea had grown cold but I forced myself to chew on crispy bread and drink lukewarm liquid.

I ran upstairs to find Elizabeth. It amused me to be a rebel while my parents were out.

My sister poked her head out of her room. 'What's all the noise about?'

'It's me.' I eased my way through her door.

'You're lucky Mother and Father are out. What's got into you?'

'I've seen how the other half live. They have fun and that's what you and I are going to have today. Where are they, anyway?'

'At a business meeting. They'll be out for most of the day.'

'Good. Get ready. One of Father's drivers is taking us into town.'

'Why?'

'To buy some fabric, so I can make your birthday present. Look.' I passed her the sketchpad.

'What on earth?'

'They're called trews or slacks, depending on the material. It's what I was telling you about last night. Remember?'

Elizabeth seemed fidgety as if she had something to say. She was trying to hide a smile. 'What is it?'

Her smile grew wider. 'Father's talking about me starting Greenemere,' she said in a high pitched voice.

'That's excellent news. Why now?'

'Daphne's leaving and Nanny's taken ill. She's gone home to be with her sister.'

'Oh dear, is she going to be all right?'

'I think so, but the doctor insisted on rest. He said she's too old to be working and should retire. Mother and Father took me to see Miss Allison to sort out the paperwork. She's looking forward to me attending and said if I'm anything like you, then I'll be a credit to the school. Father said we'd confirm later. That is, after he's decided whether you're going to college or not.'

'What difference does it make?'

'He said if you don't go then you can tutor me. So are you going?'

'Yes,' I almost yelled.

She grinned. 'There's so much to do. Will you help me pack? I know it's Martha's job but she'll pack things I don't like.'

'Yes of course. But first, let's go shopping.'

We grabbed our jackets and went downstairs to find a car. The driver was happy to oblige. He drove in silence. How I missed James's banter.

'Can you stop here please?' I asked.

The chauffeur slid the vehicle close to the kerb then got out to open the rear door.

'If you could wait, please?' I said.

'Yes, Miss.' He sat back inside.

When we opened the shop door, a bell alerted the assistant. Inside, rows of fabric rolls were laid out on the counters. My fingers glided over different textures. Wool, cotton and corduroy lay on one side. Satin, velveteen, taffeta and chiffon lay on the other. A rainbow of colours plus abstracts in brown, grey and navy.

I turned to Elizabeth. 'One day, I'll have a shop like this.'

'Father will never allow it.'

'One day. And after that, I'll have a huge store in London selling my designs. You'll see.'

She laughed. 'You're such a dreamer, Grace. I heard Father ranting to Mother about your sketchpads. He's not impressed.'

'I know, he told me. Did you know that he wants me to marry an old man?'

'I knew he was looking for suitors. How grand to be lady of the house.'

'If I tell you a secret. Promise not to tell?'

'Is it hush, hush?'

'Very much so. Mother and Father can't find out. Promise?'

'Promise,' she confirmed.

'I've met someone. His name's Jack. We're in love.'

'Is he rich?'

'No. He's Katy's cousin.' There was no way I'd disclose Jack's background, even to Elizabeth.

'Father will never allow it.'

'Jack and I have had a bit of a falling out but I'm hoping he'll write to say he can't live without me.' I fiddled with my hands. 'He's so good looking.'

'Dream, sister, dream. It will never happen.'

I was deaf to her words. I hoped she'd share in my joy. I turned my attention back to why we were there. 'Look at these materials, which one would you like?'

She selected green wool tartan and I chose satin in burgundy. The shopkeeper cut the quantities and added a couple of reels of thread to the bag before pressing the cash register. We wandered out of the shop and got into the Rolls for the short drive home.

'What do you think about *Granville Hall*, Elizabeth?' I asked.

'What a strange question? It's home of course. Why?'

'Don't you find it cold? Empty?'

'Sorry, I'm not sure what you're asking me?'

'Katy's home is warm and filled with love.'

She shrugged.

It was no use. Clearly she didn't know any different. Maybe one day she'd see.

Once back home, I was impatient to start my new project. I ventured downstairs to find a sewing machine and the butler agreed to bring it to my room. Before dinner I was in possession of a pair of trews for my sister and satin slacks for me.

Elizabeth strolled through my bedroom door. 'Wow, you've finished?'

'Yes, try them on. But don't let Mother or Father see.'

They looked perfect. She couldn't stop looking in the mirror. 'It's like someone else's reflection,' she said. 'I love them but they feel strange. Try yours.'

I stepped into the reddish-purple garment and drew them up to my waist. Wait until Katy saw them, she'd want some too. Maybe I could make money sewing when I married Jack. That would be an idea, if he still wanted me.

Loud voices and footsteps came from downstairs. Martha knocked on my bedroom door. 'Miss Grace, your father has asked for you. He's waiting in the library.'

In haste I forgot about the pants.

I ran downstairs and opened the door.

'What the hell are you wearing?' he shouted.

How could I have been so foolish to have forgotten? I bit my lip. I wasn't going to be pushed around. I hadn't done anything wrong.

'I made them.' I stared at my feet. 'I designed them too. I lifted my head up. 'Do you like them, Mother? I could make you a pair.'

Mother stood next to Father. She glared. 'Don't be insolent, Grace. Ladies don't wear trousers.'

'Go and take them off immediately,' Father ordered. 'All sewing machines will be removed from this house.'

'What? You can't do that,' I said.

'I can and I will. You were warned yesterday about fancy ideas. You're to be groomed as a lady of an estate, not a mill worker. If I have to remind you again, there'll be no more talk of college or staying with Katherine. Do I make myself clear?'

'Yes, Father,' I stuttered, hating the pompous man but for now I'd pretend to play his game. 'Sorry, Father, I was being foolish.' I turned to leave and stumbled as I contemplated the loss of my designing career.

Chapter 11

The drivers loaded two identical wooden chests into separate cars. One for Elizabeth, as she ventured off to Greenemere and one for me as I escaped to my second home in Bolton. The butler and Martha bustled around the house making sure we were fully equipped. Mother and Father, in the meantime, sat in the drawing room unperturbed that they'd be saying goodbye to their daughters for at least three months. If this had been Katy's house, her parents would have spent every last second with their children, but not here. I couldn't wait to get away and was delighted that Elizabeth was getting out too.

My sister and I were standing at the bottom of the steps when Martha came out of the front door.

'Miss Grace, Miss Elizabeth, your father has asked to see you,' she said with a broad smile showing lines on her face. She must have been close to forty now, yet unmarried.

We strolled into the drawing room, hats and coats on. Mother hinted at a smile. She went to stand up but Father summoned her to sit back down. Maybe she intended to hug us.

'Are you girls ready?' Father asked.

'Yes Father,' we answered.

'Remember you're Granville's. Don't do anything to disgrace our family name.'

'No, Father,' our voices echoed.

'Have a safe trip.' He dismissed us.

My face pleaded with Mother to say goodbye properly. Like a Mum.

She smiled. 'Goodbye Grace, be good. Goodbye Elizabeth.'

'And Grace, get rid of those fancy ideas,' Father added, 'remember after college, you'll marry. Don't let me down.'

Thankfully, he couldn't see my face. I'd no intention of giving up my designs. My sketchpad would follow me everywhere.

I hugged Elizabeth before climbing into a separate Rolls-Royce. Martha ran down the steps with hampers. The interior of the car was hot, with a sickly smell of leather. Elizabeth waved from her back window as she moved off in a separate direction.

Jack occupied my thoughts while I travelled. Why hadn't he answered any of my letters? Did this mean no more Grace and Jack? Katy said she hadn't heard from him either. My heart played tricks between excitement and gloom. I needed Jack and knew I'd agree to his terms. Even if it meant our sons, if we were fortunate to have any, would follow their father and go down the mine.

The ride was long and dull. Nothing to see except trees and passing cars. I closed my eyes for a while and was surprised to find we were pulling onto Willow Bank's drive. Katy and her parents rushed down the steps to greet me.

The driver let me out, before attending to my trunk in the boot.

I ran into Katy's arms. 'I'm here, I'm really here.'

She hugged me so tight my feet left the ground. 'Gracie.'

A warm rush swept through me. Mr and Mrs Gilmore drew close, in turn they greeted me with a hug. 'Welcome home, Grace.'

'Thank you, it's good to be here.' And I meant it, this house was my home, the mansion I'd left was an empty shell.

'Maggie's prepared tea,' Eliza said.

'Come on.' Katy led me by the hand into the house. We chatted non-stop.

Once inside I asked, 'Have you heard from Jack?'

'No. No one has heard anything. Mum and Dad are getting worried. Does he know you're coming back?'

'Yes, I told him, but he hasn't answered any of my letters.'

'Well he did say he needed time, that you both needed time. Have you made a decision?'

'Yes, I have.'

'And?'

'Whatever Jack wants.'

'Even if it means letting your sons go down the pit?'

'It can't be that bad, otherwise why do Jack and Eddie do it?'

'Eddie would stop tomorrow if he could. Sometimes I wonder? Maybe, I'm his way out.'

'No, surely not? That's no basis for a relationship, Katy. How are things, they seemed strained last time I was here?'

'All sorted, I thought I was expecting.'

I grabbed her to steady myself. 'What? And you didn't think to tell me?'

'I didn't want to tell anyone. The more I said it out aloud, the more it seemed true. Thankfully, it was a false alarm.'

'You deserve better, Katy. You deserve someone that will treat you special. Why do you stay with him?'

'I love him. Just like you love Jack. You're prepared to send your offspring down the mine. Well, I love Eddie and will put up with his little mood swings and quirks.'

Light footsteps headed towards us. 'You haven't started tea yet?' Mrs Gilmore glided over to the Royal Albert and poured me a cup. She knew exactly how I liked it.

'Thank you.'

'Have some cake,' she continued.

I selected a small slice from the cut slab of Battenberg on the tiered stand. How I adored the little pink and yellow chequered squares.

'Are you ready for college?' Katy spluttered, with a mouthful of food.

'Katherine,' her mother said, 'you've been hanging around with Eddie too much.'

'Sorry, Mum. I'm just so excited to have Gracie back.'

'I know.' Her mother laughed. Mr Gilmore joined in, he must have come in when I hadn't noticed.

'Am I in the Blue room?' I asked.

'Yes, we consider that to be your room now,' Katy's mother said. 'Eric's taken your trunk up. Would you like Maggie to help you unpack?'

'No, I'll be fine, thank you. Father said he'll send a cheque in the post, for my keep.'

'That's not necessary, Grace,' Katy's father said.

'You must accept it. He'll not allow me to stay, if you don't.'

'Fair enough. I'll put it into a savings account for you.'

'That's a good idea, Dad. Gracie that means when you marry Jack you'll have some money.'

There was a sudden silence. Mr and Mrs Gilmore looked at each other then looked at me. I wondered if they knew something that I didn't. I smiled. They tried to smile back, but instead seemed to be biting their lips.

Eventually Mr Gilmore spoke. 'Are you sure about this, Grace? Jack comes from a completely different world to you. It's not nice living in dirt and poverty. It doesn't matter how clean you are, coal dust gets everywhere. Is that what you really want? You do know Jack will never leave the pit, don't you?'

'Yes, I do. And yes, I'm sure. I've had time to think.'

He shrugged his shoulders, picked up the newspaper and left the room.

*

We ventured to college in long robes and mortar boards like everyone else. Even the staff looked the same, except for the inside colour of their hoods. Our new friends nicknamed us the twins, because we stuck together all the time.

Neither of the boys had turned up last weekend but Katy was expecting Eddie later today. There'd been no mention of Jack and he still hadn't answered any of my letters.

There was a tap on my bedroom door. 'Are you coming down, Gracie? Mum's wondering where you are?'

'Yes, sorry, Katy. I got engrossed in my drawings. What do you think of this?'

64

She took my sketchpad and nodded her head. 'Wow,' she said, 'I like that one, will you make it for me?'

'Sure, you can choose the fabric.'

'The flared skirt is fabulous for jive.'

I laughed. 'Yes that's what I thought.'

She handed the book back to me. 'Let's go downstairs. Oh that's a car, now.'

'Go on, I'll follow.' I was in no rush to see Eddie, not unless he had answers. Katy rushed out of the room and I followed in slow motion. He didn't deserve her.

A man's voice. One I'd know anywhere. Jack. My heart skipped and stomach somersaulted. Was he here to see me? Did he want me or had he come to end it? Too many unanswered questions. I walked in the direction of his voice.

As I approached, his face focused on mine. His eyes sparkled and smile widened.

'Hello, Grace,' he said, 'how are you?'

'I'm well, Jack, thank you. And you?'

'Fine.'

It was all very polite. I wanted him to tell me how much he'd missed me and how much he loved me, but nothing. My eyes pleaded for answers. 'You didn't answer any of my letters?'

'No, sorry, Da's been bad.'

'Oh dear. Is he all right now?'

'No, not really. He's very sick but stable. Look, shall we go out into the garden to talk?'

'I'll get my coat. It's a bit cold.'

'It is,' butted in Mrs Gilmore, 'don't stay out there too long. I'm sure you can find somewhere private in the house to talk, over a cup of tea?'

'Yeah, Aunty Eliza, but I need some air.' Jack looked at her for approval.

'Well don't stay out too long.'

Jack took my hand. We strolled into the garden.

'I'm sorry I didn't write, Grace. And I'm sorry for the way we parted. Have you had a chance to think?'

'Yes, I have. I'm ready to take on anything if it means being with you.'

He moved closer, held my chin and settled his soft lips on mine. He kissed me hard.

'Jack.' I pushed him away. 'You're being rough.'

'Sorry, Grace.'

He took me in his arms again but this time his kisses were soft. If he'd asked me to lie down with him, I'd have agreed. But he didn't. He moved us apart gently and took my hand to lead me back inside.

'A cup of cha, that's what we need.' he said.

We followed the clink of cups and chatter of voices to find the others in the drawing room.

Katy looked up. 'Jack, it's good to see you. Where've you been?'

'Da's been bad. It's the Black Lung. Doc's not sure how long he'll last.'

Thank goodness Jack couldn't read my mind. Hoping his father may not last long, yet bitter sweet because my relief would be Jack's pain. Sometimes, I hated myself. I decided I wasn't a nice person at all. But the picture of that vile creature from our last meeting wouldn't go away.

Katy put her hand on my shoulder. I jumped. 'Hey, Day Dreamer, where are you?'

Everyone in the room turned to look at me. I covered my face with my hands to hide the blush. 'Oops, I don't know where I was.' Strangely everyone seemed to accept that.

'Hiya,' Eddie said, 'you not speaking to me?'

'Of course, how are you?'

'I'm good. Wondered if you're up for the Palais this evening?' He turned to Jack. 'What about you Mate, did you pack your drapes?'

Jack nodded. 'I'm up for a dance, Grace?'

'I'd love to,' I said, wishing I'd run up my latest design on the machine.

'No need to ask Katy,' Eddie continued, 'she never says no to dancing.'

It was settled, we'd go into Bolton later this evening to Astoria Palais de Danse. Things appeared to be returning to normal. I caught Jack staring at me. His eyes held the love I'd seen from the start. Life was good. I had everything. A beautiful home with wonderful surrogate parents, a friend like a sister, college and most of all the love of the man I adored. What more could a person want?

*

After returning home from the Palais, we'd gone straight to bed. I was settling down when there was a small tap on my door. I thought it must be Katy, but then normally she'd knock and come in but the door remained closed.

'Hello,' I called.

'Grace?'

'Yes.'

'It's Jack.'

'What is it?'

'I need to see you. Can I come in?'

'But I'm in bed.'

'Please?'

'Give me a moment.' I scrambled out of bed to reach for my housecoat, wondering what was so urgent. 'You can come in now.'

Jack strolled in. He took my face in his hands. 'I need you Grace.' His lips touched mine, slowly at first but then more aggressively, like earlier in the day. This time he didn't frighten me. He guided me towards the bed, kissing me. His hands wandered inside my housecoat and brushed against my breast. I wanted to say no, but I was powerless.

'Jack. What about Mr and Mrs Gilmore?'

'Shh, darling.' His hands continued, moved under my nightdress and caressed my tummy. I knew I should tell him to stop. But I couldn't. His kisses became stronger, his breathing heavier. His hands settled on my stomach so I relaxed. Then they were on the move again, up to my breasts. Cupping them in his hands. I should say no, I kept telling myself, say no, but the magnetism was too strong.

'Grace, sweetheart, I love you.'

'I love you too,' I mumbled.

His hands were on the go again, this time moving lower and up my legs. I was a wanton woman. I must be strong. 'Jack, please.'

'Shh, it's all right Grace. I won't make you do anything you don't want to.'

His fingers wandered into strange territory. Now I understood how Katy had gone all the way, but I wouldn't go that far. I was listless and unsure how to cope with this sensation. There were footsteps on the stairs. 'Jack, listen,' I whispered.

'What is it, Darling?'

The sound of a door opening and closing was enough to shock me back to sanity. I moved his hand away. 'I'm not ready for this.'

'Sorry baby, I got carried away. This past fortnight has been hell and I missed you so much. It was awful after we parted. Forgive me. You're right to stop me.' He kissed me softly and climbed off the bed. 'Pleasant dreams.' He crept out of my room.

I wasn't sure what had happened there, I came close to losing my virginity which I'd promised to keep intact until my wedding night. Any more assignations like that and I wasn't sure if I'd be able to last out. Jack definitely wouldn't. I couldn't think anymore and let my eyes close so sleep could overtake me.

Chapter 12

The months passed with college through the week and the boys at weekends, apart from when I had to return to *Granville Hall* at Christmas. It had been nice to see Elizabeth and hear how she was getting on at Greenemere but I couldn't wait to return to *Willow Banks*.

In the garden daffodils bobbed their heads to remind me it was spring. Jack hadn't come to my room again, not since that night when I'd almost lost my virtue.

Katy opened my bedroom door. 'There's a letter for you.'

'Is it from Elizabeth?'

'No, I don't think so. It looks more like your father's scrawl.' She handed it to me.

'Why is he writing?' Elizabeth wrote every week, as I did to her, but my parents only wrote when there was a problem.

'Open it and you'll find out.' Katy laughed.

My tummy quivered as I tore open the letter. I balanced myself on the bed.

'What is it, Gracie?'

'It's the Anson twins. Apparently they're getting impatient. Father wants me to make a decision as to which one I'll marry. He wants to announce the engagement when I go home at Easter.'

'What? He has to be joking. Does he think we're living in the dark ages? Tell him no.'

'You don't know what he's like. He isn't like your father. Mother managed to put him off before, but now the twins won't wait. What am I going to do?'

'Have you and Jack, well, you know... yet?'

'No.'

'Well maybe you should. And get pregnant.'

'Father would kill me.'

'It'd be a way out. Get dressed, we'll have breakfast before the boys arrive. Don't worry. It's not going to happen.'

I wished I had her faith.

*

The boys arrived. It was a glorious March day, the temperature soared to sixty-nine degrees. We decided to go to Heaton Park as it was around the corner.

'Race you to the bandstand.' Katy said.

I wasn't in the mood so let her run on ahead.

'What's the matter?' Jack asked. 'You're awfully quiet. Have I done something to upset you?'

'No, it's not you.'

Katy must have overheard because she called out, 'Gracie has a problem. We need to put our heads together and come up with an answer. Let's go to the café so we can sit down, the grass is damp.'

We made our way to the tea shop. Katy and Eddie went up to the counter. Jack and I sat down.

He clasped my hand. 'Whatever it is, we'll sort it.'

I forced myself to smile but wanted to cry. How could I marry another man? How could I leave Jack? How could I let an Anson twin explore my body? I put my hand to my mouth, raced outside to the bushes. I walked back in slowly, holding my stomach. Eddie started to laugh. 'Now, I see the problem.' He turned to Jack. 'You dirty dog. You're a sly one.'

Jack grabbed him by his throat. 'What you implying, mate?'

'Well it's obvious,' he croaked.

'Stop it.' Katy said, 'Gracie, are you all right?'

Jack released him.

I wiped my mouth with a handkerchief. 'I think so.'

'We need to put our heads together,' Katy said.

'What, cos she's in the puddin' club?'

'I'm, I'm not,' I stuttered.

'She's not pregnant.' Katy slapped Eddie's hand.

'Of course she's not,' Jack said.

'Gracie, tell them about the letter,' Katy said.

70

I spoke quietly, still sick from its content. 'My father wants me to get engaged to one of the Anson twins. He wants me to go home at Easter and decide which one I'll marry.'

'What? No way,' Jack shouted. 'You're my girl and no bloody toffee nosed geezer is getting you.'

Yes, I was Jack's girl. But how did we stop it happening?

'But...' Katy said, 'I have an idea.'

Eyes darted backwards and forwards from Katy to me.

'Seeing you sick,' she continued, 'has given me the idea. You tell your father you're going to have a baby, even though you're not.'

'What, then what?' I asked.

'He'll throw you out and you come here.' She folded her arms.

Jack turned to me. 'Will it work?'

I fiddled with my pony tail. 'I'm not sure.'

Jack put his arm around me. 'If not we'll run off to Gretna Green.'

That wasn't quite how I'd planned my wedding but if all else failed then yes, we could do that. Under no circumstances would I marry either of the Anson twins.

We finished our tea and Eddie jumped up. 'Me and Katy are going for a little walk.'

Of course, I knew exactly what he was talking about. He didn't even try to hide it as I noticed his sly glint. They disappeared in haste with a quick wave.

'Come on, we'll go for a walk too,' Jack said. He took my hand and led me towards a copse secluded from the pathway. He placed his coat on the ground. We lay down and he started to kiss me. His kisses became stronger and hands began to explore. But this time, it was different, they prowled with urgency. I pushed him away.

'Don't you want to?'

'Of course, but I want to wait.'

'You know you're special. I love you, so why wait? Please, Grace. Let's?'

I shook my head and moved his hands. 'No, not like this.'

'Marry me? I was serious about eloping. I can't lose you.'

My heart pounded. I smiled. 'Yes, I will.' I had no idea how we'd make it happen. 'Mother and Father will never consent.'

'If they don't, Scotland it is. Agree? We'll go to the jewellers in Davenport Street, when you get back from down south? Once you've told your parents you're having my baby, they'll have to let us marry.'

'Yes,' I said, praying he was right.

We made our way to meet the others at the bandstand as pre-arranged. They arrived first for a change. Katy's face was flushed as usual and her clothes unkempt.

Jack dragged me gently by the hand and rushed over to the others. 'Guess what?'

'What?' Katy asked.

'We're engaged,' Jack announced.

'Congratulations, mate.' Eddie shook Jack's hand with force. 'Good on you.' He whispered something.

'No, you cheeky bugger.'

'What did he say?' I asked.

'He wants to know if you've, you know?' Katy nudged me.

My cheeks flooded. 'No, we haven't,' I said quietly.

Jack looked at his watch. 'We need to get back or else we'll miss that last train.' He tickled my chin. 'Don't look so worried, Grace. We'll work things out. I promise.'

*

Back at the house, James was standing outside the car. 'You boys ready to go?' he asked, 'Only, Mr Gilmore needs me soon.'

The boys ran upstairs, returning with duffel bags slung across their shoulders.

Jack took me in his arms and kissed me with passion. 'Goodbye, Grace, my fiancée. Don't forget, we'll sort this. You and me are meant to be together. Be brave and stand up to your father. All right?' His eyes sparkled with tears.

'Goodbye, Jack.' I nodded and wiped my cheeks.

The boys clambered into the Rolls and James drove off. We waved. Katy stood beside me and put her arm around my shoulder.

How would I survive without Jack? I didn't want to return to *Granville Hall*. I hated it. Would I have the strength to stand up to my parents? I ran into the house and upstairs to the blue room, where I lay on the bed, and cried. Afterwards I closed my eyes and fell asleep amidst dreams and nightmares.

Chapter 13

The Rolls Royce pulled up outside *Granville Hall*. My legs shook so severely that it was difficult for me to stand. If James had been my driver he'd have steadied me, but this chauffeur kept his distance. Finally, I managed to drag my feet up the steps, one by one. I knocked on the brass lion knocker. Martha promptly opened the door.

'Miss Grace, good afternoon. Your parents are waiting in the drawing room.'

'Please tell them I'll be there shortly. I need to freshen up. I've been travelling for five hours.'

'Certainly, Miss.'

I didn't wait for her to go but went straight to my room. Did I know what I was going to say or how I was going to say it? I flicked water across my face, brushed my hair and made my way to the drawing room. Mother was sitting on the chaise longue and Elizabeth was on the window seat with embroidery. Father stood by the fireplace smoking his pipe.

'Ah, Grace. Good journey I trust?'

'Yes, Father, thank you.'

'Now, as I said in my letter. The Anson twins are getting a bit impatient and they'd like the wedding brought forward to September.' He smiled.

'What?'

'So will it be Simon or Richard?'

'But you said I could stay at college for two years?'

'Yes, apologies, but nevertheless it can't be helped. Still you're seventeen now. You'll be close to eighteen when you marry.' His face was smug.

'Neither of them.'

'Don't start that nonsense again, I thought we agreed if you went to college you'd comply with the plan and do your duty.'

'I won't.'

Mother sat up, she opened her mouth and I thought she was going to say something but then she closed it again.

'They won't want to marry me now,' I said with a shaky voice.

'What do you mean? They're desperate for a prize like you.'

I stood there defiantly. 'Well I'm not such a trophy now.'

Father frowned. 'I don't understand. What rubbish is this Grace?'

I licked my lips. 'I'm going to have a baby.'

Mother nearly fell off the chaise longue, Elizabeth's eyes bulged and Father brought his arm up. Mother stood up and touched Father's shoulder.

'It's all right,' he said, 'I'm not going to hit her. Elizabeth, go to your room.'

She left but not before sending me an accusing look.

'You dirty little tramp,' Father roared. 'An animal. That's what you are, consummating out of wedlock.' He took a deep breath then stroked his chin, the way he always did when there was a problem to solve. 'We'll find someone to fix it. There's a chap down the club. He'll know someone. Cost us a fair penny but worth it.'

'Charles, an abortion? Surely not?' Mother questioned.

'I'll not have one.' I clung to my stomach protecting my imaginary unborn.

'You will if I say,' he growled.

'But Charles, an abortion? It's dangerous, not to say illegal.'

'What do you suggest, Margaret?' he asked.

'Why don't we find out about this young man? He may be a good match?' She turned to me. 'What does he do, Grace?' she asked calmly.

'He's a coal miner.'

'A coal miner?' Father shouted. 'Now it's making sense. Thinks he'll get his hands on all this?'

'It's not like that,' I stammered.

'Of course it damn well is. Do you really think he'd be interested in you if it wasn't for my money?' He turned to

Mother. 'Any more suggestions, Margaret? I'll phone that chap.'

Mother grabbed his arm. 'Charles, you can't, not an abortion. What about sending her away until she's had the baby and then it can be adopted?'

'And the twins?'

'We tell them she needs to finish college. Set the wedding for June, 1952. That allows time for Grace to give birth and fully recover by her wedding night.'

'And when the groom discovers he's married spoiled goods on his wedding night?'

'If her husband queries a broken hymen, we say it was horse riding,' she continued, 'it happens.'

He stroked his chin again making me want to yell, but I remained silent.

'Suppose I agree. Where will she stay until the confinement?'

'My cousin in Somerset. She may take her. Of course she'll never let me forget it.'

'I'm not having it adopted,' I shouted, 'I won't. I'm going to marry Jack and you can't stop me.'

'What has happened to you? We should never have let you stay with that Boltonian girl, she's obviously a bad influence. Coal miner indeed,' he huffed. 'Go to your room, we'll talk more in the morning. I need to speak with your Mother, in private.'

I walked out of the door, shaking. There was no way I'd allow them to send me away. It was appalling the way he'd spoken to me. What a price to find an escape route from the dreadful twins. I wished I could have spoken to Katy on the telephone, instead I went to my room and sat down at the desk and began to write.

Dear Jack...

*

Morning arrived too soon. Martha came to my room and told me I'd been summoned to the library by Father. I washed, dressed and drew my hair back into a ponytail before making my way downstairs. I stopped to take a deep breath when I reached the door before walking in. 'Good morning Father, good morning Mother.'

'Good morning, Grace,' she replied.

Father stood thoughtful, fingers pressed into the bridge of his nose. He slowly lifted his face and stared at me.

I waited for him to speak.

His eyebrows moved closer together. 'So Grace, have you had time to see sense?'

'If you mean have my baby adopted? Then no, I haven't.'

'That option is no longer available. Cousin Victoria isn't prepared to help and we don't have anywhere else to send you. You'll need to have it aborted.'

'No, I won't,' I screamed.

Mother intervened. 'Wait, Charles, please. Grace, does this man want to marry you?'

I saw a ray of hope. 'Yes, Mother, he does. We love each other.'

'This is outrageous,' Father raised his voice. 'You can't seriously be suggesting we let her marry him?'

'It's an option to consider, Charles?'

'I thought I made it quite clear last night. If she does that, then she stops being our daughter.' He turned to me. 'Is that what you want, Grace?'

'If I have to choose.'

'Very well. You leave this house with nothing. Is that clear? And don't come back when everything has gone wrong. You walk out of here for good. No further communication with this family.'

'But surely, I may write to Elizabeth and Mother?'

'No, you may not. Once you walk out the door, you no longer exist to us. Go and live in the gutter. In the gutter where little sluts belong.'

Mother stood up. She opened her mouth and then closed it. She cleared her throat. 'Charles, that's a bit harsh?'

'No more than she deserves, Margaret. She's disgraced this family. We're not going down with her. I'll be lenient and allow her to take a coat, whatever she can fit in a small bag and I'll even give her the train fare. One of the chauffeurs may drive her to the station. That's more than she merits.'

Mother looked at me with a thin smile. She mouthed, 'I'm sorry.'

Why didn't she stand up to him? I was her daughter. I'd never treat a child of mine like that.

As I was leaving the room I turned back. 'Father, please may I say goodbye to my sister?'

'No you may not. Leave the house now. You have five minutes to get something together and then I want you gone.' He paused. 'I'll sign the papers for marriage. Get the coal miner to post them.' His breathing became heavy, he held onto the mantelpiece and clung to the left hand side of his chest.

Mother hurried over to him, her face pale. 'Charles, let me help you. Shall I call the doctor? Sit down.'

'No, I'll be fine, once she's gone.'

'Father, are you all right?'

Mother ushered me out. There was nothing left here for me. I went upstairs. I stopped outside my sister's bedroom door, but continued to my own where I threw a change of clothes, toothbrush, comb, sketchpads and pencils into a small bag. I tiptoed downstairs and walked outside into the fresh air. Thankfully it was daylight and the sun was shining.

My eyes focused on the library window to check on Father. He was moving around which put my mind at rest. The driver was waiting at the bottom of the steps, he must have been informed. He waited for me to sit in the back before getting in the front to drive away. The railway station came into view as we approached Packhorse Road.

It was then, that the chauffeur opened his mouth. 'Are you going to be all right, Miss? Would you like me to go in and purchase your train ticket?'

'No, thank you, I'll be fine.' I forced myself to smile.

'Take care, Grace.'

I couldn't believe it. This driver had never uttered a word to me before and now he was not only being kind but speaking to me by name. He got back into the car, turned to look at me, waved and slowly disappeared along the road.

The station was busy. Travellers, carrying suitcases and bags, made their way to the cashier's office. I stood in line until it was my turn. 'A single to Bolton, please.' I passed the note that Father had given me to the desk clerk.

He handed me a ticket and small change. 'Platform three, Miss. There's a train due in five minutes.'

I hurried up the steps and arrived just as the train drew in.

The journey was long but I managed to sleep, soothed by the clickety clack. 'You're free,' I told myself. But the knowledge that I'd lost my family for good left me wretched, especially knowing I wasn't allowed to correspond. Despite Father's strictness, I still loved my parents. Suppose the Gilmores wouldn't let me stay? I wasn't sure I was ready to live in one of those small boxes with Jack in Wigan.

The sound of a whistle and a station master calling, 'Bolton' jolted me awake. It was my stop. I leant out of the window to open the door and stepped onto the platform. The whistle went again and the train slowly departed.

At the top of the stairs, I found a red public phone box. Luckily it was empty. My finger circled the wheel three times.

The operator answered. 'Number please?'

'Reversed charge call to Bolton two four five two, please.'

'Name please?'

'Grace Granville.'

'It's ringing now, Miss.'

'I have Grace Granville on the line,' the female voice said, 'will you accept the charges?'

'Yes, yes,' Mr Gilmore answered.

'You're connected,' she said. The phone clicked.

'Grace? Is that you? Are you all right?'

I started to cry. 'Father's disowned me. I'm in Bolton. Please can you send James to collect me?'

'Why? Oh never mind that, where are you?'

'I'm at the railway station.'

An old lady started tapping on the window. 'Are you going to be long,' she said in a croaky voice.'

I waved her away.

'James will be with you in a few minutes. You can tell us what happened when you arrive. I'll get Maggie to make tea.'

'Thank you, Mr Gilmore. Thank you.' The line went dead. I walked out of the phone booth and the old lady brushed past me. 'About time, you've been in there for ages.'

'I'm sorry.' I held the door open for her.

I sat down on an empty bench outside the station and waited. This bag was all I owned. How could I continue college? But at least I could marry Jack. I looked at my watch. Four o'clock. I'd been travelling all day and my stomach rumbled to remind me that I hadn't even eaten breakfast.

James drove up in the silver Rolls. He got out of the car. 'What's all this about, Grace? Not like you to come on the train? Has your father's business gone bust?'

I started to cry. 'He's thrown me out.'

James cradled me in his arms. 'Now, now, you're all right now, pet. The Gilmores will take care of you. They love you like their own.' He let go of me and opened the rear door. 'Come on, let's get you home.'

Home, I thought, yes home. A place filled with love and warmth.

Chapter 14

There was a welcoming party when I arrived at *Willow Banks*. Katy and her parents were at the front door waiting. Mr and Mrs Gilmore kissed me on the cheek in turn. Their faces held questions, yet they waited with patience. Katy gave me a huge hug. Eventually the silence was broken.

Mr Gilmore spoke first. 'It's lovely to have you, Grace, but what's happened?'

'Father's disowned me.'

'But why,' his wife asked.

Katy looked knowingly but said nothing.

'I told him I was having a baby.'

Mrs Gilmore put her arms around me. 'Does Jack know?'

'I'm not really pregnant.'

'Then why?' Katy's dad asked.

Katy jumped in between us. 'She had to.'

Her parents rolled their eyes.

'These things happen, Grace,' Mrs Gilmore said, 'but we understand.'

'She's not pregnant,' Katy raised her voice. 'They were going to make her marry some hoity-toity twin, so we had to come up with a plan.'

'They've thrown me out. What am I going to do now?'

'Stay here of course. Can't she Daddy? Mum?'

'Yes, she's very welcome,' Mrs Gilmore said.

'Father said he'll sign the papers so I can get married.'

'Are you sure about this dear?' Katy's mother continued. 'You've seen how Jack lives. That isn't going to change.'

'Let's not get ahead of ourselves here,' Mr Gilmore interrupted.

'What do you mean?' his wife asked.

'We can't just take in someone else's daughter without discussing it. There could be implications?'

'Yes, of course, Mr Gilmore, you're right. I'm sorry for putting you in that position.'

'Daddy, how could you?'

'Katy, your father is right,' I said.

'I'm not saying no,' he continued, 'I'm saying we need to discuss it. For instance, I need to call Grace's parents and we need to sit down as a family to talk things over. You've been an only child all your life, how are you going to feel about sharing your parents?'

'I don't mind, really I don't. Please, Daddy. Anyway, it's only until she gets married.'

'Grace, are you sure you want to marry Jack? Seems such a waste.' He tutted. 'I've lived amongst that coal dust and it's a tough life.'

'I love him.'

'Love isn't always enough. You've grown up in a wealthy home. If he loves you then maybe he should accept help,' Mr Gilmore answered.

'He says coal mining is his destiny and I know he's mine, so what can I do?'

He shrugged his shoulders. 'Let's go inside and have tea.'

Katy linked arms with me. She whispered. 'See? I told you it would work out.'

'But your father hasn't said yes.'

'No, but he will, you'll see.'

'I hope so.'

We sat down for tea.

'Katy,' I whispered, 'Father was awful. He called me some terrible names.'

Mrs Gilmore moved towards me. 'Stop crying now. You're making those lovely eyes red. Don't worry, we'll take care of you. If marrying Jack is what you want, we'll help.'

'Thank you.' I buried my head in her shoulder. 'You're both so kind.'

'Now pop your stuff upstairs.' She looked at the small bag on the floor. 'Is your trunk coming later?'

'No, this is all I have. Father only allowed me a change of clothes.' I bent my head.

She lifted my chin. 'Maybe your parents are expecting you to return home?'

I shook my head.

'Katy, sort some clothes for Grace. They may not be a perfect fit but I'm sure Grace can fix that,' Mrs Gilmore said.

'Yes of course, I'll do it now.' Katy shot out of the room.

'I'm certain your parents will come round, Grace. Now off you go and get settled.' Mrs Gilmore patted my arm.

I went upstairs to the blue room, sat on the bed and tipped out the contents of my bag. A cotton nightdress, clean underwear, a skirt, a blouse, stockings, pencils and a notebook.

Katy charged in with a bundle of clothes that she set down on the bed. 'Hooray, we did it. We did it.' She took hold of both of my hands and tried to pull me up. She was in high spirits. 'Let's dance, Gracie.'

'No, I don't feel like it.'

'But you're free.'

'Your parents haven't said I can stay yet. And I'll have to go and live in one of those coal dusted boxes. Suppose I have to live with Jack's father?'

'They will. What do you mean? He can't be that bad.'

'You should be glad you've never met him.'

'What do you mean? Is there something you haven't told me?'

'He touched my leg.'

Katy frowned.

'You know?'

'What? Like...?'

'Yes.'

'Did you tell Jack?'

'No. His father said I'd jumped because there was a spider, so I agreed.'

'Urgh, dirty old bugger.'

I raised my voice. 'Katy.'

'Well... what a nerve, making a pass on you.'

'I know. Then I had to kiss him goodbye. Jack insisted.'

'He wouldn't have, if he'd known. Is there room in his house for you?'

'I don't think so. There was only one bed. I don't know where Jack sleeps.'

'I'm sure Jack will rent a place for you two. Forget that for now, instead enjoy your freedom.'

'But he won't let me see Elizabeth.' The tears started again.

'Who won't? Jack?'

'No, Father. He wouldn't even let me say goodbye. And I'm not allowed to correspond. She'll think I've abandoned her.'

'I'm sure she won't.'

'She will.' I sniffed.

'Here, use this.' She passed me a clean handkerchief. 'Dry your eyes, hang these in the wardrobe,' she pointed to the clothes on the bed, 'and write a letter to Jack. He'll come up at the weekend and we can work out what happens next.'

I blew my nose hard into the handkerchief and then laughed. 'That wasn't very lady like, was it?'

Katy strolled out of the room. I waded through the pile of clothes and hung up three dresses, two skirts, four blouses and slid five pairs of new knickers, two pairs of new stockings and a nightdress into the drawer. Katy was slightly heavier than me so I would probably need to alter some of the items.

I took out a notepad and pen, from the drawer, to write letters to Jack and Elizabeth. Father would probably confiscate hers, but I had to try. When I'd finished, I yawned, stretched my arms and lay on the bed.

It was dark when I opened my eyes, I must have drifted off to sleep. Downstairs the phone rang. Eric's voice followed by Mr Gilmore's. I wondered if it was Father. I made myself presentable before going down to find the others. My stomach growled, I'd only eaten a slice of cake all day. The smell of cabbage hung in the air as I made my way to the dining room.

'Hello, lazybones.' Katy chuckled as she came up behind me. 'I wanted to wake you but Mum wouldn't allow it.'

Mr Gilmore's voice travelled through to the dining room. I heard Jack's name.

'Who's he talking to?' I asked Katy.

She shrugged.

'It's not Father is it? Only I heard him mention Jack.'

'Let's sit down,' Katy said, 'I'm sure we'll find out soon if we need to know.'

I sat down at my usual place. Mr and Mrs Gilmore's faces were strained when they walked into the room. I hoped this wasn't my doing. Once everyone was seated, Maggie served food. My tummy welcomed roast chicken, carrots, cabbage and roast potatoes. The only sound to be heard were clinks as cutlery scraped plates. Something serious must have happened. Maybe they'd decided I couldn't stay. I was fidgety. My face burned. What was I going to do? I had nowhere else to go. Father must have threatened to ruin them. I clenched my fists and waited.

Katy slammed down her knife and fork. 'Well, can she stay?'

Mr Gilmore spoke softly, 'Not now, Katy. We'll talk about it in a few days. That was Jack on the telephone.'

My shoulders relaxed.

'His dad, my brother, passed away this morning.'

Katy's mum clasped his shaking hand.

'I'm sorry, Mr Gilmore. How is Jack?' I choked.

'He's shook up, but only to be expected. I'll go down tomorrow and help him with the arrangements.'

Mrs Gilmore nodded her head. 'Yes, Max, you should be there. Such a shame the feud wasn't mended.'

'Can't be helped, Eliza. The man wouldn't budge. You know that.'

'Yes of course.'

Katy's parents, linked arms, excused themselves and left the room.

'Poor Jack,' I said, 'I should be with him.'

'He won't thank you for it,' Katy said.

My food started to back up in my throat. Jack would be in so much pain.

'Well you know what this means?' Katy folded her arms.

'What?'

'You and Jack have somewhere to live because the mining company won't throw him out. He's entitled to that house. It's tied to the job.'

Covering my mouth, I darted to the nearest bathroom to release the rejected food. Today had been too much. First I was disowned, thrown from my home and now Jack had lost his family too. Fate had hit us both at the same time. I'd scrub his bleak little house and hang gingham curtains at the window to brighten it up.

Light footsteps came along the hall. 'Are you all right, Gracie?' Katy asked.

'Yes, I'm fine now.'

Her eyes narrowed. 'Are you sure you're not pregnant? It's strange how you were sick the other day and again, now?'

'How could you even think that?' I shouted.

She stared at me.

'I understood that to make a baby you needed to have sexual intercourse. Tell me Katy Gilmore, do you know different?'

'You don't need to snap. I only asked. Have you?'

'You're unbelievable. I'd have told you if we'd gone all the way. If you must know I was sick because I was repulsed with myself. For one small moment, I was glad Jack's father was dead. There I've said it. Now you can see what a heartless woman I am.' I snivelled.

'Gracie, of course you're not. It was only for a second. No one would blame you after your experience with him.'

'I must write to Jack. I'll see you in the morning.' I stormed upstairs.

'Night, Gracie,' she called after me.

I wasn't sure who I was most angry with, Katy or myself.

Chapter 15

Katy's father was rooting through drawers in the sideboard when I came down for breakfast the next morning.

'Good morning, Mr Gilmore. Are you off to the mill?'

'Not this morning, young Grace. I'm going to see Jack to take these.' He waved papers in his hand.

My stomach leaped. 'May I come too?'

'Nah, lass, I don't think it's the right place for you. I've no idea what state the poor lad will be in.'

'Please, please let me come?'

'We'll speak to Mrs Gilmore and see what she says. Ah, Eliza, we were just coming to find you.'

'Well I'm here. Good morning, Grace, are you feeling better?'

'Yes, thank you.' I turned to Katy's father and waited.

'This young girl wants me to take her to Wigan. What do you think?'

'You're not contemplating it?'

He turned towards me and shrugged his shoulders. 'I tried.'

'Mrs Gilmore, please. I'd really like to see Jack.'

'But we don't know how he'll be,' she said.

'That's why I should be there. Don't you think?'

'She pleads a good case, Eliza. Maybe we should let her come along for the ride. I'll go in initially and see how things are.'

She sighed. 'All right, but eat something first and get Katy to lend you a pair of slacks. I'm sure you haven't forgotten what it's like there?'

'Thank you, thank you both so much.' My knees quivered and the nausea returned. I was going to see Jack but at the same time venture into that dirty dwelling.

I finished the last spoonful of porridge and drank a small amount of tea before excusing myself to find Katy who was happy to loan me an old pair of trousers. She chose a dark plaid pair.

'Are you sure about this?' she asked, 'Jack may want to be alone.'

'Yes,' I answered, not really sure at all. 'I'll see you later.' I hurried downstairs to the front door where Mr Gilmore was waiting.

'Ready?' he asked.

He took my arm and helped me climb into the Rolls.

*

The rain made the soot worse, puddles splattered black smears up our legs. Thank goodness I'd worn the trews. I covered my mouth to suppress the stench. Mr Gilmore pushed the front door open and told me to wait but I followed him in. Jack was lying on the couch. Dark shadows around his chin showed he hadn't shaved. His shirt was dirty and crumpled, bare skin was revealed around his waistline. A bottle of whisky lay on the floor.

'Uh, uh, who's there?' he slurred.

'It's all right boy, it's only me, Uncle Max.'

He looked up, eyes narrowed. 'Wha' you doin' here?'

'I've come to pay my respects.'

'Bit hypocritical?'

'Never stopped loving him, son.'

'I'm not your son.'

'Aye, lad. Whatever you say. But I'm here to help.'

'Ees gone. Ees dead. Bloody dead. I'm left on me own. Bloody lone soldier. That's me.'

'You're drunk, Jack. You need to sober up. There's a lot to be done.'

Jack picked up the bottle and slurped its contents. 'Barrrp.'

I stood by the door, covering my mouth. This wasn't Jack. This was his father.

'How many of them have you had?' Mr Gilmore asked him.

'Not enough, yu wanna get me more?'

'Come on, boy. Get yourself cleaned up.'

Jack pushed him away. 'Go away and leave me be.'

I moved slightly.

'What was that?' Jack turned to the door. His eyes held mine. 'What are you doing 'ere? Why aren't you at 'ome?'

'They threw me out,' I said in a low voice.

'Wha? Wha yu sayin'?'

'Go back to the car, Grace,' Mr Gilmore said.

I turned to leave, then hesitated.

'Now. You don't want to see him like this,' he ordered.

I took one last look. The sight of the drunk on the couch sickened me. I walked slowly back to the Rolls in the rain.

'What's up, Grace? You look terrible,' James asked.

'He was horrible. I don't know who he is.'

'Well he has just lost his dad. What were you expecting?'

'I thought he'd be pleased to see me.' I sniffed into my handkerchief. 'He didn't want me. I don't know him anymore.' I sniffed again.

'Is he on the booze?'

I nodded.

'It's just the demon drink taking over.'

I didn't like this side of Jack and hoped I'd never see it again. The car door opened, Mr Gilmore climbed in the seat next to me. 'Don't worry, he'll be fine once he's sober.'

Chapter 16

I hadn't heard anything from Jack since that dreadful morning, ten days ago. The funeral had been and gone. Mr Gilmore decided not to go in the end. He didn't think he'd be well received by the coal miners.

It was a sunny morning so I dressed in a lemon summer dress of Katy's that I'd taken in an inch, and drew my hair back in a pony tail. I was just in time to catch her on the banister when I walked out onto the landing.

'Tag on,' she called.

I climbed on behind. Whoosh - we roared with laughter.

'You look nice,' she said. 'Are you hoping Jack will be with Eddie?'

I smiled. 'Do you think he will?'

'You won't be able to keep him away. He loves you. Did you hear that? Quick that must be them, now.'

What was the point in rushing, it was probably just Eddie. To my surprise both men were coming up the steps. Jack was smartly dressed and clean shaven.

Katy ran into Eddie's arms. He kissed her briefly on the cheek then moved her at arm's length. That man didn't deserve her. What was his game?

Jack approached me in a sheepish manner. 'Grace, can we talk?'

I let him lead me into the garden. The scent from mixed coloured polyanthus tickled my nose. 'Sorry about your father,' I said and meant it.

'Thank you. Forgive me for my disgusting behaviour last time you saw me. I'm ashamed, darling. I don't know what else to say. It was such a shock when Da died, I hadn't realised it would be so quick. I'm sorry that I spoke to you badly.'

'Shh.' I traced my fingers over his mouth. 'I understand. But remember, you have me.'

He brought his face close and kissed me, his lips, soft and tender. He sobbed in my arms, I held him tight and stroked his face. 'It'll be all right, my love.'

I'm not sure how long we stood like that, probably only moments but it seemed an eternity before either of us spoke. Jack pulled out a clean handkerchief, blew his nose, then took my hand to escort me back inside.

'So, Grace, what's this about? How come you got back here so soon?'

'Let's find somewhere to sit down. The drawing room is empty.'

He guided me towards the chaise longue. 'Tell me what happened.'

'Well, you know Katy's plan?'

'Plan?'

'The one to say I was expecting. Didn't you get my letters?'

'I don't know, maybe but with everything that's gone on I probably didn't take it in. The plan, yes.' He put his hand to his mouth. 'I can't believe you actually went through with it?'

'I had to. I couldn't marry one of those twins, could I?'

'No, of course not. So?'

'Father said he knew someone that could do an abortion.'

'You're kidding?'

'Mother convinced him to send me away to a cousin in Somerset and have the baby adopted after it was born.'

'Hmm, a bit tricky when there was no baby.'

'Precisely. I wasn't sure how I was going to get round that. Anyway, luck must have been on my side because the cousin refused to help.'

'Go on.' He clasped my hand.

'Mother asked if the baby's father was prepared to marry me. Of course I said yes. But then she asked what you did. They went berserk when I told them. Father called me the most frightful names, they were disgusted with me. I was disowned and thrown out with only a small bag. He said that you weren't going to get hold of his empire.'

'I don't want his bloody empire.'

'I know that Jack, but Father could only see you as someone after his money. It was awful. So that night you lost your da, I lost my parents.'

'Carry on.'

'It was thinking of you that made me determined, but it was hard to leave my sister. Especially knowing that I might never set eyes on her again. He wouldn't even let me say goodbye. She'll never forgive me.'

'I'm sorry, darling. I'll make it up to you.'

High pitched voices came from outside the door. Katy and Eddie burst in. 'There you are,' she said. 'Have you filled him in?'

'Yes, I have.'

'Katy tells me the plan worked?' Eddie said.

'Yes, but it was a very painful experience.'

'Still, never mind. You're well out of there if you ask me,' Eddie continued.

'Except I still don't know where I'm to stay.'

'Here of course,' Katy said, 'and a wedding to organise?' She looked across at Jack.

'Nothing's settled,' I reminded her.

'What? When?' Jack asked confused.

'Dad hasn't agreed to Grace staying yet, but he will. Has Gracie told you her parents are expecting a marriage? Her father said he'll sign the papers.'

'Is that all right?' I asked.

'Of course it is, you silly thing. I couldn't think of anything better.' He picked me up and swung me around.

'I'm getting dizzy.' I laughed. 'I've got no money.' I looked across to Jack for reassurance.

'All I need is you, baby. You've made me the happiest man. When I get back to work on Monday, I'll see the Governor and ask him to put me forward for one of the new houses under construction. At least then we'll have our own lav, sorry I mean toilet, and not have to share.'

'Fabulous,' I said. 'Maybe I could get a sewing machine and take in sewing. What do you think?'

'Sounds like a good idea,' he answered.

'Eddie and I could buy you one as a wedding gift,' Katy said.

I smiled, my eyes filling. Maybe there was a future to look forward to and being a coal miner's wife wasn't going to be so bad after all.

'Right, let's go out tonight to celebrate,' Katy said.

'Palais?' Eddie asked.

'Fine with me.' Jack turned to me.

'Me too,' I added.

We approached the dining room chatting and laughing.

'You seem happier,' Mr Gilmore said as he faced Jack and I.

'I'm the happiest man alive, Uncle. Please, accept my apologies for my ghastly outburst when you came to visit. I'm sorry you didn't attend Da's funeral because of me.'

'It wasn't just because of you, Jack. You were right, it's not what your da would have wanted. It was best I stayed away.' He held out his hand to Jack. 'Let's put it behind us, lad.'

'Thanks, Uncle Max.'

'Are you young people off dancing this evening?'

'Yes, Dad,' Katy said, 'Would you and Mum like to come?'

Mr Gilmore tilted his head back as he laughed. 'I think we're a bit too old for that.'

Maggie came in pushing a hostess trolley.

'We should all sit down,' Katy's dad said.

Everyone scrambled to their seats. Despite everything, soon we were all like one big happy family.

Chapter 17

There was a tap on the door. Maggie peeped in.

'Grace, Mr and Mrs Gilmore would like you to come to the drawing room, please.'

'Yes, of course.' I quickly washed my hands, tied my hair back in a high ponytail and wandered downstairs.

The door was ajar so I could see Katy and her parents deep in conversation.

'Grace, come in. Sit down,' Mr Gilmore said. 'I phoned *Granville Hall* but unfortunately your father refused to speak to me. However, your mother did come to the phone and she said she'd appreciate any help we could give you.'

I smiled with relief. Thank Heavens that Mother at least had seen sense.

'After the boys went home, Eliza, Katy and I sat down to discuss your predicament in detail. I'm happy to say, we're all in agreement that you should stay.'

'I don't know what to say,' I stuttered.

'Furthermore, we think you should complete this term at Bolton Grange. As you know, the Principal has been made aware of your situation so I'll advise him tomorrow that I intend to continue to pay your fees until the end of this college year.'

'But I have no money to pay you back?'

'I still have the funds that your father sent last year.'

'I don't know how to thank you.'

'There's no need. We can sort out details about your wedding when Jack's here. Now I suggest you girls get your things ready for college in the morning.'

'One more thing,' Mrs Gilmore said, 'I think it's time that you started to call us Aunt and Uncle. Don't you?'

'Yes, Aunt Eliza, Uncle Max. Thank you so much.' I hugged them.

Katy dragged me away. 'Told you.' She beamed.

'I'm in your debt.' I hugged her too.

'Race you upstairs,' she said.

*

The second Saturday in June, Jack and I were summoned to the drawing room. We hovered at the open door.

'Come in,' Uncle Max shouted.

Jack stepped in and I followed. My hands were shaking.

'Hey, relax,' Aunt Eliza said. 'You're not in trouble. We thought it was time to talk about the wedding.'

'Phew,' I said, once again breathing normally.

'How about August?' Katy's father asked. 'We need to get you wed before you start to show.'

'Uncle Max, there isn't a baby,' I said.

'It's all right, Grace. Everyone makes mistakes. There's no need to lie.'

'Seriously, Uncle Max, there is no baby,' Jack echoed.

'Whatever you say,' he answered.

Aunt Eliza smiled. Clearly neither of them believed us.

'I've made an appointment tomorrow afternoon for you and Grace to have a chat with the Reverend at Christ Church. If you're happy you can book a date,' Uncle Max continued.

'And you'd better start to design your wedding dress?' Katy's mother said. 'Better make it a little on the generous side.'

It was really going to happen. I was seventeen and to be married and live in one of those bleak little boxes. How would I manage in such a confined space? How would I cope with an outside toilet? Love conquers all they say. Well I hoped it would.

As if Uncle Max could read my mind, he said, 'How's the construction going with Wigan Homes, Jack? Will they be ready by August?'

'Yes, they're due to be finished the last week in July.'

'Great news, you'll be able to get the house ready before the wedding.'

When we left the room, Eddie and Katy were hanging around outside. 'What was all that about?' she asked.

'Your parents think we should set a wedding date.'

'Can I be a bridesmaid?' Then she turned to Jack. 'And Eddie best man?'

'Yes of course,' we both answered.

'I'll start our dresses next week,' I said. 'Katy, you can wear lemon.'

Jack pulled me to the side, 'Are you sure your ready for this, Grace? After all you're not eighteen yet?'

'I want to marry you more than anything in this world, have lots of children and be a real family.'

'And so we shall,' he said and sealed it with a long passionate kiss.

*

Jack and I were just leaving the house on Sunday afternoon to go and see the Vicar when Katy called out, 'Can I come too?'

Before I could answer, Aunt Eliza touched her shoulder. 'No, you stay here with Eddie.'

Katy's eyes narrowed. I'd seen that look on Katy before.

'Can't she come too? She is going to be bridesmaid?' I said.

'This is something you and Jack need to sort out on your own,' Uncle Max said.

Jack and I strolled around to New Chorley Road.

'Christ Church,' Jack said, 'is this the one?'

'Yes, that's the name.'

It was a big old church with a lovely spire and surrounded by greenery. The photographs would be superb in this setting. The rector greeted us as we got close to the door.'Ah, you must be Grace and Jack?'

'Yes, Reverend,' Jack answered. He held out his hand to shake.

'Come in. Grace, your Aunt has told me about your circumstances. I understand your parents don't intend to attend the ceremony, but they've granted permission?'

'That's right,' I answered.

We followed him into a large dismal room. I shivered. It was chilly in here, considering it was June.

'Sit down and we'll have a chat. You're very young, Grace. Have you thought this through? Marriage is a lifelong commitment and not a five minute wonder.'

'We know that,' Jack butted in. 'Grace and I love each other. We want to be together.'

The Reverend looked at me.

'Yes, I understand. Like Jack said, we want to be married.'

'I see. I understand there's a bairn on the way?'

I could feel my face blushing. 'No, no there isn't.'

'Then why so quick. Why not wait a couple more years?'

Jack became fidgety. 'Will you marry us or what?'

I shushed him.

The vicar raised his eyebrows before standing up. 'Young man, you need to calm down. I'll make some tea.' He walked to the stove, picked up a shabby aluminium kettle, drew water from the tap and struck a match to the gas. 'I've no sugar I'm afraid.' He scooped several spoons from the black tea caddy. The kettle whistled.

'This is very kind of you, Reverend.' I gripped Jack's hand.

The vicar poured the tea. 'Milk?'

'Yes please,' I answered for us both.

He passed Jack a cup and saucer. 'Here you are, lad. Now you're a bit more relaxed we can start again.'

'Sorry about earlier. I'm a bit nervous.'

'That's very natural. Of course I'll conduct the ceremony but I wouldn't be doing my job properly if I didn't make sure that you're both ready.'

Jack nodded in agreement. I was relieved he'd calmed down.

'You're older. Maybe Grace deserves a bit more time to grow up?'

I turned to the minister. 'I'm definitely ready. I've never been surer of anything in my life.'

He stared at me for what seemed a very long moment. 'Very well.' He opened the drawer in his desk and pulled out a diary flicking through the pages. 'Let's see what we have available.'

Jack squeezed my hand and smiled.

'Is it a Saturday you'd like?'

'Yes please,' Jack said, 'I'm at work through the week.'

'I have the sixteenth of August at two o'clock, twenty-third at four o'clock or thirtieth at half past one. Which shall I pencil in?'

Jack whispered to me.

'We'll take the sixteenth at two o'clock please, Vicar,' Jack said.

The Vicar wrote in the book.

'Thank you for your time.' I held out my hand. Jack did the same.

'We'll need to read the banns, so you both need to attend church the next three Sundays.'

'We'll be there.' I turned to face Jack and smiled.

We walked back home, chatting about the wedding. It was to be a small affair as we barely had any family.

'I'd like to invite my friend John and his wife Nancy,' Jack said.

'I haven't heard you mention them before.'

'Well I work with John. He's a good mate. I'd liked to have asked him to be my best man but you know what Katy's like once she gets an idea?'

'Yes, I do.' I laughed.

'It will give you an opportunity to get to know Nancy as they'll be moving into one of the new houses too and may even be our next door neighbours.'

Chapter 18

College had finished and I wouldn't return with Katy for the final year. Still, I had plenty to focus on with the wedding in six weeks. This morning for instance, we were driving into Bolton to choose fabric for our dresses.

'Are you ready,' I called upstairs.

'Yep.' Katy appeared wearing bright red lipstick.

The car was stifling. James dropped us at the town hall where lion statues stood guard at the top of the steps, like silent sentinels.

Katy stared at me.

'What's the matter?' I asked.

'I wasn't sure what your reaction would be.' She pointed.

'What do you mean?'

'Well you know? After last time?'

'You mean Queen's Park? This isn't the same.'

She frowned. I knew she never understood.

'That was different. It was a strange sensation like gods warning me not to enter.'

Katy laughed, reinforcing my suspicion that she'd never appreciate my feelings about Queen's Park.

'You still don't understand. Anyway, I don't want to talk about it anymore.' I shivered.

'All right, whatever you say.'

To make my point I strolled over to one of the concrete sculptures and stroked its solid mane.

'What do you want to do first?' Katy asked. 'In here, around the museum, or the shops?'

'Here.' I leaned against one of the large classic columns. 'What a beautiful iconic building. Why haven't you brought me here before?'

'Because of what we were just talking about. But I couldn't let you leave Bolton without seeing it.'

'It must have taken years to build this. That clock tower is magnificent.'

'I never tire of visiting,' she said.

'It's very picturesque. I love the fountain waterfalls.'

There were more steps to climb before we arrived at the museum's entrance. A stuffed buffalo's head held pride of place high on the wall. We darted around artefacts: Egyptian mummy coffins to china dolls and woodlice.

After a couple of hours browsing we left the building and made our way to the undercover market hall to buy material.

'Mum said to go to Redman's,' Katy said, 'because she has an account there.'

We searched the stalls until we came to the right unit.

'This is it.' She looked up at the black typeset sign.

'Can I help you?' the shopkeeper asked.

I caressed the rolls of fabric that adorned the counter.

'It's Edna, isn't it? Mum, Mrs Gilmore, sent us,' Katy said.

'Oh yes, hello, err?'

'Katy. I think we may have met before.'

'You do look familiar but I'm not here very often. Mum and Dad have taken a drive over to Southport, it's their wedding anniversary today. Now what can I do for you ladies?'

'I'm looking for something special for my wedding dress. Silk, satin maybe? Lace for the underskirt and veil.'

'You're getting married. How wonderful, congratulations. You're not Mrs Gilmore's daughter though, are you? Only I thought she only had one?'

'Grace is my best friend,' Katy interrupted, 'and she lives with us.'

Edna's fingers rose to her lips. 'Ah, I think I have just the right thing. Give me a minute. Would you like some pop to cool you down in this heat?'

'Yes please,' Katy said.

'Thank you. That would be nice,' I answered.

The assistant disappeared and returned carrying a tray with two tumblers of dark liquid then vanished again.

'Sarsaparilla,' Katy said, 'my favourite.'

I sipped the welcome drink.

Edna returned. 'What about this?' She carried a cylinder covered in white shiny material.

I stroked it. 'Satin. Yes, this is lovely. Do you have it in lemon?'

'Yes, here it is.' She picked up a roll.

Katy scrunched her nose. 'I know it's your day, Grace, but please don't make me wear that. It's horrid. If you want me to be your bridesmaid...' She glared at me. 'Then I'd rather have pink.'

'We do have it in pink.' Edna passed the roll towards me.

I offered the fabric up to Katy. 'Like a rose. I did want lemon but this is striking against your skin tone. So, yes, why not?'

'You don't mind?' Katy asked.

'No, I think the colour you've chosen will be delightful.'

'What about this for decoration?' Katy pointed to some floral lace.

I touched it. 'Exquisite. This will be lovely for my veil and decorating the bodice.'

'It's new in today,' Edna said.

'May I have six yards of white satin, four yards of pink and three yards of lace, please.' I picked up some packets of small white flowers and beading. 'These too. And the thread to match please. That just leaves the underskirts.'

'What about this?' The shopkeeper pointed to some netting. 'This is what brides are wearing under their gowns these days.'

'I think we'd better have six yards of that. Do you think that will be enough for both dresses?'

'I should think so, dear.'

'I also need to make headdresses.'

'How about these little pink roses for bridesmaid and white matching ones for the bride.'

'Yes, thank you. They'll do the job nicely.'

The assistant snipped the fabrics in turn and then folded them neatly before wrapping them in brown paper.

'Would you like it delivered?'

'Will it be today?' I asked.

'Yes, I can get my brother to pop it round. I'm expecting him back any time now.'

'That's perfect. Can you add it to Mum's account, at *Willow Banks*, please?' Katy said.

'She opened a small book with columns on the pages. 'Yes, certainly. Have you thought about flowers?'

'No, not yet,' I said.

'I'm only asking because I'm a florist by trade, which is why I'm not here very often. Just when Mum needs me to help out.'

'Oh I see,' I said.

'If you'd like, I could come by your house to discuss flowers?'

I looked at Katy.

'Yes, that's a great idea, Edna,' she answered. 'Can you ring Mum and make an appointment?'

'I'll do that.' She grinned.

'We'll see you soon.' Katy waved.

'Thank you,' I said with a pang of guilt that the Gilmores were paying for everything. I'd have to find a way of paying them back.

Katy grabbed my hand. 'Come on, Grace.'

We left the shop and made our way back to the town hall.

'There's James.' Katy pointed. 'That was good timing.'

He pulled up the Rolls and we climbed in.

'Did you girls get what you needed?' he asked.

'Yes thank you. We went to the museum too, those mummies are eerie,' I said.

'They have that effect on everyone,' he answered.

It drew my mind back to the sentinels at Queen's Park. Why did I have to start thinking about them again?

*

Aunt Eliza was in the garden, stretched out on a striped deck chair with her mouth wide open and eyes shut. A book of

102

collected poems by Dylan Thomas lay upside down on her lap. I hadn't realised before that she was interested in poetry.

'Wakey, wakey,' Katy whispered. She shook her mother.

Aunt Eliza jumped. 'What? You're back. I must have dropped off to sleep.'

'I hope you haven't got sunburnt?' I said.

She held up her arm. 'I am a bit red. I should have rubbed in grease.' She smoothed out her dress as she stood up. 'Let's go and have tea while you tell me about your purchases.'

A tray with a pot of tea and a plate of bourbon biscuits was on the sideboard when we wandered into the drawing room.

'Did you find what you wanted, Grace?'

'I think so.' I started to talk about the different materials.

The doorbell rang. Shortly afterwards, Eric marched in carrying a large brown parcel wrapped with string.

'Grace it's here?' Katy said, 'Mum, we can show you.'

The butler placed the package on the coffee table. 'Would you like me to cut the string?' he asked.

'Yes please.' I knelt down on the floor eager to unpack the package.

He cut the twine with a penknife.

'Thank you.' I ripped off the paper and passed the white satin to Aunt Eliza. 'This is for me.'

'Very soft and shiny. Yes, I can see that run up as a gown,' she said.

'This floral lace is for the veil and also to go across the bodice as decoration.' I demonstrated.

'Have you designed the dress yet?'

'Yes.'

'She won't even let me see it, Mum. She said it's a surprise.'

'Look at these little flowers and beads. I'm going to use these on the veil and bodice too. And I'll make headdresses with rosebuds. And this is for Katy.' I bent my head to hide a tear.

'What do you think, Mum?' Katy asked.

Aunt Eliza was quiet. I sensed she was looking at me.

'Grace?'

'Yes?' I spluttered, hiding my tears.

'Whatever is the matter? Come and sit next to me, my dear.'

I stood up slowly and sat next to Eliza on the couch.

'Is it because I refused to wear the lemon?' Katy said.

'What do you mean, refused? It's Grace's day, not yours. Is that what it's about, love?'

I wiped my eyes with a handkerchief. 'No, not at all. I'm happy about the pink. I was just thinking how lovely it would look on Elizabeth. She should be here too, as my bridesmaid. It isn't fair.'

Aunt Eliza put her arms around me. 'I know, dear. I know.'

'And my father should be giving me away and Mother should be helping me sort out my wedding dress. You're all too kind. How will I ever repay you?'

'There's no need, Grace. We love you. I'm sorry that your little sister can't be here. I know Katy won't make up for that, but perhaps it will help. And Uncle Max is happy to give you away. He adores you. We both do.'

'Maybe I could design your outfit?'

'No, Grace. You won't have time. It's only six weeks away and the house in Wigan will come up soon. You'll need to get that ready too.'

'Well if you're sure.' I wiped my eyes and kissed her on the cheek. 'That's enough feeling sorry for myself.' I bit into the final piece of my chocolate bourbon and took a last sip of tea. 'Aunt Eliza, may I use the dining room table to cut out our dresses?'

'Of course. And Grace, you know you can always talk to me. Don't you?' She patted my hand.

'Thank you Aunt Eliza. Katy come on, I need to measure you.'

'Yes, sure.' Katy grabbed my hand as we left the room together.

Chapter 19

Maggie showed Edna into the drawing room where Aunt Eliza, Katy and I were waiting. The florist showed us floral displays and pictures while we drank tea. My wedding was three weeks from tomorrow. I'd finished making the bride and bridesmaid dresses, the flowers were the last piece of the jigsaw.

I settled on a bouquet of red roses and white gypsophila with a little bit of green foliage. For Katy, I chose pink and white michaelmas daisies tied with ribbon. Katy screwed her nose up.

'Are you all right,' I asked her.

She chewed her lip.

'What's the matter?' I asked again.

'I want roses too.'

'Oh,' I said.

Suddenly, she was a like a kettle hissing steam. 'It's not fair. Why should I have rubbish flowers when you have lovely roses?'

I was about to let her have her own way when Aunt Eliza interrupted. 'Katy, stop behaving like a spoilt child. It's Grace's wedding.'

'Grace, Grace. That's all we ever talk about these days. I don't count. Fine, I'll have the rotten daisies.' She slammed down her cup and saucer, stood up and stormed out of the room.

Edna fidgeted with her glasses before lowering her head and started scribbling frantically in her notebook.

'I'm really sorry about that,' Aunt Eliza said to her. 'I just don't know what's going on with that girl these days.' She tutted.

'No problem,' Edna said, still fidgety and looking like she wanted a hasty escape. 'Button holes? What colour is your outfit, Mrs Gilmore?'

'Navy blue.'

'How about a nice cream orchid to go with it?'

'Grace?' Aunt Eliza turned to me.

'That sounds very nice,' I said. 'And red carnations for Jack, Eddie and Uncle Max.'

'And the other guests?' Edna asked.

'We don't have very many. Jack's friends, John and Nancy, and maybe a couple of girls from college. They can wear white carnations.'

'Dad or my brother will deliver them first thing on the day. You'll make a beautiful bride. If you're taking photographs, would it be possible to let me have a couple for my portfolio?'

'Certainly,' Aunt Eliza said.

Katy strutted back into the room. 'All done?' She was smiling and seemed to be back to her old self again. 'Bye, Edna.'

'Oh er, yes.' Edna raised her eyebrows. 'Goodbye Katy, Grace, Mrs Gilmore.'

The post popped through the letterbox just after I'd closed the door and Uncle Max came up behind me and leaned down to the floor to pick it up. 'What have we here?' He sifted through the bundle. 'One for you, Grace. Sorry, love.'

I took the envelope from his hands. *Return to Sender.* 'I don't understand? Why would Elizabeth send it back when I sent it to Greenemere?'

He pointed to the telephone in the hallway. 'Give Miss Allison a ring? See if she can throw any light on it?' Uncle Max stood patiently waiting.

'Thank you. I will.' I picked up the receiver and dialled the number. Miss Allison answered. She seemed pleased to hear from me and asked how I was. Apparently, Father had requested that she opened Elizabeth's mail before passing it on. He'd given strict instructions that mine were to be returned. I put the phone down in its cradle and covered my face.

'Eh, what's wrong? What did she say?' Uncle Max asked.

'Apparently, Father's forbidden Elizabeth to receive any of my mail. I asked if I could speak to her, but she declined because he's forbidden that too. And she isn't to be told that I've written or called. It's not fair. She suggested I keep the letters, so one day I may show them to Elizabeth, so she'd see I didn't desert her. How could Father do this to us both?'

Uncle Max patted my hand. 'It'll all come out in the wash, girlie. You'll see.'

Before we had a chance to join the others the phone rang. He stretched to reach it. 'Max Gilmore speaking.' There was a small silence. 'Hello Jack, yes, she's here. I'll hand her over.' Max hovered behind me.

'Thank you.' I wondered why Jack was calling when he was due to visit tomorrow.

'Well?' Uncle Max asked, once I'd replaced the receiver. 'What did he want?'

'We've been allocated a house. It needs a good clean, apparently the builders have left it in a mess. I need to buy some cleaning products. Is there any chance you could lend me some money until Jack comes tomorrow?'

'I can do better than that. Go and find Maggie and ask her to pack scouring powder and other bits.'

'Thanks, Uncle Max.' I gave him a kiss on his cheek. I loved Uncle Max, why couldn't Father be like him. 'Katy.'

'No need to shout.' Katy rushed out of the sitting room. 'You look happy?'

'Oh, sorry.' I laughed. 'Listen, Jack's just phoned. We've been allocated a house and it's ready for us to move in, when we want. We're going down to clean it tomorrow. Will you help?'

'Err, not sure. Depends on Eddie.'

'I'd really like you with me. Uncle Max told me to get Maggie to pack cleaning products from the kitchen.'

'Come on then.' She dragged my hand and led me to find the maid.

*

'That'll be the boys,' I called.

Katy slid down the banister.

I rushed over to kiss Jack when he came through the front door. He picked me up and twirled me around the room.

'Where's Eddie?' Katy stared at him.

'He's not coming, I'm afraid. I don't think he fancied cleaning.'

'Well we didn't need to come with you.' Katy scowled.

'He said he had something else on.'

I put my arm around Katy. She shoved me away and charged upstairs.

'Is she all right?' Jack asked.

'I'm not sure. She's been a bit moody the last few days. I think I should go and see.' I ran up the stairs, two at a time, to Katy's room and tapped on the door.

'Go away,' she called.

'Katy, it's me. Can I come in?'

'I said, go away.'

I turned the handle and let myself in. Katy eyes narrowed. She was pulling clothes out of the chest of drawers and throwing them around her room. The floor was covered in petticoats and knickers.

I moved towards her to console her, but she pushed me away.

'Go back to lover boy,' she roared.

'Not until I know that you're all right.'

'Everything goes well for Miss Grace. You're getting everything that should have been mine. Wedding. House. Next you'll have a baby. What about me?'

'But you're still at college, Katy. I wouldn't be getting married if I was still there.' I didn't know what had happened to my friend. Where was the fun Katy that I'd shared a room

108

with at Greenemere for three years? Nowadays she seemed so up and down, I never knew where I stood.

'I hate you. Ever since you came here, everything has gone wrong.'

'But that's not my fault, surely?' I put my arms around her again. This time she let them stay and buried her head into my shoulder and sobbed.

I didn't trust Eddie one bit, but how did I broach that with my friend. It was something best left for later. 'Jack and I want you to come to Wigan with us. I want you to be the first to see our house.'

'You don't want a gooseberry.'

'Of course we do. What could be better, my best friend and my fiancé?'

She smiled and seemed calmer. 'I'd better clear this mess up.'

'Yes, and wash your face before you come down. I'll see you in a few minutes.' I ran downstairs to find Jack.

He was in the drawing room with Aunt Eliza. 'Is she all right now?' he asked me.

'Yes, she's coming down in a minute. I don't trust that Eddie. Why isn't he here?' I said.

'He's a bad lot,' Aunt Eliza said.

'How do we tell her that?' I asked.

She shrugged. 'There's no telling her.'

'Tell me about the house,' I asked Jack.

'It's small, two up and two down and it's got our own privy. Sorry, toilet.'

It was really happening. Was it indoors? Did it have a bathroom? Jack must have read my thoughts.

'Of course we don't have a bathroom but at least it's not a communal toilet. It's still outside in the yard but at least no one else will use it. Grace, it's ours.'

He seemed so excited about this outdoor toilet. Life was going to be quite an adjustment for me. 'How do we keep ourselves clean?' I asked.

'We'll get a tin bath and wash by the fire.'

Eliza must have seen my face. 'It's not that bad, Grace. You'll get used to it. At least you have two rooms downstairs and two bedrooms. Jack lived in one room with his father. You have a spare room too, for children.'

I thought of the numerous bedrooms at *Granville Hall* and here, at *Willow Banks*. The bathrooms almost equalled them. Oh well nothing to do about it. I had love and that was worth any price.

Katy strolled into the room and walked over to Jack to give him a friendly hug. 'They've allocated us a house,' Jack said to her.

'Grace told me. Congratulations.'

Aunt Eliza decided James should drive us to Wigan after lunch so we could start the cleaning. My knees wouldn't stop shaking. I was going to see my new home. And not only that, I had to clean it. Would I know how?

We loaded the car with tin buckets, sweeping and scrubbing brushes, Vim scouring powder, Brillo pads and Cardinal tile polish. Aunt Eliza insisted that we take her young maid, Sally, to help. She sat in front with James. I hoped that the soot wouldn't be too bad today as it was dry and sunny. Forty minutes down the road and we were there.

James stopped outside a terrace of little houses. 'Is this it?' he asked.

'Yes,' Jack said. He turned to me. 'What do you think?'

It was difficult to know what I thought yet. I hadn't seen inside. It was busy, lots of couples around the small dwellings, women sweeping floors and wiping down window frames. Jack got out of the car and took my hand. Katy looked lost. I gave her my other hand and we all walked towards the house.

Jack dangled the keys. 'Number eleven. And guess what? Nancy and John are number nine. How perfect is that?'

I smiled. Katy frowned.

Jack bounced with excitement. He was so proud. I let his enthusiasm rub off on me.

'Come on, Katy,' I said, 'come and see my new house. Eleven Bamber Street.'

She stood still.

'What's wrong?'

'You'll have a new best friend soon. That Nancy. You won't want me anymore.'

I hugged her tight. 'You'll always be my best friend.' What had happened to Katy? Why had she become so insecure? It must be Eddie, he'd chipped away at her self esteem.

'What are you girls messing at?' Jack had already unlocked the front door.

'We're coming.' I grabbed Katy's hand and pulled her along.

Jack lifted me in his arms and carried me across the threshold. I was a bit confused because I thought that was the custom once you were married, but he said we'd do it again. The front door took us directly into what I supposed was the living room with a narrow staircase towards the back. An internal door just behind held a small scullery with a stove, sink, pastel blue kitchen cabinet and a copper to heat water. I looked through the window next to the back door at the small back yard.

Jack took me by the hand and led me outside to a small outbuilding. 'This is our very own toilet.'

I opened the door. There was a wooden platform seat with a hole in it. It was going to take some getting used to. It would be no fun coming out here in the cold and dark. Jack beamed.

'Let's go and see the bedrooms then,' I said.

His smile got bigger. He guided me upstairs. Katy lingered behind with disinterest. 'You're not seriously going to live here are you?' she whispered.

'What do you suggest?' I asked.

'Come back with me, Mum and Dad won't mind. You can make a living selling your designs.'

'And you called me a snob?' I caught up with Jack and brushed a small kiss across his cheek. 'Thank you, Jack. This is a lovely house. All we need to do is clean it up and make it pretty. I'll make colourful curtains to brighten it.'

He held me. 'I love you, Grace Granville. You won't regret this.'

The house became industrious, everyone cleaning and scrubbing. Well except Katy, she sat on the step sulking. I'd never used Vim or Brillo pads before, but Sally showed me what to do. I got great satisfaction as the house started to shine. All that remained was to do the step. I relished moving Katy out of the way. 'Come on, Katy. I need to get here.' I knelt down onto old rags and rubbed red cardinal polish into the step.

A plain girl, not much older than me popped out of the house next door. 'Hello, I'm Nancy. You lot look like you could do with a cuppa. Come round to ours.'

'Thank you. I'm Grace. Have you just moved in?'

'Yeah, a couple of days ago.'

'Jack,' I called. 'Nancy's here.'

He came outside and gave her a hug. 'You got the kettle on?' he asked.

'Yeah, that's why I came round. Do you want to come to ours, or should I bring it round here?'

'We'll come around to you,' Jack answered.

James and Sally declined, they said they'd finish off tidying. Katy grunted. Nancy's abdomen was slightly raised and I wondered if she was having a baby.

'John they're here,' she said as we all trailed into her house.

'Hi mate,' he said to Jack. 'This must be the lovely Grace we've heard so much about.'

I shook hands with John. 'This is Katy, Jack's cousin and my best friend.'

'Hello Katy pleased to meet you.'

Katy forced a smile.

I walked into Nancy's scullery, she had a yellow kitchen cabinet against the wall. The cupboards at the top and bottom were stocked. A flap was pulled down to use as working space for the teas.

'We have one of these,' Jack pointed.

'Yes, except ours is blue,' I said.

'Come through.' Nancy carried a tray with five mugs of tea and a plate of cake. 'Sit down and try my Victoria sponge. It's the first time I've made it.'

The room looked delightful with ornaments on the mantelpiece, pictures and a mirror on the wall. A glass vase of summer blooms, bursting with colour, stood on a sideboard next to a clock. Nancy noticed me looking at the flowers. 'They're a housewarming present from me Mam and Da.'

'They're beautiful,' I said. 'I love sweet peas, especially purple and red. Shame we don't have gardens with these houses.'

We chatted for about half an hour and even Katy joined in. Nancy's Victoria sponge was delicious. It got me worried as I had no idea how to cook anything, I'd ask Maggie to teach me over the next couple of weeks. There was a knock on the door and the handle turned.

'Time we made tracks,' James said, 'we've locked up next door.'

I kissed Nancy and John on the cheek. We'd be back down next weekend to hang the curtains which I'd make during the week.

Chapter 20

James had dropped me off at my future home, armed with curtains, about an hour and half earlier just as Jack was taking receipt of second hand furniture.

'So did Katy say what she was doing?' Jack asked as he finished organising the latest additions to our household.

'She's gone for a walk around Wigan with Eddie. It's a shame, I really wanted her here.'

'Why my cousin is still hanging around with that tosser, I don't know.'

'She loves him.' I snapped the thread between my teeth. 'There. What do you think?' I held up the gold brocade curtains.

'They look very professional,' Jack said, 'it would have cost a bomb to have bought them.'

My eyes wandered around the room. Jack had spent last week covering the walls with gold patterned paper that almost matched the curtains. An old sideboard, discarded from Aunt Eliza's drawing room, displayed a vase of burnt orange chrysanthemums and cactus dahlias from her garden. A grey fleck settee with matching club armchairs governed the living area. In front of the fireplace lay a black floral rug. I sank into the settee. 'Where did this come from, Jack? It's a bit more comfortable than that hard chair I've been sitting on.'

'*Dawbers*, a second hand shop, near Wigan Station. Cost me a fiver. Not bad is it?'

'It's quite comfortable.' When I bounced, a cloud of dust rose in the air making me cough. 'But I think it needs a clean.' We both laughed.

Jack hung white nets, café style and arranged floor length drapes on the taut wire under the white wooden pelmet then stepped down from the ladder. We moved to the back of the room to take it all in. Yes, maybe it wasn't going to be so awful here after all. There was a knock on the door.

'Hello, it's only us,' John called. 'How's it going?'

'Wow, those curtains are incredible,' Nancy said.

'Grace made them,' Jack said.

Nancy couldn't take her eyes off the drapes. I couldn't take my eyes off the paisley patterned scarf she wrapped around her head like a turban. The other women did that too. Perhaps I should. The thought of hiding my dark bouncy locks sent me queasy, but maybe it was necessary to keep coal dust out of your hair. Nancy was timid and mouse like, different to Katy, but she seemed kind and sweet.

'Shall I put this down here?' Nancy placed a tray of mugs on the small coffee table.

'That's very kind of you,' I said, 'and I see you've brought one of your Victoria sponges too.'

Her face went red. 'This room is looking good, have you done any of the others yet?'

I held up blue gingham curtains. 'These are for the kitchen or the scullery as you may call it, and these for our bedroom.' I passed her a blue grey pair with pink roses. 'Jack has wallpapered with a similar design. We've not sorted anything for the spare bedroom yet, there's no rush.' I looked at her raised abdomen. 'When's your baby due?'

'December seventeenth.' She stroked her belly. 'I'm nearly five months. I hope it's a girl.'

'How exciting.' I wondered what it would be like having a baby so young. Seemed rather scary to me. We sat down, drank from mugs and ate jam sandwich cake. It was nice to know that when I moved here in a couple of weeks I had a friend waiting. There was a knock on the door. A visitor? Jack and I glanced at each other before he stood up to answer it.

'Surprise,' Katy shouted. 'Cover your eyes. Bring it in, Eddie.'

Jack and I dutifully obeyed.

'Ta dah,' Katy said, 'you can open them now.'

Over by the wall, stood a Singer sewing machine, set in its very own table.

'It's wonderful, Katy. Thank you so much, but why?'

'Wedding present, silly. You need one, especially after I saw you the other night with blood pouring from your thumb. You'll be able to run things up on this in no time. Ordered it from *Redman's*. James took us down to pick it up. He was sworn to secrecy.'

'That's very generous,' Jack said.

'What do you think Nassy?' Katy asked.

'It's Nancy,' I said.

'Very nice,' Nancy answered.

I hugged Katy. It was clear she was feeling threatened. 'You're such a special friend.'

'Best friend,' she said.

'Yes, best friend.'

Nancy got up. 'Would Eddie and Katy like some tea?'

'Nah, you're all right, gal,' Eddie said. We've been drinking tea most of the day. Now if you're offering beer, then that's different.'

Katy nudged him. 'Err, I wouldn't mind a piece of that sponge.'

'Of course, help yourself.' Nancy smiled.

'Come and see the rest of the house,' I said to Katy. 'Nancy, you come too.'

Katy threw Nancy a black look but she just stood up and smiled. 'That will be lovely, thank you.'

We climbed the narrow wooden steps in convoy until we reached two rooms opposite each other. 'The front one is ours,' I said.

'Oh yes, ours too,' Nancy said, 'ooh, I love your wallpaper. You're so lucky, we haven't done ours yet. And your curtains will go lovely.'

Katy bounced on the old wooden bed. 'Where did this come from? Bet you can't wait to be in here with Jack.'

My face flushed. 'Jack managed to pick it up for a few quid from someone at work. I thought I'd make a bedspread to

116

match the curtains. Nancy, I could run some furnishings up for you too?'

'Don't forget about me, Gracie. Eddie and I'll be getting our place shortly. And you'll have to make my wedding dress.'

'How could I forget you? It's starting to get dark, we'd better go back downstairs and find the boys.' I walked down the steps carefully and the others followed. Our menfolk were talking about football.

Nancy held her stomach and winced. John jumped up. 'Nancy?'

Her face was pale. 'I think it's time we went home.'

'I hope nothing's wrong.' I hugged her.

Jack saw our friends out of the house, shut the door behind them. 'I hope Nancy is all right.' He then turned to Eddie. 'Give us a hand with the rest of these curtains will you?'

'Can you pass me a ciggie first?' Katy held out her hand to Eddie.

'I thought you'd given up?' He passed her a woodbine and struck a match.

'Well, err yes. But ....' She clutched it between her shaking fingers, drew it up to her mouth and blew out smoke as she headed out to the back yard.

I didn't follow her. I was more concerned about Nancy. I didn't really know anything about having babies but she didn't seem quite right.

Chapter 21

Aunt Eliza completed my make-up and set my hair. She placed small white satin roses in the top of my dark curls and hung a double row of pearls around my neck before leaving me alone to step into my gown and look at my reflection. The pastel green eye shadow highlighted my dark eyes. White satin draped my body, hugging me at the waist and the low neckline showed off my figure without being too revealing. I clipped the short lace veil, decorated with satin roses, to my hair. I was grown up, no longer a girl, but a woman.

I picked up the lemon negligee Aunt Eliza had bought for me to wear on my wedding night. My stomach curdled. Mother should be here telling me what to expect. I folded it back in the box and stepped into silver stilettos before moving back to the mirror. There was a tap on the door.

'Are you ready?' It was Aunt Eliza. 'Goodness, Grace, you look beautiful. Where's Katy got to?'

As if on cue, she burst in. She stood there with her mouth open.

'Now who's catching flies?' I laughed.

'You look wonderful.' She adjusted my dress.

'You look wonderful too. I'm glad you insisted on pink, the colour and tiers really suit you,' I said.

Her dress flowed just above gold strapped sandals. She fixed her rose satin headdress with a silk gloved hand. She was the picture of elegance. I was proud to have her as my bridesmaid and best friend.

We descended downstairs slowly. Uncle Max stood waiting.

'What a bevy of beauties.' He looked handsome in his long jacket and striped trousers. The men had been to *Jackson's*, the tailor's in town.

Aunt Eliza fixed Uncle Max's bow tie then twirled around to show off her burgundy pencil dress and matching jacket, both trimmed with cream. She stepped into three inch stilettos that brought her closer to Uncle Max's shoulders.

'Jack's a lucky lad,' Uncle Max said. 'I'm proud to give you away.'

Oh dear, that was it, my emotions refused to stay in check any longer and a tear trickled.

'No, you can't cry,' Aunt Eliza and Katy said in unison. 'You'll smudge your mascara.'

'Sorry,' I sniffled.

'Here.' Aunt Eliza smoothed over the make-up and applied a red lipstick. She looked at her watch. 'Time to go, it's half past one. Katy and I will go first and then James will take you two.'

Once they left, Uncle Max went to the bar and poured a small sherry. 'Here, drink this slowly, it will help steady your nerves.'

The amber coloured liquid warmed me inside as I sipped.

We strolled down the steps to the Rolls, I was delighted to see the bonnet decorated in ivory ribbon and a display of pink and white roses sat on the parcel shelf. 'Katy's idea?'

'Yes love,' Uncle Max said.

It was a beautiful day for a wedding, a clear sky and the sun shining. Uncle Max guided me to the car. He was strong and comforting, a great man to give me away. But he wasn't Father. Father should be sitting here with me, reassuring me that everything was fine. Mother should have been here, elegant in a posh dress and hat. And Elizabeth... Elizabeth should have been my bridesmaid. The Gilmores were grand but at the end of the day they weren't my real family.

'Grace?'

'Sorry?'

'Your bouquet. You're going to crush it. James, pull over for a moment. What's wrong, Grace?'

'How could Mother and Father abandon me? I want to scream.'

'Do it then. Get out of the car and do it.'

I looked at Uncle Max.

'Go on.'

James opened the door and I stepped out carefully, holding my dress. I opened my mouth, let go of a high pitched shriek and climbed back into the car.

'Better?' Uncle Max asked.

'Yes.' I giggled. All those pent up feelings were expelled.

He tapped my hand. 'I'm proud to give you away and I'll do my best to be a good understudy.'

I brushed a kiss across his cheek. 'Thank you, Uncle Max.'

'You'd better put your foot down, James,' he said. 'We're going to be late.'

This was it, goodbye to my old life and hello to the new. I really was saying goodbye to my family. Father, strict but wanted the best, Mother, frightened to air her view, at least most of the time, and Elizabeth, who looked up to me, would think I'd betrayed her. I wasn't turning a page or starting a new chapter but instead I was beginning a new book. Once I became Mrs Gilmore, there was no turning back. I loved Jack but was I strong enough to live this new way of life?

'Someone's deep in thought. Jack's a good lad, Grace. He'll look after you.'

'I know.'

It was just gone two o'clock when the car pulled up outside the church. Katy was fidgeting. She glared at me. 'Where've you been?'

I lifted my dress from the ground and walked briskly to meet her. 'Has Aunt Eliza gone in?'

'Yes. We should be in there too. Jack probably thinks you've changed your mind.'

'Now Katy, leave the lass alone. It's my fault we're late.'

Katy squinted.

'Don't worry about it now. Let's go in. Grace.' He offered his arm, and took control. Katy tipped the veil to cover my face, it itched but gave me reassurance. Hidden like forbidden fruit.

The organist played *Here Comes the Bride*. That was our cue. Uncle Max and I strolled down the aisle. My bouquet bobbed up and down in my shaking hands. Katy followed behind, lifting my long train. The congregation was small, made up of a few servants from *Willow Banks*, Mr and Mrs Redman, the fabric store owners, along with their daughter, Edna, the florist, and her brother. If I'd agreed to marry one of the Anson twins, there'd be more than two hundred guests, a ceremony in a cathedral, at least six bridesmaids and a couple of page boys. But at what price? There'd be no Jack.

I looked around for Jack's friends, Nancy and John, but couldn't see them. Why weren't they here? I thought about our last meeting, Nancy's expression as she held her stomach and winced. I hoped nothing bad had happened. But surely Jack would have told me? I tried to put them out of mind and concentrate on today, which should be the happiest day of my life except for the emptiness inside and wishing my family was here to fill it.

Jack stood next to Eddie, in their matching suits that Uncle Max had insisted on buying. My heart quickened when Jack turned to face me. I couldn't stop smiling. He was so handsome. Curls that normally drooped over his forehead were gone, leaving his blue grey eyes looking larger as they held my gaze.

The Vicar opened his prayer book and lowered his head revealing a small shiny patch amongst grey wisp. Uncle Max handed me to Jack. I passed my bouquet to Katy and she lifted the veil. The sun was warm on my face as it shone through the windows. Pillar candles burnt vanilla. Summer flowers, including chrysanthemums and dahlias, mixed with green foliage, decorated the church. Their strong scent tickled my nose, making me almost sneeze. Choirboys, uniformed in white smocks, stood in pews adjacent to the altar. Soprano voices were distinct when we sang, *All Things Bright and Beautiful*, and Psalm 23, *The Lord is My Shepherd*. Was I doing the right thing? Jack stood next to me holding my hand, reminding me of our love, yet I couldn't stop thinking about my family.

'Do you Jack George Gilmore take Grace Georgina Granville to be your lawfully wedded wife?'

'I do,' Jack answered without hesitation.

'Do you Grace Georgina Granville take Jack George Gilmore to be your lawfully wedded husband?' The vicar raised his head as he waited for my answer. He smiled. 'Grace?'

My mouth was glued. Jack pressed my hand with urgency. Finally, I managed to spill out the words I hoped I'd never regret. 'I do.'

Tension slipped from Jack's face as he placed the gold ring on my finger. His smile reminded me why I loved him. I was now officially Mrs Grace Gilmore.

Jack kissed me on the lips and whispered, 'You're beautiful, Grace. You'll never regret this.' He buried my fears and I knew I'd made the right decision.

Uncle Max and Aunt Eliza had hired a photographer. He was waiting to shoot as we exited the church door. He organised us all in special poses. My dress had to trail on the ground, bouquets needed to be positioned correctly and we all had to say cheese before he clicked the camera. After thirty minutes and lots of snaps and laughs, he was finished.

It was time to return to *Willow Banks*. I was just about to climb in the car when Aunt Eliza touched my shoulder. 'Grace, would you mind if the servants joined in with the wedding breakfast?'

'No, of course not.' How could I mind? At least it would give us a few more guests.

Katy picked up my dress by the hem to help me into the Rolls. We smiled and she held my gaze for a moment.

I snuggled up next to Jack on the back seat. The church became a tiny speck as we waved out of the window. Breathing again, I turned to my husband. He gripped my hand like he'd never let me go.

'Jack, what happened to Nancy and John? I thought they were coming?'

He continued to hold my hand tight. 'She lost the baby, Grace. I didn't want to tell you before the wedding. Thank

God, Nancy's all right, but they're both devastated. John's thankful he didn't lose his wife too.'

'I'm sorry.' I moved closer to him.

When we pulled up at *Willow Banks* the others had already arrived. Maggie was at the door handing out glasses of champagne to everyone, including James as Uncle Max said he could have a night off driving.

Everyone filed into the dining room where a meal of roast turkey and vegetables was served. For the first time in my life I sat at the same table as servants. My mind wandered. I imagined having a wedding reception organised by my parents. There'd be numerous guests sitting at lots of tables and the bridal party would sit at the top. Instead, we all sat at the Gilmores' long table with flowers and candles in the centre. Uncle Max stood up to make his speech, he knew more about Jack than he did me. He ended it with a toast.

'To the bride and groom.' He raised his glass.

Everyone joined in. 'To the bride and groom.'

It was Eddie's turn next. He came out with some of the most appalling jokes. 'Here's one for you. What's the biggest horror you see come out of the pit?'

Everyone waited.

'Me and Jack crawling out at the end of the day.'

Everyone laughed even if they didn't think it was funny.

He continued, 'What's a bride's motto?'

Someone shouted, 'Don't know.'

'Three important things about a wedding,' Eddie said, 'one the aisle, cos the bride walks down it. Two, the altar,' cos she stands in front of it. Three a hymn, cos they always have one. So the bride's motto is *I'll alter him*. Gerrit?' He chuckled.

'Doh,' was the reply with a few little laughs.

'Grace, you've bagged yourself a good 'un and I hope you have lots of kids and a bright future. May all your troubles be little ones.' He raised his glass. 'To Jack and Grace.'

'To Jack and Grace.' The audience clapped.

'And over to Jack,' Eddie said.

Jack's hands trembled. 'I'm the luckiest man alive. People laugh and say there's no such thing as love at first sight, but there is. I loved this woman from the first time my eyes looked into hers and I think she felt the same.' He looked at me to clarify.

Uncle Max got to his feet again. 'And now the bride and groom will cut the cake.'

Jack and I wandered over to the three tiered beauty. I'd suggested to Aunt Eliza that we didn't need one this size, but she'd insisted it was tradition. The baker had performed a work of art. Royal icing created trails of valance trimmed with silver horseshoes and white sugared roses. A bride and groom sat on top. We stood close together, our hands touching while holding the knife in position so the photographer could take his shot. He pointed the camera. We blinked and giggled at the flash, then continued to slide the knife down like a guillotine.

Uncle Max stood up again. 'Let the party begin. Everyone to the ballroom. Grace and Jack, can I have a moment please?'

'Yes, of course.'

'You've received a couple of telegrams.' He passed the gold envelopes to me and walked away.

'Go on. Open them,' Jack said.

I ripped open the first and pulled out a gold sheet with red and black images.

'Well, read it.'

'It's from Mother.' My hands trembled.

'Dear Grace, best wishes for the future. Mother.'

'She must still care,' I said.

'How could she not and I'm sure one day your father will come round too. What about the other one?'

My hands were still shaking as I tore it open. It was similar to the one from Mother.

'Dear Grace, wishing you and your young groom all the best in your future together. Miss Allison, Head teacher, Greenemere.'

I passed it to Jack.

'That was kind,' he said.

'Yes, yes it was.'

'Hey, don't cry baby. Not on our wedding day.' Jack took the white handkerchief from his pocket and wiped my eyes. 'We'd better get to the ballroom, everyone will be waiting.' He offered his arm. 'Mrs Gilmore.'

We linked arms and I rested my head on his shoulder. 'I love you Mr Gilmore.'

'I love you too. Now we'd better hurry up or they'll send out a search party. Oh too late.'

'Hurry up you two, everyone's waiting.' Katy beckoned.

As we strolled in, there was yet another surprise. Standing on a makeshift stage were three men in black suits and a young woman in red. The band took their places. One moved to a double bass, one to the adjacent shiny grand piano, one picked up a guitar and stepped next to the girl by a microphone.

'Mr and Mrs Gilmore will now take their first dance.' Uncle Max ushered us to the floor.

Jack took me in his arms. The lights went down low and the song began. It was Nat King Cole's duet, *Unforgettable*. All eyes were on us as we twirled around the room in time to the tune. My dress shuffled along the floor with each turn. The music made Jack's closeness more magical. After the first couple of minutes everyone else joined us on the dance floor. Even the servants coupled up. It had been an amazing evening and just when I thought it couldn't get any better, Uncle Max astonished us again.

'I've booked you into the bridal suite at Halliwell Lodge for the night.' He handed Jack the reservations.

'I don't know what to say,' Jack said.

'No words necessary lad. Just take care of your girl.'

'Try stopping me,' he answered.

'Thank you, Uncle Max. I don't know how I'll ever repay you and Aunt Eliza.' I hugged him.

'There's no need, Grace. The car will be here shortly so start saying your goodbyes.'

'I need to spend a few minutes with Katy, do I have time?'

'Yes, plenty,' Jack said.

Katy was cuddling Eddie on a chair.

'Can we have a minute?' I asked.

'Of course, Gracie.' She stood up swaying. 'I won't be long, Eddie. Don't go away.'

'No problems,' he said, lifting a pint of beer to his mouth.

We found a quiet spot in the corner of the room. I was shaking.

'Gracie, what's the matter? You don't regret it, do you?'

'No, of course not. I'm a bit nervous about tonight. You know? That's what I wanted to talk to you about. I don't know what to expect.'

'It'll be fine, Jack will take care of you. It'll hurt at first but once that's over you'll be all right.'

I didn't like the sound of that. I thought love was supposed to be soft and warm, not painful.

'You won't want me as a best friend anymore,' Katy said. 'You'll be different, grown up and married. And you'll have Nancy.'

'You'll always be my best friend, Katy.' I hugged her.

'It won't be the same.' She sobbed.

I stroked her face. My fingers became moist from her tears. 'Katy Gilmore, I'll always love you and I'll never forget what you've done for me. You changed me, you showed me how the other half lived. You got your parents to take me into your home and treat me as part of the family. Nothing or no one will ever replace what we have.' We embraced again. 'I'll see you before I leave. We have to go and say our farewells now to everyone else.'

I found Jack and we waltzed around the room thanking everyone. The servants seemed to be having a lovely time. James was monopolising Sally, the young maid who had come to the house in Wigan. I wondered what was going on there. We arrived back to Katy and Eddie. She was loud and giggly with her arms slung around his neck. He slurred his words and kept moving her arms away, but at the same time kept smiling.

'Katy, we're going now,' I said.

She cuddled me. 'Be careful, it's supposed to be haunted at Halliwell.' She tittered. 'I love you Gracie.'

'I love you too.'

Aunt Eliza came over. 'I think it's time you went to bed, Katy Gilmore. Grace, you've been a wonderful bride.' She passed me a bag and whispered, 'That's your special thing for tonight. Remember?' She nudged me.

'Thank you.' The heat burnt through my cheeks. 'What would I do without you?' I squeezed her tight.

A chauffeur got out of a black Bentley and held the door open. He was more like one of Father's drivers than Uncle Max's, but then he had been hired in. I snuggled up close to my husband. My heart pumped fast at the thought of what lay ahead.

PART II

Chapter 1

11ᵗʰ June, 1962

After closing the back door behind the children, I sank into the couch. It had been a long night, the baby had me up several times to feed and then I was downstairs before light to see Jack out to work. I closed my eyes briefly. Beth whimpered. I picked her up, put her to my breast and let my mind wander back to six years ago today. I wiped my tears with the back of my hand.

Monday was washing day. I plunged sheets one by one into the kitchen sink, rubbing, scrubbing and rinsing, then fed them individually through the mangle, turning the crank. When Alice was home we pretended a monster was eating the washing. I studied the linen, it was threadbare and needed patching. The last time I'd slept on quality bedding was our wedding night at Halliwell Lodge.

As I pegged the sheets on the washing-line, little black puddles formed where water dripped.

'Bloody hell,' came from the other side of the wall.

I stood on a couple of bricks to peer over. Nancy was screwing up a dirty looking garment.

'You sound like you could do with a cuppa, Nancy?'

'Bloody coal dust. I'm going to have to wash this again. A cuppa sounds lovely. I'll bring cake.'

Within minutes she was at my back door.

'Kettle's on,' I said. Beth started to cry.

'Let me.' Nancy rushed to the carrycot. 'Better get in practise.' She patted her swollen tummy. 'I hope nothing goes wrong this time.'

Poor Nancy, I'd lost count of her numerous miscarriages. She cradled my baby. Beth closed her eyes and Nancy gently placed her back down. She was a natural.

131

'What's the matter, Grace?'

'Nothing.' But I couldn't hold back the tears.

'Whatever is it?'

'It's nothing. I'm just being silly.'

'It doesn't seem like nothing. Tell me.'

'Well, you remember Katy?'

'Yes of course.'

'It's six years ago today that she died.'

'You never did say what happened. Maybe you should talk about it? I'll get us that cuppa.' She went over to the stove and poured tea from the pot into two mugs. 'Here, get that down you,' she ordered.

I sipped from the cup and drifted back to that dreadful day.

'What happened?'

'She slit her wrists,' I whispered.

'She must have been very unhappy.'

'Yes, she was. Are you superstitious, Nancy?'

'A bit, why?'

'Have you ever been to Queen's Park in Bolton?'

'No, I've never even been to Bolton.'

'At the entrance it has these stone sentinels. The first time I saw them I was afraid. It was like they were warning me not to enter.'

Nancy prompted, 'Go on.'

'I think it was because of them... I think... that's why Katy died. Jack blamed my thinking on my hormones because Alice was only a few weeks old. He was wrong though. I know it was those sentinels. You think I'm mad, don't you?'

'No, no. I don't.' She put her arms around me.

Sweet Nancy always humoured me. We spent the day chatting, drinking tea and eating cake. It helped to lift my dark mood.

Nancy looked up at the clock. 'I must go. I haven't finished the chores and I need to get John's dinner on. Are you going to be all right?'

'Yes, thanks, I'll be fine. Golly is that the time? The kids will be home any minute so I'd better get a move on too. Thanks for today, I was dreading being alone.'

'That's what friends are for. I'm just next door if you need me.'

She'd no sooner left when the children barged through the door.

'No I won't,' George shouted.

'Yes you will,' Alice taunted.

'What's all the noise?' I asked.

Alice continued to niggle at the poor boy. They scuffled over to the stairs.

'Be quiet, you'll wake the baby. What's going on?' I said.

'She says I've gotta go down pit.'

'Well you have,' Alice chided, hands on her hips. She'd turned six in April and a real little madam. A Shirley Temple lookalike, who liked to mimic, singing *Good Ship Lollipop*. I found it hard to stay cross with her for long.

'Mam, I don't wanna go down pit. Miss says I'm good at me numbers and writin.' She says I'm too clever to go down mines. I don't wanna, Mam.'

'Talk properly, George.'

'But Mam...'

'We'll talk about it later.' It was hard to believe they were brother and sister. I wondered if George would ever fill out. Jack said he was like a streak of bacon at nine too. 'Both of you sit down at the table. Mammy's not feeling very well.'

George put his arms around me. 'Is it because of the new baby, Mam?'

'No, it's nothing to do with Beth.'

Alice whispered something in his ear. George resisted giving her another wallop. That girl never knew when to stop.

'Sit down and read your books,' I said.

'Can we watch *Blue Peter* on the telly instead?' George asked.

Jack had recently bought a small television and the children were fascinated by it.

'All right, just for half an hour while I cook dinner.'

They were mesmerised within seconds of sitting on the floor. I peeled potatoes, carrots and onions, dropping them into a large pan of boiling water on the stove, sprinkling a couple of Oxo cubes and salt to season. While it bubbled away I fed and changed Beth before returning her to the cot.

'Time to turn the television off,' I said.

'But there's somethin' else comin' on,' George said.

'Now please, George. Alice, set the table.'

'Can't George?'

'I said you. George, turn that television off.'

George switched it off and I moved back to the stove, stirring flour into the stew to thicken. Out of the corner of my eye a black statue appeared at the back door. I turned around.

'Sorry love, showers are broken at pit. I'll wash out here,' Jack said.

'I think that might be best.' I used my apron to wipe my hands. How was I supposed to keep this place clean? It was hard enough with regular coal dust everywhere without him coming home covered in it. I couldn't cope with this today. Not today. I passed him a bar of soap and bowl of hot water. 'Blind stew tonight.' He made no comment, probably because it was a regular occurrence on Mondays.

'I'll just get the worst off.' Jack dipped his hands into the water.

By the time he sat down I'd served dinner and placed plates on the table.

Jack brushed his face. 'I know, I'm still dirty but I'll have a bath after we've finished.'

'I love stew, Mam.' George never complained about his food. Whatever I put in front of him, he'd eat. He mopped up the gravy with a chunk of fresh bread and left his plate clean.

'Did you not give George any dinner, Mam?' Jack asked.

'No, that's why he's so thin,' I said.

Everyone laughed.

Jack gave me that special smile. 'The lads are going down the pub later. Do you mind if I go for an hour?'

It was obvious he hadn't remembered what day today was. But he deserved a night out after being down the pit. I'd work on my designs once the children were in bed to take my mind off things. 'No, of course not but don't make a noise when you come in. I don't want you to wake Beth.'

After dinner, Alice cleared the plates and George polished his father's boots.

Jack lifted them up to inspect. 'That's the ticket, lad. I can see my face in them.' He handed George a penny. 'That's for doing such a good job.'

'Ta, Da.' George dropped the penny in his pocket. 'Can we watch telly for a bit?'

'All right, but not for long,' I said and started to drag the tin bath from the yard.

'Grace, let me.' Jack said.

He did try to look after me, especially since Aunt Eliza and Uncle Max wanted nothing more to do with us. They blamed me for Katy's death. It must have been horrific to find your daughter drowned in a bath of blood. It made me shiver. Jack said they had to blame someone.

'George, Alice, Dad's going in the bath.' They barely moved their eyes from the screen. I closed the door.

Jack hauled the tin container into the kitchen, added buckets of hot and cold water before stepping into it. I scrubbed his back and splashed his face playfully.

'I love you,' he said, 'thanks for not being cross.'

How could I be, when his smile melted my heart every time? He climbed out of the water and I wrapped a towel around his sleek body. He never looked any older. A real Peter Pan.

Jack went upstairs to get ready and came back down looking very handsome in a white shirt. 'You kids, go up to bed when Mam says.' He pecked Alice on the cheek, patted George's head and peeped at Beth in the carrycot. He put his arms around me and kissed me. 'I won't be late, love.'

'Don't forget, no noise when you come home,' I said.

After washing the baby in the kitchen sink, I passed her to George and Alice in turn to cuddle before bed.

'Alice, George, time for bed now,' I said.

'Ah, do we 'ave to?'

'George, it's have. And yes you do. After I've fed Beth I'll come up and read a story.'

They ran up the steep staircase.

After draining the milk from my breast, Beth fell asleep, so I settled her back in the carrycot and carried it up to our bedroom. The children were eager for their story. It was Alice's turn to choose.

'*Milly Molly Mandy*,' she said.

'Ugh no, that's for girls,' George said.

'Shh, George, it's Alice's turn. One chapter won't hurt you.'

He lay down on his pillow squeezing his eyes shut. I read from the book and Alice was asleep before I'd finished. I tucked them both up.

'Nan-night, Mam.' George kissed me on the cheek.

'Nan-night, George darling. Sleep tight.'

I crept downstairs, switched on the television and picked up my sketchpad to scrawl some sketches. *All our Yesterdays* ran in the background, I wondered what the fashion in Paris was like at the moment.

I must have dozed off because the loud buzz of the television woke me. My sketchpad and pencil had dropped to the floor. I switched off the set and got halfway upstairs to bed when there was a big crash. I made my way back down.

Jack was singing, '*Show me the way to go home*.' He fell against the back door, looked up at me and put his finger on his mouth to signal Shh, and giggled.

'Jack, you promised.'

'Sorry. Give us a kiss.'

I tiptoed upstairs and threw down a pillow and blanket. 'You can sleep on the couch.'

'Aw no, please, not the couch.' He grinned and pleaded, but I refused to give in.

The alarm clock jogged me awake, it was still dark when I rolled out of bed. I went downstairs, turned on the copper and laid the fire using scrunched up newspaper, small sections of firewood and a few pieces of coal. One thing we were never short of was coal, because Jack managed to bring some home each night.

I turned on the stove to cook breakfast for Jack. The fat from bacon splashed in my face as it sizzled. Beth screeched.

Jack woke up and held his head. 'Is she all right?'

'Just hungry.'

'My head hurts.'

'Self inflicted, Jack.' I put his plate of bacon and eggs on the table.

He stood up and went to kiss me.

'Eat your breakfast. I've got to see to the baby.'

I fed and changed Beth. She was back in the cot before Jack was ready to leave.

'I'll see you later Grace.' He put his face close to mine, I turned away. 'Ah come on Gracie.'

He very rarely called me that, it had been Katy's pet name for me, but on occasions when he was in trouble he knew how to get around me. He put his arms around my waist and planted kisses up my neck until I couldn't stay cross any longer. I turned and kissed him. Marrying Jack had been the right thing. Our love had grown richer over the years. He was a good husband and father. I wondered what Katy's life would have been like if she'd married Eddie. I always knew he was a bad one, stringing her along all those years and then getting a younger girl pregnant. It was his fault she took her own life, not mine. I fought the tears. I think baby blues must have kicked in as I coped quite well on the whole. Well, except when it first happened. Then I was in a dark place but after a few months Jack and the children brought light back to me.

'What's the matter, Grace?'

'Nothing.'

'Darling, what is it?'

'You'll think I'm daft but it was six years yesterday since Katy died.'

'Why didn't you say something? I'd have stayed in last night.'

'You deserved a night out with the lads.'

He looked up at the clock. 'We'll talk tonight, I must go or I'll be late.' He picked up his sandwiches. 'Have a good day. Try not to be too sad.'

I watched him leave the house in half-light.

I thought of my last day with Katy, it wasn't a happy memory. We were alone and I broached the forbidden subject, Eddie. She retaliated by scratching my face and drawing blood. 'Lies, all lies,' she'd shouted. Her last words were, 'I hate you and never want to see you again.' She never did and my last memory was seeing her coffin lowered into the ground.George and Alice charged down the wooden stairs.

'Shh,' I said, 'you'll wake the baby. Come and sit down. Jam on toast.' I poured them both a beaker of warm milk.

George shovelled food into his mouth while Alice ate hers delicately.

'George, manners. Eat nicely,' I said.

Once they were ready for school, I dug into my purse to find them both a penny for break so they could buy a jammie dodger to eat with their milk. They both left the house and I began my daily chores, starting with sweeping and polishing.

I was disturbed by a knock on the front door. It was very rare for anyone to use that entrance. A skinny young woman stood on the red painted step.

'Good morning, Mrs Gilmore.' She held out her right hand. 'Do you have a few minutes? I'm Miss Jones, George's afternoon teacher.'

'What's he done now? Come in, I'll put the kettle on.' I rushed around picking baby clothes off the couch so she could sit down.

Miss Jones peeped into the cot. 'She's bonny, how old?'

'Two weeks.' I scooped tea into the teapot, adding boiling water and settled two mugs on a tray with a plate of freshly baked fruitcake. 'She's a good sleeper.'

I sat down next to Miss Jones and poured the hot liquid. 'So what's young George been up to then? Must be something serious?'

'No, Mrs Gilmore. On the contrary, the reason I'm here is to talk about his capabilities. I'm not sure if you know how bright he is?'

He'd always been quick to learn.

'We've had a meeting about him at school and it's unanimous that it would be a tragedy for George to follow in his father's footsteps down the mine. He could get a scholarship, go to grammar school and have a good career.'

'But he's only just nine.'

'Yes, and he's brighter than most of the eleven-year-olds in school. I know it's traditional for miners' sons to go down the pit like their fathers, but when a child as gifted as George comes along... Well, I'm sorry but I can't sit back and do nothing. I'm prepared to come around once a week and do some extra classes to get him ready for the eleven plus. He could take it when he's ten. Anyway, I'll leave you to think about it as I need to get back to school.'

'Thank you Miss Jones. I'll discuss it with my husband when he comes home from work.'

Butterflies worked overtime inside my stomach. I was so proud. This opportunity could be my prayers answered. I'd always dreaded the idea of George going down the mine when he left school but Jack had been adamant about convention. Once he heard how bright George was, he wouldn't want him to go down there either. I'd speak to him this evening.

Chapter 2

Miss Jones left by the front door. Twice opened in one day must be a record. I looked at her details on the scrap of paper and wondered how I'd approach the subject with Jack. It was wrong of me to have been irritated with him last night. So what if he'd come home a little inebriated and happy. He'd given me that clown smile, which normally softened me, but having a new baby made me less tolerant and a bit grumpy. At least I wasn't cross when he went off to work. He was due home before the children today, so that would give us the opportunity to sit down and talk about George.

I opened the sideboard drawer to store the teacher's particulars and took out a pile of envelopes tied in ribbon. The sheet from the last envelope read:

Dear Grace,
Hope you're well and happy.
Mother

It had arrived just before last Christmas. Snatched messages, obviously when Father wasn't around.

'Yes Mother,' I said out loud, 'Yes, I'm very happy. I'm married to the most wonderful man and have three beautiful children.' The only thing that could have made it better was if my parents had taken me and my family into their fold. I'd marry Jack again, no regrets.

I wrote home regularly and occasionally received a short scribble back but most of my letters came back, *return to sender*, probably when Father got the post first. I retied the ribbon and returned them to the drawer.

Suddenly there was a whining noise. A siren from the mine. The sound miners' wives dreaded. 'Oh God, there must have been an accident.' I scooped Beth into my arms and charged outside. Women from all down the road were coming out of their doors. Nancy came out the same time as me.

'Oh my God, what is it?' I asked.

'It must be the men at the mine. There must have been an accident,' Nancy said.

Toddlers were running down the road with their mothers. Women held babies in their arms, like me, while others pushed prams. A convoy rushed towards the mine.

As we got closer, I noticed the ample figure of Mrs Deane, flagged by two other wives coming back. Knowing her as a reliable sort I ran towards her.

'They're not letting us through,' she said, 'they've put up a road block. We've been told to go back to our houses and wait.'

There was uproar, women shouted, pushed and shoved, children screamed.

Mrs Deane stood in front and clapped her hands to silence the crowd. 'We all want to know what's going on, but we've got to let them do their job. We've got to let them get our men out.'

'Do you know what's happened?' I asked.

'A rockfall. Other than that they wouldn't tell us anything.' She made a cross of her hands on her chest. 'Dear God, keep our men safe.'

'What should we do?' Nancy covered her face with her hands and screamed.

'It'll be all right.' I put my arm around her. My insides crumbled but we had to try and stay calm.

A cluster of women gathered. One made herself the speaker. 'I think we should march down and not take no for an answer. Who's with me?'

'Me, me,' they shouted in turn holding their hands up.

'It's no use,' Mrs Deane said. 'They won't let you through. We'll have to wait. Go home to your houses and put the kettle on. Get your bairns inside, it's too hot out here. Support each other, no one stay on their own. I'll make a list of who is with who to give to the authorities.'

'Who made you spokesperson?' one woman said, dangling a cigarette from her mouth.

'The Police. Anything else?'

The woman stepped back.

'Mrs Baines, go to Mrs Gilmore's, she'll look after you. You shouldn't be on your own in your condition.' Mrs Deane patted Nancy's shoulder.

I nodded. 'I'll take care of her.'

The women dispersed in small groups. The siren kept whining.

Everyone walked back slowly, some in hysterics while others stayed calm.

Nancy and I arrived back at my house. I put Beth in the cot. 'I'll put the kettle on.' We drank numerous cups of tea, sitting in trepidation, praying Jack, John and the other men would be safe. The china rattled in our hands.

'They'll be all right, won't they Grace?' Nancy asked.

'Yes. Yes, of course they will.'

Beth started to cry. I picked her out of the cot and held her to my breast.

Another hour went by. Still nothing. The children would be home soon. There was a loud knock on the front door.

Nancy and I looked at each other. I held my breath. Was the knock for her or me? I didn't want anything to happen to John but if I had to choose?

I opened the door to find a man and woman in uniform.

'Mrs Gilmore,' the policeman said.

'Oh no.' I held the door to steady my balance.

'There's been an accident...'

'Not Jack? Please, not Jack.'

'I'm sorry but Mr Gilmore, Jack Gilmore is one of the men on our list. I'm sorry but Jack's dead. It would have been instant...'

His mouth continued to move but there was no sound. The room was spinning. When I opened my eyes again, the policewoman was holding smelling salts under my nose. Nancy was wailing in the arms of the policeman. Her face had bleached white. I stood up to hug her.

We watched the policeman and woman continue to walk a few doors up. There was an overwhelming silence outside now the siren had stopped. I wondered how many men had been lost today. My biggest fear, every miner's wife's fear, had happened.

*

When I looked in the dressing table mirror, my face was pale and my eyes puffy and bloodshot. What would Jack think? An oval photo frame housing a pressed red rose reflected back at me. I strolled across, took it down from the wall and stroked the glass before hugging it close to my chest. Jack had given me this rose on our first Valentine's. I closed my eyes and took myself back to that first meeting at the Palais. I'd sniggered at his shabby suit, but once he smiled, none of that mattered. I loved him from that moment and our love went from strength to strength, despite all the obstacles in our way. 'Jack, my darling Jack,' I said aloud. After kissing the frame, I returned it to its pride of place and reached for a sphinx pink lipstick from my make-up bag on the dressing table. Tracing the outline of my lips brought more tears as I remembered Jack's kisses. Pulling myself together I smoothed the slight creases in my black skirt and picked up the matching jacket from the bed. 'I'll make you proud, Jack Gilmore.' I positioned the small black hat on my head.

George crept into the room. 'Mam, Mrs Deane's just come.'

'Thank you, Darling.' I dropped the netted veil in front of my face, took his hand and followed him down the small narrow staircase.

'Mrs Deane, thank you for coming.'

'How you bearing up, deary?' She held me close and I cried into her shoulder. 'Am I just taking the babby or all of them?'

'Just Beth please. She's in the pram.'

'Are you sure? Funerals aren't places for bairns?'

143

'He was their father. If I don't allow them to go they may never forgive me.'

'Fair enough.' She turned to George. 'Look at you, all grown up in a suit.'

'I'm man of the house now. I need to take care of Mam and me sisters.'

She stooped her large body down to him. 'Don't forget you're still only a wee lad. Let your Mam and others look after you too.'

I touched his hand. 'That's right.'

A small tear trickled from his eye. 'I need the lav.' He raced out the back door into the yard.

Mrs Deane pushed the pram outside. She tapped my hand. 'Sorry I can't be there with you and Nancy, but best I take care of the babby.'

George ran back in as she left.

Alice sobbed softly into the cushion, hunched into a little ball.

I tapped her gently. 'Come and sit with me. Both of you.' I signalled to George and sandwiched myself between them on the couch.

Alice wiped her nose using the back of her hand. 'Is Daddy coming back?'

'Here, use this.' I wiped her nose with my handkerchief. 'Pop it into your pocket, I'll get another one. Daddy's gone to Heaven and one day we'll see him again.'

She sniffled. 'Why can't we all go to Heaven?'

'One day we will, but not yet.'

'But I want to see Daddy.' This time she howled.

George put his arms around her. 'I'll look after you, Alice.' He was definitely old for his years. He looked smart in his little black suit. His spindly legs dangling from the three quarter length trousers almost made me smile.

*

We strolled towards the churchyard in hazy sunlight. The dimlit church had been suffocating and the sickly taste of

144

flowers lingered in my throat. A soft breeze blew the netted veil against my face. I held my children's hands tightly, Nancy close to my side. Her elegant black skirt emphasised a flat stomach. We tailed surviving miners with Jack's coffin on their shoulders, to his parents' burial plot. Crowds trailed behind.

The coffin was partially lowered in the open grave. I wanted to run away but stayed for the children's sake. Their little not-knowing faces tore me inside.

The vicar held a prayer book. Once everyone was gathered he began. 'On behalf of Grace and her children, I'd like to thank you all for coming today. We're here to say goodbye to a loving husband and father. Please let us pray together as we entrust our brother Jack to God's mercy.'

Everyone joined in prayer but their voices became muffled as I drifted into Jack's arms. Our first kiss, our first dance and our first passionate embrace. I didn't want it to end.

The vicar continued, 'We now commit Jack's body to the ground.'

The coffin was lowered. 'Earth to earth.' He threw a handful of soil onto the coffin. 'Ashes to ashes, dust to dust.' He prompted me to come forward and throw a handful of soil and floral tributes.

The children and I moved closer. We each sprinkled dirt and threw a red rose in turn. I wanted to scream. Uncle Max's words were in my head. "Scream. You'll feel better."

I crumpled to the ground, opened my mouth and shrieked as loud as I could.

There was a man's voice. 'Nancy, take the kids. They shouldn't see her like this. I'll take care of Grace.' Strong arms pulled me up.

A familiar face through a mist of tears but older than I remembered. 'Eddie?'

'Yeah, it's me. Don't worry about Alice and George, Nancy has them.'

'But how, how come...'

'Me and Jack never stopped being mates. Let's get you a cuppa.' He led me to the house.

Nancy had laid sandwiches out on the table and was making tea and coffees. It amazed me how well she was coping. She'd lost everything. At least I still had George, Alice and Beth.

'Where are the children?' I asked.

'Mrs Deane's,' Nancy said.

We buried our heads into each other's shoulders and sobbed. Somehow we'd get through this together. Eddie circled his arms around us both.

Chapter 3

It was four thirty in the morning when I slid out of bed in the dark to go downstairs. I turned on the copper, laid the fire and sloped into the kitchen to light the gas on the stove. It was only when I reached for the frying pan that it struck me. Jack was no longer here. He was gone. My stomach raged. What was I going to do? It had been two weeks since he left me. Left us. How could he have done that to us? He promised to always be with me. Seven miners killed in the rockfall, including Jack and John. Seven funerals had been and gone. Roses, carnations, gladioli. White lilies and green foliage. So many wreaths. So colourful, blue, white, pink and magenta. So many tears of sadness.

The same questions whirled around in my head. How would I manage to feed and clothe my three children? I could take in sewing but would that be enough? What about our home? Would they want to put in a new family? If they let us stay, could I cope with so many memories? There was nothing else for it, I needed help. My parents' help.

I sat down at the table to write, leaving ink smears from my tears on the notepaper.

Beth screamed. I put the letter in the envelope, addressed it to *Granville Hall* before going upstairs. I picked her up, sat on our bed to feed and change her then returned her to the cot. The smell of Old Spice lingered on Jack's pillow. I drew it to my face to inhale the last of his scent. Why had this happened? What had I done that had been so awful? I wasn't a bad person. Why did our happiness have to be ripped away?

I must have fallen asleep as the next thing Alice and George's fighting rang in my ears.

'What's the matter with you children?'

Alice clung to me. 'He said Daddy's not coming back.'

'No, he isn't darling. He's gone to Heaven. You remember we talked about it? George, come here too.' I cuddled them. How would we get through this? 'Let's go downstairs and get breakfast before school.'

'I don't want to go to school, Mammy,' Alice said.

'You'll feel better playing with your friends. George will look after you. Won't you darling?'

'Yes Mam. Shall I bring the carrycot down?'

I lifted Beth out. 'Yes please, George.'

We carried on as normal. Like any other day. Breakfast, wash, dress, brushing teeth and taking a penny out of my purse to buy a biscuit at milk break.

I wrapped a white cotton bonnet on Beth's head and attached a canopy to the pram. 'I'm going to walk with you this morning.'

'Ah no, Mam,' George said.

'I want Mammy.' Alice pushed him.

'Please don't fight. George, you walk on in front if you like?' I tipped the pram down the small step and out into the back yard. Alice held the side of the pram rail.

My mind drifted to the last night with Jack. I saw his cheeky grin. Felt his palm cupping my cheek. Smelt his scent. Why didn't I let him come to bed? Instead I'd thrown him a blanket and pillow. If he'd come to bed we'd have had one more night cuddled close, but instead we slept apart.

'Mammy, we're here.' Alice nudged me. 'I don't want you to come in. I'm not a babby.'

'All right honey.' I kissed her cheek.

George stood by the school wall. He put his hand across his mouth. 'I don't want one.'

I waved goodbye to my children and watched them run into the playground before returning home. As I pushed the pram towards the yard, sobbing sounds came from Nancy's. I opened her back gate and found her sitting on the doorstep, head buried into her lap, the washing only half pegged out.

I put the brake on the pram and rushed over. 'We're in this together.'

She wept on my shoulder.

'Come round and have tea,' I said. 'I've got cake.' I took her hand to guide her.

'Thank you, Grace. It wasn't meant to be was it? I wasn't meant to have a child. I suppose in a way it's lucky because now I've only got myself to think about. What are you going to do? It's going to be hard with three children on your own.'

'I don't know.' I parked Beth up in the yard leaving the back door open so I'd be able to hear if she cried.' In a trance-like motion, I filled the kettle and placed it over the gas then scooped tea from the caddy and cut cake.

We sat close on the couch, neither sure what to say to the other. I could hear myself talking nonsense but it was better than thinking of what lay ahead. I dabbed my eyes and looked at the monogram on my handkerchief. 'Do you know how old this is?'

Nancy stared at me.

'I've had this since I was a girl. I've written to Mother and Father, asking for help. They may let me and the children live at *Granville Hall*. Of course it all depends on Father.'

'I suppose I could go back to Preston and live with Dad,' Nancy said. 'But he'll have me running round like a skivvy now Mam's mind has gone.'

'Do you think the mining bosses will look after us?'

'According to Mrs Deane, it's up to the government. She said they won't throw us out. But I'm not sure, how does she know? It hasn't happened to her, has it? These houses are meant for miners and their families. But surely they won't push to get us out.'

'When did you see Mrs Deane?'

'She and some of the other women have been popping around regularly to check on me.' Have they not been to you?'

'No, no one. They've never really accepted me, have they? I think they only put up with me for Jack.'

'Mrs Deane helped at the funeral.'

'Yes, that's true. But no one has thought to check on me since.'

Beth started to cry.

Nancy stood up. 'Let me go.' She rocked the baby in her arms and sat back down on the couch cuddling Beth and singing, *Brahms' Lullaby*.

'You've got a lovely voice.' I smiled.

She smiled. Yes, we could still smile.

Chapter 4

Every surface had been scrubbed and polished including the front doorstep. The house was spotless. I dragged the tin bath into the kitchen and filled it with buckets of water.

'But Mammy?' Alice said, 'It's not bedtime.'

'It's not Sunday either,' George said.

'We've got a special visitor coming. Remember I told you last night? Your grandmother's coming today.'

Alice bathed first. 'It's in my eyes. The soap's in my eyes,' she screamed.

'That's because you keep rubbing them. Keep your hands down and it'll soon be over.' I continued to rinse her hair.

She climbed out of the bath and I patted her all over with a towel. I lifted the lemon flower-print dress over her head and she pushed her arms through the sleeve. 'That's you done. Now don't get dirty. Go and read a book and send George in.'

George stormed in. 'I don't need one, Mam.'

'Yes you do. I've brought down your best shirt and suit, ready.'

'I don't wanna wear them. They remind me of Da's funeral.'

'I told you, Grandmother's coming.' I hugged him. 'George, I need you to put them on. Would you do that for me, please?'

'Yes, Mam.'

'Good boy. Now get ready.'

I left him in the kitchen and went to dress Beth. She looked so bonny in her pastel pink smock. Mother wouldn't be able to resist her.

*

'Come here.' I cuddled Alice and George. 'Now promise to be on your best behaviour.'

They both nodded but George didn't look convincing.

There was a knock on the front door. Well this was it. Hopefully our troubles would soon be over.

I brushed my hands down my dress, took a deep breath and opened the door. 'Hello Mother.'

She walked in, her nose high. 'Good afternoon Grace. I trust you're well. Our condolences at your loss.'

'Thank you,' I said. Why didn't she hug me? Show me some form of affection. I stepped towards her but she turned away.

'Sit down, I'll make tea,' I said.

Her black pencil skirt rose slightly as she sat down on the couch and crossed her legs, showing off expensive stockings and high heel shoes. She removed the pillbox hat from her head, placed it on the cushion next to her and circled the room with her eyes. 'So this is why you gave up *Granville Hall*?'

'I gave it up for love.'

'It's cramped. I can't believe five of you lived here. The furniture's seen better days too.'

I signalled George and Alice to come over. 'These are your grandchildren. Alice and George. Beth's asleep at the moment but she'll wake shortly if you want to hold her.'

George held out his hand.

Mother looked at my children and offered a small nod. 'How do you do, George?' She turned to me. 'They could do with some new clothes.'

'These are me Sunday best,' George said.

'Mine too.' Alice joined in.

'Well I'm sure we can do better than that,' Mother said.

That sounded hopeful. I waited for her to tell me that we could all return home to Gerrard's Cross. 'I'll put that kettle on while you all get acquainted.' As I drew the water, I could see George and Alice moving to sit next to their grandmother on the couch.

'Mind the hat,' she scolded.

Alice jumped. 'Sorry Grandma.'

'Grandmother, I'm not Grandma.'

'Sorry Grandmother,' Alice said.

'Me teacher says I'm very bright,' George said, 'really good at numbers and writing. She wants me to go to grammar school. She says I can do me eleven plus when I'm ten. Doesn't she Mam?'

'Yes, George.'

'Don't you teach your children to speak properly? Me. Mam. Common. I thought we'd brought you up better.'

'Yes I do, Mother. But it's hard when they're around the local children. I don't want them to be different.' I carried a tray holding Royal Albert china. It was a wedding present from the Gilmores and I cherished it. I poured out the tea. Milk and sugar, Mother?'

'Milk but no sugar, please.' She took the cup and saucer. 'Thank you.'

'Cake?' I passed her a plate of Victoria sponge. 'I made it myself.'

'Just a small piece.' She took the plate and delicately teased crumbs of the jam sponge onto the fork. 'This is delightful, very light. Where did you learn to bake like this?'

'Practise, Mother.'

Once her mouth was empty she spoke. 'Your father has agreed to help you.'

'He has? We can come home?'

'No, I'm sorry, Grace, he's not ready for that. But he won't see you on the street. He's bought you a lease on a unit in London with a flat upstairs. It's only the East End but better than here. You can open up a fabric shop. We remembered you loved working with cloth. I presume you still do?'

'Yes, Mother. I'm still designing. Would you like to see?'

'That won't be necessary. Now as I was saying, your father's purchased the lease and written a cheque for two thousand pounds. Enough for stock and to get you on your feet.'

'That's very generous, Mother. Thank you.'

She opened her purse and passed me a five pound note. 'This should cover the train fare. I suggest once you get to London you get yourself a bank account if you don't have one already.'

George's face beamed when he saw the blue note. 'Wow, can I see?'

I passed the note to him.

'Is that the Queen?'

'Yes.' I laughed.

'There's plenty more where that came from, George,' Mother said.

I thought that was a strange thing to say to a nine-year-old child.

Alice brought over a glass of pop. 'Would you like some, Grandmother?'

Mother shook her head. 'What is it?' she asked me.

'It's Sarsparilla. You should try it,' I said.

'I don't think so,' she answered.

Beth gave a cry. I wandered over to the other side of the room and lifted her from the carrycot. 'Would you like to hold her, Mother?'

'No, don't worry Grace. It's not necessary. I can see her from here.'

I sat down and rocked Beth in my arms. It was going to be all right. They didn't want us at *Granville Hall* but they were willing to provide.

'There's a condition?' Mother said.

'Condition?'

'Yes, your father wants George to come and live at *Granville Hall*.'

I laughed. 'This is a joke?'

'No joke, Grace.'

'No, no we stay together. We'll all come and live with you. Alice, George, go out to play for a while. I need to talk to Grandmother alone.'

The children charged out of the door. I'd never seen them move so fast.

'What are you saying, Mother?'

'Quite simply that your father wants George as his heir. It's a great opportunity for the boy.'

'No, Mother. I'm not giving up my son.'

'It's up to you, Grace. This way you get a chance to make a good life for you and the girls. You get the ability to have a shop and sell your own designs. The boy would get away from this village and coal mine. You don't want him ending up like his father. What do you say?'

'I can't give him up. He's my first born. He's part of Jack.'

'So what then? You all end up on the street?'

'Mrs Deane said they won't evict us.'

'Who is this Mrs Deane?'

'She's one of my neighbours.'

'What does she know? They won't let you stay here for free, so how are you going to find the money for rent?'

I became fidgety and stood up to put Beth back in her cot. 'Mrs Deane said the government will pay a widow's pension and I can take in sewing.'

'Be realistic, Grace. Look at what your father is offering. A good home and family for George. A good start for the girls. Do you really want handouts and your children to walk around in cheap cast offs all their lives?'

'But to give George up...'

Mother stood up and took my hand in hers. 'It's for the best. You must see that. Think of the privileges you grew up with. Do you really want to deny your children the same? George would go to a good school and become Master of *Granville Hall* one day. With the shop and funds, you have the capacity to make sure Alice and Beth have a good start too.'

'How often will I see him?'

Mother lowered her head.

'I will be able to see him?'

She lifted her head, slowly. 'Your father won't allow it. I'm sorry, perhaps in time he'll relent.'

'No. No. He's not having my son.' I thrust the five pound note into her hand. 'My son is not for sale.'

'You're thinking of yourself Grace, as always. Still as selfish as the day you walked out and left your sister without a thought.'

'No I'm not. And I didn't walk out on her, I wanted to see her. Father wouldn't let me and now you want me to do the same with my son?'

'He needs a male influence. Do you want him to grow up a mummy's boy?'

'No, of course not. How is Elizabeth, anyway? Is she married? She never answers my letters.'

'Yes, she married into a very influential family. Regrettably, like you, now a widow. Her husband died a few months ago from tuberculosis. Unfortunately, she wasn't blessed with children. She's back home at *Granville Hall* and eager to spend time getting to know George.'

'I'm sorry she's lost her husband but that doesn't mean she can have my son.'

'She's not having your son, he's not a possession. George would go away to school once he's settled. The same path he'd have taken if you'd married correctly.'

'You want to send him away? He's too young. He's only just nine.'

'Your father went at eight. Boys need toughening up. You're being self-centred.'

I didn't know what to say. Was she right?

Mother slid the five pound note back inside her purse. She stood up and smoothed down her skirt. 'I'm staying in a hotel tonight so I'll call back tomorrow afternoon at four for your decision. But please, make sure you think of him and not yourself.' She brushed her lips against my cheek and walked out of the front door without saying goodbye to the children.

Powerless to move, all I could do was contemplate Mother's words. Maybe I was selfish and self-centred not wanting George to go. Perhaps I should let him live with them, after all it would only be a matter of time before Father relented. George would go to a good school away from here. He'd definitely not end up down the pit. He dreaded that.

156

Beth's cry shook me. I gathered her up thinking that I couldn't expect any affection from Mother but perhaps today was a start.

*

The children sat down at the table to eat. George slurped his soup and Alice dipped in the homemade bread.

'George, please,' I said.

'What Mam. What's wrong?'

'Eat nicely, don't slurp.'

I wondered what Father would make of George's table manners.

'Is there any pudding?' Alice asked.

'Yes, I've made jelly.' I opened the pantry and brought out the mould.

'Strawberry, my favourite.' George rubbed his hands in anticipation.

Alice served the sweet into small dishes and passed one to George.

'When you've finished,' I said, 'could one of you pop to Nancy's, and ask her to come and see me this evening? About eight o'clock.'

'I'll go, Mammy,' Alice said.

'George, would you like to feed Beth?'

'Yes please, Mam.'

'Can I?' Alice said.

'No, you're going next door. George will feed Beth and I'll wash the dishes. You can dry them when you get back.'

I took down the drum of National Dried Milk from the shelf and made up the formula. My breast milk had dried up after losing Jack, but at least she'd had a good start.

George picked up Beth from the cot and sat on the couch. I passed him the bottle and watched him place the teat to her mouth. He'd become quite adept at feeding.

The children were all tucked up in bed when Nancy tapped on the back door and walked in.

'It's only me,' she said.

157

The kettle was on and I scooped tea from the caddy. 'Thanks for coming.'

'Are you all right? I presume that was your mother?'

'Yes. I'm fine. I wanted to mull some stuff over with you. Yes, that was Mother. Very elegant, isn't she?'

'That's one way to describe her.'

I passed Nancy a mug of tea. 'Father's purchased a lease on a shop with a flat for me. It's in London.'

Nancy's face dropped. 'I see.'

'Would you come with us?'

'Oh, oh I don't know. I'm not sure.'

'What else will you do? You don't want to go and live with your father. Anyway, that's not the only reason I asked you around. They've offered a shop and two thousand pounds.'

Nancy sat with her mouth open. Eventually she spoke. 'That's a lot of money, Grace. They've forgiven you then?'

'Not exactly. Father's made a clause.'

Nancy looked confused.

'He wants George.'

'What do you mean, he wants George?'

'He wants him to go and live at *Granville Hall*.'

'You said, no?'

I shook my head. 'I need time to think about it.'

'I can't believe you're even thinking about giving your child up.'

'It's like Mother said, it's an opportunity for us all. You know how George worries about going down the pit. This way he'll be away from here and it would never happen.'

'But Grace?'

'You don't think I should?'

'Definitely not. What does George say about it?'

'He said he didn't want to go away but what does a nine-year old know.'

'Listen to your heart, Grace. What does that tell you?'

'I don't want to give him up. Of course I don't but I can't see any other way out. George's teacher said he's very bright and can go to grammar school.'

'So what's the problem then? He can stay with you and get a good education and still make something of himself?'

'Can you imagine the folk around here accepting that? They'll have seen Mother and the expensive chauffeur driven car. They're not going to like the idea of my son getting a better education than theirs. I can hear them now. We'll all be tormented. I don't think there's any other way.'

'There's always a way, Grace.' Nancy kissed me on the cheek before leaving.

I turned the key in the lock and flicked the big bolt at the bottom before turning the light off and making my way up to bed.

I peeped into Alice and George, they were both sleeping sound as was Beth in our room. After undressing I slipped into the empty double bed, staying on my half. 'Jack, Jack,' I said out loud, 'help me, Jack. I don't know what to do.' If I let George go with Mother, he'd have a good life, *Granville Hall* would be his one day. How would he feel later in life if I denied him this chance? If he went to grammar school here then he'd be different to the other children. He could end up being bullied especially living in a female household. Mother was right, he needed a male influence and toughening up. I was being selfish. It had been an emotional day, my eyes refused to stay open so I stopped fighting and let myself slip into sleep.

Chapter 5

Four o'clock she'd said. I'd made up my mind, George would stay with me. George was my son, not Father's. Just because Father wanted a son didn't mean he could have mine. George's friends were here. I watched him from the front window kicking a ball around with a couple of boys from down the road. Alice was playing hopscotch with a little girl from number seven. We had a roof over our heads and each other. No, I'd tell her he was staying.

The table was set for lunch but first Beth needed a bottle. She'd gained weight much quicker since being on formula. I'd just finished changing her nappy when Alice started screaming.

'Mammy, Mammy.' She was holding her knee, dripping with blood.

'Shh, it's all right Alice. Mammy will make it better.'

She shook intermittently. I bathed the graze and dabbed witch hazel on the wound.

'It stings, Mammy. It stings.'

'I know darling. Mammy will give it a magic kiss.' I kissed her knee. 'That's better, isn't it?'

'Thank you, Mammy. Is it dinner time?'

'Yes, we need to get your brother in. You sit down at the table and I'll get him.'

'George,' I called out of the window.

He waved and in no time at all came flying through the back door.

'Sit yourself down. I'm just pouring the soup.'

'I'm starvin.' He picked up a piece of bread and rammed it into his mouth.

'George,' I said in disappointment.

'Sorry Mam. Is Grandma comin back? You won't send me away, will you?'

'Yes, she is and no I won't.'

The room was silent except for the clink of cutlery on the dishes, slurps of soup from George and his chewing noises. If I did let him go, Father would send him back after a day.

'Clear the table Alice. George, wash the dishes please.'

I went upstairs to my room, adjusted my hair and put on a threadbare summer dress. At least it was freshly washed and ironed, I'd worn my best yesterday. The children would be wearing patch ups, but they'd be clean. If only I'd been able to buy a new sewing machine when the old one packed up a couple of years ago. I looked at my gaunt reflection. My frock hung like a sack. I grabbed an apron out of the drawer and tied it around my waist to conceal the bagginess. Jack stared at me from the photograph on the bedside cabinet. Our wedding day, we looked so young and happy. I slipped the frame into the apron pocket, maybe Mother would like to see?

As I stepped down the steep stairs I could hear the chink of plates being placed on the draining board.

When I got to the kitchen, Alice was screaming and hitting George.

'What's going on? Can't I leave the room for five minutes? You'll wake up Beth.'

'He flicked soap in my eyes.'

'George?'

'It's her fault. She keeps saying I'm goin' down pit but I'm goin' to grammar school and gettin' a good job. Miss Jones said so.'

'Yes, George. You are. Alice, stop tormenting your brother. Let me look at your eyes.'

She came over and snuggled into my apron.

'Let me see then?'

She lifted her face.

'They look fine, Alice. You'll live. Let's get you washed. George, can you sit with Beth while I clean your sister up please?'

After drying the dishes, I poured boiling water from the kettle into the sink, ran cold water from the tap, wiped the draining board and sat Alice on top with her feet in the sink.

I removed the dirty dress and passed her a warm flannel. 'Wash your face.' I sponged her all over, then dried and dressed her in the tatty garment. The hardest thing was combing her curly hair without screams. 'You'll do.' I lifted her down to the floor. 'Go and get George.'

I swilled the dirty water out of the sink before refilling fresh for George. A clean pair of shorts and t-shirt hung over the dining chair.

'Beth's still asleep, Mam,' he said.

'Thank you, love. Now come and get washed.'

'Ah do I 'ave to?'

'Yes you do. Grandmother will be here soon. She doesn't want to see a dirty urchin, does she?'

He stood by the sink and washed his face.

'Don't forget to strip,' I reminded him before leaving the room.

Alice was lying on the floor looking at the pictures in a Rupert book. George could read the whole book at her age.

'I'm just popping upstairs to put lipstick on,' I told her.

'Can I have some too, Mammy?'

'Not today, darling.' Sometimes I'd put a tiny bit on her lips.

I stared into the mirror but didn't recognise myself. I applied my lipstick with care before returning downstairs to check on Beth. She was still asleep, hopefully she'd stay that way for another couple of hours. 'George, how are you getting on?' I called.

He wandered into the sitting room. His t-shirt looked like moths had been having a feed and his shorts were frayed at the legs. But at least he was clean.

I looked at the clock, five to four. She'd be here any moment. Mother was always punctual. As if on cue a car pulled up. I glanced out of the window and sure enough the silver Rolls was parked outside. The chauffeur got out and opened the passenger door. Mother stepped out of the limousine, pulling her skirt down as she stood up.

'She's here,' I said to the children. 'Now remember, best behaviour, just like yesterday.'

They sat on the floor completing a jigsaw puzzle of the seaside.

'Mammy,' Alice whispered, 'can we go to the seaside one day?'

'Yes of course, we will.'

The metal knocker banged loudly against the wood. I opened the door. Mother looked stylish in her fitted cobalt blue skirt suit. A lampshade hat framed her small face. Dropped pearl earrings swayed as she offered me her cheek.

'Grandmother's here,' I said to the children.

'Hello Grandmother.' Alice and George stood up.

Mother offered her cheek, once again. She certainly seemed more mellow today. 'Sit down, children. Carry on with your puzzle.' She picked up the lid of the jigsaw box. 'This looks like Brighton to me.'

'Have you been there, Grandma?' George asked.

'Oh yes, frequently. At least once a week during the summer months. Your mother used to go to school there. Didn't she tell you?'

George stared across to me.

'Remember, I told you about boarding school near the sea?'

George nodded. 'I wanna go to the seaside. Would you take us one day, Grandma?'

'It's Grandmother, remember? But yes, I'm sure that can be arranged, George.'

He gave a huge smile showing gaps in his teeth before nestling back down to the puzzle.

'I've baked a fruitcake, Mother. Would you like some?'

'That sounds delicious. Thank you.'

I moved to the kitchen and put the kettle on the stove. I listened carefully.

'I love that big hat, Grandmother. May I try it on?' Alice asked.

'Certainly,' Mother answered.

I peeped through the door, Alice's face was hidden and they were all laughing. Mother seemed almost human today. I wondered what was going on. She looked like my mother but it was like she'd been injected with a new personality.

The china clattered on the tray as I walked through to the sitting room. I passed Mother a cup of tea and a slice of fruitcake. 'Alice and George, milk and cake on the table.' I turned to Mother, 'They know they have to eat out there.'

She nodded with approval. After the children left the room, she spoke to me quietly. 'Have you made a decision?'

'Yes, I have. I'm sorry Mother but he's staying.'

'You've not thought this through.'

'I've done nothing but think it through since you left yesterday. He doesn't want to go.'

'What does he know? He's a child. Those children are close to neglect. Look at their clothes, patched all over, even if nicely done. I can see you try your best but if you couldn't manage when you had a husband, how do you expect to manage now? And you've an extra one to clothe and feed as Beth was only just born.'

'We'll manage.'

'Will you? I wouldn't be surprised if the authorities take them away.'

'Why? How could they be better somewhere else than here, where they're loved?'

'Did you notice the look on their little faces when I mentioned Brighton? Have they ever been to the sea?'

'We took George before Alice was born, but it became difficult to afford the train fare.'

'I'm offering you this chance, now. George will want for nothing and you'll have the means to take care of the girls.'

'Nancy said I shouldn't give George up?'

'Nancy, who's she?'

'My best friend. She lives next door.'

'You mean the plain woman with her nose at the window. What does she know?'

'She said a mother should never give up her child.'

164

'So you don't want better for your son?'

'He can go to grammar school here.'

She tilted her head back and let out a loud laugh. 'Do you really think that people around here will accept that? He'll become well spoken and what then? Yesterday you told me you didn't want him to be different. Now you're saying you'll make him different. Make up your mind, young lady.'

Mother could make me feel so inadequate and sixteen again. 'I'm sure we'll manage.'

'Grace, you won't. Now I suggest you stop being selfish and start thinking about those children. Now call the boy in and tell him what's happening.'

'But Mother?'

'Do as you're told girl, you know it's the right thing. Do you think that you'd have learned what you know about designing if you hadn't gone to a decent school? Give your children the chance they deserve. Call him.'

I sat silently. Was she right? Would the authorities take my children?

As if she could read my mind she suddenly said, 'I'm warning you Grace, if you don't, I shall be contacting the relevant authorities first thing in the morning and reporting you for neglect. They'll take away all the children and you'll be left with none. Is that what you want?'

I shook my head.

'Call him in.'

I sobbed silently into my handkerchief, then dabbed my eyes. 'George, can you come in here please?'

'I'm just finishin' me cake, Mam.'

'All right, honey.'

Mother took my hand. 'You're doing the right thing, Grace.'

'Am I?'

'Yes, yes of course you are.' She opened her handbag and passed me the cheque and the bundle of papers that she'd shown me yesterday.'

George walked into the room. 'Alice is just finishin' off.'

'It's you we want,' Mother said. 'Come here, lad.'

He strolled over to the couch. She took his hand. 'You're coming home with me. You're going to live in a big house called *Granville Hall* and I'll take you to see Brighton.'

'What like a holiday?' His eyes lit up as he smiled.

'No, not a holiday, forever.'

I'd turned away so he couldn't see me crying. Was I doing the right thing? What else could I do? Suppose she was right and the authorities took all my babies away because I couldn't provide properly for them. I hadn't considered it neglectful if their clothes were tattered, as long as they were clean. But maybe she was right.

'Mam?' He ran into my arms.

I hugged him tightly.

'Mam, you promised?'

'I know, I'm sorry. But it's for the best, George. This way, there's no chance that you'll ever go down the pit. You'll go to a decent grammar school and who knows, maybe university.'

'But why can't we all go and live with Grandmother?'

'That's not possible, I'm afraid,' she answered. 'Your Grandfather won't allow it.'

'Well I don't like him. I think he's a horrid man and I don't wanna go and live in his great big house. I wanna stay here with Mam and me sisters.'

'You don't know what you want, you're too young. Why don't we have a trial? If you don't like it after a month then you can return home to live with your mother.'

A spring of hope ran through me. A month's trial sounded good. We'd be set up in London by then and he could join us. I smiled.

'Will you take me to the seaside next week?' George asked Mother.

'That can be arranged,' she answered.

'And what about our Alice? Can she come to the beach too?'

'Not this time,' Grandmother said.

'Do I need to pack?' George started to run upstairs.

'Perhaps something for tonight and the morning, then we can get you some new clothes.'

George returned with Jack's old duffle bag. I closed my eyes and thought of the times that I'd seen Jack carrying it in the same manner. 'Mother, I'm not sure about this,' I said.

'Don't start the boy off again, Grace.'

George looked at me, his eyes questioning.

Alice came into the room. 'Where's he going?'

'He's coming home with me to *Granville Hall*.'

'Mammy, what does she mean?'

'George is going away for a little while.'

'I don't want him to go. No, Mammy, don't let him go.' She clung to my dress.

George rushed to my arms. 'Mam, I'm not sure. I don't wanna go away.'

'It'll be all right, George. You'll have a great time.' I pulled the photograph frame out of my pocket. 'Here, take this.' I thrust it into his hands. 'Just remember, I love you. I'll always love you. If you're not happy then tell Grandmother you want to come back home. We'll be waiting.' I hugged him tight and he even kissed me.

Mother stood up and took George's hand. 'Say goodbye to Alice.'

'No, No. Don't go, George. Please don't go. I'll stop fighting you. I promise. Please don't go.' She clutched his arm.

Mother plucked her away and pulled George out of the front door into the car.

George looked back over his shoulder with pleading eyes.

Alice thumped me, continuous pounds. 'I hate you, Mammy. I hate you.' She sobbed into my skirt.

I sobbed too. What had I done? What could I do? We watched the Rolls drive away with my small son peering out of the rear window.

Chapter 6

I cried into Jack's pillow. Mother's words echoed in my ear, 'Neglect.' Had I been neglectful? I thought back to the crash of waves at Greenemere and how soothing I'd found them. I was fortunate to listen to that sound almost every night for three years. Yes, it was neglectful that I'd never taken my children to the seaside. Why hadn't I thought about it? Surely we could have managed a trip to New Brighton, Southport or Blackpool. I should have made more effort. I closed my eyes and imagined George on his first visit to Brighton beach, his eyes big with wonder, saying 'wow,' over and over. I smiled, tears dripped onto my cheeks and lips. As soon as we were settled in London, I'd organise an outing at the weekend to Brighton to see Alice's eyes light up. Maybe Mother would bring George and Elizabeth to meet us? I inhaled the last of Jack's scent from the pillow.

*

Nancy poured tea and passed me a mug. Alice was at school and Beth was in her pram, out in Nancy's backyard, enjoying the sunshine.

'You did what?'

I couldn't look at her.

'You let her take him? What were you thinking?'

'I had no choice, she said she'd report me to the authorities for neglect and they'd take all my babies.'

Her voice rose. 'Neglect?'

'Neglect, yes.' I sipped my tea.

'I've never in my life seen children further away from neglect. Little Jonny Brown, down the road maybe, but not George, Alice or Beth. No one would try and take away your kids.'

'Mother said they would. And with my parents' money and contacts, they'd make it happen. I couldn't take that chance. Do you know I've never taken my children to the seaside? What kind of mother does that make me?'

Nancy coughed. 'So because you spent money on food rather than an outing to the sea, that makes you a bad mother?'

I shrugged. 'Well no, of course not. But I should have tried to take them.'

'Grace, I've never been to the sea and I certainly wasn't neglected.'

'Haven't you? We're going to go to Brighton as soon as we're settled in London.'

'Err; I haven't said I'll come yet.'

'But you will? Please? We can both work in the shop.' My words became hurried. 'I'll design us both a uniform. You can help with sewing too.'

'It's tempting but I don't know whether I'm ready to move away from memories of John.'

'Surely memories are held in your heart not a place. I don't think I could watch the other men come home every day to their wives and know mine wasn't with them.' I put my mug by the sink. 'Let's go for a walk in the park. It's a lovely day. We can feed the ducks. You can push.'

'All right, I'll just get something for my head. I don't want to get heatstroke. Grab that chunk of stale bread on the dresser.'

I picked up the bread and wrapped it in muslin before popping it into a wicker basket. I was lucky the sun didn't bother me; the thick mass of hair across my neck probably helped. Nancy wrapped a paisley scarf across her head.

Although it was another hot day, the slight breeze was inviting and the rustle of leaves on the trees had a calming effect. Birdsong was loud and lively. I imagined a hidden conductor. The park was busy, women pushing prams and toddlers playing. As we approached the pond my mind flipped back to the first day I'd fed the ducks when I was with Katy and Jack.

169

Neglect. Mother said, neglect. She'd tricked me. I felt my face heat up as I tried to control the rage. Surely it wasn't me that was neglectful, but Mother? All their money, yet no affection. Taken to the park by Nanny who never allowed me close enough to water to feed the ducks. My children not only experienced this pastime from an early age but made daisy chains, played mud pies and even boiled up flower petals to make perfume. My tears tumbled. I turned to Nancy. 'I need to get my boy back.'

'That's more like it,' she said, 'I was wondering how long it would take you to regain your spirit.'

We sat on a wooden bench by the water. I pulled out the portion of bread and snapped it in half, passing Nancy a share. A raft of ducks hovered close to the bank. I threw in a piece of crust, a mallard caught it in its beak, a drake spread his wings, shook its head and tail before somersaulting. I tossed more scraps. Nancy joined in and we laughed. We laughed properly for the first time since losing our men.

'So Grace, what's your plan to get George back?'

'Mother mentioned a month's trial, so I may not need to do anything.'

'What about the money? Will you give back the cheque?'

'No. I need it to set us up in London.'

'You're still going to take it then?' She rocked the pram. 'Even if you get him back?'

'Don't you think I should?'

Nancy shrugged.

'Mother took George. She trapped me into handing him over. If he's unhappy after a month it isn't me breaking the condition. I've kept to my part of the agreement.'

'She did manipulate you. But do you think it's right to keep the money?'

'Maybe not. It can be a loan. I'll pay them back every penny. I'll pay by instalments. Does that sound like a plan?'

Nancy nodded but didn't look convinced.

'We need to leave in two weeks, after Alice finishes the summer term. Once the month is over, I'll visit Gerrard's

Cross to check the situation. George will be ready to come home by then. Both children need to be enrolled in the new school for September. Please say you'll come to London with us. I really need you.' I pressed Nancy's hand.

'Why not? I'll give it a try.' She leant over the pram and stroked Beth's face. 'She's adorable. Aren't you two due a check up with a doctor or midwife?'

'Yes, you're right. Beth's over six weeks. Thank you for reminding me.' I looked at my watch. 'We should start to think of making our way back. Alice will be home shortly.'

We threw in the last particles of bread and I held onto the idyllic picture of ducks. 'I hope she's been all right at school today.'

'It certainly hasn't been easy, first losing her dad and then her brother.'

'I know. I'm wondering how to make things up to her.'

'Why don't you come round for tea? Alice can help make fairy cakes.'

'That's very kind. Thank you, Nancy.' As we approached home I saw my little girl, all alone, dragging her heels up the cobbles. 'There's Alice.'

'She doesn't look very happy. Why isn't she with friends?'

I took the pram from Nancy and pushed faster. 'Alice,' I called.

She turned around. 'I don't want to speak to you. I hate you. You made George go away.'

'I know, Darling. I'm sorry.' I hugged her tight. 'We're going to Nancy's for tea. She said you can do baking while I see to Beth. Would you like that?'

She ran into Nancy's arms. Not only had I lost my husband and given away my son, it now seemed I was losing my eldest daughter. She hated me. Beth started to cry. She was probably hungry as we'd been out for a while. My stomach rumbled, I'd forgotten I hadn't eaten since breakfast.

Chapter 7

The bedroom floor was full of old clothes as I tossed things out of the wardrobes and drawers. Most of this had seen its day. Once in the shop I'd run up new outfits for us all.

School had broken up and Alice was almost back to her old self. It had been heartbreaking when she'd shouted that she hated me.

Alice charged into the room. 'Mam. What you doing?' She picked up one of her dresses. 'Why are you throwing my stuff away?'

'Because my little lovely.' I swung her in my arms. 'When we get to London, I'm going to make you some pretty new frocks.'

'Are you going to make George new clothes too?'

'Of course.'

'When's he coming home?'

'Soon I hope. He'll be back before we know it. In the meantime, you can enjoy some special spoiling time.'

A chant came from outside. 'Any old rags? Any old rags?' The words echoed over and over.

'It's the ragman. Can I go and see his horse?' Alice asked.

'Yes, but wait, if we take this lot, he'll give you a balloon.' I quickly scooped up the pile of old clothes before making our way downstairs.

The grey haired man stopped outside our house with his cart.

Alice rushed to stroke the brown pony. 'Look, Mam, he's wearing socks that match his hair.' She pointed to his mane.

I giggled and threw the rags onto the cart. The ragman handed my daughter a blue balloon on a stick. Women and children raced outdoors, arms piled high with old garments.

Alice clung to the cane, the balloon swinging. 'Isn't his horse lovely? Will you buy me one? Will you buy me one when we're in London?'

'One day maybe.' We strolled back into the house. Cardboard boxes were stacked high. The removal men would pick them up tomorrow while we travelled by train. It was quite exciting, despite mourning Jack and missing George. I hoped he was enjoying his holiday.

Nancy popped her head around the back door. 'How are you getting on? Did you catch the Rag and Bone?'

'Yes we did. We're doing well. How about you?'

'I'm almost finished. Hard getting rid of John's things.' She leaned into me and began to cry. I comforted her holding back my own tears.

'They're not coming back, are they?'

'No, Nancy. They may be gone but they'll always be with us.' I pressed my palm to my heart. 'In here. We'll never forget them. Let's have a cuppa.'

The kettle whistled. I poured water into the pot for tea and tipped warm milk into a tumbler for Alice. Nancy opened a packet of morning coffee biscuits and placed them onto a plate. We all sat down and talked about tomorrow's trip.

'How long will the train take, Mam?'

'A few hours. It's a long way to go. It will stop and start lots of times. We can read and write, maybe sing a bit too?'

'I like singing. Will my new school have a choir?'

'I'm sure they will. And they'll want your sweet little voice in it.'

Alice clapped her hands before slurping her drink. Once we were away from here I'd be able to make sure the children held onto good manners.

Nancy looked at her watch. 'I'd better get on. Still a few things to do before bed.'

'Are you going to be all right? You can stay here, if you like?'

'No, I'd like to spend the last night in my own little home. What time is the van arriving?'

'Just after eight o'clock. They'll have a head start. I thought we'd take a picnic as it's a long journey.'

'We can make it between us?'

'Good idea. I'll make potted beef sandwiches for us and jam for Alice.'

'Maybe I could do hard boiled eggs and some fruitcake?'

'Smashing.'

'See you tomorrow.' She kissed Alice on the cheek and left through the back door.

'Bedtime for you, young lady,' I said.

'Ah do I have to?'

'You do. I'm going to give Beth a last feed and then go myself.'

'I miss George.' Alice rubbed her eyes.

'Me too, honey. If you go to bed I'll be there to tuck you up in a minute.'

'Want a story. Want George to read me a story.' She galloped upstairs.

'Be careful,' I called. The last thing we needed was an accident.

Beth was still sleeping so I carried her up in the cot. I read Alice a short chapter from Rupert before kissing her goodnight. 'Night night, precious.'

Once downstairs I made up Beth's feed. I looked around the room. Memories flooded back. The very last morning Jack had gone to work. Intimate bath times by the fire when the children were in bed. The first day this house became our home. So many memories, moments I'd take with me. I thought of when the policeman and woman visited with the devastating news that Jack was dead. 'Stop it,' I said out loud. I wiped my eyes and went up to Beth. I lifted her out of the cot, picked up the bottle and fed her. She gulped back the milk and burped before I attempted to wind her. I laid her on our bed, changed the terry nappy and then settled her back down to sleep.

Memories surrounded me of our first night in this house, this room, this bed. Jack taking me in his arms, making love to me. It wasn't fair. I wanted to scream but instead I punched the pillow with my fists until I was spent.

Chapter 8

The removal men stripped the house of furnishings and boxes including the pram and carrycot. Mrs Deane managed to borrow an old pram from one of the neighbours for Beth to sleep in for now. Alice's interpretation of Shirley Temple echoed around the house. I looked around at the empty shell, home for more than ten years. Such happy moments but also so much sadness. How my life had changed since Greenemere. I'd lost Katy, her parents, Jack and now George, but I was going to get him back.

Nancy tapped on the door and walked in. She stared up at the ceiling. 'Someone's having fun.'

'Yes, she seems happy. Well I suppose we should make our way to the station, the train leaves at nine thirty. At least it's dry. Alice,' I called, 'time to go.'

'Can I bring my balloon?'

'No, not really love. Why not leave it for the new little boy or girl who's going to live here.'

'All right, I'll put it in my old bedroom.' She ran up and downstairs at great speed.

'Mrs Deane's coming to collect our keys,' Nancy said. 'Oh look, she's here.'

Our friend walked through the door. 'You ready to go? Come here.' She hugged Nancy tight. 'Write and let me know how you get on.'

'Yes of course, you've been like a mum to me.' Tears trickled down Nancy's cheeks.

'Don't,' I said, 'you'll start me off.'

'And me,' Mrs Deane said before giving me a hug too.

I locked up my house for the last time and handed over the keys to our neighbour. I shivered.

'I know,' Nancy said, 'it's scary.'

'Why are you all crying?' Alice asked.

I cuddled her. 'We're just a bit sad.'

The women down the street came out of their houses. Some waved while others ran up and shook our hands. They were there for Nancy, they'd never really accepted me. The taxi arrived, women crowded to say goodbye as we stepped into the black cab. Alice was fascinated by the little seat that dropped down from between the rear seat and the driver's partition screen.

'Mam, can I sit here?'

'Yes, you may. I'd like you to try and start calling me Mum or Mummy. Do you think you can manage that?'

She frowned. 'Why?'

'Because that's how the children down south will speak.'

'All right, Mum.' She laughed.

The cab pulled up outside the station. It reminded me of the times Jack and I came here with Katy and Eddie. It was all such a long time ago. Eddie had made me promise to keep in touch. I'd never really liked him but he'd been good to me at Jack's funeral. I walked over to the clerk in the window. 'Two and a half to Euston, London, please.' I handed over the money.

'Thank you.' She passed me the tickets and change. 'Platform two, it leaves in ten minutes.'

Thankfully, we didn't have any stairs to climb. A train chugged down the track but didn't stop. Alice's eyes widened as she took in the running engine with steam circling the platform. She coughed and waved the smoke away. It was only a few minutes before ours pulled in. Nancy climbed on with Alice and I followed carrying Beth. We were lucky, it was quiet so we had a carriage to ourselves. The train whistled and let out its steam before racing along.

'Listen to the train,' I told Alice, 'listen, it's saying, go to sleep, go to sleep.'

She stopped to pay attention. 'Yes, it does Mum. I can hear it. Go to sleep, go to sleep. Chuggedy chug, chuggedy chug.'

We all laughed. Nancy pulled the Rupert book out of her bag.

'Rupert! You didn't let the men take it.' Alice kissed Nancy.

'It was Mummy that kept it for you. I only carried it.'

'Thank you, Mum.' She turned around and gave me such a sweet kiss and hug. 'You're the best mum in the world.'

My face tingled. We trundled along until we came to Crewe where we had to get off and change to a diesel-electric locomotive. Alice twirled while singing and lost her footing, her hand came away from Nancy's grasp and she tripped inches away from the edge of the platform.

'Alice.' I snatched the belt on her summer dress to rein her back in.

Nancy's face flushed. 'I'm sorry Grace. I couldn't keep hold of her. I'm so sorry. Alice, are you all right?'

'It wasn't your fault,' I reassured her.

Alice looked up at Nancy. 'Yes, course. Why?'

She was a wild one, no fear of danger, so different to George. I thought of him, what would he think of the train? He'd be standing close to me and probably nervous at Alice's daredevil antics. I wished he was with us. I missed him so much.

Once we settled in our carriage, I passed a jam sandwich to Alice and offered the potted beef to Nancy. Beth was awake so I gave her a bottle and laid her on the bench seat to change her nappy. 'Alice,' I said, 'now that we've finished eating, why not lie down on the opposite seat and have a little rest?'

She jumped up and took her teddy. Hopefully she'd sleep for a while as it would be a few more hours before we arrived at Euston.

My arms became numb so Nancy offered to hold Beth for a while. I took the opportunity to pull out my sketchpad and flipped through the pages to show her my latest designs.

'They're impressive. How do you come up with your ideas?'

'I tend to look in newspapers and see what everyone's wearing. Once I've got an idea I think of something different, sometimes something to shock.'

'They're really good, Grace. Have you ever sold anything before?'

'No, but I'm sure we'll learn. It can't be that hard.'

'I'm not as confident as you. I hope I don't let you down and you regret bringing me along.'

'Of course I won't. You'll never let me down, how could you? You've been a great friend, sister in fact.'

'Thank you, Grace. I don't know what I'd have done without you.'

'Likewise, Nancy. I need you as much.'

Alice lay sleeping on the patterned seat. She purred like a cat. Nancy and I giggled quietly.

'Thank Heavens for your quick reflexes.' She clenched my hand. 'I thought she was a gonner when she tripped. Especially when that next train came whizzing through. I just froze.'

'It wasn't your fault.'

'Thank you.'

Beth opened her eyes briefly but closed them again when I rocked her and sang, 'Go to sleep. Go to sleep,' in tune with the train. Nancy shut hers for a while too. I watched the countryside rush by. Another couple of hours and we'd be there.

Alice sat up. 'Are we there yet, Mum?'

'Not yet darling. Would you like to play snakes and ladders?'

She rubbed her eyes and nodded.

'Get it out my bag and lay it on the seat between us.'

She pulled out the game and shook the dice in a small cup. 'We have to get six first.'

'Yes we do.'

Eventually we were both on the move, climbing up ladders and sliding down snakes. Nancy slept soundly. Alice was nearly home on ninety-five when she threw a four and landed on a snake. It took her back down to eighty-seven. Lucky for her it was only a little drop.

'That's not fair.' She stood up and stomped.

'Ssh, Alice, it's only a game. You'll wake up Nancy.'

Nancy opened her eyes. 'What's going on?'

'That stupid snake ate me up,' Alice said.

Nancy smiled. 'That's the idea of the game.'

'But Mum's going to win. It's not fair.'

I shook the cup and prayed I'd land on number ninety-nine too. I did.

This time Alice chuckled, took her turn and overtook me. Ten minutes later, she'd finally hit home.

'Hooray, I won.' She clapped her hands.

I glanced at my watch. 'We should be coming into Euston in about fifteen minutes. Hopefully there'll be a cab outside.'

Nancy stood up and stretched. 'I can't say I'll be sorry to get off. It's been a long ride.' The train slowed and we drew into the station. Nancy stepped down with Beth in her arms and I guided Alice. 'Hold my hand until we're clear of the platform.'

The sun was setting. A row of cabs sat outside the station. I approached one at the head of the queue. 'Could you take us to Wilson Street, in the East End please?'

'Yes, climb in.'

Alice scrambled inside and found the pull out seat. Nancy and I followed with Beth.

'Are you visiting?' the driver asked.

'No, we're moving down here. I'm opening a fabric and haberdashery shop. It's called *Grace's*. Please tell your clients and friends.'

'Certainly will Ma'am. My wife likes dressmaking. I'll get her to pop in. When do you open?'

'Monday, 13th August, with a sale.'

'This is it.' The driver stopped the car. 'I'm sure I'll see you again. My name's Ted.'

'Thank you, Ted. Do bring your wife.' I gave him a small tip.

We stepped out of the cab and looked up at the shop window. It was dull grey and weathered. I'd paint it pink. Alice and Nancy could help. There were two front doors, one to the shop at an angle, and the other, flush with the window, was the entrance to the flat. I unlocked the door. I flicked the light switch and picked up a duplicate door key that the removal men had posted through the letterbox.

I took Alice's hand and climbed the steep stairs ahead following Nancy. She pushed a door open when we reached the top. We strolled into what I supposed was the sitting room. It was huge, twice the size of our little houses put together. Our small amount of furniture looked lost. This led on to the kitchen, again massive, larger than Father's study. There was a big kitchen sink, cupboards and worktops and a pantry.

'What's this Mum?' Alice stood next to a tall white appliance.

'It's a refrigerator.' I opened it up and sniffed, it had a funny smell. I plugged it in and it began to whirr. We hadn't had one in Wigan, the cold shelf on the pantry had to suffice. We could get lots of food in here. No more sour milk. The removal men had placed the kitchen table and chairs in the centre.

'I wonder if we can paint these.' I pointed to our dressers, one blue and the other yellow. 'What colour do you think?'

'We could keep them as they are and have the decor blue and yellow?' Nancy said.

'We'll think about that. We don't have to decide now. Let's go upstairs.'

Alice charged on ahead. 'Wow.'

Nancy caught up with her. She echoed, 'Wow.'

We had five bedrooms, two double and three single but one nothing more than a box room. 'What's in here?' I pushed open a door. An indoor bathroom, after all these years. 'Look, Nancy.'

She stood with her mouth wide open. 'Wow, no more going out in the cold for a wee or breaking our backs dragging out a tin bath.'

Alice's corkscrew curls tossed backwards and forwards across her face as she jumped with excitement. 'Oh wow. Wait till George sees. Which room's mine? Will we share?'

'You can both have your own. Beth will come in with me for now in one of the doubles, leaving the other one for

Nancy.' As soon as we had the money we'd get more furniture, after I'd paid back Father of course.

Alice held her tummy. 'I'm hungry.'

Nancy looked at me. 'There's a chippy across the road. I noticed it when the cab pulled up. Shall I get fish and chips?'

'Yeah,' Alice shouted.

'Sounds good. I'll go down and put the kettle on.' I reached the gas stove and struck a match. The gas roared.

Chapter 9

Nancy had always been a great friend but even more so since we'd moved to London, although the first week had been strange, suddenly living together. Keeping busy helped. It was fun brightening up the shopfront with pink paint. Even Alice joined in. I stuck a sack over her clothes to keep her clean. She looked a picture, so much so that the man in the chip shop came across and offered to take a photograph.

It was now a month since Mother had taken George. I'd heard nothing. She said a month's trial, yet she hadn't answered my phone calls or letters.

'Nancy, are you able to look after the children this morning?'

'Yes, where are you off to?'

'I'm going to get a bus to *Granville Hall* to bring George home. He needs to be enrolled in the new school and we're running out of time as the term starts in a couple of weeks. They wear uniforms down here, so I'll need time to run them up on the machine.'

'Of course you must go and bring him back.'

'There's probably going to be a supplier's delivery today too. Can you open the shop to let them in?'

'No problem, Grace. Alice and I will bake. Beth sleeps most of the time so she'll just need a bottle and nappy change.'

Although still in August the weather was more like autumn so I put on my long tweed coat and hat to combat the wind. 'Alice.'

'I'm here.' Alice skipped into the hall.

'Mummy's got to go out this morning to bring George home. Be a good girl for Nancy.'

'I want to come too. I've never been to Grandma's house.'

'Not this time, sweetheart. Let's get George back where he belongs first.' I kissed her on the cheek and left the house. I caught a red bus at the end of the road and sat on the long bench seat at the front.

The conductor came to collect my fare.

'Gerrard's Cross please.'

'Where about?'

'*Granville Hall.*'

'We don't stop there so you'll need to get off a block before. Sixpence, please.'

I passed him the money.

He reeled out the ticket and passed it to me.

'Thank you.'

The bus trundled along, stopping every few minutes. I rehearsed my speech. Mother said a month's trial so why hadn't she kept to her bargain? I couldn't see George wanting to stay, he needed to be home with his family. I was fully armed if she threatened me with neglect. She wouldn't get to me this time. Heavy rain pounded on the window. The bus drew up at a stop.

'You need to get off here.' The conductor winked.

'Thank you. Goodbye.' I climbed off the bus and watched it pull away.

My coat blew open making me wet and cold. I ran through the wrought iron gates and down the winding path dodging puddles. I stepped up the wide steps leading to the mansion and tapped the brass knocker. The flower beds were adorned with my favourites, burnt orange cactus dahlias and chrysanthemums. Maybe Mother would let me take some home.

Martha opened the door. 'Miss Grace?'

'Hello Martha, I've come to collect George. Is Mother in?'

'If you'd like to wait here, I'll go and see.' She closed the door and left me standing on the step.

Mother opened the door. 'Grace? What are you doing here?'

'I've come to collect George.' Rain dripped from my face.

'He's settled.'

'What do you mean? You said a month's trial.'

'And he's happy.'

'I want him back with me. You took advantage when I was vulnerable. I'll repay every penny.'

'Don't be foolish, girl. We offered your son a good home and made sure your other children weren't taken by the authorities.'

'You tricked me. You said they'd take all my babies.'

'And so they would.'

'No, you're wrong. You took advantage of me. Now please hand over my son.'

'I've told you, he's settled.'

'Please, please Mother. I need my boy.'

'Selfish, Grace Gilmore, selfish all over. You'll never change.'

'No, I'm not. I'm not, you're wrong. It's you that's selfish. You've stolen my son. Now please let me take him home?'

I backed away from the steps and looked up at the window. George, I could see George. I waved, I shouted, 'George, George, I've come to take you home.'

George waved back but then two large hands pulled him away.

'You need to leave before your father returns. There's nothing left to discuss, Grace. Go back home. Your business here is finished. Don't try and make contact again.' She tried to close the door.

I pushed it open and managed to slide into the hallway. 'I'm not leaving without George.'

'Don't force me to throw you out, Grace,' Mother said softly.

There was still hope. 'I'm not leaving without my son.'

A tall male servant I didn't recognise marched into the hall. 'Would you like me to call the police, Madam?'

'Yes, call the police. I'll tell them she stole my son.' I pointed to Mother.

'That won't be necessary, Barnes. It's fine, leave us be.'

He walked away.

'Grace, Grace. You silly girl,' Mother continued, 'do you really think they'll believe such nonsense? Carry on like this and I'll organise the authorities to take away your girls. You're emotionally unstable and not fit to look after them.'

'You won't get away with this. I'm not giving up. Couldn't I just see him? Please, Mother, please.' Tears streamed down my face.

She looked at me with compassion. 'I'm sorry, Grace. It isn't possible. Your father has given strict orders.' She opened the door. 'Now come along and go back home to your children.'

I stood on the step, pleading.

'Please don't come here again. It's too painful for us both.' Mother closed the door in my face.

'No, No, No.' I hammered with my fists. I pressed my head into the door and sobbed, continuing to pound on the wood. No one answered. I walked away and looked up at the empty window. Rain poured from the thunderous sky.

Chapter 10

I adjusted a garment on the dressmaker's dummy. It took pride of place at the front, so it was the first thing clients saw when they walked in. Nancy was serving a customer, Beth was asleep in her pram at the back and Alice was at school. The last year had flown by and things were ticking over nicely or they would be if I'd managed to retrieve George.

The bell on the shop door pinged. A well-dressed woman breezed in.

'Good morning,' I said.

She shook out her umbrella. 'I've seen better ones.'

'It's probably just a shower,' I said.

She touched the tailored dress hanging on the dummy. 'Did you make this?'

'Yes, I designed it too.'

'You must be Grace?'

'Yes, ah, the shop name gave it away?'

'No, you're the talk of the East End. The debut designer tucked away. That's why I'm here.' She stroked the shiny satin fabric. 'Forgive my manners.' She held out her hand. 'Charlotte Cunningham. I'm very pleased to finally meet you. Don't look so confused dear, I told you, everyone's talking about you.'

'Well you know I'm Grace but it's Grace Gilmore.'

'Do you have any more designs?'

'Yes, I'll get my portfolio.' I stepped over to the counter where Nancy was cutting crisp cotton fabric for her client. I reached underneath for the large folder.

Charlotte followed. She flipped through the pages. 'These are outstanding? Did you train in Paris?'

'No, I've never been to Paris.'

187

She turned the pages in my portfolio, browsed rows of fabrics and checked each area of the shop before looking at her watch. 'I've got another appointment. May I come back later, once you're closed? Six o'clock? I have a proposition.'

'Yes certainly.'

Charlotte opened the door and flipped her umbrella up as she ventured outside to battle the rain.

Nancy folded the fabric into a brown paper bag, took the client's money and pressed the keys of the cash register. 'Goodbye Madam, hope to see you another day.' She opened the door to see out her customer.

'Who was that?' Nancy said. 'She looked posh.'

'Her name's Charlotte Cunningham. She's coming back this evening. Are you able to look after the children? This woman says she has a proposition. I wonder what that could mean.'

'Yes of course. It sounds exciting. The postman was here earlier. Did anything come from *Granville Hall*?'

'No, still nothing. All my letters come back *return to sender*. Sooner or later they'll have to let me see him. Won't they?' I rubbed my eyes.

'Don't give up, Grace.' She gripped my hand.

'I won't. I want my son back.'

A cry came from the pram. I lifted Beth out and she toddled over to Nancy. 'I'm going to have to sort out proper childcare. The shop's getting busier and now she's mobile it's more difficult.'

'We could put an advert in the newsagent's window across the street?'

'That's not a bad idea, Nancy. Just for a couple of hours a day to start with.

In-between, you and I could take turns.'

'I'm going to take Beth upstairs for a bite to eat and bake a couple of cakes,' Nancy said, 'and then we'll swap so you can have something. You collect Alice from school at three and I'll take over when you get back. That way you'll be available for the smart lady.'

Nancy baked a fruitcake to offer the visitor for tea. I swept the floor, cashed up and locked the day's takings in the safe. There was a tap on the shop door. The elegant woman stood at the other side of the glass.

'Good evening.' I let her in. 'At least it's stopped raining.'

'Yes, thankfully,' she said. 'Sorry about rushing off earlier.'

'Come through to the back.' I led her to a small room housing a couch and coffee table. 'Do sit down. Tea?'

'That would be nice. White no sugar.'

'My friend's made a fruitcake. Would you like a slice?'

'I shouldn't really.' She patted her tummy. 'But yes, why not? It looks delicious.'

She held the china cup gracefully, using her thumb and index finger, as I'd been taught myself. She reminded me of Mother. This woman was obviously well bred so what was she doing in a little East End shop like mine?

'You're probably wondering what I'm doing here?'

'You could say that.'

'As I said earlier today, I've a proposition for you. Is it possible to have another quick peep at your portfolio?'

'Yes, I've got it here. If you'd like me to make one of the designs, I'll need a deposit.'

Charlotte laughed. 'No that's not what I'm here for. Although I wouldn't say no to a few new outfits.'

'What then?'

She continued to flip through the folder. 'These really are very good. I'd like to invest in your business. We'd become equal partners. My money, your expertise?'

'I already have a partner.'

'We'll share three ways. I'm happy with that.'

'Why do you think I'd need your money? We're doing fine.'

'Grace, Grace. You can do so much better than fine. Let's turn this little haberdashery into a fashion boutique with full body mannequins rather than one outfit on a dressmaker's dummy.'

She was offering me what I'd visualised but could only hope for.

'With my money we can make up dozens of outfits to display as well as taking orders.'

'We'd need extra staff for that sort of turnover.'

'That would be up to you, Grace. I wouldn't interfere.'

'I'll need to talk it over with my partner. Do you have anyone who can vouch for you?' Father's business sense had stayed with me.

'Certainly. Very wise, I could be anyone. I can give you a list of connections for you to contact. How long do you need? Will a week suffice?'

'A week sounds fine.'

She set down the cup and saucer, stood up and opened her bag. 'Here's my card, and I'll send you on a list of names who'll confirm my credentials. Give me a call once you've made a decision and we'll talk figures.'

I shook her hand. 'Thank you, Charlotte. I'll be in touch.'

*

It had been a busy four months since we'd closed for refurbishment. Fabric was ordered and stored in the back room. Rolls of different materials stood on shelves by the wall ready to make clients' orders. Beth had a part time nanny, and Joan, my friendly taxi-driver Ted's wife, had come to work as a seamstress. She jumped at the chance when I mentioned the position. A partition was set up in the shop to make a small room to house two sewing machines. Changing cubicles with curtains had been installed for clients to be measured and fitted. The shop floor and window randomly displayed numerous full bodied, long, short and curly haired mannequins wearing outfits in different styles and textures.

Alice had settled back in school. I'd still had no luck getting George back, despite traipsing to Gerrard's Cross almost every week. I'd contacted the authorities many times, but as soon as I mentioned Father's name they'd clam up and not want to know. A similar response came from solicitors' offices that I toured. Everyone wanted to help until I revealed the name Granville and then suddenly became mute. I wasn't going to give up.

The shop now had a brand new name, *House of Grace*. Maybe once monies started to come in I'd have more ammunition to fight my parents. They may have won the battle but not the war.

Nancy and Joan stood in position as I opened the door to the queue outside. Our advertising of the new opening had been successful. There was a mixture of clientele, working and upper class. Charlotte had used her contacts.

'Good morning and welcome. I'm Grace. This is Nancy and Joan. They'll look after you today. Do look around.'

Customers browsed the store, touching garments and talking to each other.

The bell chimed from the shop door. 'This is impressive. Height of industry. How's it going?' Charlotte asked as she walked in.

'They seem to be enjoying themselves but no orders yet.'

'Give them time, treat them special. Have you got tea and cake?'

'Yes, Nancy made a large batch last night. We have fruitcake, Victoria sandwich, Madeira and Angel.'

'That sounds like a lovely collection. Leave the sales to me.' Charlotte circled the room stopping to chat to individual clients. 'Grace, let me introduce Mrs Katherine Windsor.'

'How do you do?' I shook her hand.

'Katherine's looking for something special to wear for her daughter's wedding. Do you think you can help?'

'Certainly, come this way?' I led her to the seating area in the back room. 'Would you like some refreshment?'

'Yes, that would be nice. The Victoria sponge looks inviting.'

I passed her the cake and a cup of tea. 'Did anything on display catch your eye? Or how about something quite different? This is my latest design.' I pointed to a drawing in my folder. 'It's like a suit but all in one. The top half shirt-like, a belted waist that falls into a pencil skirt. You could easily carry this off with your slim figure.'

'Do you think so?'

'Yes. I'm thinking silk, emerald or cobalt blue.'

'How delightful.'

'Let's get you measured up. Joan, look after Mrs Windsor please?'

'Of course, would you like to come this way, Madam?' She led her to one of the cubicles.

A similar routine was repeated throughout the rest of the day. Charlotte passed clients to me, I'd work out what they required and then Nancy or Joan would take over. I closed the shop at five thirty. We were all exhausted.

'Joan, you can get off now if you like. We'll start the orders tomorrow,' I said. 'Are you coming up to the flat, Charlotte?'

'Yes, I will. We need to work out where to go from here.'

Chapter 11

The last few weeks had been hard work, clientele increased daily. We employed a couple of casual staff to help with the overload after the sales promotion. It was difficult juggling extra labour and childcare. I was careful not to neglect my children so tried to be with Alice after school, although lately she pushed me away. She'd lost trust in me after my broken promises that her brother would come home.

Last month Nancy and I decorated George's room in hope of his homecoming. I let Alice choose the wallpaper. She decided on *The Beatles*, mainly because her brother's name was printed on the covering. It didn't matter that Paul, Ringo and John's were there too. I ran my fingers over the repeated blue pattern, touching the black inked italicised George on the white background.

A wooden chest of drawers displayed a variety of Matchbox cars. I picked up a maroon Cortina that looked just like my first car. No, I mustn't give up hope of getting George home.

Beth was asleep in her cot and Alice was downstairs engrossed in the television. We were going to Victoria Park today for a picnic. I hoped Charlotte would come along too as I wanted to speak about using her connections to help me get my son back.

I closed his bedroom door behind me and made my way to the bathroom to freshen up. I didn't want Alice or Nancy to see I'd been crying. I scooped tepid water in my hands and splashed my face before venturing downstairs to the kitchen.

Nancy was spreading butter on the bread. 'Are you all right, Grace? You look a little tired.'

'I'm fine thank you. It's been a busy few weeks. You must be exhausted too?'

'Yes I am, but very happy.'

I touched my friend's arm. 'I'm pleased. What can I do?'

'Pack up the picnic if you like?'

I filled the bag with sandwiches, hard-boiled eggs, potato crisps and garibaldi biscuits. Nancy passed a batch of freshly baked fairy cakes before she filled a flask with hot coffee.

There was a knock on the door.

'I'll go,' Alice shouted. Her programme had obviously finished. She ran downstairs and reappeared with Charlotte.

'I'm so pleased you could make it.' I shook her hand.

'It will give us a chance to get to know each other.' She smiled.

'I'm looking forward to it,' I said.

'No business talk.' Nancy wiped her hands down the apron before untying it and throwing it over a chair.

'Quite right too,' Charlotte said, 'today will be about getting acquainted as friends. I'd like to be around the shop a bit more in the future, if that's all right with you two?' She turned towards me.

'Yes, that sounds good. Shall we go?'

We headed outside. Beth was strapped in the pushchair and Alice strolled ahead with Nancy. It was a lovely April day, blue skies and the temperature around seventy Fahrenheit.

Beth's little legs kicked with excitement as we approached the park. 'Quack quack,' she mimicked.

Alice had been teaching her to say that, all week. Today was to be a family day, all of us together. There hadn't been enough of those recently. Shame George couldn't be here with us too, but hopefully after my conversation with Charlotte later, that would soon be rectified.

At the entrance Alice ran on ahead.

'Let me take Beth,' Nancy said, 'we'll go on ahead and feed the ducks. You and Charlotte chat.'

'Thank you.' I released the pushchair.

Charlotte and I strolled along the dried mulch footpath until we came to a wooden bench close to the spot where Nancy and the children were already throwing bread into the water.

'Let's sit here,' I said. 'We can watch Nancy and the girls. We've never really had a chance to talk properly before about personal issues, have we?'

'No, we haven't. It's all been business. That's why I thought it would be nice today if you told me about yourself.' Charlotte adjusted her already immaculate hair.

'Have I mentioned that I've another child?'

'Yes, yes, you have. You went to see him a few weeks ago, didn't you?'

'Well I tried. Charlotte, I was hoping you may be able to help me?'

She frowned. 'Yes, of course, if I'm able.'

'My parents tricked me into taking my son and now they won't return him but worse than that, they won't let me communicate with him.'

Charlotte patted my hand. 'That must be dreadful for you darling. But where do I come in?'

'I've toured solicitors and contacted the authorities but *no one* will take on my case. Do you think you could use your influence to find someone to help me?'

Charlotte opened her handbag and took out a small notebook and pen. 'What's your father's name and address?'

'Charles Granville. *Granville Hall*, Gerrard's Cross.'

'Not Lord Granville?' Charlotte's mouth remained open.

'Yes.' My hands shook.

Nancy twisted towards me. 'You never mentioned your father was a Lord.'

'It's not something I'm proud of.'

'This conversation isn't over.' Nancy turned back and focused on the children.

Charlotte pulled out a packet of Woodbines and a lighter from her pocket. She flicked a flame into life and then drew on the cigarette as she lit it. 'Darling, you can't be serious.'

'Deadly. Can you help?'

'Go up against Lord Granville? Your son, he's George?'

'Yes, have you seen him?'

'No, but the rumours say your parents took him in after he was orphaned.'

How could they tell everyone that he was an orphan? I couldn't believe it. Suppose they'd told George I was dead too. I pulled my handkerchief from my pocket to dab my eyes.

'Sorry, darling. I didn't mean to upset you. It's the talk of the city, Lord Granville and his young grandson George. Seriously Grace, I'd stop worrying. He's being well looked after.'

'You've never had children, have you? I can't expect you to understand.' I rubbed my eyes. 'So you won't help me then?'

'It's not the case of won't but can't. No one will cross Lord Granville, too many ramifications, darling. He'd ruin me and any of my contacts that try to interfere. The boy will get a great start.'

'You sound like Mother.'

'It makes sense, Grace. I'm not saying to forget about your son. By all means keep fighting your father to have contact but don't try and take him away. He's got a good life ahead of him.'

Charlotte started to irritate me. I was wishing that I hadn't asked her to the picnic. Today was supposed to be about relaxation but that was impossible now. It was good to hear that Father cared for George. He'd always wanted a son. But George wasn't his. No, no, I wasn't going to give up, I'd have to do this on my own. I couldn't really blame Charlotte for not wanting to risk losing everything and she was right, Father most certainly wouldn't stop until she had. Why hadn't I thought of that? I'd have to think of another plan.

'Let's go over to the children and feed the ducks.' I pulled my camera out of my handbag.

Charlotte gripped my hand. 'Look, Grace, I'm sorry. I wanted us to be friends.'

'No, I shouldn't have asked you. I'd like to be friends too.' I smiled. 'Alice, Beth, say cheese.' I clicked the camera. I'd send a copy of the photo with my next letter to George so he could see we hadn't forgotten him.

Chapter 12

Charlotte strolled through the door with the mail in her hand. 'For you.'

My heart hammered as I flicked through the letter pile and spotted two small white ones. Disappointment rose when I noticed the usual black diagonal lines struck across the address, 'Return to Sender.' One had been to George and the other, Elizabeth. Every week I wrote to them both with the hope that one day I'd receive an answer. A tear fell, smudging the ink on an envelope.

'I'm sorry,' Charlotte said. 'Keep writing, one day you may get a reply. If George ever comes looking for you, he can see that you never stopped fighting for him.'

Why was I surprised? Why should it have suddenly changed? George was probably away at school anyway. I went into the living room and pulled open the top drawer of the sideboard and took out a bundle of similar letters. All alike, they'd been returned. I untied the ribbon, inserted the two new additions and retied.

'Right, go and put your face on so we can look at these properties,' Charlotte said.

'I'm not sure. The girls aren't well.'

'What is it you're worried about?'

'They seem a bit warm, especially Beth.'

'It's probably just a cold. Nancy's here, she'll take care of them.'

'I'm not sure, Charlotte. I have a feeling, like someone or something's telling me not to leave them.'

'Don't you think that sounds a bit melodramatic, Grace?'

'Possibly, I don't know.'

Nancy strolled into the room. 'Are you ladies off then?'

'Grace is having second thoughts. She's worried about the children.'

'Don't worry, Grace, I'll take care of them.' Nancy patted my hand reassuringly.

'I'm not sure,' I repeated.

'Look I've just given them both aspirin and if there's any change I'll contact the doctor. You're only going to be away for a couple of hours, it's not like you're leaving the country.' Nancy flicked her long fringe away from her face.

'I'll just take one last peep and see how Alice feels about me going out.' I left the room and went upstairs to find the girls. Their bedroom looked cramped as Beth was in with Alice while her room was being decorated. She only had the box room but it was adequate for the moment. Nearly two years of age so she needed a little girl's room rather than a baby's. She was also too big for her cot so a new bed was on order.

Alice was lying on the pink candlewick bedspread in her winceyette pyjamas, reading a *Famous Five*, by Enid Blyton. Beth was playing with wooden coloured bricks on the rag-rug Nancy had made.

'Alice, I'm going out to look at some new properties but I can stay here if you're not well.' I felt her head, it was still warm but hopefully the aspirin would soon do its job.

She sneezed. 'I'll be fine, Mum. Nancy's here.'

I felt a little irritated; Alice always chose Nancy over me these days.

Nancy breezed in. 'You'd better hurry, Charlotte's getting impatient. She says you're going to be late for the agent after he's made an exception to meet you on a Sunday.'

Beth lifted her face. I leant down towards her. 'Is that a rash?'

Nancy peered at Beth's face and neck. 'It's probably where she's cutting those last teeth and I expect she's dribbled on her neck making it sore. It can't be anything serious, she's playing happily enough.'

'I suppose so, but promise me, if there's any change you'll call the doctor straight away.'

'I promise.' Nancy touched my arm. 'You know I love these children like my own. There's no way I'd put their health in jeopardy.'

'Thank you.' I turned to Alice. 'Be a good girl and help Nancy look after Beth.' I kissed both of my children on the cheek. 'Mummy won't be long.' I turned to Nancy. 'Three hours at the most.'

The click clack, click clack of heels echoed outside the room. Charlotte appeared. 'Are we going or not?'

'Give me five minutes,' I said, 'I'll follow you down.' It didn't feel right. I had a strange feeling, almost as strong as that first day at Queen's Park when I faced the sentinels.

*

Nancy was halfway downstairs as we opened the front door.

'Thank God, you're back,' she screamed.

'What's happened?' I ran upstairs to meet her.

'The doctor's just arrived; Beth took a turn for the worse. Come quickly.'

I rushed past Nancy and up the next flight of stairs to the girls' bedroom. The doctor was leaning over Beth's cot, shaking his head. She lay listless.

I put my hand to my mouth. 'What is it?' Please let Beth be all right.

'I need to call for an ambulance. Do you have a phone?'

'Yes, I'll show you,' Charlotte said.

'I knew I shouldn't have gone out,' I cried.

'But it wouldn't have made any difference, Grace. I called the doctor as soon as there was any change. She was fine one minute and then like that the next.' Nancy turned her head towards Beth in her cot.

'I'll never forgive myself if anything happens.' I held my head.

The doctor rushed back in. 'The ambulance is on its way. It should be here in a few minutes. I just hope we're in time.'

'What's the matter with her? What do you think it is?'

'Looks like Scarlet Fever, she'll need antibiotics. Your eldest daughter is fine, she's just got a bit of a cold.'

Alice stood up. 'What's that noise?' She moved over to the window. 'Mum, there's a big white van outside with a blue light on top. Is that the ambulance?'

'Yes,' the doctor said before heading downstairs.

Heavy footsteps stomped on the stairs and two men wearing dark uniforms appeared carrying a stretcher. 'She's a tiny one,' the taller of the two said as he looked over towards the cot.

'I knew I shouldn't have gone. You promised me, Nancy. And you, Charlotte, you made me think that I was being overly protective. I knew I should have stayed at home. I could lose Beth.' I covered my eyes.

'What's happening, Mum? Why's Beth got to go to hospital? She isn't going to die is she?'

'Come here.' I held Alice in my arms. 'Beth's very poorly but the doctors will try very hard to make her better. I have to go with her, so be a good girl for Nancy, while I'm gone.'

She hugged me. 'I will Mum.'

'I'll follow on in the car,' Charlotte said.

*

Beth was surrounded by doctors and nurses while they wired her up to tubes.

'It's not as scary as it looks,' the nurse said. 'We need to get antibiotics into her bloodstream quickly. The best way is intravenously.'

'The mother shouldn't be in here,' the doctor said. 'The child's contagious.'

'Please, Doctor, please let me stay.'

'Can we not make an exception, Doctor? She could wear a mask?'

'Very well, but make sure she stays out of the way while we treat her daughter.'

The nurse handed me a white mask to put over my face.

Charlotte burst in. 'How is she?'

'She'll have to wait outside,' the doctor said, irritated.

'Sorry.' Charlotte backed out of the door.

'Mrs Gilmore,' the doctor said, 'Mrs Gilmore, your daughter is very poorly, I'm not sure if we've got the antibiotics to her in time. The next few hours will be critical. If she gets through the night, then we have hope.'

The room went black. I opened my eyes to find I was sitting in a chair next to Beth.

'You fainted,' the nurse said. 'I'll get you a cup of tea.'

'Where's the doctor gone?' I asked.

'He's done all he can. It's a question of waiting.' The nurse touched my shoulder lightly and exited the glass door.

I sat next to Beth, holding her hand and prayed, 'Please don't let me lose my baby.'

My mind drifted back to the night she was born. Jack had run to get the midwife and she arrived only just in time. 'Seven pounds five ounces,' the midwife said. She was a bonny little thing even then. Of course Jack never got the chance to know her and she'd never known what it was like to have a daddy, just two Mums, Nancy and me.

I squeezed her hand. 'Please my little Beth. Please wake up for Mummy. I need you.' Beth's eyes remained closed and her breathing was shallow. Her fever was still high. 'Nurse,' I called.

The nurse entered.

'Nurse, she's still burning up. Do you have a flannel so I can bathe her forehead?'

'The doctor's given her aspirin to reduce it but I don't see any harm in giving her some extra help. I'll get you a basin.'

'Don't worry, Beth, Mummy's here. Mummy will make you better. I'm not going to lose my precious little girl.'

The nurse strolled back in. 'Here you are, Mrs Gilmore. The water's tepid so should be just right.'

I swilled the flannel into the bowl before wringing it out and laid it across my daughter's forehead. At least I felt like I was doing something. The room was silent except for the loud tick of the clock. Three minutes past two. I asked whether

Charlotte had gone home, the nurse said she was waiting outside and she'd put her in the picture.

Over the next few hours different nurses came in to check on Beth and replaced the bowl of water.

'Are the antibiotics working?' I asked the latest one.

She shook her head. 'The fever still hasn't broken and her pulse is getting very weak. I think you need to prepare yourself for the worst.' She touched my shoulder lightly like the other nurse. 'I'll get you a cup of tea.'

I wanted to scream, 'I don't want a cup of tea. I want my baby to be better.' But instead, I looked up and gave a small smile.

The clock showed half past four when the doctor walked in with the nurse. He strolled over to Beth and held her wrist to take her pulse. He shook his head. 'Mrs Gilmore, would you like to hold your daughter?'

'Yes, yes please. Is she going to be all right?'

'I'm sorry, I don't think she is. You need to prepare yourself for the worst.'

Those words again, that's what the nurse said. What do they mean, prepare myself for the worst? What were they saying? The nurse handed me my baby, still attached to tubes. She lay listless in my arms, her breath shallow. I kissed her face. 'Please little girl, please come through this. Please God,' I prayed out loud.

Beth took her last breath at half past six that morning. My little girl had gone. I rocked her in my arms willing it not to be true until the nurse prised her away from me. 'She's gone, dear. I'm so sorry.'

'No, no,' I screamed. I ran out of the ward, down a flight of stairs and stood outside in the cold. Why was this happening to me? Why was I being punished?

Charlotte came up behind and took me in her arms.

Chapter 13

I stood in the mirror. Same black suit, same black hat but a different face, a thinner, more haggard face than the last time I'd worn this outfit. Not even two years since I'd buried Jack and now I must go through the same ritual for our baby girl.

If only I hadn't walked through those stone sentinels at Queen's Park that day. Maybe then, just maybe then, none of this would have happened. That day sealed my fate. My fate to lose everyone close to me. I had no right to Alice or George, they were better off without me. Nancy loved Alice and would always be there for her. George was safe and comfortable at *Granville Hall*. No, they were better off without me.

'Are you ready? They're here.' Charlotte put her hand on my shoulder.

'I don't want to do this, Charlotte.' I nestled into her chest and sobbed.

'Shh, we need to go, Grace.' She led me downstairs and out of the door. It was pouring, the rain dripped down my face while the cold wind cut through the thin cloth of my suit. Nancy and Alice hovered under the shop window, shivering. I stared into the black hearse that housed a tiny white coffin covered in daffodils and narcissi, wishing it wasn't my little Beth inside. I turned away and buried my head again into Charlotte.

'Come on.' She guided me to the black limousine behind the hearse. Nancy and Alice followed.

We reached the church and the driver held the door open while we stepped outside and rushed into the dry, trying to avoid the puddles. Alice clung to Nancy. At Jack's funeral the church had been packed with coal miners and their wives, but today there weren't many people. Just the couple of staff I'd employed to work in the shop and dressmakers including Joan. Her husband, Ted, the taxi driver, sat close, holding her hand.

Daffodils filled the church. Their fragrance was sickly and overpowering combined with the sweet aroma from the candles. I had to steady myself on the pew as everything started to go black. Nancy gripped my hand. Alice didn't look at me.

The minister mumbled words and the small congregation sang but all I remember was *All Things Bright and Beautiful* and *The Lord's Prayer* before being invited to follow the small casket out to the burial ground.

Once everyone was gathered the vicar said a prayer before signalling for the coffin to be lowered. I collapsed to the ground longing to be with my daughter. Charlotte dragged me back. I was ashamed but I couldn't stop. I was a useless mother. I'd given away one child and now I'd lost another.

My hands, knees and face were slick with mud. Charlotte took out her handkerchief to clean the black smears. Nancy spoke to the small group of guests and invited them back to the flat for coffee and cake. I forced myself to offer my hand to Alice. She looked at me, frowned and turned back to Nancy. I sobbed for my dead daughter, I sobbed for my lost children too.

Nancy hugged me but Alice turned away.

I threw a red rose onto the white casket. 'Goodbye my baby.'

Charlotte patted my hand. 'Let's get you home and run a hot bath.' She steered me towards the car.

Chapter 14

Nancy and I were sitting on the settee, she was trying to make conversation but I just uttered sounds back. Alice was face down on the floor drawing a picture. During the last few months I'd lost interest in everything, the shop, my designs and my daughter.

Alice picked up her notebook. 'Look Mum, I'm drawing, like you.'

I brushed the book away. She kept pushing it in my face so I flicked it and sent it flying across the room, making her cry. I wanted to comfort her but couldn't. Nancy frowned at me before getting down on the floor with Alice to reassure her that everything was fine.

Charlotte rushed in. 'What's all the noise about?'

Nancy shrugged her shoulders and turned her head towards me. I jumped off the seat, charged into the bedroom, grabbed my design sketchpad and a marker pen and began scrawling over my sketches, faster and faster until they became unrecognisable. Once I started, I couldn't stop.

'Grace, what the hell are you doing?' Charlotte snatched the pad away from me. 'What have you done? These are your latest.'

I ignored her.

'You've got to pull yourself out of this. We can't keep tiptoeing around you forever. It's tragic you lost Beth but what you seem to be forgetting is that you have another child who needs you.'

'She doesn't need me.'

'That's where you're wrong. That girl needs her mother now more than she's ever needed her before.'

'She's got Nancy.'

'Nancy isn't her mother.'

'I don't deserve to be a mother. Everyone close to me is taken away. She's better off without me. It's my own fault for walking through that park entrance.'

'What are you talking about, Grace?'

'When I was sixteen, the stone sentinels at Queen's Park warned me not to enter. But my friends made me. And now I'm paying by losing everyone. First Katy, the Gilmores, Jack, George, Beth. It's only a matter of time before Alice is taken from me too.'

'Do you know how melodramatic that sounds, Grace?'

'You don't understand,' I screamed.

Charlotte slapped my face leaving me stunned.

'I'm sorry, Grace.' She stroked my hair and moved it gently behind my ears. I lay face down, closed my eyes and slowly became calm.

Nancy rushed in. 'There's a phone call.'

'Take a message,' Charlotte said.

'He sounds young but very insistent that he wants to speak to Grace.'

'He's probably looking for a job. Take his number. Grace is in no fit state to speak to anyone at the moment.'

The door closed. Charlotte massaged my shoulders. I missed Jack so much. Why wasn't he here to help bear this pain? I must pull myself together. I'd been feeling sorry for myself for far too long.

*

The following morning I woke up to birds singing and that feeling of isolation had evaporated, maybe the sadness of the past few months were behind me. I had a good feeling about today. I'd make things right with my daughter. After bathing, I paid particular attention to my appearance, including brushing my hair one hundred times, something Katy and I used to do every day at Greenemere. I patted my face with powder and guided a red gloss stick over my lips. Yes, I had a good feeling about today.

Nancy and Alice were eating porridge when I walked into the kitchen. They were chatting and hadn't heard me enter the room.

'Good morning.' I smiled.

Nancy grinned with approval. 'Morning, Grace.'

Alice looked at me and returned to her porridge.

I could hardly blame my daughter for not wanting to know me, but I was really going to try. Today I'd go to the cemetery and say goodbye properly to Beth so I could attempt to move on. I'd pick up some lilies to put on her grave. Afterwards I'd concentrate on showing Alice how much I loved her and resume the letters to George in my fight to get him back. I needed to work hard to regain Alice's trust. I sat down at the table, next to my daughter, and touched her hand. 'Alice, may I see that drawing again, please? The one you showed me yesterday.'

She remained focused on her breakfast.

'Alice, Mummy's speaking to you,' Nancy said.

Alice lifted her face towards me. 'I hate you.'

'I know and I don't blame you. I've been a rotten mum. I'll try and make it up to you. Please let me see your drawing.'

She placed her spoon down in her empty dish and left the table, returning with a notebook and slapped it into my hand. 'There.'

I looked at the pencilled figures in dresses and skirts. I was impressed. My daughter had potential. 'These are very good.'

Alice shrugged her shoulders.

'Maybe you'll be a designer like me one day.'

She shrugged again, snatched the book back and left the room.

'She's never going to forgive me.'

'She'll come round.' Nancy tapped my hand.

'I'm going to the cemetery today,' I said.

'Do you need company? I could come with you, or Charlotte, if you prefer?'

'No, this is something I need to do on my own. Maybe you could watch Alice?'

'Yes, of course, but before you go anywhere, you need food inside you.' She placed a bowl of steaming porridge in front of me.

I teased my spoon around the dish. I wasn't hungry and this newfound bravery of mine was rapidly slipping away. Suppose I wasn't ready to move on. My tummy curdled. I picked up the bowl and left it in the kitchen sink.

'I'm off now,' I called.

'Take care.' Nancy ran through and pecked me on the cheek. 'I'm proud of you.'

I decided to walk rather than take a bus, that way I could think. The sun was shining so I didn't need a cardigan. It was a beautiful August morning. August, I'd missed so much time. The children's birthdays had gone by without me realising. Alice had turned eight in April and I hadn't even acknowledged it. George's eleventh birthday had been in May and I hadn't sent a card. My lovely little Beth would have been two in May and I hadn't even taken flowers to her grave. What sort of mother did that make me? Tears fell, salt lingered on my lips. I wiped my eyes. 'Pull yourself together,' I told myself. 'This won't do. You have a family to repair.'

I approached the florist near the cemetery gates and looked in the window before strolling inside. The shop was empty. I expected a lot of people had taken the opportunity to go to the park or seaside in the warm weather.

I picked up a handful of lilies and handed the money to the sales assistant. Thankfully she didn't try to start up a conversation. Maybe she sensed that I didn't want to talk. I sniffed the white-belled flowers and sneezed. I crossed the road to go through the wrought iron gates, along the gravelled footway until I reached my daughter's grave. I read the words out loud.

Beth May Gilmore,

25th May 1962 – 29th March 1964

Daughter to Grace and Jack,
Sister to George and Alice.

Sleep in Peace, little Angel,
until we meet again in Heaven.'

Hopefully, Beth was reunited with her father. I knelt on the dry ground to place the flowers. The vase was empty, we'd had no rain for days. I dragged myself up and staggered over to a tap set in a wall close by. After filling the container with water, I returned to the stone to arrange the lilies. My mind wandered back to the last time I held Beth in my arms. Kneeling down I thumped the ground and wept silent tears.

I brushed dirt and leaves away from my dress before making my way back towards home in a trance like state.

The sun burnt my face but I didn't care, at least I was feeling something. I turned into the road and could see the flat. I hoped Nancy and Alice weren't in but I was out of luck. They were in the sitting room. Chubby Checker's plastic disc, *The Twist* was spinning around on the record player. Alice and Nancy were doing the motions while giggling.

'Come and join us,' Nancy said.

'Errm, I'm not sure, I think I'll go and sit down for a while.'

'Come on Mum,' Alice pleaded.

'Not now.'

Her face fell, she turned off the music and slumped on the sofa. She muttered something to Nancy but I couldn't make it out. Nancy cuddled and tickled her, making her giggle.

'You're just in time for tea,' Nancy said, 'Charlotte's due shortly.'

Tea. Had I been out that long? It was strange how time had passed so quickly. I wanted to put my arms around Alice and show her that I loved her but something stopped me. The image of Beth lying limp in my arms and the nurse prising her away wouldn't go away. I wanted my family back, Jack, George, Beth and Alice. We were happy, what had I done to deserve this? Of course I knew the answer, I should never have entered Queen's Park. I should have heeded the warning.

'Mum.' Alice shook my shoulders.

She made me jump. I wanted to be left alone. 'Not now, Alice.'

But she kept leaning all over me, nudging my arms and peering into my eyes. 'Mum.'

'Not now.' I pushed her away.

She stumbled, caught her balance then stared at me. Tears streamed down her face. She shrieked, 'I hate you,' and ran out of the room.

'I'm sorry, Alice. I'm so sorry,' I called. Whatever possessed me? I heard Jack's voice in my head. *I'm ashamed of you. How could you treat our daughter that way?* Oh my God, what had I done, how could I behave like that?

Nancy glared at me. 'Do you know how long I spent getting her to forgive you? You don't deserve her forgiveness. You don't know how lucky you are to have such a beautiful daughter. She's kind, loving and patient.' She brushed past me.

'I know, I'm sorry,' I shouted, but it was too late, she was gone. I ran into my bedroom and dropped onto the bed.

Soon there was a tap on the door. Charlotte entered. 'Grace.' She sat next to me and cradled me in her arms. 'Hey, come on. What happened to that new beginning?'

'I've made such a mess of things. Nothing will ever be right. I've let Jack down.'

'Shh, it'll be all right.' She kissed me lightly on the cheek.

'It will never be all right and it's all because I walked through those stone sentinels. No matter how hard I try, things will keep going wrong.'

Charlotte shook her head. 'You and I are going on a little trip. Pack a small bag. I'll sort it with Nancy. Get yourself ready, wash that face, then go and see that daughter of yours.'

'What about the shop?'

Charlotte tilted her head back and let out a loud laugh. 'Now you're worried about the shop. It will carry on the same as it has for the last few months. A couple more days without you won't make any difference.'

She left the room, I began sorting clothes and wondered where she was taking me but didn't argue. Once I'd packed, I swilled my face with water before going to find Nancy and Alice.

'I'm sorry, Alice. Please forgive me. Charlotte's taking me away for a couple of days. I promise when I'm back I'll make it up to you.'

Alice barely looked at me. Nancy gave me a false smile. 'I hope so,' she said.

Chapter 15

'Where are we going?' I asked Charlotte as I climbed into the passenger seat of the car.

'Close the door.'

'Are you going to tell me?'

'We're going to put an end to this overactive imagination of yours.'

'What do you mean?'

'We're going to Bolton to visit Queen's Park.'

'You can't be serious?'

'I am.'

It wasn't long before we linked up with the M1 and drove in silence along the motorway. Luckily the travel sickness I'd experienced as a sixteen-year-old had resolved itself. Charlotte was going to make things worse. She couldn't force me to walk through the entrance. I wouldn't. She couldn't make me. As we raced past the countryside other cars went faster and overtook. Oncoming headlights made my head hurt. Part of me wanted to be there quickly while the other part didn't want to arrive. How could she think this would make things right? She didn't understand. Those sentinels had haunted me since the day I'd been encouraged to enter. Everything had gone wrong since that day. My parents disowning me, Katy's suicide, losing the Gilmores, Jack, George and then Beth. Eventually I'd lose Alice, Nancy and Charlotte. I'd be left alone. Alone like I deserved to be. All I did was bring unhappiness to everyone. If only I'd never gone to Bolton but then I wouldn't have met Jack. If, if, if, I screamed silently.

'We'll be pulling onto the M6 shortly,' Charlotte said. 'Nearly there. We'll stay in a hotel overnight and then go to Queen's Park in the morning. The weather forecast is dry and sunny.'

'Do you think we could drive over to Wigan before we go back home?' I asked, 'I'd like to visit Jack's grave.'

'Of course.' Charlotte placed her hand on my arm. 'I thought we'd stay the night in Halliwell Lodge. It's supposed to be exquisite and has a good history.'

'No, Charlotte, not there. That's where Jack and I spent our wedding night.'

'Sorry, Grace. I'd no idea. We'll find somewhere else.'

I thought back to that night, the night I lost my virginity and became a woman in the full sense. I pictured Jack's caresses and tried to imagine his scent but I couldn't remember. Why couldn't I remember, why did it have to fade? My beloved Jack whom I'd let down, just as I'd let my children down. Charlotte felt she was going to make everything right with this trip but how could she? What did she know?

She pulled up outside a small inn. *The Frogsman Arms.* It looked dingy, not that it bothered me but I was surprised Charlotte had chosen a place like this.

'This will do,' she said, 'we need to get some sleep. I'm too tired to drive any more. Let's hope they have room at the inn.' She laughed at her joke.

We walked through the door. Workmen were leaning at the bar, drinking pints of beer. Wolf whistles were directed at us, although why anyone would find reason to offer me one I'd no idea.

'Do you have a twin room with an ensuite?' Charlotte asked the barman.

'We 'aven't got one of them I'm 'fraid. We're not that posh, we donna 'ave that kind of luxury, but we do 'ave a room with a bathroom opposite,' he said. 'Top of stairs, second on right.' He handed her a set of keys. 'Du want somethin' to eat? Can't offer anythin' cooked but me wife could rustle up some sarnies if ya like?'

'That would be nice. Coffee too?'

'Yeah sure. Go on up, ya donna wanna hang around 'ere.' He looked around, signalling at the rowdy crowd.

213

We strolled across the low-beamed room and up the steep narrow stairs. Charlotte turned the key in the lock and pushed open the door.

'It doesn't look too bad,' she said.

I looked around, twin beds with matching blue covers and a small mahogany chest of drawers in-between. A large matching wardrobe and dressing table stood on the opposite wall. It was quaint but not what Charlotte was used to, although she didn't seem to mind at all.

'Take the bed by the window if you like,' she said.

'Thank you.' I bounced on the bed to test its comfort.

There was a tap on the door. Charlotte opened it to find a young girl around fifteen-years-old holding a tray stocked with plates of sandwiches and coffee. Charlotte placed some change into the girl's palm before closing the door. We screwed up our noses as we chewed on the sandwiches and then undressed for bed.

'Try to sleep. It'll be a long day tomorrow,' Charlotte whispered.

*

We stepped out of the car, Queen's Park faced me. I tried to avert my eyes so I wouldn't see the statues but slowly I forced myself to look. They looked like sentinels from here. I walked closer, still nothing. I lifted my hand and touched one with the tip of my finger, brushing it across a small stone cross on top. I didn't understand. 'These are what I've been so fearful of.'

'Are you afraid now?'

'No.' I laughed. 'It seems ludicrous that I was. They're just like little church windows, set in rock. I don't know why I feared them so much. It's just an entrance. This must have been what the others saw.'

'Exactly. At sixteen you had an overactive imagination and you've carried that memory with you all these years.'

'How could I have been so stupid?'

214

'Not stupid, impressionable. I'm surprised you never became a writer, but then I suppose you used that imagination to create fascinating fashion, instead.'

'So it wasn't my fault. It wasn't my fault that all the bad things happened?'

'No.'

'All these years I've tormented myself.'

As we walked through the opening and around the park, I reminisced the good times I'd shared with Jack and Katy. This time without feeling I'd sealed their fate. We stopped at a round stone bank, I'd sat there with Jack. 'This is known as the Pie Crust, I said. 'It was a meeting place for courting couples. If you look across over there you can see the mill chimneys.'

She used her hand to shield her eyes from the sun. 'Oh yes. Is this where you shared your first kiss?'

'No.' I thought back to the first time Jack kissed me, it was only a peck on the cheek but it was the first time any man had shown that kind of interest. It was after our first meeting in the Palais. The night my life changed.

'Come on, let's go.' Charlotte took my arm.

We climbed back into the car and drove towards Wigan.

'Are you hungry, Grace?' Charlotte asked.

'Not especially. You?'

'To be honest, I'm famished. We only had those awful sandwiches for dinner last night. Do you mind if we stop at a café and get some food?'

'No, of course not.'

The roads were fairly empty so we had a smooth drive and arrived in less than thirty minutes. Charlotte parked the car.

'There used to be a café around the corner,' I said.

We hurried out of the vehicle and made our way around. It was still there. Many a cup of tea and snack had been shared in there with Jack, Katy and Eddie. That all seemed a lifetime ago now. The café was empty. We pushed the door open and a dark-haired man smiled. I didn't recognise him but then it had been many years since we'd made our regular visits. It looked the same inside.

215

'What can I get you lovely ladies?' the waiter asked.

'Egg and chips, twice?' Charlotte looked at me to confirm.

I smiled. 'And a pot of tea for two, please.'

It wasn't long before steaming plates of dinner were placed in front of us. The smell of salt and vinegar made my tummy rumble.

'How are you feeling now,' Charlotte asked as we ate.

'Quite relieved to be honest. But I think it's going to take me time to be normal again.'

'Grace, of course it will take time, but you've climbed the first step.'

'It seems silly but I'm really nervous about visiting Jack's grave. I feel like he'll know what I've done and condemn me for it.'

'You're grieving, Grace. If Jack was here he'd tell you the same.'

'There used to be a florist close to the cemetery, I'd like to pick up something to put on Jack's grave before we go in.'

'Of course.' Charlotte patted her stomach. 'That's better, I was very hungry.'

I managed to eat most of mine too, although I thought I wouldn't. Charlotte left a few coins on the table for a tip.

We made our way to the little florist and I purchased one red rose. That's all I wanted. I held it carefully to avoid the thorns sticking in my fingers. My nose became itchy almost immediately. 'Hayfever,' I said.

'Would you like me to come in with you?' Charlotte asked as we approached the gates.

'Why don't you wait on a bench inside so I can visit Jack on my own?'

Our shoes crunched on the gravel footpath. I left Charlotte sitting on a wooden seat, quite close to the entrance and wandered towards Jack's final resting place as I clung to the deep coloured bloom.

His grave was bare, but then there was no one to bring flowers. He lay here with his mother and father. I felt ashamed that I hadn't been back before.

'Jack, my darling Jack. I've let you down so much. I gave George up, let Beth die and Alice, poor Alice. I stopped being a mother to her. I've turned into a bad woman and not the loving, kind one that you married. This all ends now. I promise you, I'm going to try to put things right. I'll get George back and I'll make it up to Alice. Forgive me, dear husband, forgive me,' I sobbed.

I kissed the red rose before laying it on dry dirt. It was time to begin again. It wasn't going to be easy but I had to attempt to put everything behind me. Thankfully I had good friends and a daughter that needed me. I knew what I had to do.

Chapter 16

It took over six months to regain Alice's trust but gradually we rebuilt our bond. That wasn't to say I didn't have moments where I slid back into darkness, because I did, but at least I was slowly moving on.

I started writing to George again but the letters always came back unopened. More than once I trekked down to *Granville Hall* to see him but never got past the servants, nor did I ever see Mother.

Alice and Nancy walked into the sitting room, curious.

'What's all this about?' Nancy asked.

Charlotte and I had been talking and after making a few preliminary decisions, we'd come up with a plan. Now we needed Alice and Nancy to approve it. Hence a family meeting.

'You'll see.' I smiled. 'Wait until Charlotte arrives.'

'Please, Mum. Can't you tell us now?'

'No.' I tickled my daughter around the waist. She giggled loudly. 'You can pour tea for the grown-ups, and squash for you. And don't eat all the cake.' I laughed.

The doorbell rang. 'That'll be Charlotte. Can you let her in please?'

Alice skipped out of the room and returned arm in arm with my friend. It seemed my daughter had three mums.

Nancy and Alice sat sipping their drinks.

'Charlotte and I have been talking the past few weeks about our future. We think we need a fresh start. A house with a garden, away from London for starters. Would you like that, Alice?'

'Yes, I'd like to play outside in a garden,' Alice answered.

'And how do you both feel about Charlotte moving in with us? After all she spends most of her time here.'

'Yes please, Mum.'

'Nancy?'

'Yes it sounds good but we need to choose a place big enough for us all. We've got used to all this space.'

'Naturally,' Charlotte said, 'we're thinking a large detached house. Take a look at these, what do you think?' She passed some leaflets to Nancy.

'Can we afford it?'

'Yes we think so. The shop profits are up and I will have money from the sale of my flat,' replied Charlotte.

Alice looked over Nancy's shoulders. 'Cheam, where's that?'

'It's just outside London,' I said, 'but a nice area and good schools.'

'Will George be able to find us?'

'Yes, I'll make sure he knows where we are.'

'Is there a reason why there's a cottage on the land too?' Nancy asked.

'Yes, for Ted and Joan. They will come too. We need a driver to ferry us backwards and forwards to London and Joan will take on the post as housekeeper.'

'But Joan's our best machinist,' Nancy said.

'She can still sew at home. However, we need to employ more staff as that's not all the news.'

'What else, Mum?' Alice asked.

'We've had an offer accepted on a large unit in Oxford Street.'

'Oxford Street?' Nancy grinned.

Our dream to be up there with *Selfridges* looked like it was finally going to happen. I had lots more to tell but I wanted them to take things in slowly. The plan was to start designing children's clothing too and have a pre-opening fashion show in the new store.

'What about this shop,' Nancy asked, 'is it going up for sale?'

'No, we'll get a manager.'

There was a lot to be done, staff to interview, designs to complete as well as finding a new home, and a school for Alice.

'I like this one, Mum.' Alice passed the paper. It was detached with ten bedrooms, a side cottage and set on an acre of land.

'That's my favourite too. We'll look at that one first.'

Signs of normality were creeping back into our lives after what seemed a very long time.

*

Charlotte sat behind the steering wheel. I was in the passenger seat, holding a map, acting as navigator, while Nancy and Alice spread out behind us on the bench seat.

'This looks like it.' Charlotte drove the car through the metal gates.

I gazed out of the window as we entered the driveway. Branches swung on blossomed trees, daffodils and tulips bobbed their heads in the soft breeze. It was a beautiful clear blue sky. They say spring is for new beginnings. This was a new beginning for us all. I had high hopes about this house, something inside told me it was going to be just right.

'Wow, it's enormous,' Alice said.

Surrounded by a brick wall and trees was a pillared porch. The cottage was quaint and situated near the gate entrance. I imagined Jack and I could have been happy living there.

A van pulled up and a young man wearing glasses stepped out. 'Ah, Mrs Gilmore and Miss Cunningham, I'm pleased to see you again.' He held out his right hand. After greeting us he took a bunch of keys from his pocket. 'Would you like to see the house first and then the cottage?'

I looked across at Charlotte. 'Yes, that sounds like a good idea.'

He unlocked the door and we ventured into a large room with stone flooring and a wide stairway in the middle of the room. 'This is the hall,' he said.

'Wow,' Alice said.

It had bay windows, and large yucca plants stood in pots on the floor. The spring scent from the garden hung in the air. We stepped upstairs and one by one peeped in at each of the six double bedrooms, four single rooms and three bathrooms. We made our way back downstairs and found a large kitchen, dining room, living room and library. Yes, this seemed perfect. I turned to Alice. 'What do you think?'

'I love it Mum.' She hugged me tightly.

Charlotte and Nancy peered out of one of the downstairs windows. 'It's wonderful to see all the greenery,' Nancy said. 'I've never lived anywhere with a garden, never mind all these fields and trees.'

Of course I'd experienced a much bigger garden and home but that was a lifetime ago. Nancy had only ever lived in a two-up and two-down terraced. Charlotte was used to living in a large home with a garden but she'd be gaining company as part of a family.

'There's still the cottage to see,' the young man said. He led the way.

The walls were painted white with a pillarbox red door, window frame and sills. The agent turned the key and we followed him in. He stooped to avoid touching the low beams. 'It only has two bedrooms, is that enough?'

'Yes, that's quite sufficient.' Thank goodness Ted wasn't very tall, he wouldn't have a problem banging his head. I took note of the small sitting room and kitchen. As I climbed the steep narrow stairs it took me back to my home in Wigan. The two bedrooms were about the same size too. This little cottage, however, had a bathroom added on downstairs, unlike our old home. Ted and Joan could be happy here, it was more than adequate. They even had their own little garden where daffodils bobbed in the light wind.

Conversation was busy, everyone excited and talking at the same time. Charlotte cornered me. 'What do you think? Shall we make an offer?'

'Without a doubt,' I said.

She took the young man to the side and they shook hands.

Chapter 17

Wooden crates stood high in the new house as the removal men continued to bring in furniture. I peered out of the window into the large garden where June roses bloomed. I had to wait until around August before my favourite flower, the burnt orange cactus dahlia displayed its beauty. Part of me felt like I'd come home.

I turned back to the box in hand and pulled out a gold frame housing an old school photograph of George and Alice. It was the last one of them together. George's skinny limbs and beaming grin made me laugh. Alice had changed a great deal. Long straight hair replaced short blonde curls and the mischievous little girl had become serious. I wondered what George was like now.

'When will George come home, Mum? I still miss him. Do you?'

I hadn't realised that Alice had come into the room. 'I don't know, darling, but I'll never stop trying to get him back. There isn't a day that goes by that I don't miss him.'

'I miss Beth too. Why do bad things have to happen?'

'Come here.' I hugged my daughter. 'That's all behind us. We've got a fresh start in this lovely house and you'll be starting a new school next week.'

'How many weeks are there, before summer holidays?'

'Only about four, but long enough for you to make new friends,' I answered.

'I'm going to tell Nancy.' Alice ran out of the room.

I wondered if George had filled out. He was thirteen now. Was he quiet, shy and serious or confident and funny? My parents could have kept in touch. They could have sent photographs and let me know how he was getting on. How could they be so cruel? I put the photo down on the windowsill and reminded myself that this was a new beginning.

I must remain positive, one day I'd see my son again. I heard footsteps behind me.

'What's going on here?' Charlotte laughed. 'You haven't time to go down memory lane today, there's too much to do.' She picked up my design pad and flipped through. 'These are looking good, are you finished?'

'Nearly there, just a few touch ups to do.'

'Wow, Grace, I love the contrast with the flirty miniskirts and maxi dresses. And the fabrics, plain against psychedelic spots and stripes.'

'What about the teen range?' I asked.

'Love it,' she said, 'the plaid pleated skirts are so fetching and checked flared dresses belted at the waist, so flattering. And the slacks, I love the patterned ones. Are you going to do slacks for ladies too?'

'Yes and I intend to do an underwear range.' This fashion show had been exactly what I needed to start again and think ahead to the future. I thought back to the first pair of trousers I designed for Elizabeth and myself. The night Father first turned against me. He wasn't always bad, when I was little he used to take me into his study and show me how the business worked. I think he had high hopes for me until he discovered I was set on my dress designing which he saw as rubbish.

'Grace?'

I jerked back to reality.

'No time for daydreaming. I was saying, are you going to do some of those new push up type bras?'

'Sorry, yes, I am.'

'Look we've got time for a quick coffee. There's something I want to talk to you about, now the removal men have gone.' Charlotte left the room and returned with a tray holding two cups and a plate of plain biscuits. 'Come, sit down.' She ushered me to the table and chairs that had appeared a few moments before.

I wondered what she had in mind this time. We'd managed to acquire two units in Oxford Street, upstairs and downstairs.

The shopfitters were working at it now. Charlotte had sorted that side of things.

She passed me a cup of coffee. 'I want you to meet someone. Adriéne Ardant, he's a French fashion designer that specialises in menswear.'

I could see where she was going with this. I hadn't really got into menswear, although I'd explored the possibility and the store could do with a section.

'What we want is to get the whole family in and shop. Also, Nancy has expressed an interest in textiles. I think we should send her to college. What are your feelings?'

'It's a great idea.' I didn't know why I hadn't thought of it myself. Nancy had always been creative in her little house in Wigan. It was quite unique with rag-rugs and café style curtains.

Charlotte brushed her hands together and stood up. 'That's settled then. I'll get in touch with Adriéne and arrange a meeting in town tomorrow. The Savoy or the Ritz?'

'I think I prefer the Savoy.'

'I'll book us in there then. You'll like Adriéne, he's a lovely chap, good looking too.'

I laughed and felt my face flush.

'I'll get Nancy to start looking for courses to start in September. I'll leave you to your designs.' She left the room.

I stayed sitting at the table and added a few finishing touches, they needed to go off to the cutters by this evening and the machinist's tomorrow. We had three months before the store pre-opening evening fashion show. It really was quite exciting. I wished that George could be here to share it too. I decided that I'd write another letter. He'd be home from school shortly for the summer vacation.

*

Charlotte and I were meeting Adriéne at four for tea. Nancy and Alice were going to the park. I dressed carefully with sophistication. I wanted to make an impression on Adriéne, show him that I'd only accept top class fashion. The purple linen jacket hugged my waist while the matching skirt showed my slim figure. I stepped into black stilettos and slipped a handbag over my shoulder.

'Ah, you're ready?' Charlotte said, 'Ted's outside waiting.'

Ted and Joan were settled into their little cottage and already they'd been out in the garden making their mark.

'Bye,' I called upstairs to Alice and Nancy. 'Have a nice time at the park. Joan's making dinner for seven thirty. We'll be home by then.'

The door slammed as it shut. I took the steps slowly in my high heels and climbed into the car. Not quite a Rolls but a nice silver Daimler. Ted looked handsome in his grey uniform and matching peak hat.

'We're going to The Savoy, Ted,' Charlotte told him.

He put the car into gear and began our journey into London. Luckily the traffic wasn't too bad and we managed to get there within half an hour. It was warm and sunny, I felt a bit hot in my linen suit and longed to slip off the jacket.

Before we got out of the car I noticed creases in my skirt. I should have thought twice about wearing this fabric. 'Look at the state of me.'

'It'll drop out, Grace. It's only a couple of wrinkles.'

'Well I hope so. I want to make a good impression. I don't want him to think we'll accept sloppy workmanship. Nothing but the best for *House of Grace.*'

'He's meticulous Grace. You'll see. You're going to love him.'

My heartbeat quickened. What was the matter with me? I was behaving like a school girl on a blind date. This was a professional appointment not social. I took out my lipstick and compact from my purse. My hands shook as I traced the red crayon around my lips. Good God woman, this was a business meeting.

Ted opened the door and took my hand to aid me out of the vehicle.

'Come back at six thirty,' I told him.

'Very well, Grace.'

I was on a first name basis with all of my staff. I didn't feel superior to any of them. In fact a lot of them had never been as low in class as I was when living as a coal miner's wife, not that I'd have changed a moment of that. They were the happiest days of my life, albeit the toughest.

We walked through the foyer of the hotel.

A uniformed porter smiled with recognition. 'Good afternoon, ladies. If you'd like to go on through to the restaurant.'

We strolled on and the maître d' greeted us. 'Your table's ready, Mrs Gilmore, Miss Cunningham.' He put up his hand and a young waitress came over.

'Follow me,' she said.

Normally I liked to sit by the bandstand to listen to the piano but as it was a business meeting, Charlotte had requested a quiet position. As we approached our table I could see a dark haired man in a suit, seated already. He stood up when we arrived.

'Charlotte.' He kissed her hand. 'And this must be the lovely Grace?' He kissed my hand too.

'How do you do, Adriéne?' I willed my heart to stop pounding, I felt sure it would give me away. This man was gorgeous with his bronze tanned skin, sleek hair and immaculate clothing. Just as Charlotte promised.

'You like to see my designs?' He pulled out a notebook, not dissimilar to the ones I used myself. I flicked through the pages trying to hide my enthusiasm. He was very talented. Yes, we should have him on board with *House of Grace*. The waitress came along with the trolley. It was crammed with finger sandwiches, scones and cakes. She filled our cups with tea, while I continued to study Adriéne's drawings.

'You like?' he asked.

'I like.' I laughed. 'I think this calls for champagne. Waitress, can you bring a bottle please?'

She was back in no time, uncorked the bottle and poured fizzy liquid into fluted glasses.

'To new beginnings,' I said.

'New beginnings,' Charlotte and Adriéne replied in unison.

Chapter 18

Three months whizzed by. Thankfully everything was in place for the pre-opening fashion show, to be held in the new shop at Oxford Street, opening on Monday. *House of Grace* was going big and it would soon be a match for *Selfridges*.

Alice settled well into her new school before the summer holidays and she was looking forward to returning next week to be with her latest friends. Adriéne had not only become an asset for the business but also a close companion. Together, we enjoyed the theatre, ballet and opera. It was nice to benefit from male company. I think he wanted more than to be 'just good friends,' and although I was very tempted, my energies had to lie with taking care of Alice, getting George back and concentrating on the business, apart from the fact I didn't think any man could ever take Jack's place.

'Are you ready?' Charlotte popped her head into the lounge. 'We need to go.'

'Yes, I am.'

'How are you feeling?'

My stomach felt like it was doing flips. 'A bit nervous to be honest.'

'Lucky you've got Adriéne to hold your hand,' Charlotte said, 'where is he? He's cutting it fine.'

I laughed. 'Don't tease. I've got you, Nancy and Alice too, you know. He's meeting us there.' I followed her out to the car. Nancy and Alice were already inside.

'You get in the back with the others and I'll sit in the front,' Charlotte said.

Alice squeezed into the middle. Ted drove the Daimler into London and dropped us outside the shop. I looked up at the banners and coloured balloons hanging from the front.

*

The teenage boys and girls were on first. Alice took the lead. Although only ten years old, she was tall and carried off young fashion just as well as the thirteen and fourteen-year-olds. She stepped into green kitten heel shoes which set off her gold multistripe minidress. To finish it off she flicked a matching jacket across her shoulder, holding it casually in her right hand. She strolled down the catwalk, stopped at the end, twirled, turned back and walked across the stage. The audience clapped loudly. I quivered with pride. Considering everything my daughter had been through, she still bounced with confidence. The other girls followed in different styles of miniskirts, dresses, stripes, spots in linen and cotton textures. Girls in slacks trailed behind. The applause continued. Cameras flashed. It was the boys' turn next. How I wished George could be here to model too, although I wondered if he'd have the same self-assurance as Alice. The first youth, a skinny fourteen-year-old with red hair, headed onto the stage. Black pointed shoes squeaked as he walked across in beige trousers, waistcoat and brown jacket. The rest followed, some with similar styles in a variety of patterns and textures, others in a range of checked shirts and casual, polo knitted jumpers tucked into jeans.

It was half-time, a buffet reception was set up at the side of the show. Waiters and waitresses served champagne while finger food, chicken breasts, devilled eggs, spicy stuffed mushrooms, smoky porcupine cheese balls and various other savouries had been laid out on tables for the audience to consume during the interval.

'What do you think?' Adriéne put his arm around me. I let it linger, enjoying a mixture of security and sensitivity, until I saw Alice heading our way.

'It's going well.' I slipped out of his hold. 'I must congratulate Alice and the other models.'

Alice skipped towards me with Charlotte and Nancy. They each gave me a hug.

'They love it.' Nancy clapped her hands.

'So far so good,' I said. 'Women and menswear next, let's hope we get the same response to them. Alice, well done, darling, I'm so proud of you.' There's no way I could have walked across the platform like she did.

Alice beamed.

'I must go backstage and speak to the boys and girls. Do you want to come with me?'

'Yes Mum.'

We sauntered behind the scenes and one by one I congratulated the young teenagers and handed each of them a brown envelope with their wage. 'I hope you make it to the next show.'

They all nodded with enthusiasm.

'You can go and find your parents now and get something to eat and drink before the start of the second half. You'll find orange juice on the tables.'

Charlotte suddenly appeared. 'Grace.'

'What's the matter?' I asked.

'There's a man in the audience asking for you. He's got a northern accent and said his name is Gilmore.'

Gilmore? Was this some sort of joke?

'Grace, are you all right. Sit down.' She eased me into the nearest chair.

'Jack is the only Gilmore I knew, unless...'

'I'll send him away.'

'No, wait. I need to see. It might be someone else I once knew.'

The blurriness gradually disappeared and I lifted myself slowly from the seat before proceeding to the front of the stage to where the man stood. Was it him? But he looked older. I walked closer.

He smiled, 'Grace?'

'Max? Uncle Max? It is you?' I hadn't seen him for ten years, he'd aged. The lines on his face and greying hair exceeded his years.

'Yes, it's me.' He hugged me tightly. 'You've done very well for yourself, not that I ever doubted it.'

I wondered why he was here now, after all these years. 'Aunt Eliza?'

'No, she isn't with me. She's in America. I was in Bolton, checking on the mill when I saw the headlines in the newspaper about a pre-opening fashion show for *House of Grace*. I'm always on the lookout for new business so thought I'd contact the proprietor to see if I could become a supplier. I'd no idea it would be you until I saw you on the stage. I should have realised. I mean how many more Grace Gilmores into dress design could there be?'

'The mill? I thought you'd sold it?'

'No, I put a manager in. It was all very quick. Have you time for a catch up and coffee later?'

'Yes, of course but after the show. Are you enjoying it?'

'Very much so.'

Charlotte made an announcement using the microphone and asked everyone to return to their seats for the second half. The lights in the audience lowered and the models began to flow. We'd teamed up a male and female together to start off the show. The young woman stepped forward in a green tweed suit trimmed with fur on the collar and cuffs, while her partner held her hand and showed off his black and white checked V-neck jacket. The other females followed in turn, straight plain minidresses with high boots. Then tight jumpers and slacks, but I think my favourite was a purple dress that hugged the waist and twirled when the model swung around. There were cries of approval, whistles and claps. We'd done it. *House of Grace* had definitely arrived.

The press continued to take photographs and at the end came over for a press release. Charlotte took the lead and offered them a statement before more snaps were taken of

Adriéne and me. Bustling crowds left the shop full of chatter. Monday morning was going to be busy.

Once everyone had gone, Adriéne kissed me affectionately on the cheek. 'Dinner?'

'I need to speak to someone first.'

'I was wondering who that old man was?'

'He's kind of a relative. He's my late husband's uncle but more than that, he was like a father to me a long time ago. Let me speak to him and then I'll invite him to join us.'

He took my hand and kissed it. 'Very well, Chérie. Don't be too long.'

I walked over to Max and hugged him.

'That was an amazing show, Grace. You really are very talented, but then I think we always knew that.'

'Come and sit down.' I led him to the side of the room where the chairs hadn't been cleared yet. 'How have you been? And Eliza?'

'I'm fine. As I said earlier, I'm still in textiles and over here for business.' His eyes focused on my face. 'Grace, I can't tell you how good it is to see you again. I expect you wondered why we disappeared from your lives so suddenly.'

'I did wonder. Of course I knew you both blamed me for Katy's death, Jack told me that.'

'I never blamed you Grace, but yes, Eliza did. She needed someone to blame and that was you I'm afraid. She felt if we'd never taken you into our lives then it would never have happened. I couldn't go against my wife's wishes, you understand that?' He pressed my hand. 'Good God, Grace. This feels so good to be here with you. You were like a second daughter to me. It ripped my heart out leaving you after already losing one child.'

'It's all right, Max.'

'I blame myself for Katy's death. I saw her mood swings and should have insisted she saw a doctor. I tried to talk to Eliza but she was blind to it all. I ought to have been firm and made her see.' He wiped his forehead. 'I'd seen moods like that before.'

'Jack's mother?'

'Yes. He told you about her?'

'He worried about Katy too.'

'I know. He brought it to my attention and what did I do? Nothing. I was too weak to argue with my wife that something was wrong with our lovely girl.'

'Max, stop punishing yourself.'

'After the funeral, Eliza...' He gripped my hand tightly. 'After the funeral Eliza couldn't cope with being in England so we packed up and went out to America. Down south, Georgia, a small town, Savannah. I tend to come home, I still call England home, once or twice a year. Unfortunately my wife never returns with me and she's spent the last ten years in and out of mental institutions.'

'I'm so sorry, Max.' I touched his hand. 'We're going for a celebration dinner. Would you like to join us?'

'I don't want to intrude. Perhaps we could meet up tomorrow for lunch, just the two of us? You can tell me what's been happening and what you've done with that fine nephew of mine, Jack.'

'Oh my God, Max. You don't know?'

'What?' Max's face became ghostly white.

Chapter 19

31st July, 1968

Max and I met up several times before he returned to America and then every couple of months or so. It had been comforting having him back in my life over the past two years. He was horrified to hear about Jack's accident and what followed later with George and Beth. *House of Grace* signed a contract to buy his cotton fabric from the mill, although he was rather uncomfortable about it, not wanting to take advantage of our personal connections. But after all, business was business and it was a good arrangement for us both.

The postman disturbed my thoughts as he pushed a bundle of mail through the letterbox, two items in particular were of interest. A brown envelope with a Brighton postmark was the first, I recognised it straight away. It was from Greenemere. Alice had been pestering me for months to allow her to board there. Later on we'd sit down together and browse the brochure. The second, a white, handwritten one with *Granville Hall* stamped on the back was more of a mystery. I ripped it open and pulled out a quality sheet of stationery. It read:

Dear Grace,

Please can we meet? I've made a reservation at The Savoy on the afternoon of 10th August, 1968 at three. I'll try and bring George as he's home for summer vacation.

Yours truly
Elizabeth.

My hand shook. I was going to see George. At last I was going to see my son. 'Charlotte,' I shouted.

She came hurrying into the room. 'What's up? My God you look like you've seen a ghost.'

I held out the letter.

She read it. 'Why now?'

'I don't know but she says she'll bring George.'

'Grace, don't get your hopes up. It says, she'll try.'

'He'll be there. You'll see.'

'I think you'd better sit down. I'll get some tea.' She rang the bell.

Within a few minutes Joan stood in front of me holding a tray. 'Is everything all right, Grace? Have you had bad news?'

'It's actually good news, but a bit of a shock.'

She poured the tea and then tapped my hand. 'That's nice to hear, dear.' She smiled and left the room.

We were due to fly out to Paris a week on Saturday to explore the possibility of setting up a new branch. It made sense with Adriéne's contacts. But it was the same date, August 10th. It was no good, they'd have to go without me.

'Are you going to meet her?' Charlotte broke my thoughts.

'I must go. You do understand? George comes before the business.'

'Yes of course. Don't worry about France, Nancy and I will go. Adriéne can stay here with you.'

'He's not going to like that.'

'Are you kidding? Do you think I haven't noticed?'

'Nothing's happened.'

'Not yet, but only a matter of time. Your secret is safe,' Charlotte said in almost a whisper.

'As long as rumours don't end up in Alice's ears. She's far too impressionable at her age.'

Charlotte hugged me. 'She'd cope fine. You know, Grace, you deserve some happiness. We all need someone.'

'Yes I suppose we do.' I picked up my cup and sipped the warm tea. I wondered when my best friends would find happiness too. It was strange how Charlotte had never married. The letter rustled in my lap and reminded me of my son. How was I going to get through the next ten days? The brochure, yes, I'd show Alice the brochure but she mustn't know about George or the visit. Not yet.

Nancy stormed in. 'What the hell's going on? Why are you sending her away?'

'I'm not. It's Alice's decision. She's been begging to go for ages. You know that.'

'And we said no. And now you've gone ahead.' She pushed the brochure at my face.

'I haven't gone ahead. It's just information.'

'But she's too young.'

'She's twelve, Nancy. By the time she goes, if she goes, she'll be thirteen. Think of her, stuck around the three of us all the time. She needs to be amongst young blood and have opportunities.'

'What, the same opportunities that threw you into the arms of a coal miner?'

'If that's what she does with them, then so be it. But she deserves to have them. It's not like we can't afford it.'

Alice crept in around the door frame. She waved a white handkerchief. 'Is it safe to come in? I can hear you both upstairs. What's going on?'

'It's this nonsense about your mother wanting to send you away.'

I wanted to scream that it wasn't me that wanted her to go away, it was Alice's decision but Nancy wasn't going to listen to any of that. I'd never seen her with so much rage. It was like she hated me. Instead I said softly, 'It's just to look at, that's all.'

'Nancy, it's not Mum, it's me. Mum doesn't want me to go.'

'But why? Are you sure it's what you want?' Nancy was still waving the pages around.

'I don't know, we're just exploring. And maybe if it's the right place. If George ever comes home, then maybe not. I don't know. We've got over a year to decide as Mum says I can't go until I'm thirteen. I want to go to Brighton and wake up to the sea every morning. I want to ride down Bernie the banister and hide from the Head. I want to have a special

236

friend like Mum's Katy. I'm fed up being around the three of you. Look at me, Nancy, I'm not a little girl anymore.'

Now might have been a good time to tell Alice about George, but then I thought, no, it may fall through. We didn't have to make any decisions about Greenemere yet, we hadn't even talked about it and then we'd need a visit and tour. There was still plenty of time.

'I'm sorry, Grace,' Nancy said, her voice still shaking.

Chapter 20

I looked out of the window at my favourite flower, the burnt orange cactus dahlia. It always reminded me of my first time in the Blue Room at *Willow Banks*. Such happy times, such kindness from Katy and the Gilmores, after my parents had thrown me out. So much had happened since.

Last night, Adriéne proposed to me again and like several times before, I turned him down. 'But Chérie,' he'd pleaded, 'why not?' There was too much going on in my life at the moment, my children took precedence. How could I commit to marriage when my first priority lay with getting George home?

I was deep in thought and didn't hear Nancy come in.

'Grace, the phone's been ringing.' She picked it up. 'Gilmore household. May I help you?' Nancy beckoned me. 'And who should I say is calling?' Nancy held the receiver towards me. 'It's Elizabeth.'

I took the phone from her. 'Elizabeth...' As I listened to the voice I stumbled.

'Grace, are you all right?' Nancy dragged a chair over to where I was standing and guided me to sit down.

'Tomorrow then,' I said into the mouthpiece before returning it to its cradle.

'Grace, what is it? You're making me nervous sitting there with your mouth wide open?'

'It was a shock hearing her voice after all these years.'

'You look like you need a drink.' Nancy moved over to the cocktail cabinet.

I stared into space as fluid trickled into crystal.

'Here, drink this.' She pushed a glass of sherry to my mouth.

'It's a bit early.'

'Medicinal. She hasn't cancelled, has she?'

I sipped the warm liquid and raised my face. 'No, she wants to meet a bit earlier, at two.'

'And George?'

'She said, hopefully.'

'Don't get too excited in case he isn't there.' She tapped me affectionately on the shoulder. 'The colour's coming back into your face. You had me worried there. Don't forget Charlotte and I are flying out to Paris first thing?'

'No, I hadn't forgotten, I've arranged for Alice to stay with Joan.'

'You don't think she should go with you?'

'No, not yet.'

'What about Adriéne?'

I shook my head. 'I need to do this on my own. I don't want George to think I've replaced his father.'

'Ted can drive you. He'll be back from the airport by then.'

*

'Good luck.' Charlotte hugged me.

'Thank you. Good luck in Paris too. Phone me and let me know how it goes.'

'Give George a huge hug from me,' Nancy said, 'that's if he remembers me.'

'I hope he remembers me,' I said quietly to myself as they left.

Sleep had refused to come last night as my mind worked overtime. Would George recognise me? Would he hug me? Would he come back home? It was five in the morning before my eyes eventually gave way.

I went to my bedroom and pulled out the batch of letters tied in ribbon from the dressing table drawer. I'd take them with me to show George I'd never forgotten him.

*

Ted dropped me off outside The Savoy and the concierge recognised me immediately.

'Good afternoon, Mrs Gilmore.'

'Good afternoon.' I smiled and continued through to the restaurant.

Although nervous about the meeting, I felt confident about my appearance as I carried off one of my designs in green tweed. Its tight skirt clung just below my knees, and a French knot held my hair neatly in place.

The Maitre d' greeted me at the entrance. 'Mrs Gilmore, nice to see you again. If you'd like to follow me.'

Coloured murals and statues decorated the arched walls and crystal chandeliers hung from the high ceiling. No matter how many times I saw them, they never failed to impress me. I followed the Maitre d' to a table towards the bandstand where a pianist was playing a tense piece of music that matched my mood.

Nervous and excited I pulled out a copy of *The Times* and tried to focus on reading. The music switched to *Flight of the Bumble Bee*, and I wondered if someone was telling me to run. However, at that moment, high-heeled footsteps approached and I looked up to see a woman who seemed familiar.

Stunned, I stood up. 'Elizabeth?' She looked like Mother. The resemblance was uncanny.

'Yes.' She kissed me on the cheek. 'I have the benefit of seeing your photograph from the news.'

I looked around. 'Where's George?'

'He'll be along later. I need to speak to you. Let's sit down.'

My heart was like an erratic drum as I watched her pull back the chair. There were so many questions but where did I start? 'The reservation was in the name of Granville. Why didn't you use your married name?'

'Mother and Father suggested I return to Granville after Gregory died. Particularly, as we weren't blessed with children.' She changed the subject quickly. '*House of Grace* is doing well.' Her eyes focused on the newspaper lying on the table. 'You got what you wanted then? A career as a dress designer.' She paused and looked me directly in the eye. 'And the love of a coal miner.' She clasped her hands. 'I expect you're wondering why I asked you here.'

'Well yes, I was surprised to suddenly get a letter, especially after all of mine have been returned. Why did you never answer?'

'Father forbade it.'

My chest tightened. 'Why didn't you stand up to him?'

'Like you did, when you handed over your son?'

'That's cruel, Elizabeth. You don't know the full story.'

'Maybe I don't. But I do know that if I'd been lucky enough to have had a child, I'd never have contemplated giving him or her up. No matter what the reason. And especially not for money.'

'It wasn't like that. They tricked me. I was desperate. Mother said she'd report me to the authorities and all of my children would be taken away. I couldn't let that happen. I'd just lost my husband and was vulnerable.'

Elizabeth stared back at me, her eyes moist. 'Grace, I had no idea. It must have been awful for you. That's quite a different story to the one Mother and Father tell.' She stood up and put her arms around me.

'Elizabeth, help me get my boy back. Please.'

'I'll do what I can. After we've finished discussing the reason for our meeting, I'll go and find him. Father's ill and wants to see you.'

I was shocked. Had he had a change of heart? 'And Mother? How's she?'

'Not coping at all. Most of the time she sits staring into space by his bedside.'

'Why does he want to see me, after all this time?'

'He's dying. Maybe he wants to put right his wrong. I don't know, but he's been asking for you. He hasn't long.'

'How can he think I'd want to see him after the hell he's put me through? No, I'm sorry.'

'Please, Grace, you're not like Mother and Father. Look inside your heart. Try and forgive.'

'So what's wrong with the mighty man?'

'Cancer. They gave him six months at the beginning of the year, so you see, he's on borrowed time.'

I laughed. 'He's lying, I bet he isn't dying at all. He just wants to manipulate me a bit more.'

'Come and see. Make up your own mind.' A tear caused her mascara to smudge.

'All right then, as it's you who has asked, I'll come. Can you go and bring George in please?'

'Yes, I'll try and tempt him in with the cakes and clotted cream scones. He's got quite a sweet tooth your son.'

She stood up and left me alone at the table. I tried to concentrate on the pianist who was now playing a melancholy piece. My eyes moved to the newspaper where *House of Grace* was featured on the front page, about it going international. A photograph showed Adriéne standing at my side. I rummaged in my bag to make sure the bundles of letters were still at hand. I looked up at the entrance and thought I was seeing a ghost. My breath became short. George? It was George but his shoulders had broadened. He'd become a handsome young man.

I stood up, leaning on the table to steady myself and greeted him. 'George, darling, it's so good to see you.' I went to hug him but he moved away. 'You're the image of your father.'

He shrugged his shoulders.

'Let's all sit down,' Elizabeth said.

George eased the chair from under the table, his face held no emotion.

'I've waited so long for this day,' I said to him.

'Really? I can't think why,' he threw back.

'What do you mean?'

'You sold me. You're a Judas, only you got a bit more than thirty pieces of silver for me, didn't you?'

Just at that moment the waiter appeared at the table. There was silence as he arranged the finger sandwiches, scones with jam and cream and small delicate cakes. It seemed like forever before he finally placed a choice of sliced gateaux in the centre

242

and left. The whole time, George's accusing eyes never moved from my face.

'I didn't sell you,' I said in desperation. 'I was put in a predicament where there was no choice but to let you go with Mother.'

'George, look at all these lovely cakes,' Elizabeth said.

He ignored her and focused on me. 'Have you any idea what it was like to be ripped away from your family, straight after your father's died?'

'I can imagine.'

'No, I don't think you can. Stolen away. Stolen away not just from my mother but my sisters. Where are they? Or did you sell them too?'

'Alice is at home, eager to see you.'

'And Beth? Not that you gave me the chance to know her. She must be about six? Does she look like Alice? Has she got the same Shirley Temple curly hair?'

I wiped my eyes. 'I'm afraid, Beth died.'

'What? When?'

'It was Scarlet Fever, when she was nearly two.'

'Oh my God, it gets better. Now I'll never get the chance to know her. It didn't occur to you to let me know? I should have been allowed to attend the funeral.'

'I tried, George. Really I did. I haven't stopped trying. Not just to tell you about your sister but to get you back home. I've been trying since the day Mother took you, six years ago. I've been to *Granville Hall*, I've written to you, Mother and Elizabeth.'

He looked at Elizabeth. She nodded back in acknowledgement.

'Then how come I never got a letter? Once, I saw you come to the Hall, I tried to wave but the maid pulled me away from the window. I thought you'd come to get me but you didn't. You left me there. Deserted me. You deserted me again.'

'I did come to get you. But she wouldn't let me in.'

'I phoned you once, but you were too busy.' His eyes narrowed.

'Did you say who you were?'

'No, because I could hear you shouting that you didn't want to be disturbed. Too busy for me. After all I was only your son. Why would I count?'

'You've always counted. If I'd known... The last few years have been dominated by trying to get you home.'

'I'm sure. Don't make me laugh.' He picked up the newspaper. 'You're far too busy with your fancy man.' He flung the paper towards my face.

'He's my business partner.'

'Didn' take yuze long to replace me da, did it?'

'George, don't be too harsh on your mother. There are things you don't know. Not just about the letters, but other things that I didn't know about before today. You need to give her a chance.'

He sat still for a moment before dragging his chair back. 'I don' wanna know. I've 'ad enough of this. I wanna go 'ome. I told you I didn' wanna cum.'

I rummaged into my bag and pulled out the large wad of envelopes. 'George, take these, please. Read them and then hopefully you'll understand.'

He snatched the batch from my hands, stood up and left the restaurant without looking back.

'I'll try and make him understand. Give him time. As I said earlier, Mother and Father's tale is quite a different story.' Elizabeth kissed my cheek. 'You'll come to Granville, tomorrow at two?'

'Yes, I'll be there.' I watched her catch up with George, picked up the newspaper to hide my face and sobbed in silence.

244

Chapter 21

The meeting with George spun around my head all through the night. I slept a maximum of two hours. I couldn't believe the resentment and hate in his eyes. Yes, I'd known it wasn't going to be easy after we'd been estranged for six years. However, I did think he'd let me try to explain.

I opened my wardrobe door and took out a lightweight, shift dress. I could get away with its large checks on my slender figure. It was one of my latest designs, smart but fashionable. I wondered why I wanted to impress Mother and Father, after all I didn't really want to see them again. Then I remembered my dream from last night. Jack holding me and caressing me and just before I'd woken with a start, his words, *fight for our son*.

Adriéne had phoned earlier but I feigned a migraine. I didn't want to tell him what was going on. It had nothing to do with him. In fact, I'd made a decision, there was only one man for me and that was Jack. I'm not sure why I contemplated anything more with Adriéne, obviously I'd been momentarily weak but the decision was now made. We needed to resume a purely professional relationship. Getting George back home was my priority.

The house was quiet, Ted and Joan had taken Alice on a picnic. I didn't want to answer any questions as to where I was going so decided to drive myself. I looked at my watch, twelve thirty, time I should be making tracks. I grabbed a long cardigan, draped it over my shoulder and made my way down the steps to my car. At the press of a button the soft roof lowered. I pulled my hair back into a ponytail to keep it away from my face.

*

I waited at the door in trepidation. The last time I'd been here, Mother had been vile. Would it be the same again today? Did she know that Elizabeth had contacted me? Still her threats wouldn't work now, no one would contemplate taking Alice away and I was in a stronger position to fight both her and Father in a court of law to reclaim George.

After what seemed an age Martha opened the door. She hadn't changed much but then I suppose it had only been six years.

'Miss Grace.' She offered no smile.

'Martha.' Who was she to judge me? What did she know?

She showed me into the reception room. 'Miss Elizabeth will be along in a moment.'

I sat down on the chaise longue, it reminded me of the night I'd announced I was pregnant to my parents, my one lie.

A shadow brushed past the open door. I walked over to the opening to catch George rushing towards the stairs. The lemon Ben Sherman tucked into tight denim jeans accentuated his tanned skin and showed off his slim physique.

'George,' I called.

He turned around. 'Oh it's you.'

'Can we talk?'

'There's nothing to say. Have you come with more lies? Grandmother said you always were a liar.'

'Did you read the letters?'

'No need. Nothing will convince me that you didn't sell me.' George took the stairs two at a time and was soon gone.

I wiped my tears. This was going to be harder than I thought, but I didn't want Mother and Father seeing me in a vulnerable state. I closed my eyes and took a deep breath and when I opened them Elizabeth was standing in front of me.

'Are you all right?' she asked.

'I've just seen George. He's still angry.'

'It'll take time, but you have that. Father's waiting.' She took my hand and guided me to a room next to the library. 'Mother converted it for Father as it was easier on the staff than expecting them to go up and downstairs all day.'

Elizabeth opened the door to the old day room. Its previous light and airy feel had gone, instead it was replaced with a dark and dismal look, mainly due to the curtains drawn at the window. Mother sat by the side of the bed reading a book. She looked up at me. 'Grace, so pleased that you made it.'

'Mother.'

She pointed to a high backed chair the other side of the bed. 'Sit by your father. He's sleeping at the moment but I'm sure he'll be awake soon.'

This couldn't be Father. Father was a big strong man, yet here lying in front of me lay a shrivelled prune with tubes connected. His body had barely more flesh than a skeleton. He opened his eyes.

'Grace. Grace is that you?' he said in a soft croaky voice.

'Yes, Father. It's Grace.'

He turned to the nurse who entered the room. 'Help me sit up.'

She rushed to his side and placed more pillows behind his head and leant him back.

'I knew you'd come,' he said to me.

'Did you?'

He signalled to Mother and she turned to the nurse. 'Ellie, take a break. I'll call you if I need you.'

'You too,' Father said.

'I'm just next door.' She left the room leaving Father and I. The door clicked shut.

'Come closer, child,' he said.

His breath smelt sickly and sweet. I put a hand towards my mouth to stop myself from gagging.

'You've done well for yourself. I've been following you. I was wrong in trying to stop you drawing and sewing as a child.'

'Yes you were.'

'But I wasn't wrong about the coal miner.'

'Excuse me?'

'Admit it. If he hadn't died you wouldn't be where you are today. I was right. He was no good for you.'

'How dare you? Is this what you've brought me here for? To tell me that you were right. I don't believe you.'

Mother rushed in. 'What's going on?'

Father put his hand to his chest. 'Grace,' he gasped.

'What have you done?' Mother yelled. 'Ellie come quick. It's all right, Charles.' She took his hand. 'Ellie's here.'

'I'm sorry. I didn't mean to.' I recalled the last time he'd held his chest when we'd argued. I may have despised him but didn't want him to die by my hand.

Ellie dropped a tablet onto Father's tongue and put a beaker of water to his mouth.

'Go now.' Mother nudged me.

'I'm going, but rest assured I'm going to get my boy back.'

Father tugged at my hand. 'No, don't go. Not yet.'

'Why do you want me to stay?'

'I think that you need to rest now, Lord Granville.' The young nurse, whose face was now ashen, stayed calm. She removed the pillows to allow Father to lie back down.

Father released his hold and I sped out of the room, my hands and knees still shaking. Elizabeth was waiting for me.

'You can see he's dying, how could you upset him?' She pulled me towards the library. 'Martha's made tea. You can pour.'

I tipped the pot and the dark fluid trickled into the familiar china. My stomach rumbled so I lifted a bourbon biscuit from the plate. Of course, no wonder I was hungry, I'd skipped lunch.

'What happened in there?' Elizabeth said after a long spell of silence.

'He wanted me to admit that he was right about Jack.'

'Maybe he was. Have you thought about that?'

'How on earth can you say that?'

'Would you be a successful dress designer if he'd lived?'

'I don't know. Possibly. But even so I'd rather have continued life in our little box with Jack than all the money and success in the world. Can't you understand that?'

She didn't answer but stared, puzzled.

248

'You've never been in love, have you?'

'No. Father arranged my marriage.'

'It's different when you really love someone. You become one and know what the other is thinking before they even say it. The day Jack was killed, a spark in me died. My heart was broken. I could never feel like that about any other man, ever again.'

'What, not even that good looking French partner of yours?'

'No, not even Adriéne. No one could make me feel like Jack did.'

'Then you're lucky, Grace, to have experienced such a love.'

'Yes I am. I'm grateful for the happy years that Jack and I had together and for our children. This is why I must get George back. I miss him so much and he belongs with me and Alice.'

'Maybe he belongs at Granville now. He's not the same little boy who arrived here six years ago. He's matured, goes away to a good school. Intelligent. He'll go far.'

'That was the last thing his teacher said to me. *He'll go far.*'

'Then why try and take him away?'

'Because he belongs with his family. He can still go away to school if that's what he wants. I can afford the fees.'

Elizabeth shrugged her shoulders. 'Ask yourself, are you doing this for George or yourself. Mother said you always were selfish.'

I was raging but kept my cool. 'Mother said a lot of things and most of them lies.' I picked up my cup and swallowed the lukewarm liquid before standing. 'Do you think George will see me?'

'No, no chance today. It's going to take time. Will you come again to see Father?'

'I don't think so.'

'I think you should. Please say you'll come again. I'll phone you. By the way, that's a lovely dress. Is it a top seller of yours?'

'It's original, the one and only, Elizabeth. One of my latest designs and I'm keeping it purely for myself. Of course some of the lower market companies will try and make a copy but it won't be the same. I'll design a frock for you too, if you like?'

'That would be lovely. It's nice to see my sister again. Takes me back to the trousers you designed for my birthday. Do you remember? Before everything exploded.'

I laughed. 'Oh yes, you had the first pair that I'd ever done.' I looked at the tailored black pair that she was wearing. 'I see they must have had an impact?'

'It's acceptable now for a lady to wear them. They're comfortable and make me feel more in control.' I watched the smile disappear from her face.

Mother came into the library. 'What are you still doing here? Haven't you done enough damage? He's going to be all right but that's no thanks to you. I can't believe you, Grace, your father invites you back into the home and this is how you repay him. You should be ashamed.'

'I should be ashamed? You should be ashamed, you and him. You stole my son.'

'We gave him a good home. He's been better off here than with you and your corrupting ways.'

'So you admit it. You stole him.'

'Call it what you like. What would you have done if we hadn't given you the money? Where would you be? Where would the children be? As it stands George is doing very well.'

'You could have helped me, Mother, and let me keep George,' I said in a soft voice. 'Or you could have let me stay in touch with him. Sent me photographs, at least, let me know how he was getting on. Let me speak to him on the phone. But no, you cut me off completely and now he thinks I sold him.'

'You did. What else can you call it? You took the cheque and let me take your boy.'

'But I was vulnerable. My husband had just died and you threatened me. And you threatened to have Alice and Beth removed and put in a home if I ever came here again.'

'It was necessary. Your father and I did you a favour. Do you think that you'd be where you are today if I hadn't done that?'

'Unbelievable. And you have the audacity to say I'm selfish.' I picked up my bag from the chair. 'You haven't heard the last from me, Mother. I'll see you in court if necessary.'

Mother smirked. I left the room in a hurry before she could see my wet eyes and made my way outside and into my car. Before turning the key in the ignition, I sobbed.

Chapter 22

Was I a wicked person? Should I have had more compassion for Father? I didn't remember receiving affection from him or Mother but I had respected him until the day he threw me out. Mother lost all rights to respect the day she stole George. So no, I didn't think I was wicked.

Elizabeth asked me to visit the Hall again, but should I? Did I want to? Should I, out of duty? If only Charlotte and Nancy were here then maybe I could talk things through with them. I looked up at the clock. It was only eight, so the middle of the night in the States. I couldn't ring Max now but maybe later?

The clatter of crockery made me turn to the dining room door. Joan was bringing in breakfast. I'd promised to spend today with Alice and take her to Brighton. We were going down by train to visit Greenemere and then make a day of it along the promenade and have fish and chips on the pier. Ted offered to drive but I wanted time alone with Alice, even if it did mean getting a taxi to the school.

'Joan, why don't you and Ted take the rest of the day off? Alice and I can clear up after breakfast?'

'Are you sure, Grace?'

'Yes, it's a lovely day, shame to waste it.'

'I'll make up a picnic hamper for you before I go.'

'No, it's fine. We'll eat out. Go and find Ted, take the car and go somewhere special.' I opened my purse and passed her a twenty pound note.

'Thank you, Grace. But that's too much. It's almost a week's wages.'

'You deserve it. I don't know what I'd do without you and Ted. Apart from anything else you keep me sane.'

As Joan walked towards the door, she bumped into Alice. 'Hey, little one, what's the rush?'

Alice laughed. 'Mum's taking me out and I've overslept. We're supposed to be getting the ten o'clock train.'

'Have a lovely time, Pet.' Joan patted Alice's head before disappearing from view.

Alice and I sat down to eat. She chattered as we drank fresh orange juice and ate buttered toast.

'Time to make tracks,' I said.

*

The taxi pulled up outside Greenemere Abbey. Alice jumped out and stared at the large building as I paid the driver.

I took my daughter's hand. 'Let's go and find Miss Allison.' I'd spoken to her on the phone a couple of weeks ago so I knew she was still there. The six foot wrought iron gate creaked and groaned as I opened it.

'It sounds like a haunted house.' Alice giggled.

'Yes, it does a bit. Think of the stories it will inspire you to write.'

'I'd like that, Mum. Next to designing, writing stories is my favourite. I don't like Maths, not like George did. I wonder if he still loves numbers.'

'I'm sure he does.' We reached the oak front door and I lifted the large knocker.

'Grace, how wonderful to see you. Come in, come in.'

Her face looked vaguely familiar, of course it must be Miss Allison but she'd aged quite a lot over the years. Her hair was salt and pepper, fine lines and wrinkles creased her face. She had the same soft voice though.

She opened the door to her office, marked *Headmistress*, just the same as I remembered from all those years ago. 'Shall we have a chat and then I'll show young ...'

'Alice,' my daughter announced.

'Oh yes, of course it's Alice, your Mother did tell me. My memory isn't what it used to be. I'll show you around after we've had tea. Sit yourselves down. Of course it's quite different with the girls away on vacation. I miss the hustle and bustle of young ladies running along corridors and sliding down banisters when they think I'm not around.' She winked at me before pouring two cups of tea and offered Alice a biscuit from a flowery china plate.

'Ginger nuts, my favourite.' Alice took a bite.

Miss Allison handed my daughter a beaker. 'And Ribena for you.'

'Thank you,' Alice said.

'Grace, it's been amazing to follow your career. I'm so proud. Whatever happened to Katy? Katy Gilmore? Are you still in touch?'

'Unfortunately, she committed suicide when she was still young. Nineteen-fifty-six, I think. Such a waste. I've recently reunited with Uncle Max, her father. He and his wife emigrated to the States after Katy died.'

'Oh I see. How sad. I'm so sorry.' Miss Allison squeezed my hand. 'Now, did I mention that I'm retiring at Christmas?'

'No, no you didn't.'

'This of course means that I won't be here when Alice starts but she'll get a chance to meet the new Head before you commit. How old is Alice?'

'I'm twelve,' my daughter answered.

'She was twelve in April,' I added.

'When were you thinking you'd like her to start?'

'Next September.' I looked at Alice to confirm.

Miss Allison continued to ask more questions before getting Alice to sit a small test. 'This will just give me an idea where you're at with your schooling. If you do well then you'll be invited to come along and sit an entrance exam with the other girls.'Afterwards, Miss Allison showed us around the school, it was surreal walking around empty corridors and strange to think of everything that had happened since Katy and I had shared together.

'Please can I see Mum's old room?' Alice asked.

'Yes, I don't see why not. Of course your mother had the finest room in the house. Nothing but the best for Lord Granville's daughter. Grace, how is your father?'

I wasn't sure what to say. If I told her he was dying then Alice would know I'd seen him. It made me think of his emaciated figure and strangely enough this brought a tear to my eye.

'Oh my dear. What is it?' Miss Allison moved closer.

'It's nothing. It's just that I've had nothing to do with my parents since they disowned me when I married Jack, my late husband.'

'Really? I'd have thought that Lord and Lady Granville would be extremely proud of their talented daughter.'

I shrugged my shoulders. We reached my old room. 'Here it is,' I said to Alice and she ran in.

I held Miss Allison back. 'Actually, I've recently seen my parents, but I don't want my daughter to know yet. Father is dying. Cancer.'

'Oh dear, I'm sorry. I'm surprised it hasn't been on the news?'

'I think they're trying to keep it quiet.'

'Mum, come and see. It's better than you said.' Alice led me by the hand into the room and across to the window. The tide was coming in and we watched a large wave crash to the edge.

I'd forgotten how magnificent this view was.

'May I have this room if I come here, Miss Allison?'

'I'm not sure Alice, it would be up to your Mother.' She looked across at me. 'It is the most expensive.'

'Money won't be a problem,' I said. 'Of course, you'd have to share, it's a two person room. Isn't that right, Miss Allison?'

'Yes, it is, dear.'

Alice's eyes matched her smile. 'I hope I make a special friend like you did. I love it here, Mum. Please can I come?'

'We'll talk about it at home. But I can't see why not. If that's what you want?'

'Thank you, Mum.'

'We've taken up enough of your time, Miss Allison, but I'd like to come and see you again before you retire.'

'I'd like that too, Grace. I look forward to it.' She shook my hand before turning to Alice. 'It was good to meet you, young lady, I'm only sorry that I won't be around when you start. Your mother was one of my favourite pupils you know?'

'Really?' Alice and I said in unison.

'Really.' Miss Allison laughed.

As we wandered out I thought about my life since the last time I walked away from this place. So much had happened. I'd been disowned, married, had children, widowed, lost George and then Beth. I'd gone from wealth to poverty and built an empire. I suppose I had Mother and Father to thank for my determination. Nothing else though. I'd phone Max when we got home and ask his advice as to whether I should visit Father again.

Chapter 23

Adriéne was flying out at noon to finalise things with his contacts. The new shop and factory should be open within three months. This meant he'd need to spend a lot of the next year in Paris, probably a relief to us both. For me, so I didn't get his persistent proposals and puppy dog eyes and it would give him space after I'd supposedly broken his heart.

It was now over a week since I'd been to *Granville Hall* and I still hadn't made a decision whether to return. If I was going to go then I needed to do it before George went back to school, on the off chance that I'd see him. I'd hoped to have talked things through with Max but unfortunately when I telephoned I was informed that he was in China on business and wasn't expected back for another couple of weeks. I was just finishing off my lipstick when there was a tap on the bedroom door.

'Joan? What is it?'

She squeezed my hand tightly. 'Grace, your sister Elizabeth has been on the telephone.'

I'm sure there were questions that she wanted to ask as she'd never heard me talk about a sister. 'Does she want me to ring her?'

'She said to come quickly. She said your father only has a few hours left.'

I still hadn't had time to talk to Charlotte. What should I do? Joan answered for me.

'You should go quickly. Ted's got the car ready outside. I'll get your raincoat, it's pouring.'

'Don't mention this to Alice. Please.'

'I won't. Go, you'll regret it for the rest of your life if you don't.'

'Tell the others that I've had to go out on business.'

She put her finger to her lips. 'Your secret's safe with me. Hurry.'

I made my way downstairs, taking care not to wake the rest of the household so I didn't have to answer unwanted questions. Ted was waiting as promised. I stepped into the car and we drove off in silence. The windscreen wipers danced backwards and forward aggravating my nausea.

*

I climbed out of the car and stepped into a puddle. The rain was torrential and it took me back to the day all those years ago when I'd seen George at the window. Why hadn't I been more persistent? He said he thought I'd come to fetch him and felt deserted. If only I'd been stronger but suppose Mother had carried out her threat, how would that have helped George, Alice or Beth?

Eventually, Martha opened the door.

I shook out the umbrella and passed her my drenched coat. 'I know where to go.' I rushed along the corridor and found the door open, it was crowded inside. Mother was by the bed, George's arm around her shoulder. Elizabeth was on the other side of the room, deep in conversation with a doctor. My sickness increased with the stale stench.

Elizabeth spotted me and signalled. 'He's been asking for you,' she said, before taking my hand. 'It won't be long now.' She wiped her eyes.

Mother sobbed. Her whole body shook. George was trying to hide his tears.

'Father, Grace is here,' Elizabeth said.

'Grace?' he whispered.

'Yes, Father, it's me. I'm here.' I couldn't believe the change in just over a week. His voice was so tiny that I could barely hear, and the small amount of flesh that had covered him on my last visit had left his body.

'I'm sorry,' he whispered.

'Sorry?'

'Sorry, Grace.' He touched my hand and closed his eyes. The machine bleeped. Mother gasped. The doctor hurried over, lifted Father's eyelids to shine his torch.

The bleeps stopped, leaving a straight line.

Mother pushed past me and fell on Father, wrapping her arms about him.

Elizabeth was at her side. 'Come along Mother.' She lifted her and directed her out of the room.

I reached out to George but he moved away towards the door. I followed.

Elizabeth was waiting for me. 'How do you feel?' She clasped my hand.

'I'm not sure.'

'Don't you feel anything?'

I shrugged my shoulders. 'And you?'

'Sick, that's how I feel. I can't believe that you don't feel anything. He's our father. Perhaps it's time for you to go. I'll be in touch about the funeral.'

'Please do,' I said. We walked along the hall and caught up with Mother.

'Why couldn't you have married one of the Anson twins, like he wanted?' she said to me.

'What?'

'There's nothing wrong with an arranged marriage. Mine was arranged and we grew to love each other, you'd have done so too. Instead your poor father died full of regret. You wrecked our family.'

'It's all right, Mother, Grace is going now.' Elizabeth led her to the library and signalled me to leave. 'The doctor wants to give you a sedative.'

Martha was ready at the front entrance with my Mac and umbrella. She opened the front door. 'Miss Grace.'

It had stopped raining. Ted was at the bottom of the steps and opened the car door. 'Are you all right, Grace?' He tapped my upper arm.

*

Charlotte was at the window when we returned.

'My God, you look terrible,' she said.

I sobbed in her arms.

'You need a drink.' She strolled over to the cocktail cabinet and poured a sherry. 'Here, drink.'

I sipped the warm fluid.

'The colour's coming back into your face, you gave me a fright. You need to tell Alice,' she announced. 'She has the right to know about her brother before he suddenly turns up out of the blue.'

'I don't want to get her hopes up.'

'She's old enough to cope and she'll never forgive you if she hears it from someone else. Tell her where you've been. You don't have to tell her about the earlier meeting but she needs to know where you've been today and about her Grandfather's death. It's going to be on the news. She knows that Lord Granville has been standing between you and George. You must tell her.'

Alice walked in the room.

'No time like the present,' Charlotte said.

'Tell me what?'

'Sit down, Alice.' I looked up at Charlotte.

'I'll leave you to it,' she said.

'I've been to *Granville Hall*,' I said.

Alice sat still on the couch. 'Did you see George?'

'Yes but we didn't speak.'

'Why not?'

'Wait, Alice, there's more. The reason I went there this morning was because my sister telephoned to tell me to come.'

'For George?'

'No, because my father was dying and wanted to see me.'

'And did you?'

'See him? Yes. He died a few minutes after I arrived.'

'Does that mean George can come home now?'

'George is very upset about losing his grandfather.'

'How could he be? Grandpa was wicked. He kidnapped George.'

260

'We have to be patient. I'm hoping in time that he'll read our letters and then know the truth.'

Chapter 24

A week later, Ted drove me to St James's Church. Elizabeth and I decided it was best that I made my own way rather than leaving from the family home. At least the sun was shining. Lettered wreaths labelled *Husband* and *Father* lay across the mahogany coffin carried on the shoulders of six men. My flower arrangement of white chrysanthemums, red roses and trailing blue lobelia lay on the ground.

Mother stood by the door with the minister, her plain black suit accentuating her thinness. My eyes focused on the back of the young man next to her in the expensive tailored suit. From this view I could be forgiven for not at first realising it was my son.

Elizabeth, her bun hidden under a net veiled hat, signalled me to join her. 'I'm glad you came. But no scenes please. Today is about burying Father.'

'I'm here for you and George.' I took a moment before adding. 'Mother too, if she needs me.'

The pallbearers began their journey down the aisle, Mother and George behind, and in turn we followed the procession until Father was set down and the family directed to the front pew.

Elizabeth ushered me to the opposite side. 'It's for the best,' she said, 'I'll sit with you.'

The church filled. Men and women were uniform in black. Choir boys, dressed in red and white, led the congregation in song. I didn't recognise the hymn and was unable to focus on the words but it was dull and gloomy, a complete contrast to Jack's funeral. Prayers were said including The Lord's Prayer, a few verses from the Bible and a Eulogy conducted by a friend of Father's. I wondered why I was here, after all he'd disowned me years ago.

The coffin carriers picked up Father and began the procession outside towards the graveyard. So many people, there must have been more than two hundred, so many more than Jack's. And poor Beth's was a very quiet affair. I hung back with Elizabeth to let Mother and George go ahead.

Elizabeth passed me a white rose. 'For when it's time.'

I shook my head. 'No, I don't think so.'

'Grace, please don't show Mother up in public. The Press are here and they'll pick up something isn't right. Please?'

I took the rose. Why did people drop roses? A rose for Jack, a rose for Beth and now a rose for Father. But it was different for my husband and daughter, their flowers were full of love but what did this one say? It was for show. Nothing more.

Elizabeth linked her arm in mine as we strode across to the open grave.

The Minister acknowledged us with a nod then began reading from a prayer book. 'We commend to the Almighty God, our brother, Charles Andrew George Granville, and we commit his body to the ground, earth to earth, ashes to ashes, dust to dust. The Lord bless him...'

I stopped listening and began to relive Jack and Beth's committal.

Elizabeth mistook this act as distress over Father and comforted me in her arms. 'It's time now,' she said and held out her hand.

I let her lead me to the grave and we dropped the white roses to symbolise love before turning and moving away.

'You'll come back to the Hall?' Elizabeth asked.

'No, I don't think so. I don't want to upset Mother or George.'

'If you think that's for the best. You know Grace, Mother isn't so bad. Not really.'

'You think what she did was right?'

'No of course not. But you know Mother didn't think it was right either. She fought with Father and she begged him to let you see George. She never wanted to take your son away but loved Father so much that she carried out his wishes.'

I thought back to that night when I'd announced I was pregnant. Father wanted me to have an abortion but Mother came up with a plan and suggested I stay with her cousin. When that fell through, she said I should marry Jack, it was preferable to killing an unborn baby. But that didn't stop me remembering the day she walked out of my house with George and that day at the Hall when she threatened to have all my children taken away if I ever stepped foot there again. Could I ever forgive her?

Mother walked slowly towards the limousine, her arm linked in George's. She looked extremely ill. She really loved Father and I expect the last few months of worry had done this to her. But why couldn't she have kept some of that love for her children? I loved Jack but it didn't stop me showing affection to George, Alice and Beth. There was more than enough love to share. Yet Father and Mother gave us none. George looked towards me. I thought I saw a small smile. Was I getting somewhere at last?

Chapter 25

Be patient, Elizabeth said. I struggled to concentrate, getting the latest designs ready for Paris. I dropped my pencil to the desk and walked over to the office window. Red leaves fell like rain.

Three weeks and not a word from my sister. George's new school term would have started, he most likely left at least a week ago. I'd lost him. Father was dead. No one to stand in George's way, certainly not Mother, she was in no state.

I heard loud voices. Max stormed in.

'I rang the house but Joan said you were here, at the shop. I've only just heard.' He waved a newspaper showing a headline.

LONDON MOURNS GRANVILLE

'I spotted it a couple of days ago in China and got the first flight to Heathrow.'

'You must be tired?' I hugged him.

'Yes, but never mind about me. How do you feel, now he's dead? Are you all right?'

He stepped back and looked me directly in the face.

'I'm fine, Max. Father asked to see me before he died.'

'Really? Did you go?'

'Yes.'

'And?'

'He said he was sorry. Nothing else, just sorry.'

'So he did have a heart after all.'

'But George still hasn't come home. I thought with Father gone that he'd read my letters and know I hadn't abandoned him. It's been weeks now and not a word. I've lost him.'

'It's a lot for a young lad to deal with in one go, Grace. How old is he?'

'Fifteen. But he hasn't even asked to see his sister.'

'There you are then. He's probably trying to cope with the grief of losing his grandfather. From what I've heard through the grapevine, the old man took him along to many meetings. People said Lord Granville was grooming his grandson to take over one day. I should imagine young George became very fond of him.'

'That did certainly seem to be the case.'

'Then he needs time. Be patient.'

Those words again, 'Be patient.' Hadn't I been patient for long enough? I'd been waiting more than six years, was it wrong for me to want my son home now? A peep peep sound filled the room. Max looked around.

'It's my alarm clock,' I told him. 'I get engrossed when working, so don't notice the time and I like to be home before Alice gets in from school.'

'I'll come with you. I'm looking forward to seeing the young lass again.'

It was wonderful to have him with me, he was the dad I never had.

'Are you staying a while, or charging off on business?' I asked him.

'A couple of days if you'll have me? Give me a chance to get over the old jet lag before popping up to Bolton.'

'Fabulous, I'll phone ahead and get Joan to make up your room.'

'Thanks, lass. It'll be nice to catch up. It's been a while as I've been so busy the last few months.'

'Do take care of yourself, Uncle Max.' I brushed my lips lightly across his cheek. 'You're not getting any younger.'

'Hmm, how come I always become Uncle when you're wearing your Mother Hen hat?'

We both laughed. I rang Joan before collecting my coat from the cloakroom, said goodbye to the staff and found Charlotte.

'Max, Darling.' Charlotte hugged him. 'It's good to see you, what brings you here, personal or business?'

'I'm here for Grace.' He was still holding the out of date newspaper. 'I've only just heard so got straight on a plane.'

'I'll see you back at the house this evening. Something tells me there's going to be a very happy little girl when I arrive home.'

'A big one too.' I chuckled. Meaning me of course. I was in my element and Max had taken my mind off George for a while.

*

The coloured lights twinkled on the six-foot tree. I stepped up on a leather pouffé to add the final touch, the same fairy that topped the tree since Jack and I had our first Christmas together. He'd been thrilled when he saw how I'd transformed a penny plastic doll using white netted fabric.

'You're getting a bit old and shabby, girl,' I told her. Maybe next year I should replace her clothes. No, I didn't like that idea. If I kept her as she was, it was like having a piece of Jack.

Elizabeth had been in regular contact, she'd met Alice and we'd even visited the Hall a couple of times to have tea. Mother hardly came out of her room and when she did, she never spoke.

'I'm worried about her,' Elizabeth said. 'I don't know what to do. It's like she's dying of a broken heart. Is that possible?'

I thought back to when Jack died. If I hadn't had the girls and had to fight for George, I could have quite easily hidden myself away in a room. Then when I lost Beth. 'Yes, I think perhaps you can,' I told her.

George asked Elizabeth to pass on a letter to Alice but there was nothing for me. She'd been ecstatic. The note was short but clear that he wanted to meet up with her when he came home for Christmas. She was with him today at *Granville Hall* and had been almost every day this last week.

I pinned up the final chain decorations that Alice and I made last evening. The fire was running low so I gave it a poke then stoked it up with coal. It didn't take long to produce a roaring flame.

The phone rang, I picked it up. 'Grace Gilmore speaking.'

It was Adriéne, he was back from Paris. He wanted to bring a female guest for Christmas.

'That'll be fine.' I placed the receiver into its cradle. It seemed rather sudden and tactless of him.

Surrounded by Christmas paper and parcels, I found I was still thinking about Adriéne's request. There was a knock on the front door. It must be Max.

'Grace, Happy Christmas.' Snowflakes covered his hair. 'Where shall I put these?' His arms were laden with gifts.

'It's snowing?'

'Brr...' He shivered.

'Here let me.' I knelt on the floor and carefully placed his parcels. 'I'll get you a towel.'

'No need, Joan's going to bring one.'

On cue, she appeared with a white fluffy towel over an arm and a tray in her hands. 'Hot chocolate, to warm you up.' She passed a mug to us both.

'Thanks Joan.' He turned to me. 'Where's our Alice?'

'She's with George.'

'Our George?'

'Yes, I'm hoping he'll want to see me soon too.'

'I'm sure he will, lass. I'm sure he will.'

After sounds of scuttling and rustling, Alice hurried into the sitting room. 'Uncle Max.' She hugged him tight. 'Don't you just love the snow? Mum, close your eyes. I've got an early Christmas present for you.'

'Can we do it later, darling? Tell me about George, first. How is he?'

'Close your eyes, Mum. Then I'll fill you in.'

Grudgingly, I allowed myself to do as she asked and tried to be patient, yet again. Alice spun me around three times and led me out of the room like *Blind Man's Buff*. A hand touched my shoulder and a familiar male voice spoke.

'Hello Grace.'

I opened my eyes. 'George.' I moved over to hold him but he distanced himself. 'Come through and sit by the fire.' As we entered the room his eyes focused towards Max, accusingly.

'I'm your Great Uncle Max. Your dad was my dad's brother.'

George gave a half smile.

'Alice, let's leave your mum and brother to chat. We'll go and see what Joan's got cooking in the kitchen and get her to make tea.' He took my daughter's hand and winked at me.

My stomach churned as we sat down by the fire. I noticed George was also nervous, fiddling with his hands.

He looked around the room before finally saying, 'The tree's pretty, bit bigger than what we had in Wigan. Ours used to sit on the sideboard, do you remember?' He strolled over to it. 'No, it can't be. Is that our... Tinkerbell?'

'Yes, George. I remember. There was no room for it on the floor. And yes, it's the same Tinkerbell.'

'I remember when Da used to lift me on his shoulders so I could place her at the top.' He turned his face but not before I noticed a tear trickle down his cheek. 'You've done very well for yourself, Grace. Was it worth it?'

I wished he'd call me Mum and not Grace but I didn't say anything. 'Worth it?'

'Two thousand pounds. Was I worth it?'

'It wasn't like that. I thought you understood. The letters?'

'Yes, I read the letters and listened to what Alice and Aunt Elizabeth said so I know you didn't abandon me, but that doesn't explain why you let me go in the first place.'

'I had no choice.'

'Surely, there's always a choice?'

'I don't believe there was. After your father died I contacted my parents for help. Mother, you may remember, came to the house?'

'Yes, I remember that day. I also remember you promised you wouldn't let her take me away.'

'I did promise, and at the time I meant it. However, when your grandmother arrived she gave me no option.'

269

'Why, because she offered money?'

'No, because she said the authorities would take away all my children. Foolishly, I believed her.'

'I'm struggling to understand. Whichever way you say it, you sold me.'

I stood up, moved closer to him. 'No, George, I didn't.' I reached for his hand.

He circled the room. 'Was it because I was naughty?'

'No, darling of course not.'

'Then why me? Why not Alice?'

'Father wanted you. I didn't want to let you go. Alice must have told you.'

'Yes, she did.'

'All I can say, George, is I wasn't thinking straight. Your father had just been killed, I had three children to feed, no money and the only help I could get was if I let you go with your grandmother. I didn't want you ending up down the mine.'

'I may not have. My teacher, what was her name, err Miss Jones, she said I could go to grammar school.'

'It wouldn't have happened. The villagers would never have allowed it. They never accepted me because of my class and endured me purely because of your father. I only ever meant for you to go to *Granville Hall* as a temporary measure. Mother promised that if you were unsettled you could come back home. I knew you would want to. I went back for you but she wouldn't let me see you.'

He picked up my portfolio from the sideboard and flipped it open. 'Are these yours?'

'Yes, they're for the Paris shop.'

'I like drawing too, you know?'

'No, I didn't know.'

'Not clothes though, buildings.'

'That's wonderful, George.'

'When did you know that you wanted to be a designer? I remember you used to draw once we went to bed.'

'I think since I was ten years old.'

'That's around the time I started drawing too. The old man hated it. Told me to get that nonsense out of my head.'

'Sounds familiar. He said the same to me.'

'He said he'd brought me to *Granville Hall* to learn to run the estate. I don't want to do that though.'

'And you don't have to, George. It's your life and Grandfather isn't here so there's no one to stand in your way.'

'But what about the estate?'

'A manager can be hired, or maybe Elizabeth may like to run it. I'd like to see some of your drawings, may I?'

He smiled with enthusiasm. 'Yes, I'll bring them next time. I want to be an architect.'

My son, an architect. It was going well, there was going to be a next time.

'I don't think Elizabeth would be interested in running it though,' he said.

'Someone will need to take over anyway as you're only fifteen. There's no reason why they can't carry on indefinitely.'

'I'd like to get to know you, but do you think we can take it slowly?'

'We can take it as slow as you like, darling.' I was overjoyed, the first step of what was probably going to be many, but a first step nonetheless to bringing my son back home.

'Would you like to stay for dinner?'

'No, I can't unfortunately, Elizabeth has made plans, but I've got an hour before she picks me up, so maybe tea?'

'Did someone mention tea?' Uncle Max sauntered through the door, a tray in his hands and Alice in tow.

'How well did you know my father?' George asked Max. I noticed he refrained from using the northern dialect.

'We were very close. Has your mother told you how much you look like him?'

He smiled. 'Err I think she did mention it at some point.'

'Jack used to come and stay in Bolton with my family, he was very close to his cousin Katy. He had his own room, as did your mother, years later.'

271

George's face beamed as he lapped up the conversation. 'He was a fantastic father, so attentive with Alice and me. Do you remember, Alice?'

'I think so. I know he took us out a lot.'

'He used to give me a penny for cleaning his boots.'

'I remember that.' I laughed.

The hour whizzed by reminiscing, eating cake and drinking tea. George stood up. 'Elizabeth will be here in a few minutes. I'd better start to get ready. It's been lovely meeting you, Uncle Max.'

'What are you doing for Christmas, George? Would you and Elizabeth like to come here?' I asked.

'That's very kind, but I think arrangements have been made. I could come for a couple of hours in the afternoon, on Christmas Eve. If you like?'

'That would be fabulous.'

Elizabeth collected George. She didn't come in as they had plans to have dinner with friends of Father's. I was up in the clouds, totally elated. For the first time in years I'd had time with my son.

'What do you think?' I asked Max, once they'd gone.

'He's a great lad. Chip off the old block, Jack would be proud.'

'But what do you think, do you think he's coming around?'

'Definitely.'

'I wish he'd have called me Mum or even Mam.'

Alice came over and hugged me. 'Don't worry Mum, I'm sure he will soon.'

*

It was Christmas Eve and 1968 would soon be over. Snow had been falling, on and off, for days, creating a thick white carpet on the ground. I hoped it wouldn't stop George getting here.

'Do you think he'll get here?' I asked Max who'd arrived earlier.

'The roads aren't too bad, Grace. He'll be here.'

I heard crunching sounds and looked out of the window, a Silver Rolls glided to a stop. 'It's him. He's here,' I called to the others.

The room looked inviting with coloured lights twinkling and an open lit fire. Mulled wine scented the room.

'Hi Alice.' George hugged his sister. 'Uncle Max.' He shook his hand. 'Grace.' He brushed his lips lightly across my cheek. Still not calling me Mum, but almost a kiss so we were moving forward.

'Let's play Monopoly.' Alice held the game in her hands.

Everyone was in agreement, after all there's nothing like a board game to break the ice.

'George, you choose first, who would you like to be?' Alice asked.

'I'll be the dog. I've always wanted a dog.'

'You can be dog then. Here you are. I'll be *top hat*, Mum, what about you?'

'I'll be *iron*. Max?'

'What's left?'

Alice passed him the *wheelbarrow* and we began the game. The room was filled with laughter as we made our way around the board. George managed to buy the purple properties, Mayfair and Park Lane and it wasn't long before he planted hotels on them, thus bankrupting us all. I think I spent more time in jail. It was fun and I was getting closer to George.

After the game Alice and Max left me alone with him. 'Did you bring your drawings?' I asked.

'Yes, I brought some. They're out in the hall, I'll get them.'

He left the room for seconds and reappeared with a foolscap folder.

I led him to the chaise longue so we could sit next to each other. He passed me the file filled with drawings on white sheets of paper.

'These are incredible, George.' The pages were full of different designed houses, Georgian and Tudor style. Offices, with windows for walls, showing trees around them. 'This is how you see the future?'

'Yes, it is. These windows will bring in more light, meaning less fuel required for electricity. The workers would benefit too, seeing the sun.'

'You should train to do this, George. Seriously, don't let anyone stand in your way. You have a gift.' I was filled with pride.

The doorbell chimed. There was a rush of steps and greetings at the door. Max wandered in. 'Look who we found at the door,' he said.

Elizabeth strolled in with Alice at her heels.

'We've been playing Monopoly, Aunt Elizabeth,' Alice said.

'And I won.' George laughed.

'Are you in a rush Elizabeth?' I asked her.

She looked at her watch. 'I have time for a sherry.'

'Fabulous.' I wandered over to the sideboard and poured three glasses, handing one to Max and Elizabeth.

'What about us?' Alice said.

'You're too young to drink alcohol, Miss,' Max scolded, before I had the chance to say anything.

Alice and George sat in the window seat, chatting. I could see her pushing him in play. She'd missed that. My family was close to becoming full again.

'It looks like the afternoon has gone well,' Elizabeth said.

'Yes, very. I think he's starting to warm to me.'

She gripped my hand. 'He'll come around, you'll see.' She turned to him, 'George, I think we should leave in a few minutes. We need to be at The Ansons' by eight.'

'Before you go.' I reached under the tree and retrieved a small wrapped parcel. 'George, this is for you. You can open it now.' I passed a small present to Elizabeth too.

'Yours are with Joan,' Elizabeth confided.

George tried to shield his face, but not before I saw it flush red. 'Thank you. I'm sorry I haven't anything for you.'

'You've given me the best present being here.'

He ripped off the paper like any other teenager and stared at the gent's watch.

'It was your father's,' I said. 'It still works. It's a good one, Uncle Max and his wife bought it for his twenty-first. The strap was a little shabby so I had it replaced with this gold bracelet.'

'To have something of Da's. I can't tell you how much that means.'

It amused me how he switched to the northern dialect when talking about his father. 'Go on, put it on.'

He slid it over his hand and checked the time. After staring at it for moments, but it seemed longer, he looked up at Elizabeth and announced, 'We should be going.' Then he turned back to me. 'But I'll see you again soon. I promise.' He gave me a peck on the cheek and gently tapped my upper arm.

I watched my son walk out of the door, but this time I felt we were closer to reuniting fully.

Chapter 26

The house bustled around us Christmas morning as we sat around the tree opening presents. Adriéne brought his young lady, and I mean young, she looked straight out of school. Easily half his age. Pretty though, straight blonde hair that touched her shoulders.

I opened my present from Elizabeth, she'd actually written George and Mother's names on the tag too. I held it up in the air for the others to see.

'Is that Chanel No. 5?' Charlotte asked.

'Yes, would you believe, I've given Elizabeth the same?'

Everyone laughed. Alice ripped open presents, one after another. Woollen hat, scarf and gloves, Timex watch, Bunty and Judy Annuals, high kinky boots, Tressy doll, transistor radio and of course a special gift from me.

She opened the small package and drew out a gold locket. 'Mum, this is beautiful.'

'Take a look inside,' I said.

'She opened it. 'George?'

'Yes, he was eleven. Elizabeth gave me the photograph.'

'I'll treasure it.' She rushed over to Nancy.

I turned to chat to Charlotte. 'How did the staff party go? I'm really sorry I didn't make it.'

'They really enjoyed it and loved the contents of their little brown envelopes.'

I liked to look after the employees, they worked hard and were very loyal. Charlotte said it was too generous when I placed a five pound note in each. We had quite a number now working in the shops and factory, as well as a couple of juniors I'd taken on to train as dress designers. Ted and Joan were more like family and always joined us for Christmas lunch, including today.

Max opened his present. 'Cufflinks. These are lovely, Grace. MG. The monogram matches my car.' He laughed.

Everyone sat down to eat, the clink of glass rang loud as everyone lifted wine goblets to toast. Knives and forks clicked on the plates, and various conversations were active at one time.

After dinner we amused ourselves with Charades. The phone rang and Joan jumped up to answer it.

'No, leave it,' I said, 'it's your day off. I'll get it. Carry on with the game.' I picked up the handset. 'Grace Gilmore, speaking.'

It was Elizabeth. She wished me Happy Christmas and we laughed about the perfume. I asked to speak to George but he wanted to speak to Alice.

He didn't want to speak to me. I wiped my eyes, I couldn't let anyone see how I was feeling. I had to take it slowly, maybe next time he'd talk to me.

I could hear Alice telling George about the locket. 'It's got a picture of you in it.'

I returned to the others, still playing charades, Max tilted his head back and Charlotte nearly fell off her seat with laughter. It provided lots of fun but enough was enough. I waited for Alice to finish her conversation on the telephone before suggesting she perform a song and tap dance while I played the piano. It was a good day, I wished George could have been with us or at least spoken to me. However, progress had been made. Yesterday, I'd seen him for a couple of hours.

When Adriéne's girlfriend Susan left the room to powder her nose, he didn't waste any time to be at my side. 'Just give me the word, Grace, and I'll end it.' He touched my arm. 'I still want you.'

'It can't happen, Adriéne. Be happy.' I kissed him on the cheek and moved away quickly before my face gave away the tingle rushing under my skin. Why was he doing this to me? I had far more important things to think of in my life right now, George took priority and he'd taken an instant dislike to Adriéne, just from the newspaper photograph.

Joan stretched and yawned. 'Come on, Ted love, I've a big day tomorrow, lots of cooking for the visitors.'

'It's time you were going to bed too, young lady,' I said to Alice.

'Just ten more minutes. Please.'

'No, it's nearly eleven, it's been a long day. Say your goodnights.'

'Ahh.' She scrambled up from the carpet where she was sitting cross-legged.

Adriéne and Susan retired too. Joan had made up his regular room and allocated the girlfriend a smaller one. I didn't think there'd be room swapping during the night, Adriéne was far too much of a gentleman for that.

One by one everyone left, except Max and me. We chatted for an hour about Jack, Katy, Eliza and of course my dear Beth, the baby that Max never got to meet. Christmas was hard for us both.

He clapped his hands. 'Now Gracie, it's time you had some beauty sleep, not that you need it of course. Thanks for a lovely day.'

'Thank you.' I gave him a big hug and he kissed me on the cheek.

Chapter 27

We didn't see George again over the Christmas period, he'd gone skiing with friends in The Alps and then returned to Westbridge. The earliest I'd likely see him would be the end of March for Easter. I knew Alice would get letters from him, maybe he'd write to me too.

I'd taken the day off work, Charlotte decided we needed to talk, just the two of us. She walked in with a tray of tea. 'We haven't done this for a while have we?'

'What, drink tea?' I teased.

'Talk, just you and me.' She laughed.

'And what are we going to talk about? Sales? Designs? New Premises?'

'No business today. We're going to talk about you, Grace.'

'What's there to say?'

'Adriéne for starters,' she said.

'What about him? He's history.'

'I don't believe that for one minute and I don't think you do either.'

'It doesn't make any difference, he's got a new girlfriend.'

'What, Susan?' She shook her head. 'You really have no idea, have you?'

'What?'

'He's not interested in her? He brought her to get a reaction from you.'

'I'm just getting somewhere with George. It's not fair to keep Adriéne hanging on.'

'But I've seen the way you look at him.'

'There's magnetism, I won't deny. But what's the point? It can't go anywhere.'

'Don't dismiss it, Grace, that's all I'm saying. You need to work in close contact with each other, and to be honest you won't be able to fight those feelings forever.' She poured the tea and passed me a cup. 'Let's finish this and then go shopping for shoes?'

'If you insist.' She was right of course, my feelings for Adriéne ran deep. I wondered if I was in love with him, but it felt different to Jack. Maybe that's because he was my first love. Still, I didn't see how anything could come of it. George had to be the priority. In the meantime I'd go shopping with Charlotte and have some fun.

'How about a visit to the hairdressing salon? I asked her. 'I think it's time I had my hair cut and restyled.'

'What, lose those long locks?'

'I think it's time, I'm thirty-five in March.'

'A change will do you good. I'll ring Gino's and book us in at four, give us time to shop and eat lunch. Nancy's taking Alice out to tea after school, so we don't need to worry about her.'

Just as she reached for the handset it rang. 'Gilmore household, Charlotte Cunningham speaking.' She gave me a nod. 'Elizabeth. Yes of course, she's right next to me. I'll put her on.'

'Elizabeth. Let me check. We were on our way out.' I turned to Charlotte. 'She's worried about Mother and wants me to go over there.'

'Then you must go. Shopping can wait. I don't really need that pair of shoes.'

I spoke into the mouthpiece. 'I'll come straight over and we'll sort something out. Bye for now.'

*

It was just before twelve. I stood shivering on the step at *Granville Hall* waiting for Martha to answer the doorbell.

'Miss Grace,' she said in a judgemental tone.

'Martha.' I passed her my coat. 'Where's Elizabeth?'

'She's in the drawing room.'

'I'll find my own way.' I brushed past her.

'Grace, thank you for coming. Mother's barely eating. She hardly comes out of her room. I just don't know what to do. I wondered about Cousin Victoria. What do you think?'

'Hey, slow down.' I held Elizabeth close, she sobbed in my arms. 'Sit down and I'll get you a drink. Scotch?' I didn't wait for an answer. I strode over to the cocktail cabinet and poured out the liquor. 'Here, drink this. It's medicinal.'

'Thank you.' She sipped from the tumbler.

'Are you suggesting that Mother should go down to Somerset? Have you been in touch with Victoria?'

'Yes, it was her suggestion but what do you think?'

'I think they were close as children. Has she seen the doctor?'

'The doctor wants to admit her to a psychiatric hospital. But I can't let that happen. I just can't, Grace.'

'Don't upset yourself. We'll work something out. I need to see Mother, is she in her room now?'

'Yes. I'll come with you.'

With dread I made my way up the staircase and along the corridor. Elizabeth followed. I wasn't sure what I was going to see or if Mother may turn on me. I gently pushed the master bedroom door open and walked inside. The curtains were closed but it was light enough to make out a hunched up figure on the edge of the bed gazing into air.

'Mother.' I tapped her shoulder.

She looked up, her face thin and haggard.

'Mother, it's me, Grace.'

She didn't answer but stared through me. I remembered the time I'd been like this after Beth died. If I hadn't had Charlotte, who knows what would have happened. Elizabeth was right. Mother should go to stay with Victoria, she could show her that life was worth living again. Mother needed quiet, beautiful countryside and support, not a mental hospital.

'I think you should phone Victoria,' I said to Elizabeth. 'She can't stay like this indefinitely. She'll starve to death. There's barely nothing of her.'

'I'll go and do it now.' My sister left the room.

I sat next to Mother and held her hand. She didn't move away or say a word but she looked at me momentarily before staring into space. She must have loved Father very much. I put my arm around her shoulders. 'It's going to be all right, Mother. Don't worry, you'll see.' I kissed her lightly on the cheek before leaving.

'Any luck?' I asked Elizabeth when arriving back downstairs.

'Yes, she's happy to help. Simon's going to drive us down.'

'Simon?' I thought he must be a new driver, although we'd never used names when I lived here.

'Anson. Simon Anson. She needs to be with family and friends that care for her. I don't want her going down with a chauffeur.'

'The Anson twins, I assume they're married with families?'

'Richard is, but Simon's a widower.' She blushed.

'You and him? Are you together?'

'We started seeing each other after Father's funeral.'

'But he's old. He must be nearly fifty.'

'He's forty-seven actually and age doesn't matter. He's kind and would like children too. His wife was unable to have any.'

'I'm pleased for you, if he makes you happy. How does George feel about this relationship?'

'George. George doesn't mind. He's pleased to see his old aunt happy. Simon said once we're married he'll take over running the estate and teach George everything he needs to know when he comes of age.'

'So when's the happy day?'

'Not for a while, we need to have a respectful mourning period first.'

'Do you know George doesn't want to run the estate?'

'Of course he does. Father's been grooming him for years.'

'He doesn't Elizabeth and I'll do everything in my power to make sure he isn't forced. Father's not here anymore and George is my son.'

'I'll not stand in his way if there's something else he'd rather do. Of course, I can't answer for Mother, when she recovers that is.'

Martha tapped on the door. 'Miss Elizabeth, Mr Anson is here. Lady Granville's suitcase is packed ready.'

'Thank you, Martha. Show him in please.'

'It's cold out there,' I heard him tell the maid before entering the drawing room.

'Elizabeth.' He kissed her cheek.

'Simon, you remember Grace?'

'Of course, it's been a while though. You look well, Grace.' His six foot frame had widened since I last saw him, grey thinning hair showed how he'd aged.

'Thank you. It's good to see you.' I shook his hand then turned to my sister. 'Would you like me to come too?'

'No, there's no need. Simon will look after me.'

My eyes were drawn to the patterned cravat around his neck. '*House of Grace* designs for men too.'

'Sorry?' he said.

'For the wedding, I mean.'

He laughed. 'I'll bear that in mind.'

I was happy my sister had found someone. He wasn't my choice but then Elizabeth and I had always been different. Martha brought my coat.

'Let me know how Mother settles.' I kissed my sister.

Chapter 28

While Mother appeared to be settling in Somerset, Elizabeth and I were slowly rebuilding our relationship. In fact, she'd asked me to design her wedding dress.

I felt the warmth of the sun on my face as I walked around the garden cutting flowers: daffodils, tulips and wallflowers. The latter were my favourite, in particular the purple.

'The post is here,' Charlotte shouted from the French doors.

I waved.

'You'll want to see this.' She walked outside towards me. 'Look where it's from.'

I threw off the gardening gloves and took the envelope in my hand. 'Mrs G Gilmore.'

'I'll leave you to it,' Charlotte said. 'Joan's making tea.'

My eyes didn't leave the letter, concentrating on the Berkshire postmark I'd seen on the many occasions Alice had received one. I stooped down to sit on the step and ripped the envelope open.

Dear Grace,

Thank you for your letter and your interest in my drawings. Yes, I've drawn a few more and I'll bring them with me when I come to see you next week, once I'm home. I spoke to my Technical Drawing Teacher like you suggested and he thinks I could have a career as an Architect.

See you soon.

Love

George

xxx

I rushed inside. 'Charlotte. Charlotte.'

'Are you all right?'

'Yes, yes. Read it.'

'That's promising, he's coming to visit.'

'I know. And look, he ended with three kisses.'

'I'm pleased for you, Grace. It sounds like your patience is paying off. The drawings are the common denominator that will bring you back together.'

'Yes, I think you're right. Do you fancy celebrating? Maybe shopping and a trip to the hairdresser's? I never did get that restyle.'

'I'll ring Gino's now.'

*

It was April Fool's Day, Alice had broken up from school for Easter and spent most of the morning catching me out. I needed to be on my guard.

'Mum, Aunt Elizabeth's car has driven up and George has just got out,' Alice said.

I glanced at the clock, it was only eleven thirty, surely she wouldn't joke about something like that. 'Are you playing tricks?' I asked her.

'No, see for yourself, he's coming now.' At that point I heard 'ding dong,' from the front door. It was Joan's day off so I rushed to answer. 'George, Elizabeth, so good to see you both. Come in.'

'I'm not stopping,' Elizabeth said, 'I'm meeting Simon for lunch but this young man wanted to come around here. Is that all right?'

All right, it was more than all right. 'Yes, yes of course. Come in George.'

'I'll pick him up at five,' she said.

I closed the door on her and led George towards the dining room. He was clutching a large A3 folder.

'Your hair's different. You look like that pop singer Cilla Black,' he said.

'Do I?' I laughed. 'Well I think she's pretty, so thank you.'

'I've brought my drawings.'

'Excellent, I'm looking forward to seeing them. Would you like something to drink?'

'Yes please.'

I walked towards the doorway. 'Alice, it's George. He's come for lunch. Can you get drinks please?'

'Yes, Mum.'

'Let's sit up at the table,' I suggested to George.

He took out half a dozen sheets of large paper from the folder. 'What do you think?'

I scanned the drawings. Most of them were offices but there was a house and bungalow too. 'Do you prefer to draw these?' I pointed to the office drawings.

'Yes. I like the idea of large windows for business buildings.'

'These are so impressive and the windows are eye catching. I thought that last time I saw them. It's marvellous you know what you want to do. And not even sixteen yet.'

'You've made me believe I can. Aunt Elizabeth seems quite keen on the idea too, she said Simon will take over the estate. There's only Grandmother to convince, if she ever gets well, that is.'

Alice strolled in carrying a tray with two glasses of orange squash and a mug of coffee. 'What have you got there, George?'

'My designs. I want to be an architect, remember I told you? Would you like to see?'

'Oh yes, of course. Do you have to go to university to do that?' Alice asked.

'I'm not sure. But I'm going to Cambridge anyway. My tutor at school said I'll have no problems getting in.'

'Can I, Mum?' Alice asked

'Can you what?'

'Go to Cambridge.'

'We'll talk about that when you're older.' Alice wasn't bright like her brother, she was a talented artist but as for academic studies, she was only average for her age.'

'George, I'm going to Brighton to boarding school in September. I can't wait to be down by the sea,' Alice said.

'Yes, you told me last time. I'd like to be by the sea too. Perhaps we can all go down there during the holidays? You can show me where you're going.'

'Mum?' Alice asked.

'I don't see why not, we could take a picnic,' I said.

'I'll speak to Aunt Elizabeth,' George replied.

'Are you coming to my birthday party?' Alice asked.

'Yes, I think so. It's this Sunday, isn't it? Alice, would you mind if I had a chat on my own with Grace? You and I can catch up after lunch.'

I found it hard to contain my excitement. My son wanted me all to himself.

Alice wasn't put off by his request. Instead she smiled. 'No of course not. I've got stuff to do upstairs anyway. Call me when it's time for lunch.'

'I will,' I said, 'thanks darling.'

George and I sat and talked about his drawings a bit more. He wanted to know how I got started and I told him it was making the items in the shop. For him it would be different, but the university would offer plenty of advice.

He suddenly changed the subject. 'Grace, do you think you could take me to Da's grave?'

I was taken aback.

'I asked Grandfather before he got sick, but he wouldn't let me go. Elizabeth didn't know where he was buried. Will you take me?'

'Yes of course I will. When would you like to go?'

'Before I go back to school. Just you and me? I love Alice but I don't want her to be there.'

'I'll discuss it with Elizabeth and firm up on a date. When do you go back to Westbridge?'

'Not until the twenty first.'

'We'll sort something out. Don't worry. I gripped his upper arm lightly and he didn't shy away. Would he ever call me Mum?

'I'd better make a start on lunch. Would you like to help?' I said.

'Yes, I'd like that.'

On our way to the kitchen we bumped into Alice.

'I'm starving,' she said.

'We're just going to make lunch. Do you want to help too?' I asked.

'This is going to be great fun,' she said.

'What shall we have?' George asked.

'Sausage, egg and chips? Please Mum.'

'Is that all right with you, George?' I said.

'Wow, yes. I can't remember the last time I had that.'

We became a team, George cracked and cooked eggs, Alice and I peeled potatoes. It wasn't long before the hot meal was on its way. After eating, my children went outside in the garden, and I could hear Alice bossing George about. It was almost like old times. I may still have been Grace to him but at least now he was happy to be in my company.

*

Last week we had a party for Alice's birthday. It was a great success. My sister brought Simon along. He seemed a nice enough chap and was making her happy.

Cousin Victoria advised Elizabeth that there was no real change in Mother but she was comfortable and getting lots of fresh air. Time would tell, it seemed.

I spoke to Elizabeth about taking George to Wigan and she had no objections, in fact she saw it as a positive move that he was coming around to accepting me. We decided on the fourteenth, the week before he went back to school. Nancy, suggested she should take Alice to Dorset for a couple of days. It was better she didn't know my arrangements with her brother. I agreed it was a good plan so they'd set off last night.

Ted and I picked George up first thing so we could get the eight o'clock train. Ted wanted to drive us to Wigan but as George had never been on a train I declined this offer, even if it did mean a few changes, across London to Euston. The journey there and back was too much to do in one day so I booked us a room each at *The Bellingham*.

George was quiet on the train so I didn't push him to speak. He was engrossed in reading Graham Greene's *Brighton Rock*, so I took the opportunity to carry on with *One Flew over the Cuckoo's Nest* which I'd started a couple of nights back.

The journey was finally over. I flagged down a black taxi to take us close to the cemetery.

'Would you like some lunch first?' I asked, after stepping out of the cab.

'No, I'd like to see where Da is first, please.'

I liked the way he said 'Da' rather than Father.

'There's a florist over there.' He pointed. 'Is it all right if I buy some flowers?'

'Of course.'

We walked into the shop and George made his way towards the elderly lady behind the counter.

'Good afternoon,' she said, 'how can I help you?'

George looked to me.

'Roses were his favourite but as it's only April we can't have them but he loved daffodils too,' I said.

'I'll have bunch of those please,' he told the assistant. 'What are you getting?' he asked me.

'Gladioli.'

We left the shop with a mixture of yellows, purples and reds.

The cemetery was across the road and we strolled through the wrought iron gates. I remembered exactly where Jack lay and followed the path until arriving at his resting place. The grave was bare but tidy. We laid our blooms on the ground.

'Would you like some time alone?' I asked George.

'No.' He took my hand and held it tight. 'Why did that accident have to happen? If only Da was still alive then things would have been different.'

'But you've had a good life, George?'

'Yes, but it wasn't always so.'

'No?'

'I don't want to talk about it. Is Beth here too?'

'No, she's in London. Would you like to visit her too, sometime?'

'Yes, maybe in the summer holidays. Will you take me?'

'Of course.'

He released his hand from mine, wiped his eyes when he thought I wasn't looking and then began to speak fast. 'I'm starving, shall we find somewhere for lunch?'

'There used to be a little café where Da and I liked to go. Shall we see if it's still there?'

'That's a good idea. I'd like to know more about him. I don't remember a lot. Where did you meet him?' he asked as we were walking.

I told him about the Palais in Bolton and how I'd laughed at his shabby clothes and then felt bad.

'This is it,' I said. 'And it's open.'

It looked dull and gloomy but brought back a lot of memories. The young waiter brought us steak and kidney pudding, chips and peas. 'Your da's favourite,' I told him. 'How about we order a glass of Sarsaparilla? You can't get it down south.'

He nodded eagerly. In a couple of minutes the waiter returned with the brown fizzy liquid.

George took a sip. 'I remember this. I'd forgotten. Shall we take back a couple of bottles for Alice?'

'Hmm,' I pondered. I wasn't sure if that was the right thing to do. 'Let's leave it for now, George. She doesn't know we're here and may get upset about being left out. Perhaps we can come again, all of us?'

This seemed to satisfy him, which meant he was happy to come again.

After eating we caught a taxi to the hotel, we needed to rest and get an early train in the morning to return home. It had been a strange day, filled with emotion. Standing at Jack's graveside stirred sad feelings but it had been wondrous spending time with George. I could feel my son and I slowly bonding.

Chapter 29

Max only arrived late last night so we hadn't had a chance to catch up properly. I had a lot to tell him. He wanted to come to the store with me today to have a look at the latest men's fashion. I slipped on my jeans and white t-shirt. Not bad for a thirty-five-year-old who'd given birth to three babies, I thought, admiring my figure in the mirror.

I caught up with him as he sloped down the stairs. 'Good Morning, Max.'

'Morning Grace.' He kissed me on the cheek.

'Breakfast?' I led him into the dining room. 'Alice has gone off to school. We let you sleep as you're probably jet-lagged.'

'Thanks, I'm famished, the food on the plane was atrocious.'

'I was going to suggest a light one but in view of your last comment I'll get Joan to make you a full English.'

He circled his stomach. 'Sounds good. It means we can catch up properly before we go out.'

Joan pushed a hostess trolley laden with food and drink into the room. 'Max, I've taken the liberty of cooking you bacon and eggs. I know you always say they don't make it right in the States.'

'You know me too well, Joanie.'

She giggled. 'Just toast for you, Grace?'

'Thank you.'

Max cut into the bacon before Joan had gone through the doorway. I poured tea and passed a cup to him.

'I've got lots to tell you,' I said.

'By the look of that twinkle in your eye, I'm assuming all good?'

'Yes. It's about George. I tried ringing you but your office said they couldn't contact you.'

'I was offsite. Now don't keep me waiting. Tell me.'

'George has been visiting. And last week.' I couldn't stop smiling as I spoke. 'Last week we went to Wigan together, he wanted to see where Jack's buried. Max, I think he's coming back to me.'

Max put his knife and fork down. 'Grace, that is good news.'

'There's more. We went down to Greenmere, Alice too. He wanted to see where she was going to school in September. I think perhaps he wanted to see where I went. And he wants me to show him where Beth's grave is. He said in the summer holidays.'

'Where's George now?'

'He's gone back to school, but he'll be home in July. And then of course we have Elizabeth's wedding at the end of August.'

'Elizabeth's getting married?'

'Yes and you'll never guess who to?'

'Err...'

'Simon Anson. He's one of the twins Father wanted me to marry. Do you remember me telling you about them?'

'Yes, I do. Quite a lot older than you. Is that right?'

'That's right. Elizabeth said he's forty-seven. Still, she's happy and he treats her well. I'm pleased for her. She wants me to design her dress.'

'That's exciting, Grace. Everything is coming together. How about your mother?'

'She's still not well. Elizabeth goes down to see her once a month, but she says Mother doesn't recognise her.'

'That's very sad, I can understand. Of course you know what happened to my wife after Katy died.'

'How is Eliza?'

'In hospital again. She keeps going deeper into herself. I hope that doesn't happen to your mother.'

'Oh Max, I'm so sorry. It must be hard on you.'

'I'm lucky. I have you and all your family.' He clenched my hand. 'What's happening with Adriéne and you?'

'Nothing at the moment, but he hasn't seen Susan again, or any other girl from what I can gather. Who knows what may happen one day?'

*

The organist played Mendelssohn's, *Wedding March*. Alice and I followed Elizabeth down the aisle. She looked beautiful. The empire line cut on her broderie anglais dress flattered her figure. It skirted satin, high-heeled shoes. Light brown spiral curls hung under the headdress which allowed a netted veil to hang low. She held a trailing bouquet of white roses, mingled with green foliage. George walked by her side, arm in arm. My heart skipped. He reminded me of Jack, maybe a little more handsome. The dress suit and bow tie made him look older than his years.

Elizabeth came to a halt as she reached her groom and Richard, Simon's twin brother. I lifted the veil from her face before standing behind with pride.

The vicar welcomed the congregation with prayers, beginning with 'The Grace of our Lord Jesus Christ...' Then the preface, how we'd come together to witness the marriage between the bride and groom followed by the declaration.

'First, I am required to ask anyone present who knows a reason why these persons may not lawfully marry to declare it now,' he said.

The church was silent.

He proceeded to advise the bridal couple of the importance of the vows they were about to make in the presence of God.

'Simon Archibald Anson, will you take Elizabeth Anne Granville to be your wife? Will you love her, comfort her, honour and protect her, and, forsaking all others, be faithful to her as long as you both shall live?'

'I will,' Simon answered.

The rest of the service was hazy as I drifted back to my own wedding day. Jack and I saying those words. Don't cry, I told myself, you'll smudge the mascara but tears still trickled. I hoped no one would notice. I missed Jack, but it was more than that. I missed the close affection that you had with marriage. Did I really want to be on my own for the rest of my life? Would Jack expect me to?

'I pronounce you Husband and Wife,' the vicar said.

Simon kissed his bride.

The organist hit the chords of *Amazing Grace* and the congregation joined in. Alice nudged me. George turned to me and smiled.

At the end of the service Charlotte, Nancy and Max joined the other guests to throw confetti over us all. Adriéne watched me from the side. Elizabeth had very kindly invited them all, including Joan and Ted. She saw them as extended family.

Back at *Granville Hall* the reception was in full swing. George, Alice and I shared the top table with the bride, groom and best man. I sat next to my son and Simon's brother, Richard.

George stood up to do his speech. 'Elizabeth is a kind, generous woman. Over the years, she's been a fantastic aunt and friend. It gives me great pleasure to welcome Simon into the Granville family. To the bride and groom.' He held up his champagne flute.

'To the bride and groom,' everyone echoed.

As the guests started eating and chatting, George turned to me and whispered. 'Grace, if you and Adriéne, well you know, if you wanted him as your boyfriend, I wouldn't mind.'

'You wouldn't?'

'No. I've seen the way you look at each other and I can see how lonely you are. I think Da would want you to be happy.'

I touched his arm and kissed his cheek. 'Thank you, George.'

The band assembled on the stage and began to play The Beatles' *Hey Jude*. Simon took Elizabeth in his arms and twirled her around the room.

Adriéne approached. 'Would you like to dance?'

George nudged me. 'Go on.'

I let Adriéne take my hand and lead me to the dance floor. We joined the bride and groom and circled the room. My pulse quickened at his touch. I looked into his eyes, he smiled. No words were said. Out of the corner of my eye I noticed Max escort Charlotte to the floor and soon after George followed as he guided his sister.

We were all invited to stay the night at *Granville Hall*, so once everyone else had gone to bed, I retired to my old room.

I stared at my reflection in the mirror and sensed Jack by my side. 'I'm proud of you, Grace,' I heard him say. 'Life is for the living, make every day count. You deserve happiness.'

I removed the locket from around my neck, opened it and gazed at his photograph. 'Thank you, Jack.' I knew from tomorrow I would start living life again and it wouldn't be long before George would call me Mam.

*

After the wedding I was busy getting Alice's trunk ready for Greenemere. She was so excited. I remembered the day I'd first started. Apprehensive but excited at the prospect of being away from Mother and Father. However, I wasn't sending her alone in a chauffeured car but going down with her to make sure she settled in. George wasn't leaving for Westbridge until next week so he'd asked if he could come too.

'Alice, are you ready?' I heard George say.

'I'm here.' She met us in the hallway.

'You look so grown up, darling. Come here.' I hugged her tightly. 'I'm going to miss you.'

'I'll miss you too, Mum. But don't worry, we'll both be fine. I'm going to concentrate on my studies and make lots of new friends and you've got *House of Grace* and Adriéne.' She blushed.

'You don't mind then?'

'It's about time. George said he's fine about it, too. Didn't you?'

'Yes, I told Grace at the wedding.'

'Where's Nancy,' I asked, 'We need to leave now.'

'I'm here. Sorry.' Her eyes were red.

'Oh Nancy, you've been crying.' Alice wrapped her arms around her.

'It's just so hard,' she said.

'I'm thirteen. It's time you thought about your own life. Take a leaf out of Mum's book, get yourself a boyfriend.'

Nancy laughed in-between sobs. 'Who's going to look at an old frump like me?'

'Mum, can't you help her choose a new wardrobe. She's not much older than you and you don't dress like that.'

'I have offered. Would you like that, Nancy?'

'Yes, I think I would. Perhaps I should get my hair cut like yours. It seems to be all the rage now.'

'Maybe Adriéne can fix her up with a blind date?'

'Oh I'm not sure,' Nancy said.

'It will do you good,' Alice said, 'won't it Mum? George, what do you think?'

'Go for it,' he answered.

'Yes it will.' I looked at my watch. 'But can we discuss this later, we're going to be late.'

Nancy put on her coat. 'We can talk about it in the car. I'm coming too.'

'What? Why didn't you say earlier?' I asked.

'I presumed it was obvious. Alice has been like a daughter to me. It's all right isn't it?'

'Yes of course but hurry up and let's go.'

'Alice's trunk is in the boot and Ted's waiting,' Joan said, appearing from nowhere. 'Here take this.' She handed George a picnic basket. 'You don't want to be hungry.' She took hold of Alice and gave her a huge cuddle. 'I'm going to miss you, little one.'

'I'll be back before you know.'

Nancy squeezed between Alice and George in the back leaving me no option but to sit in the front with Ted. I took a deep breath and kept silent but hoped my friend wasn't going to break down at school.

The car was full of chatter, mainly Alice. She didn't seem to stop, but then she was always like that when excited.

'I hope I make a friend like your Katy, Mum,' she said.

'I hope so too,' I said. 'Ted, do you think you can pull in along the promenade. It would be nice to picnic before dropping Alice.'

'What about here?' he said.

'Perfect, we can sit under the shelter.'

We hunched up together to keep the wind at bay. I passed around the egg and cress sandwiches and coffee to wash it down. Alice was still chattering and not letting George get a word in edgeways. Nancy sat quietly while barely eating. I breathed in the sea air. Why hadn't I come here more often? I'd forgotten how glorious it was. I looked at my watch. 'We ought to make a move.' I resealed the flask and packed it away.

After only ten minutes we arrived at Greenemere. I took a variety of photographs and Nancy asked one of the fathers, with a young girl wearing plaits, if he'd mind taking a group one.

'What's your name?' Alice asked the girl.

'Rebecca. It's my first day here.'

'Mine too. Let's go in together.' Alice linked arms with the girl. We all followed.

A woman who looked in her forties greeted us at the front entrance. 'Hello, I'm Miss Henderson. Headmistress. And who do have here?'

'Alice Gilmore. Mum came here when she was my age. Grace Granville?'

'Oh yes of course. How do you do?' She shook my hand. 'Miss Allison spoke very highly of you. And Alice, I see that you've met Rebecca Weller.'

'Yes, outside.' She was still linking arms with the quiet girl.

'Rebecca is to be your room mate,' Miss Henderson said.

'Fantastic. Did you hear that, Rebecca. Is it all right if I call you Becky?'

'I'd like that,' she answered in a small voice.

Ted brought Alice's trunk to the door. 'Where would you like this?'

'Just leave it there for now,' Miss Henderson said. 'I'll get the porter to take it up later. These two are the last to arrive. Now girls, say goodbye to your families and let's get you both settled.'

Alice hugged Nancy. 'Don't worry about me.' Then moved on to George. 'I'll miss you.'

'Don't forget to write. I've got a new room.' He passed her the details.

'Mum. I love you. Don't worry about me. Be happy,' she said.

A tear ran down my cheek. 'I'm just being daft.' I laughed.

The girls followed the headmistress upstairs. They turned around and waved.

Rebecca's father looked lost. 'I don't know what I'm going to do without her. There's just been the two of us since her mother died. Kevin Wise.' He held out his hand to Nancy.

'Nancy Baines. Where are you from? We're in Cheam.'

'What a small world. I'm down the road in Carshalton.' Kevin was obviously struggling.

'Do you have time for a drink?' I asked him. 'We're calling into The Queen's Head, a nice little pub, on the way home.'

'Yes, I know it. That would be nice, thank you. I'm not in any hurry to get home.'

'That's great,' Nancy said. 'Will you follow us?'

We arrived at the venue in no time at all and ordered drinks. George sipped Coca-Cola through a straw and crunched on crisps. He offered me the packet. Today was the last day I'd see him until he came home from school for Christmas.

Nancy held on to Kevin's every word.

He passed her his business card. 'Call me. Maybe we could go out to dinner sometime?'

'I'd like that.' Her face flushed.

George teased her on the way home until he closed his eyes. He leant his head on my shoulder. Things were coming together. Adriéne and I were back on, and it looked like my son was ready to forgive me.

Chapter 30

The pine needles made my nose itch as I dressed the tree in the corner. I was sure Ted had bought a taller one this year. It was at least seven feet high. I decorated the branches with coloured lights then added baubles and tinsel. I really enjoyed this job, even at my saddest times I found it gave me hope. Parcels I'd gift-wrapped earlier sat on the floor. This year the Gilmore household would entertain lots of guests on Christmas Day. I was elated when George had written that he'd be here with Elizabeth and Simon. His school term finished in a couple of days, so it was agreed he'd come around to show me his latest drawings.

Alice was enjoying Greenemere, she'd become very good friends with Rebecca and asked if she and her father could share Christmas Day with us. That would certainly please Nancy as she'd been out to dinner with Kevin a few times.

'Hello Darling.' Charlotte waltzed in carrying bundles of parcels. 'Shall I slide them under?'

'Yes, I've just about finished.' I stood back to admire my handiwork. 'I love the transformation, don't you? Oh hang on.' I rooted in the bottom of a box. 'I nearly forgot poor Tinkerbell.'

'We can afford a new one, you know Grace? She's a bit old and tatty.'

'I know but she's special, so stays.'

We both laughed. Charlotte held the stool to keep me balanced and I stretched high to the top. 'This one's definitely taller than last year.'

'She's a beauty,' Charlotte said. 'Have you time for a chat and tea before everyone comes in?'

'Yes, sure. Is there a problem?'

'No, just thought we'd catch up.'

'I'll go and get tea.'

'No need, Joan said she'd bring it in.'

We sat close together on the chaise longue. Charlotte was silent.

'Well?' I asked.

'There's something I wanted to run by you, but first, how are things with you and Adriéne?'

'Good. I've a feeling he may propose again at Christmas. But this time it'll be different.'

'You'll say yes?'

'I think so. Alice loves him to bits and George is fine now. So why not? Jack wouldn't want me to spend the rest of my life on my own.'

'No, he wouldn't Grace. We all deserve happiness.' She sat quietly fiddling with her hands.

'Charlotte, is there something you'd like to tell me?'

'Err. Yes, there is actually.' She hurried her words.

'Go on.'

'Remember Elizabeth's wedding, Max and I danced?'

'Yes, I remember.'

'After the celebrations we chatted into the night, you know...'

'You didn't?'

'Not that. But we did kiss. We've been writing since he went back and would like to continue seeing each other and see where it goes but...'

'You're worried about me?'

'Yes, we both are. Max in particular, he's concerned how you'll take it, because of Eliza.'

'It's not for me to judge. He's lonely, I can see that. But the age difference. You must be twenty years younger than him?'

'Age doesn't matter.'

'Then you have my blessing. I thought perhaps you preferred female company.'

'Because you've never seen me with a man?'

'Mmm.'

'I had a bad experience when I was younger. Maybe one day I'll tell you. Max has made me feel like I can move on.'

'Then I'm happy for you. How could I not be?'

'Thank God for that.' Charlotte relaxed. 'I need a cigarette.'

'But you gave up years ago?'

'The stress levels have given me a craving.'

'Eat some chocolate cake instead.'

*

The dining room was packed with people. It was lovely to hear so much chatter around the table. 'Thirteen,' I'd said to Charlotte last week. 'Who else can we invite?'

'Stop being silly,' she'd said, 'your superstitions were put to bed years ago.' She was talking about the stone sentinels of course and I knew she was right. It was Christmas Day and everyone sat around the table.

I had insisted on employing outside caterers to ensure Joan had a proper day off. 'You're family,' I told her, 'and I want you to be waited on for at least one day a year.' She accepted grudgingly, but she seemed to be enjoying herself.

The table was set with Max at the head. 'Grace. I don't deserve this honour.'

'Yes you do, Uncle Max. You're the nearest I have to a father.'

'Well if you're sure.' He began to carve the large bird.

The uniformed waitresses weaved in and out serving roast potatoes with vegetables while the penguin waiters served wine. Paper crackers were pulled and several conversations were conducted at the same time. Joan observed the staff critically, she wasn't used to sitting back and relaxing, unlike Ted who didn't seem to have a problem at all.

'Loosen up, Joanie, drink some more wine.'

'I'm not sure that I should.' She giggled.

'Of course you should,' I said. 'Ted's right, you need to unwind. Charades after dinner, you're up first.'

Brandy was poured over Christmas pudding, struck with a match and burst into flames. Everyone clapped. Mince pies and coffee followed. By this time everyone felt uncomfortable around the waist.

'I think I'd like to go for a walk. Anyone else?' I asked.

Adriéne jumped at this idea.

'It's too cold. I would like to play Monopoly.' Alice grabbed the game from a cupboard.

'I think I need a snooze,' Joan said.

'That's a better idea,' Ted agreed.

'Why don't you two go, Grace, and the rest of us can play,' Nancy took the box off Alice. 'Unless anyone else would rather...?'

'Well if you don't mind. Kevin? Charlotte? Max?'

'I'm happy to stay, think I've had a bit too much wine to risk walking on that ice,' Kevin said.

'Are you going to be banker, Alice?' Elizabeth opened up the Monopoly board.

'Charlotte, do you fancy a bit of fresh air?' Max asked.

'Why not, but I'll need to wrap up warm, it's chilly outside.'

So it was decided that the four of us would go for a stroll while everyone else stayed and played Monopoly.

'We'll be back before three,' I said. 'We don't want to miss the Queen's speech.'

*

I shivered as we turned along Ewell Road into Nonsuch Park. Adriéne put his arm around me. The ground crunched as we trudged on. I was glad of my fur ankle boots. The frost was refusing to budge but thankfully the fog had lifted. Silver trees glowed across the landscape.

'We'll leave you young lovers alone for a while,' Max winked at Adriéne. 'See you back here at two thirty?'

It reminded me of all those years ago in Queen's Park when Jack and I were left alone but I mustn't think like that. This was different. Adriéne was different.

'Let's walk around the mansion,' he said.

I never tired of the massive sixteenth century building in the park. It reminded me of *Granville Hall* with its castle like appearance.

302

'You probably guessed that I had a quiet word with Max.' Adriéne took my gloved hand.

'I did wonder. What's this all about then?'

'I needed a chance to get you on your own. You know I adore you?'

'Yes, I do.'

'Come and sit down.' He led me to a bench, rummaged in his pocket and brought out a small box. 'I hope you'll forgive me if I don't get down on the ground.'

My stomach stirred, I shook all over but how much was due to being cold or due to excitement, I wasn't sure.

'I know we've been here before, but I think this time it's different. Grace, will you do me the honour of becoming my wife?'

'Yes. Yes I will.'

Adriéne removed my glove and slipped the diamond ring onto my finger. He kissed me firmly on the lips. 'I knew you were ready when I noticed your wedding band from Jack had disappeared. I love you and promise to do everything in my power to make you happy.'

'I love you too,' I said, and meant it.

'Let's go and find the others.'

Max and Charlotte were at the meeting spot as promised.

'Well?' Max asked, 'don't keep us waiting.'

I held out my hand.

'Congratulations, darling.' Charlotte kissed me.

'I'm happy for you.' Max gave me a hug. 'It's about time. Are you going to make the announcement when we get back to the house?'

'No, not yet.' I turned to face Adriéne. 'I want to tell George and Alice first. I'll need to take the ring off. Do you mind?'

'Of course not. I understand.'

*

The television was on and everyone sat close to the roaring fire, drinking tea and watching in anticipation. The Queen

303

began her speech, my mind wandered. I rehearsed what I'd say to George. I just needed him alone. Intuition told me he'd be fine, I knew Alice would be ecstatic. She loved Adriéne.

I looked around when I heard a gentle purring coming from Joan. Ted was also snoring. Bless them. Sitting in a warm room after too much eating and drinking was a recipe for sleep. I refused to wake them when Nancy declared it was time to play Charades. This activity seemed to go on forever.

I stood up and stretched my arms. 'Tea, anyone?' I'd sent the caterers home. 'George, would you like to help me?'

He looked at Nancy.

She said, 'You go. The rest of us will carry on.'

*

The stone floor felt cold under my feet. It took me back to our little house in Wigan, when George as a small boy used to do his best to help me with the tea.

'Let's sit down for a minute.' I pulled out a chair from under the freshly scrubbed table. 'It's not that different to the one we had at home, is it?' I asked him. It was better quality of course but its purpose was the same.

George sat down. 'What is it?'

I took his hand. 'I wanted to know...'

'He's asked you then?'

'You don't mind?'

'No, I told you at Elizabeth's wedding. He's a nice guy. I'm happy for you. Does Alice know?'

'I wanted to tell you first.'

'I'm glad you did, Mam, Mum. What do I call you?'

'I think I'll always be your mam. I can't tell you how long I've waited to hear you say it. I love you, George. I never gave up on you.'

'I know. I love you too.' He stood up and wrapped his arms around me.

A tingling sensation ran through me. 'Does that mean you want to come home?'

'Yes, Mam.'

304

'And are you ready to announce it to the others?'

'I'm ready to shout it to the whole world. I feel like a little boy again in me mam's arms, warm and comforted, pain washed away from the past seven years. I think although you'll always be me mam, I'd better call you mum or mother in public.' He held my hand and led me back to the lounge where everyone was still playing Charades.

'We have an announcement.' George turned to me.

They stopped the game. Eyes focused on us. Waiting, wondering what we were going to say. I kept them waiting a little longer, hugging the news to myself for a few more seconds, holding onto a rich smile.

'Well?' said Charlotte, breaking the silence.

I took a deep breath, tears flowed.

Eyes fixed, wondering what was wrong.

'My son has returned. George has come home.'

I looked around at my family's faces, yes family. They may not all be blood related but they were family. I gazed at them in turn, enjoying their joyful reaction. Nancy, a true friend, we'd been through so much together. Not just a friend but a sister. Max, more of a father to me than my own had ever been, since that first day I'd stepped into *Willow Banks* when I was only sixteen years old. Charlotte was wise and always brought me to my senses. I thanked God for the day she sauntered into my little shop. She was the big sister I'd never had. Elizabeth, we'd lost contact for so many years but she was still my sister. We'd never share the same bond as I had with Nancy and Charlotte, but slowly we were building a connection. Simon, I buried the painful past, he was my sister's husband now, my brother in law. I'd always wanted a brother. Joan and Ted, ready-made grandparents. Joan always there with a cup of tea and piece of chocolate cake to make things better and Ted, well Ted was Ted. He'd sit at the steering wheel and know when to pass over a handkerchief or just drive. Kevin and Rebecca looked at each other, I sensed their embarrassment. They felt they didn't belong. But they did. Soon they too would become part of the picture.

Alice, my Shirley Temple. The little girl that had to grow up too quickly to support her mother. The little girl who cried every night for her brother. The little girl who was growing into a beautiful, young woman.

Then there was Adriéne, my husband to be. I beckoned him.

Alice ran over to George and teased him affectionately. Adriéne took my hand.

It was time to move on, time to move forward, time to put the past behind. Beth would always be in my heart, and Jack. I'd never forget him but it was time to say goodbye and move on. Our son had come home and it was time to bury the ghosts. My family deserved all of me and that's what they would have. My all.

'Champagne,' I said to Charlotte.

She poured into thirteen flutes. I'd never be superstitious again. I raised my glass. 'To George, my son. To family. To the future in nineteen seventy.'

Everyone raised their glasses.

Tomorrow Adriéne and I would announce our engagement. Tomorrow not today. Today was for George.

Acknowledgements

I'd like to thank members of my online forum who participated in feedback and members from The Palais De Danse Bolton, 50s & 60s Bolton and Bolton Lancashire Bygone Days Facebook groups for their generous help in my research.

Finally, I'd like to thank my husband, children, family and friends for their continued support and faith in me.

Patricia M Osborne was born in Liverpool and spent time in Bolton as a child. She now lives in West Sussex. Apart from novel writing, Patricia writes poetry and short fiction. Her poetry and short stories have been published in various literary magazines and anthologies. She is studying for an MA in Creative Writing with University of Brighton. *House of Grace* is her first novel.

Manufactured by Amazon.com
Columbia, SC
11 April 2017